R. Barri Flowers is an award-winning author of crime, thriller, mystery and romance fiction featuring three-dimensional protagonists, riveting plots, unexpected twists and turns, and heart-pounding climaxes. With an expertise in true crime, serial killers and characterising dangerous offenders, he is perfectly suited for the Mills & Boon Heroes series. Chemistry and conflict between the hero and heroine, attention to detail and incorporating the very latest advances in criminal investigations are the cornerstones of his romantic suspense fiction. Discover more on popular social networks and Wikipedia.

Nationally bestselling author **Patricia Sargeant** was drawn to write romance because she believes love is the greatest motivation. Her romantic suspense novels put ordinary people in extraordinary situations to have them find the 'hero inside.' Her work has been reviewed in national publications such as *Publishers Weekly, USA Today, Kirkus Reviews, Suspense Magazine, Mystery Scene Magazine, Library Journal* and *RT Book Reviews*. For more information about Patricia and her work, visit patriciasargeant.com

Also by R. Barri Flowers

The Lynleys of Law Enforcement

Christmas Lights Killer
Murder in the Blue Ridge Mountains
Cold Murder in Kolton Lake
Campus Killer
Mississippi Manhunt

Hawaii CI

Captured on Kauai
Honolulu Cold Homicide
Danger on Maui

Also by Patricia Sargeant

The Touré Security Group

Down to the Wire
Her Private Security Detail
Second-Chance Bodyguard

KILLER IN SHELLVIEW COUNTY

R. BARRI FLOWERS

COLTON'S DEADLY TRAP

PATRICIA SARGEANT

MILLS & BOON

First Published in Great Britain 2025
by Mills & Boon, an imprint of HarperCollins*Publishers* Ltd
1 London Bridge Street, London, SE1 9GF

www.harpercollins.co.uk

HarperCollins*Publishers*
Macken House, 39/40 Mayor Street Upper,
Dublin 1, D01 C9W8, Ireland

Special thanks and acknowledgment are given to Patricia Sargeant for her contribution to *The Coltons of Arizona* series.

ISBN: 978-0-263-39700-0

0225

This book contains FSC™ certified paper and other controlled sources to ensure responsible forest management.

For more information visit: www.harpercollins.co.uk/green

Printed and Bound in the UK using 100% Renewable Electricity at
CPI Group (UK) Ltd, Croydon, CR0 4YY

KILLER IN SHELLVIEW COUNTY

R. BARRI FLOWERS

In memory of my beloved mother, Marjah Aljean, a devoted lifelong fan of Mills & Boon romance and romantic suspense novels, who inspired me to excel in my personal and professional lives. To H Loraine, the true love of my life and very best friend, whose support has been unwavering through the many terrific years together, as well as the many loyal fans of my romance, suspense, mystery and thriller fiction published over the years. Lastly, a nod goes out to my great Mills & Boon editors, Denise Zaza and Emma Cole, for the wonderful opportunity to lend my literary voice and creative spirit to the Mills & Boon Heroes series.

Prologue

The last thing Tris remembered was hiking in the Manikeke Crossing of the wildlife management area in Shellview County, Georgia, on a Wednesday afternoon, hoping to take full advantage of the inviting natural setting during the summertime for some wildlife viewing—such as red-cockaded woodpeckers, gopher tortoises and other endangered or threatened species. Apart from loving nature, including the abundance of longleaf pines, wild orchids and other features of the rich landscape, she welcomed a reprieve from both the overprotective mother she currently lived with, as well as the overzealous, underachieving boyfriend whose house she'd recently moved out of. As far as she was concerned, the relationship had run its course and she just wanted to get on with her life. Maybe even start over in another state altogether. At twenty-five, she still had her best years ahead of her. Hopefully, she would share them with someone who respected what she brought to the table and could offer as much in return, minus all the drama.

But then something totally unexpected happened.

The man that she had run into on the trail, who had seemed friendly enough, turned out to be anything but. Before she could even react, he had whipped out a stun gun and placed it squarely on her upper chest. She quickly lost all control of her mind and body, which twitched uncontrollably. She must have passed out when she'd fallen and hit her head on the ground.

Now awake, with a splitting headache, Tris managed to open her sore blue eyes and take in the surroundings. She was still in virtually the same spot where she had been zapped by the man. But where was he? Her clothes hadn't been removed, so there seemed to be no sexual assault. Why had he attacked her unprovoked?

Tris then remembered that someone had been strangling people in Shellview County for several months now. The press had referred to the perpetrator as the Shellview County Killer. But none of the murders had occurred in or around Manikeke Crossing. Surely the killer would not be so bold as to target someone—her—in broad daylight in a popular area for hikers, hunters and others?

Come to think of it, Tris realized that she had not actually run into anyone else lately while hiking.

No one except for the man who had used the stun gun on her. So where was he? Should she be worried that he might come after her again?

She struggled to get to her feet. *I have to get out of here and go for help*, she thought, while trying to regain her equilibrium and find the right direction to get out of the Manikeke Crossing.

Tris had only taken a few steps when she suddenly heard a noise behind her, indicating that she wasn't alone. She glanced back over her shoulder and saw him. He had a big grin on his face, as though having planned this moment all along, and was getting some sort of perverse thrill in watching her squirm in fear.

With wobbly legs, she tried to make a run for it, but

somehow ended up flat on her face. That was when he pounced on her, and she knew there would be no escape from what he had in store for her.

HE HAD PLANNED every step, wanting to leave little to chance. Just like the other times. Seeing the terror in the eyes of his victims was half the battle. The other half was finishing what he set out to do, knowing there was nothing that could stop him. Unfortunately for them, escape was impossible. Not when he was so determined to complete his mission.

But that didn't mean he wasn't above at least giving the target a fighting chance. So he allowed that tiny glimmer of hope for survival to be out there. Only to snatch it away in the blink of an eye, like taking candy from a misbehaving child.

It was time to put an end to this, once and for all. When she was put out of her misery, he would be out of his.

At least for the moment.

He sucked in a deep breath and then ended her life, so that he could celebrate his great victory thereafter.

Chapter One

Tisha Fletcher drove her state-owned black Ford F-150 truck onto the Manikeke Crossing in Shellview County on Friday morning. The wildlife management area was part of her jurisdiction as a game warden first class in the Region 5 Law Enforcement Division of the Georgia Department of Natural Resources, headquartered in Albany, Georgia. She took note of the built-in laptop with computer-aided dispatch system, along with a high-powered radio. Then there was the Glock 43 single-stack, 9mm Luger pistol she carried in a waistband holster as a uniformed officer of the law and for her own protection. She also had a smartphone-based body camera attached to her shirt.

All part of the daily and necessary equipment for a Georgia Peace Officer Standards and Training Council certified game warden tasked with enforcing environmental, wildlife, and boating state and federal laws; holding violators of these laws accountable; and educating the public on proper and safe use of Georgia's natural resources. Six years ago, she had attended and graduated from the DNR Game Warden Academy in Forsyth, Georgia, gotten married and been assigned to the work section in Shellview County, a mix of rural and urban landscapes in the southwest part of the state.

Now twenty-eight years old, Tisha was a young Korean American widow. Three years ago, her husband, Bradley Fletcher, an environmental technologist, had died suddenly of a massive heart attack at the age of thirty-two, leaving her devastated and alone. They'd seemingly had their whole lives ahead of them. Until they didn't.

Her small hazel eyes glanced at the 14K gold wedding ring on her finger. She had been reluctant to remove it for what it represented, though she had put the worst of that painful chapter in her life behind her, just as Bradley would have wanted. For the most part, Tisha had focused on her work, which she loved, and it paid off in ways she could never have anticipated. At the start of the year, she had received the prestigious Torch Award from the DNR Law Enforcement Division, as a means of encouraging the progress of young game wardens who happened to be current members of the North American Wildlife Enforcement Officers of America.

Tisha smiled at the honor and was certain that her late husband would have been proud of her for picking herself up and finding a way to excel professionally. Romance was a different story. Her romantic life had been pretty much nonexistent for the last three years, as she never seemed to connect seriously with anyone who met the high standards for what she looked for in a man. Maybe she had set the bar too high. Or maybe finding true love was one and done for her.

She pulled her truck into the parking spot next to the black Ford F-150 she knew belonged to Sherman Galecki, a senior game warden, who last year had received his own special recognition by the DNR, being named Game Warden of the Year. They had both been sent to the Manikeke Crossing to collect and study data on local wildlife and their habitat to help determine abundance, distribution and mortality rates, and then formulate strategies to maintain it.

Emerging from her vehicle, Tisha glanced down at her patrol boots and squared the shoulders of her slender, five-seven frame. She tucked an errant strand of her long brunette hair, fashioned in a low bun, behind one ear and watched as Sherman climbed out of his cab. Tall and firm in his uniform, at thirty-five, he had short dark brown hair styled in a burst fade cut and blue eyes behind round glasses. He had recently ended a long-term relationship and seemed to be content right now just playing the field.

Tisha was glad he hadn't tried to hit on her. Though he wasn't too bad on the eyes, Sherman wasn't really her type. Not to say that she was necessarily in the market for starting a relationship with anyone, even though she was single and available, more or less.

"Hey," Sherman said easily, sporting a grin on his oblong face as he met her halfway.

"Hey." She twisted her thin lips. "Sorry I'm a little late. Got stuck finishing up some paperwork involving a boating accident."

"No problem. Just got here myself, after bumping heads with a couple of illegal and intoxicated road hunters."

"Ouch. Hope you've got a hard head," Tisha quipped with a chuckle, though she knew any such investigation could be dangerous. Especially when alcohol or drugs were involved.

"I do. Them, not so much." He laughed. "Let's do this."

"Alright." She headed into the WMA with him, and they collected data together, observing small game in their habitat amid the green ground cover, sand dunes and longleaf pines.

"Why don't we spread out and double our reach," Sherman suggested.

This made perfect sense to Tisha, considering that she often worked alone, which was par for the course for most game wardens. She told him, "Good idea. We can meet back at our trucks and compare notes."

"Sounds like a plan," he agreed. "See you in a bit."

Tisha headed north and through a grove of turkey oak trees and vegetation, while considering the restoration and fire management of the ecosystem. When she neared a hill, something odd caught her eye. What was that?

As she grew closer, Tisha winced when she realized that the object in question was, in fact, a human being.

It became obvious to Tisha, based on the deteriorating condition of the young female lying awkwardly atop some foliage, that she was dead.

Tisha immediately got on her radio and told Sherman the disturbing news. "There's a dead woman lying here on the hill," she said flatly.

"What?" His voice rang with shock, then he said evenly, "Tell me where to find you..."

After giving him her coordinates, Tisha waited for his arrival while standing guard over the clothed body and trying to ascertain if this was an accident, suicide, or foul play. The area was a hot spot for hunters, which could have resulted in an honest and tragic mistake...or even one unbeknownst to the shooter.

Except for the fact that there was no sign that the woman had been shot.

With no blood coming from a wound, Tisha ruled out stabbing, as far as a deliberate attack. The body didn't seem to have been prey for a wild or bloodthirsty animal, either.

When she heard the sound of footsteps, Tisha turned

to see Sherman moving briskly toward her. He furrowed his brow while regarding the dead woman and snorted out an expletive, then said, “Yeah, she’s definitely no longer among the living.”

“What do you think happened to her?” Tisha asked tensely, having her own suspicions.

“Without contaminating the body or scene by touching anything, judging by the position of her body, if I had to hazard a guess, I’d say she was killed by someone or something…”

“I was thinking the same thing,” she told him, “but more likely the *someone* angle.”

“Yeah, probably,” Sherman agreed, and took out his cell phone. “Better alert the sheriff and get the Georgia Bureau of Investigation medical examiner down here.”

“I’ll call the latter,” Tisha said, lifting her own cell phone from a side pocket.

She reported the news of a dead body to the medical examiner’s office. Though all possibilities for the cause of death were on the table, instinct, as well as that some similar corpses discovered over the last six months in the county had been classified as serial homicides, left Tisha fearful that a serial killer may have struck again.

GEORGIA BUREAU OF INVESTIGATION Special Agent Glenn McElligott sat at his L-shaped black espresso-colored wood corner desk in the Region 2 Investigative Office on Beaver Run Road in Midland, Georgia. He was a year removed from his assignment to the Region 12 Investigative Office in Eastman, in Dodge County. As deep gray eyes perused information on his laptop regarding the latest case involving a serial killer prowling the streets of Shellview County, one of several counties within his present jurisdiction, Glenn was tempted to say he was getting too damn old for this.

But having just turned thirty-two, he was hardly ready to check himself into the senior living facility that wasn't too far from his property in the county, in the town of Akerston Heights. Hell, if he was being honest about it, he would admit that being a GBI agent was right for him and something he took pride in. After all, he'd been at this for nearly a decade now, becoming a certified Georgia peace officer upon passing the special agent exam and successfully completing the 16-week GBI basic agent course at the Georgia Public Safety Training Center in Forsyth. Before that, he had received his bachelor's degree in criminal justice and criminology from Georgia Southern University's Armstrong Campus in Savannah.

Through the years, Glenn had been involved in his fair share of tough investigations, dealing with a wide array of criminal activity: mass murders, missing person cases, sex offenses, human trafficking, cold cases, and more. But his latest assignment was every bit as unsettling and perhaps even more mystifying. Someone was strangling people to death—female and male victims—and leaving the corpses in both plain view and less visible spots throughout the county. So far, three people had been murdered in the past six months and they were linked to one unsub, whom the local press had given the moniker the Shellview County Killer.

So far, no identifiable DNA or prints and no reliable info on a physical description of the perpetrator had surfaced. The modus operandi was ligature strangulation of the unsub's victims, while doing so brazenly, and had proven quite elusive. This frustrated Glenn, even though he was certain it was only a matter of time before the killer's luck ran out and the perp was locked up where such offenders belonged for the rest of their miserable lives.

That can't happen soon enough, Glenn told himself keenly, running a hand through his short dark hair. No one else had to die. At least that was his fervent hope. When in college, a friend had gotten into a barroom brawl, only to be strangled to death by a jealous boyfriend. Glenn wouldn't wish that kind of attack on anyone. Least of all some innocent people who were apparently being randomly targeted by a serial killer.

When his cell phone buzzed, Glenn, in his short-sleeved, flex collar blue shirt, turned and grabbed the phone. He saw that the call was coming from the Shellview County Sheriff's Department.

This can't be good, Glenn thought, sensing as much given the timing, as he answered routinely, "Agent McElligott." He listened as he was told about the discovery of a dead female in the Manikeke Crossing on Foxx Road. The circumstances of the death were described as suspicious. "I'm on my way," he said, after taking down the GPS coordinates.

Glenn rose to his full six feet, three inches height. He had a SIG Sauer P320-M18 modular handgun system 9mm Luger sidearm inside a leather pocket holster on his slacks, along with a Taser. Just as he was about to brief the special agent in charge, she stepped into his corner office.

Rhianna Kingsley was African American, in her early forties and around five-ten with a medium frame. She had blond hair in a curly bob and was frowning as her brown eyes gazed at him. "I take it you heard about the body found in the Manikeke Crossing?"

"Yeah, just got off the phone with the sheriff's department," he confirmed bleakly. "I'm headed over there right now."

"Good. Our crime scene specialists will meet you at the wildlife management area."

"Okay." Glenn paused, reading her thoughts about the worst-case scenario, which in this instance was more evidence of a serial killer at work. "I won't jump to any conclusions," he offered. "Maybe this will turn out to be something that won't necessarily require the assistance of the GBI."

"One can only hope," Rhianna said. "We certainly have enough other investigations on our hands, including the one you're working on now. We don't need any more bodies to have to deal with in the process."

"I agree." He paused thoughtfully. "Only one way to find out."

She lowered her chin. "Don't let me stop you, Agent McElligott."

Glenn nodded. Shortly, he was out the door and into his black Dodge Durango Pursuit SUV. It was equipped with an AR-15 semiautomatic rifle as backup firepower, if needed in the course of his duties.

During the drive, he considered that the independent GBI's assistance had been requested in what turned into a serial killer investigation, with him taking the lead in trying to solve the case, while at the same time fully cooperating with the sheriff's department in the pursuit of justice for the victims.

After arriving at the Manikeke Crossing, Glenn flashed his identification in what had clearly become a bona fide crime scene, with the yellow tape cordoning off the area in question. He got the general sense that the situation would likely get worse before things got better. This was confirmed, more or less, as he conferred with the GBI crime scene specialists, who had already begun to process the immediate surroundings.

He made his way farther inside the WMA and approached the sheriff, who was talking with two game wardens—one male, the other female. The three turned Glenn's way in unison. Shellview County Sheriff Marjorie Pierce, of medium build and in full uniform, was in her fifties, with green eyes and crimson hair in a pixie cut. Glenn was glad to be able to assist in this investigation that was within her jurisdiction, having worked together before on a joint task force involving sex trafficking in the state.

"Sheriff Pierce," Glenn said in a friendly but ill-at-ease tone, "I got the call about a dead body found…"

Marjorie nodded dourly. "Unfortunately, that's what we're looking at."

He gazed at the male game warden, who was about his height and build, and said, "GBI Special Agent Glenn McElligott."

"Sherman Galecki," the game warden introduced himself.

"Nice to meet you." Glenn shook his hand with a firm grip and eyed the female game warden.

"Tisha Fletcher," she said, her tone even.

It took only a moment to assess the attractive game warden. She had pretty hazel eyes and her brunette hair was obviously long and pulled up from her heart-shaped face into a bun, with curtain bangs. Even in uniform, he could see that she was well-proportioned on a slender frame.

"Hello," Glenn said respectfully, and stretched out his long arm to shake her hand. He couldn't help but notice the wedding band on her other hand and told himself that her husband was a lucky man. Something that Glenn had thus far found himself falling short on—though not from lack of trying. He wanted to meet someone who was marriage material and a person he could grow with.

They released hands and Marjorie said, "Warden Fletcher is the one who found the body."

Glenn eyed the game warden again and asked, "Where?"

"Just up this hill," she responded, and began to lead the way. "Sherman and I were collecting data in different parts of the WMA, when I spotted her lying on and partially covered by some underbrush..."

When they arrived at the spot, Glenn bent down and studied the deceased female. She was slender and had medium-length light blond hair tied in a ponytail. He guessed that she was in her late twenties to early thirties. She was lying on her side, wearing a carrot-colored cropped tank top, black high-waist leggings and white sneakers. It seemed apparent to him by her pallid coloring that she had been dead for more than a day. He noted the discoloration around her neck, suggesting she could have been strangled. Furthermore, there appeared to be two small puncture wounds on the part of her chest that was exposed, consistent with use of a stun gun.

"And this is exactly the way she was found?" he asked, having no reason to believe either game warden would have tried to move the body, potentially corrupting evidence of a crime.

"Yes," Tisha assured him. "We had no desire to complicate the investigation in any way."

Sherman backed her up on this. "Once Tisha alerted me as to what she'd found, I came over and we both inspected the dead woman without touching her."

"Just checking," Glenn said, regretting putting the two on the spot, knowing they were all on the same team. "Judging by her attire, it appears that she was hiking or jogging, before something happened—"

"So what do you think we're looking at here?" Sheriff Pierce asked urgently.

Glenn understood by her expression that she was cutting to the chase as it related to the possibility that the deceased was another victim of a serial killer.

"Could this be the work of the so-called Shellview County Killer?" Tisha asked bluntly, with unease, before he could respond to the sheriff.

"Well, without getting ahead of ourselves," he answered coolly, "and pending an autopsy, it appears that she was accosted by someone, who either came with her or followed her into the Manikeke Crossing, or she ran into by chance, such as a hunter..."

"If a hunter did this, we should be able to narrow down some possibilities based on hunting licenses issued for hunting on this WMA," Sherman stated.

"That would help," Glenn said, while considering that the unsub serial killer could be a hunter as well. "Do we know the name of the dead woman?"

"Not yet," the sheriff said sadly. "Appears her identification is missing. Assuming she came here alone and ran into harm's way, it was either left behind or taken by her killer—"

"We'll need to identify her as soon as possible," he stressed, knowing that this could be a key factor in the circumstances that led to her death.

"As part of the DNR Law Enforcement Division," Tisha said, "whatever we can do to assist in the investigation, Agent McElligott and Sheriff Pierce, just let us know."

Glenn could tell by her tone that she was as eager to see this death solved, occurring where it did, as he was, giving him a certain sense of anticipation of them working together toward a common goal. Sherman seconded this.

"Okay," Glenn responded. The sheriff also welcomed their cooperation.

Signaling for the crime scene technicians to begin working the area around the body before the medical examiner arrived, Glenn instructed that they use a Leica C10 laser scanner for a three-dimensional scan of the crime scene and how it may have been used as a death trap for the hiker or jogger.

The hard part, Glenn knew, was to put these pieces together to make a case for what likely was a murder of the as-yet unidentified victim, who had undoubtedly been in the wrong place at the worst possible time before her death.

Chapter Two

Tisha wondered if she had gone overboard in stating the obvious to the GBI special agent, along with the sheriff, in volunteering assistance in what would almost certainly be a homicide investigation. After all, the woman's death had occurred within a DNR wildlife-management-area work section. Not to mention, after having discovered the body, Tisha felt it was incumbent upon her to see this through to its conclusion to the extent possible in her position as a game warden, her regular duties and life away from work notwithstanding.

She gazed at Glenn McElligott as he orchestrated the movements by the GBI crime scene investigators in combing the area to collect evidence. Tall and in his early thirties, with jet-black textured hair in a stylish undercut, arresting gray eyes, and in really good shape, Tisha couldn't help but think that the good-looking, square-jawed special agent with a five-o'clock shadow was totally her type. Or at least she felt he could be if the situation presented itself, since she was a widow, too long without real companionship, and wanted to believe someone else might still be out there for her in this world.

Dream on, Tisha told herself, as she let the thought pass and got back to the moment at hand, while watching the associate medical examiner and his team arrive and take possession of the decedent, with an autopsy forthcoming to determine the manner and circumstances of what had already been classified as a suspicious death.

Tisha could only wonder if a serial killer had made his way to the Manikeke Crossing to cause trouble in a major way. When the dust settled and everyone had begun to clear out from the main crime scene, she found herself being approached by Agent McElligott.

"You have a cell phone?" he asked.

She batted her eyes and quipped, "Doesn't everyone?"

"Can I see yours?" he asked with a straight face, even as Tisha removed the phone from her pocket and handed it to him. She watched as he put in his cell phone number and said, "In case you happen to come upon anything relevant to this investigation, feel free to call me anytime…"

"Will do," she promised, and sent him her own cell phone number should he wish to contact her pertaining to the case. Or maybe he might want it someday outside of the investigation. Who knew?

"Thanks." He gave a crooked little grin and walked away, meeting up with Sheriff Pierce and some of her deputies.

A few minutes later, Tisha had walked back to the parking lot with Sherman, where their Ford F-150 trucks awaited them.

"Been a hell of a way to start our day," he moaned.

She sighed. "Tell me about it."

Sherman eyed her. "You going to be okay?"

"Not like I have much of a choice," Tisha answered truthfully. After all, as an armed game warden, she had to be up to the task of dealing with whatever—or whomever—she encountered. That included dead bodies. Didn't mean she had to be comfortable with it. "I'm sure that Agent McElligott and the sheriff's department will get to the bottom of the poor woman's death, whether it's tied to a serial killer or not."

"Yeah, one can only hope. We don't need that type of trouble while doing our jobs." He touched his glasses and headed for his truck.

"Catch you later," she called out to him and got into her own cab. There, Tisha watched Sherman drive off, then she got out her cell phone to give an update on the latest happenings to the work section boss, Sergeant Fritz Alvarez.

When his full face appeared on the small video screen, surrounded by black hair in an Edgar cut, Tisha followed up on their earlier chat. "The GBI is looking into the suspicious death of the female hiker, which appears to be homicide."

Tisha could see the intensity in his deep brown eyes as Fritz, in his midforties, said, "Sorry you had to be put through that, and sorrier about the hiker."

"Me, too," Tisha commented, covering both fronts.

"Do they know who the victim is yet?"

"No, they're still trying to identify her." She could only imagine the heartbreak of the woman's family or close friends, upon learning what would be unthinkable for most people. Until it happened.

"Well, I'm sure the authorities will get to the bottom of it," Fritz said.

"Hope so." Tisha took a breath, fearing they might not like what they discover, if in fact the death could be tied to a serial murderer.

"Sherman was shaken up by it, too," the sergeant remarked. "No matter your toughness, this type of encounter never goes down easily."

"No, it doesn't," she admitted.

"Unfortunately, it can come with the territory, which, in this case, is the entire county."

Tisha met his gaze knowingly. "We'll get through it."

"I know you will," Fritz said confidently. "In the meantime, we'll certainly step up our patrols of the hot spots within our jurisdiction, which, if nothing else, will hopefully help give visitors some added peace of mind."

"That will be good."

"Yeah."

"Well, I better get back to work," she told him, neither requesting nor expecting to be given time off to come to terms with the trauma of finding a dead body. That would need to work itself out on its own schedule.

After disconnecting, Tisha started the truck and headed out. She thought briefly about Agent Glenn McElligott, wondering what he could discover about the dead woman. And what might remain unknown. That would be for him to determine. Along with the other aspects of his investigation, over and beyond his personal life, however that played into working for the GBI.

GLENN WAS ALREADY on his way home for the day when word came in that the dead woman had been tentatively identified. According to a member of his crime scene investigators, the driver's license and cell phone belonging to a Tris Lindberg had been found scattered in undergrowth just outside the crime scene. Now, this information needed to be confirmed by the sheriff's department, along with getting the results of the autopsy, in piecing together a timeline and exact cause of death.

I have a very bad feeling that the Shellview County Killer has struck again, Glenn told himself bleakly. But he knew he couldn't get ahead of himself just yet in this investigation. Whatever the case, a woman was dead, and someone needed to be held accountable.

He pulled his SUV into the driveway of his two-story, three-bedroom custom home on Fennly Street. It sat on forty acres of rolling hills and mature pine trees, not far from Lake Oliver. He had purchased the fenced property after being reassigned to the area a year ago. It had pretty much everything he wanted in a residence, other than perhaps a human companion to share his life with. He held out hope that could still happen for him as a healthy man with a lot of loving to give to the right woman.

The instant he stepped inside the house, Glenn was practically bowled over by his lovable black Labrador retriever named Riley, whom he'd had for three years now.

"Hey, boy. It hasn't been that long since I left for work," Glenn told him with a chuckle, while petting the dog's head. "Love you, too, Riley."

He played with the dog for a bit, then let him go. Riley ran across the hand-scraped, engineered hardwood flooring, into the U-shaped kitchen and back out, disappearing down the hall.

Glenn glanced around the open-concept first floor with its picture windows with vertical blinds and relaxed modern furnishings. After heading up the winder staircase, he put away his firearm safely and freshened up while trying to decide what to have for dinner.

Back downstairs, Glenn fed Riley some dry dog food, then decided to have leftover cheese and pepperoni pizza, washing it down with beer as he ate standing up.

Once done, he settled onto the midcentury-modern armchair in the great room, where, with Riley lying at his feet, Glenn grabbed his acoustic guitar and started to play. Ever since his parents had gotten him a guitar at ten years of age, playing the instrument had been one of his favorite pastimes. As well as a means to relieve some of the stress that life brought.

He thought about his current investigation. At the moment, that was the death of Tris Lindberg. Had someone targeted her in particular? Did she know or recognize her attacker?

If only she could speak from the grave, it would save me from needing to speak on her behalf in nailing her killer, Glenn told himself. His thoughts gravitated to the pretty game warden who discovered the body, bringing it to his attention.

He wondered if coming upon the victim would leave a lasting impact on her. Or had she hardened her ability to deal with such incidents by virtue of a law enforcement profession that required toughness and fortitude?

Something told him that she would want to be kept in the loop on how this case unfolded, seeing that the game warden had been inadvertently drawn into the murder investigation. He was more than happy to oblige her from one professional to another…while knowing that on a personal level, as a married woman there were no possibilities that his attraction to her would go any further than appreciating her from a safe distance.

SHELLVIEW COUNTY SHERIFF Marjorie Pierce hated this part of her job—the part where she had to notify one or more family members of a murder victim that the person was dead. And, as such, would not be showing up for breakfast, lunch, dinner, or whatever, again. But unfortunately, this was par for the course. Someone had to be the bearer of bad—make that very bad—news.

That would be her.

She got comfortable behind the wheel of her black Ford Explorer SUV and headed out to the address on Millburn Lane in the county town of Breyford, where Marjorie had been told that Tris Lindberg lived off and on with her mother, Alyssa Lindberg. Or at least she used to when still among the living.

It struck Marjorie to the core when she thought of her own daughter, Sarah, who wasn't much younger than the victim. She could only imagine how it would tear her up inside were Sarah to lose her life in such a tragic and senseless way. Having raised her on her own, by and large, as a divorcée, she wanted her daughter to have everything in life she deserved. That included attending Princeton University, where Sarah was in graduate school and working on her PhD in electrical and computer engineering. Pity that Tris Lindberg was destined to never be afforded that same courtesy in living out her dreams.

When Marjorie reached the ranch-style house, she parked along the curb, then headed up to the door, past a red Honda Accord in the driveway. It took a couple of rings of the doorbell before the door opened.

Marjorie looked into the face of a petite, fortysomething woman with short brown and gray hair, and said to her, "I'm Sheriff Pierce. Are you Alyssa Lindberg?"

"Yes," she responded, seeming ill at ease. "How can I help you, Sheriff?"

Marjorie waited a beat, before she responded in the only way she knew how, and that was to get right to the heart of the matter. "I'm afraid I have some bad news… It's about your daughter—"

AFTER HER SHIFT ENDED, Tisha drove to Blair Bay, where she lived in a two-bedroom town house on Tallins Drive, near the Chattahoochee River. She had moved there shortly after her husband's death, knowing she couldn't bear to continue living in the Georgian cottage they shared. She opted instead for a fresh start.

Or at least to give herself a chance to recalibrate her life and see what else—and maybe who else—was out there for her.

Glenn McElligott entered her head, but Tisha quickly let the thought slide. The truth was that she knew far too little about the good-looking special agent to get too carried away by his appearance and the few words that had passed between them. If they ever got the chance to really talk, and he was available, too, well, who knew where it could lead.

She reached her place and used the remote to open the attached garage with an entryway into the corner two-story unit that sat beside a cluster of pink flowering dogwood trees. After driving inside, she closed the garage and left the car.

Before even heading into the town house, Tisha could hear her dog, Jacky, barking in anticipation of seeing her.

Back at you, she thought, as Tisha went in and greeted the German shepherd warmly. She had inherited, more or less, the ten-year-old retired DNR Law Enforcement Division K-9 Unit dog, after his handler had been given a younger partner to fight crime.

Tisha considered the two of them to be a good fit in fighting off each other's loneliness. She watched as Jacky licked her hand playfully, and Tisha wondered if the dog was eager to be let out into the big fenced-in backyard for some exercise.

Instead, Jacky abruptly scurried away from her, across the bamboo flooring, past rustic furnishings and large windows with faux wood blinds in the spacious living-and-dining-room combo, and up the stairway to the second floor.

I'll be up shortly, she told herself, and headed into the open kitchen with its granite countertops and black stainless-steel appliances. She took a goblet out of the wood cabinet, opened the fridge, removed a half-filled bottle of red wine and poured it.

After sipping a bit of wine, Tisha filled a dog bowl with chicken-and-white-rice dog food for Jacky, and then got out some leftover tuna noodle casserole to microwave for herself.

As if sensing dinner was about to be served, Jacky came back downstairs and went right to her meal.

Tisha smiled and went upstairs, where she put her firearm away and changed into more comfortable clothing—a yellow T-shirt and brown shorts. She washed her face and let down her hair, which fell below her shoulders.

Twenty minutes later, she was sitting barefoot in a wood-ladder side chair at the round pedestal dining table, eating alone once again. She wondered if this would change anytime soon. Or was this destined to be the story of her life, whether she wished to move forward or not, in longing for human companionship, taking nothing away from her lovable former K-9 dog.

THE FOLLOWING MORNING, after taking Jacky out, Tisha drove to work, patrolling Shellview County rural areas for any violations pertaining to wildlife, waste and litter laws. She couldn't help but think about yesterday's unfortunate turn of events and the sad reality of how one wrong move in life could ruin it forever, as was the case for the dead female hiker.

Just as Tisha was about to check in with Sherman, to

see if he, too, had to come to grips with what went down at the Manikeke Crossing, her cell phone rang. She saw that the caller was Agent McElligott and that immediately commanded her attention.

"Hello," she said, putting him on speakerphone.

"Hey. In case you haven't already heard, we've identified the woman you found in the WMA as Tris Lindberg, a twenty-five-year-old from Breyford."

"No, I hadn't been briefed," Tisha confessed, while picking up noise from the road in the background, indicating that he was also in his vehicle.

"Well, I thought you ought to know."

"Thanks for the update. Have you learned anything else about her that's pertinent to the investigation?"

"Well, apart from being the apparent victim of foul play, Ms. Lindberg may well have been targeted..." he said, leaving it at that.

Tisha sighed, though wasn't really surprised, in remembering the signs that suggested as much. "I'm sorry for her," she said nonetheless.

"Me, too."

She couldn't help but wonder if he had connected this to the serial killer case.

Glenn cut into Tisha's thoughts when he uttered, "In any event, I'll be giving a full briefing on the death at eleven thirty this morning at the sheriff's department. If you'd like to attend, given your involvement in discovering the victim, you're welcome to. Same with Sherman Galecki."

"Yes, I would definitely like to be there." She suspected the same would be true for Sherman, who may as well have found the body himself, seeing that they had both been collecting data in the same area.

"Good..." The GBI special agent paused, as if wanting

to say something else to her, but had a change of heart, then simply replied, "I'll see you then."

"Okay." Tisha disconnected, eager to hear what he had to say and, truthfully, keen to see him again, while uneasy at the same time, as she anticipated the murder would be linked to several others in recent months who had died in a similar fashion.

She gave Sherman a buzz and he quickly said, "Heard the victim has been identified and that she was killed by someone."

"Yes, sadly."

"Agent McElligott invited us to his joint update with Sheriff Pierce," Sherman noted.

"I just spoke to him," Tisha confirmed. "Are you going?"

"Yeah. Maybe we'll get some more definitive answers as to why this happened in one of our WMAs and whether or not we need to be on the serious lookout for a killer..."

"I agree." She hung up, thoughtful, before touching base with Fritz Alvarez about the status of the investigation.

Chapter Three

Glenn had to admit that he liked the sound of Tisha Fletcher's voice when he heard it again. Or was even that stepping over the line when talking about a married woman? Why should it be? No harm in admiring a pleasant-sounding voice. Or even an attractive face with a nice body—from what he could interpret of the game warden in full uniform—for that matter.

The important thing was that she and Sherman Galecki deserved to know what they had learned thus far about the dead female Tisha had come upon.

Glenn believed he would have more answers about the death of Tris Lindberg at the briefing today and, very likely, some connecting of dots to the broader serial-killer investigation.

He pulled up to the Georgia Bureau of Investigation's medical examiner's regional laboratory on Deckler Street in Shellview County, where the autopsy on the victim had taken place this morning.

After stepping inside the building and flashing his ID, Glenn made his way to the lab, where the associate medical examiner, Dr. Ned Karakawa, was on his cell phone, but waved him over.

In his early sixties, Dr. Karakawa was lean and had short

white hair in a quiff style. He had on brown rectangle eyeglasses, a stained white lab coat and latex gloves. While waiting for him to end the phone chat, Glenn glanced at the nearby autopsy table, where Tris Lindberg's corpse was covered by a sheet up to her neck.

"Agent McElligott..." the associate medical examiner got his attention after hanging up.

Glenn regarded him with a nod. "Dr. Karakawa."

"Sorry, didn't mean to keep you waiting."

"No problem." Glenn cut to the chase. "What can you tell me about the death of Tris Lindberg?"

Karakawa touched his glasses and frowned. "Well, it wasn't pretty. As I indicated in the preliminary report and have now confirmed, Ms. Lindberg died of ligature strangulation from what appears to be some type of thin cotton cord," he said matter-of-factly. "I'm ruling the death a homicide."

Glenn muttered a sound of resignation and then asked, to be sure in his suspicions, "What about the injuries to her chest?"

Karakawa moved over to the body and slid the sheet down to her chest, pointing at the marks. "Similar to recent postmortems, these puncture wounds indicate that the decedent was subjected to some kind of stun gun, making it easier for whoever killed her to gain complete control, before finishing her off."

"How long was she dead?" Glenn questioned.

"I'd say anywhere from twenty-four to thirty-six hours or so."

Glenn mused about that. "Any chance she could have been killed elsewhere and the body dumped where it was found?"

"There's always a chance," the associate medical examiner replied. "But given the rather steep and dense location, and good possibility of detection were that to have occurred, I'd say the decedent was almost certainly killed close to where she was found."

"I agree." Glenn eyed the victim again, almost feeling the pain she must have endured both physically and psychologically from her ordeal. "Were there any signs of a sexual assault?"

Karakawa shook his head. "Not that I could detect."

"Just thought I'd ask." Glenn was pensive, before he asked curiously, "Could this be an isolated incident?" *Or, in other words, unrelated to the serial killings?* he thought.

Karakawa sighed. "I'll leave that for you and the sheriff's department to determine, Agent McElligott." He paused thoughtfully. "That being said, after conducting this postmortem examination, the particulars of the homicidal death in relation to the aforementioned murders make me believe it's unlikely to be an isolated attack. Simply put, the murders were much more likely to have been committed by the same person."

"My sentiments exactly," Glenn said soberly, while getting what he needed from the associate medical examiner, in linking the murder to a serial killer.

TISHA FINISHED HER morning rounds by citing three minors who were caught drinking alcohol near Lake Oliver. She hoped, but doubted, that they would heed this moment as a predictor of future trouble, should they continue down a path that could well escalate into more serious problems.

She drove up to the Shellview County Sheriff's Department on Twelfth Street in Blair Bay and parked in the lot, then headed inside to get the scoop on the death of Tris

Lindberg and its relationship, if any, to other deaths that occurred in the county in recent months.

The briefing was held in a conference room on the first floor. Inside, as members of law enforcement stood around, Tisha spotted Sherman, who had beaten her there and was chatting away flirtatiously with a pretty blond-haired deputy. *Good for him*, Tisha thought, while not knowing if he was actually hitting on the deputy or not.

"Hey." She heard a voice from behind and turned to gaze into the sharp eyes of Glenn McElligott.

Tisha grinned softly. "Agent McElligott."

"Feel free to call me Glenn, Warden Fletcher," he said smoothly, and as an obvious move to reduce the formalities both ways.

She happily took the bait and responded accordingly. "Only if you'll call me Tisha."

He flashed straight, white teeth. "Deal."

"So where do things stand in the investigation?" she asked, suspecting what his answer might be.

"Well, we're about to give an update," Glenn told her. "Afterward, if you have any further questions, I'll be happy to answer them."

"Fair enough." She smiled at him and watched as he headed toward a podium, joining Sheriff Pierce.

Tisha listened as the sheriff was all business in laying out the case in general terms for what was believed to be a strangulation-style serial killer in their midst, with Tris Lindberg as the latest victim.

GLENN WAS ALL ears as Sheriff Marjorie Pierce gave the foundation for their joint effort and paved the way for him to spell out the specifics of the case. He glanced at Tisha, wondering if she was up for hearing some of the unsettling details. The game warden had likely seen her fair share of criminal activity within her territory. But he suspected that serial murder was not amongst the criminality she encountered. Didn't mean, though, that Tisha would shy away from having a better handle on the circumstances involving the homicide victim she'd happened to come upon.

Marjorie was finishing her briefing in a somber tone of voice. "We're all in this together. We'll do whatever it takes to crack this nightmare case and make Shellview County a safe place to live and visit again..."

When Glenn took to the podium, he didn't mince words in getting to the heart of the matter. "We're almost certainly looking at a serial killer on the prowl, who the press has given the moniker the Shellview County Killer. I'm sure they're seeking to dramatize it, borrowing from other notorious serial killers' names, such as Jack the Ripper, Boston Strangler and Green River Killer. What we can ascertain, whatever the unsub's handle, is that he seemingly has no qualms about targeting the growing number of victims, which currently stands at four. All of them died from ligature strangulation in different locations and were subdued by the perpetrator with the help of a stun gun."

Holding a stylus pen, Glenn turned toward a large touchscreen display and brought up a split-screen image of the first victim. One image was of the victim still very much alive, and the other was as seen when the remains were discovered.

"Patsy Dunnock, a twenty-seven-year-old African American hairstylist and part-time model, was found strangled to death six months ago inside her white Acura Integra that was parked outside her apartment on Keblan Avenue in Akerston Heights. The killer had apparently been hiding in the back seat and caught her by surprise."

Glenn took a moment to look at the victim's attractive oval face with big brown eyes. It was surrounded by long and curly hair in a pink-to-copper-ombré style, parted on the right side. He allowed the stark living image to sink in before moving on to the second and third victims.

"Walt Patrick, an IT manager, age thirty-four, and his girlfriend, twenty-nine-year-old artist Patti Arnaz, were found strangled to death three months ago at Brenner Park in Nelse's Creek."

Glenn put their pictures on the screen, before disaster struck the nice-looking couple. Patrick, who was white, had dark hair in a buzz cut and blue eyes. Arnaz, Hispanic, had brown eyes and wore her brown hair with blond highlights in a spiky style. Glenn switched to the harsh but necessary corpse images of the pair from the morgue. "This is what became of them," he muttered, and then replaced it with the split screen of before and after images of the homicide victims.

Lastly, he put up the split-screen images of the most recent victim of the serial killer, and said sourly, "Yesterday, the body of twenty-five-year-old Tris Lindberg was discovered by game wardens at the Manikeke Crossing." Glenn regarded her attractive face, with blue eyes and long blond hair with retro bangs. He glanced at the picture of her corpse and then eyed Tisha, knowing that reliving the moment of discovery couldn't have been easy. But she had wanted to be here, to catch the briefing. "The bank teller was apparently hiking when the unsub used a stun gun to subdue and then strangle her. According to the associate medical examiner, the victim had been left there by her killer for as long as thirty-six hours, before the crime came to light."

Glenn turned off the monitor to spare them any unnecessary discomfort in viewing, then continued, "That makes three women and one man that we believe were victims of the so-called Shellview County Killer. Surveillance video was able to pick up a tall and slender white male with short dark hair, either leaving or in the vicinity of some of the crimes around the time they occurred. As of yet, we haven't been able to get much more than a general description and guesstimate his age range at anywhere from early thirties to midforties. No reliable DNA or prints have been collected and no witnesses have surfaced to pinpoint the unsub's identity. Nor have we been able to lock down a solid motive or connection between the victims. The current thinking is that the unsub targeted the females—perhaps randomly or intentionally—and the male victim was there by happenstance or simply in the way when going after the intended target."

Glenn sighed with frustration but refused to affix blame on the sheriff's department investigators, or himself, for that matter. They were all doing their respective jobs to the best of their abilities, as would be expected. Still, he knew that as the GBI special agent assigned to the case, he needed to find the serial killer and expose him for all the world to see. Then make sure that he was held accountable to the fullest extent of the law for what he'd done.

TISHA LISTENED WITH interest and sadness as Glenn linked the death of Tris Lindberg to a serial killer. Though this had been expected, all things considered, it was still a blow to think that Tris had been murdered in a wildlife management area that fell within Tisha's jurisdiction. That hadn't been the case for the earlier murders attributed to the Shellview County Killer, but it was no less unsettling. One murder within her territory as a game warden was one homicide too many.

I'd like to get more insight into the investigation, she told herself sincerely, if only for her own peace of mind, while the case went on. Not to mention, it would help her to be on the lookout for any other threats that could present themselves in the course of her work from the at-large serial killer.

"So what do you think?" Sherman asked as he walked up to her, snapping her out of her reverie as the briefing was ending.

Tisha met his curious gaze while wondering if he had gotten the number of the cute deputy he had been talking with. "I think we need to be vigilant in our duties while the killer's out there," she replied flatly.

"Aren't we always?" he queried. "We handle all types of law violators. This isn't any different, other than the fact that he's probably hidden in plain view and is, more likely than not, looking for soft targets that he can get the jump on, and out of the reach of game wardens, for the most part."

She couldn't help but chuckle. "I'd say that makes it just a bit different than the norm, wouldn't you?"

"Yeah, I suppose it does." He laughed. "We'll keep our eyes open for anyone acting suspicious."

"That's a good idea," Glenn said as he approached them.

Tisha smiled at him. "Hey. Thanks for giving us an update."

"Happy to do so." He grinned evenly.

"Hope you get this bastard soon," Sherman stated.

"You and me both," Glenn assured him. "We're working on that but can always use any help we can get."

Sherman nodded. "If anything draws our attention, you'll be the first to know."

"Good." Glenn patted his broad shoulder.

"If you'll excuse me, I'd like to have a word with Sheriff Pierce," Sherman said, and gazed at Tisha. "See you when I see you."

"Okay," she told him, and turned to Glenn, offering him a nervous smile.

He smiled back and said, "So do you have any questions?"

Tisha thought about it for a moment or two, before looking him right in the eyes as she responded whimsically, "Would you like to grab a bite to eat?"

"Not exactly what I had in mind." Glenn chuckled. "Uh, sure, I'm down with that. Starved, in fact."

How embarrassing would that have been if he'd turned me down, Tisha told herself, coloring nonetheless. "Cool," she responded, knowing it was lunchtime. She added candidly, for the record, "I do have some questions as well, pertaining to your investigation into Tris Lindberg's murder..."

He nodded. "Alright."

She lifted her chin. "We can take my vehicle."

"Lead the way," he told her.

As they headed outside, their hands touched inadvertently, and Tisha felt a sudden tingling ripple throughout her body. She wondered if he'd felt the same strange sensation. Or was it just her?

GLENN HAD TO admit that the last thing he expected was to be invited to lunch by the striking and married game warden. But then again, there was no harm in wanting to learn more about the investigation over a meal. Especially now that she had been drawn into the case indirectly. He turned in his seat and gazed at her profile for a moment while she drove, then asked curiously, "Where are we going?"

"There's a great place on Batten Avenue called Pauletta's Café that pretty much has everything," she told him.

"I'm familiar with it," he said, having gone there a few times since his transfer. "Good food there."

She smiled. "I agree."

He was curious to know more about her, and asked, "Are you from around here?"

"Depends on what you mean by around," she replied.

"The local area," he clarified.

"I grew up in DeKalb County, Georgia. My parents still live in Stone Mountain there, having emigrated to this country from South Korea before I was born."

Glenn nodded interestedly. "I see."

"What about you?" Tisha asked him. "I'm guessing that you haven't always lived or worked in or around Shellview County?"

"You guessed correctly." He grinned. "Until about a year ago, I was working for the GBI in Eastman. I'm actually from Sandy Springs, Georgia, where my mother and stepfather reside. My dad lives in Topanga, California."

"Cool," she uttered thoughtfully.

He felt the same way in getting some info on her geographical background as another native Georgian and hoped to discover more about the game warden.

Ten minutes later, they were seated in a window booth, where Glenn chose the steak burger and fries off the menu and Tisha went with a turkey BLT sandwich. Both ordered black coffee.

After some brief small talk, she asked him, "Is it possible that Tris Lindberg could have been stalked by her killer, so he knew exactly where she would be when he attacked her?"

Glenn considered what they knew, thus far, about the murder. "That is a possibility," he admitted, biting into a fry, knowing how some stalkers operated by tracking a victim's every movement. "We're looking into every angle to try and piece together Ms. Lindberg's movements in the forty-eight hours before her death to see if there was an indication that someone was stalking her. Or otherwise threatening her. Beyond that, there's also the matter of investigating her death, specifically, with the bigger picture of four deaths in total likely perpetrated by one individual."

Tisha nodded. She bit into her turkey BLT, chewed a bit and wiped her mouth with a napkin—she seemed ill at ease. "It's chilling to think that a serial killer is operating in Shellview County, right under our noses."

"Yeah," he concurred. "No one ever likes to think it can happen where they live. Unfortunately, these things can take place anywhere, at any time. Serial killers tend to pick and choose their killing locations based on wherever they happen to be that provides enough targets to go after, while having cover in one way or another to avoid capture. But the good news is they all slip up, sooner or later, and give us what we need to bring them down."

"That's comforting to know," she said softly. "I just hope it's sooner than later, so that residents and visitors alike, along with game wardens, can get on with their lives without this specter hanging over us all."

"There's every reason to believe that will be the case. The investigation is ongoing, and we won't stop till we have our man in custody." Glenn tasted his coffee, wishing he could reassure her more. But he understood that the only real remedy for that was to make an arrest, or otherwise stop the unsub from hurting anyone else. He regarded Tisha sipping her coffee and focused especially on her wedding band, which prompted him to ask what had been on his mind. "So how long have you been married?"

Tisha touched her ring self-consciously. "I'm a widow," she informed him. "I lost my husband three years ago to a heart attack."

"I'm sorry to hear that," Glenn uttered, hating to think that she was such a young widow.

"It's o-okay," she said with a stammer, as if to keep him from feeling sorry for her. "It was devastating for sure and came before we could add children to our marriage… But as hard as it's been, I've managed to move on with my life over time." She paused and gazed at the ring. "I've continued to wear it mostly for sentimental reasons and not as an indication that I'm unavailable to anyone."

"I understand." He ate more of his steak burger, while finding himself emboldened in knowing that she was open to romance again should the right person come along.

"How about you?" Tisha asked, getting his attention. "Married? Kids?"

"Not married and no kids," Glenn told her. "But not for lack of want in both instances." He sighed. "I suppose that between the demands of the job and rotten luck in developing a successful relationship, things have yet to work my way in that regard."

"I wouldn't give up on a happy ending," she said, smiling at him over her coffee mug. "You have plenty of time to find who you're looking for. Or be found by her to your mutual satisfaction."

He grinned back, intrigued by her, along with the possibilities that had presented themselves. "I'll keep that in mind."

"So how long have you been with the Georgia Bureau of Investigation?" she asked him.

"In September, it'll be ten years," he said proudly.

"That's a long time." She grinned. "You obviously enjoy what you do."

"Not always. It can be pretty demanding, if not downright frustrating at times, but it does have its rewards." *Meeting an attractive game warden has been one fringe benefit*, Glenn told himself. "How long have you been a game warden?"

"Not quite as long as you've been a GBI special agent." She laughed. "Six years and counting."

"Nice." He grinned sideways, impressed. "It obviously agrees with you."

"Not always, as you put it," she confessed. "But for the most part, it's a great job for a person who loves nature and the outdoors." Her expression became downcast. "At least until yesterday, when I discovered a dead body under the worst possible circumstances."

"I'm sorry you had to go through that," he said candidly. "But I'm sure it will pass with time, as do most things we could do without." He hoped she understood that he was referring to those types of tragedies, in particular. As opposed to losing a husband in the prime of her life and likely his.

"I'm sure you're right," she agreed quietly, "especially once her killer is apprehended and Tris is able to rest in peace…"

Along with the other victims of the unsub, Glenn mused, as he drank coffee and thought about the road ahead in that regard.

When Tisha dropped him off at his own SUV, he told

her, in noting that she had insisted on paying for the meal, "Thanks for the lunch."

"Thank you for agreeing to it," she countered with a grin.

"Next time it's on me." He wasn't sure if there would be a next time, but Glenn was definitely open to it, if she was.

"Deal." Tisha flashed her teeth, making it clear to him that she was on board.

Chapter Four

Later that afternoon, Glenn paid a visit to Tris Lindberg's mother, whom she had apparently been living with at the time of her death. He hoped to establish a timeline of her movements in the days prior to being killed.

"GBI Special Agent McElligott," he said, identifying himself to Alyssa Lindberg after her friend Irene Jenkins, a pregnant, thirtysomething, blond-haired woman, invited him inside.

Alyssa stared at him blankly through tearstained blue eyes as the three of them stood in the contemporary furnished living room. Her voice shook as she asked, "Do you have news about who killed my daughter...?"

"We're still investigating what happened to her and who was responsible," he responded honestly. "I need to know when you last saw your daughter."

Alyssa drew a breath, as Irene held her hand supportively. "On Wednesday morning, before I went to work. I own a boutique at the Hubbard Mall."

"I understand that Tris worked at a bank?"

"Yes, the Munroe Bank in Breyford. Wednesday was her off day. She loved to go hiking."

"Did she typically hike alone?" Glenn asked. "Or go with someone?"

"Both," Alyssa declared. "Sometimes it was with friends. I have no idea if she went by herself or not that day."

He gazed at her. "Do you know of anyone who might have wanted to harm your daughter?"

Alyssa stared at the question before answering with a hint of suspicion. "Why don't you ask her ex-boyfriend, Michael Beal? Tris lived with him before moving back home last month after Michael lost his job. They had a volatile relationship. He wasn't happy when she left him." Alyssa pursed her lips. "When she didn't come home that night, I feared that Tris had actually gone back to Michael, having done so before. Now, I'm left to wonder if he might have killed her—"

Glenn contemplated if the ex could have resorted to murder as payback for an ended relationship. It was not at all uncommon in modern times in intimate relationships gone sour, including hiring someone else to do his dirty work. But whether this amounted to serial murder, before and after, was a different matter altogether, though he believed that anything was possible and needed to be checked out.

"Where can I find Beal?" he asked.

Once he was given an address, Glenn left the women, while promising to keep Alyssa Lindberg informed of any new developments.

TISHA FELT HAPPY to get to know Glenn McElligott a bit better. Yes, there was still more to learn both ways, but she liked the idea of seeing if there was anything there that could be developed between them.

Glancing at her ring while driving, she realized that it could scare off men, making them believe she was either spoken for or unable to let go of the past. She hoped that Glenn now understood that it was neither. And that she was open to pursuing whatever came her way, if the person had the right character and was serious about getting involved.

Was Glenn such a man? She considered that he seemed ready to open his heart to someone who could relate to his focus on his career, while not holding that against him.

We'll see where it goes, if anywhere, Tisha told herself, as she parked her truck near Bartin's Creek. She got out and approached a couple of anglers, who were fishing in a prohibited area. The flaxen curly-haired male and a female with short beet-red hair were in their early twenties and exchanged a passionate kiss before realizing they had company.

"Hey, you two," Tisha said in a serious tone. "Didn't you see the sign? This area is off-limits for fishing."

"Must have missed it," the tall and lanky male said sardonically, his fishing line in the water.

Tisha was not amused. "Excuses, excuses," she said. "This isn't a game."

"We're sorry," the female said, holding her own rod unsteadily. "We just thought this was the perfect location to snag some bass for dinner. Can't you cut us some slack?"

"No can do." Though sympathetic to a point, Tisha wasn't quite enough to let them off the hook, no pun intended. "The rules are meant to be followed. You have to leave here, but not before you're both cited. Then you can find a spot to legally fish."

The male grumbled more than the female, but both took their lumps and moved on, with no fish for their trouble. Tisha was satisfied that she was back in gear with her normal work as a game warden, even if the ghastly thought of Tris Lindberg's body as she had found it still loomed large. And that would likely continue to be the case. Until her killer was brought to justice.

GLENN LEFT HIS vehicle on Baker Street and approached the bungalow, where he saw a man sitting on the stairs of the front porch, smoking a cigarette. He was in his midthirties and slender, and had long, layered dark hair swept backward.

Glenn walked up to him. “Are you Michael Beal?”

“Yeah. Who are you?”

“GBI Special Agent McElligott.” He flashed his identification.

Beal furrowed his brow. “Let me guess—you’re here about Tris…?”

“Good guess,” Glenn said sarcastically. “I’m investigating her death.”

“And I bet you’re wondering if I had anything to do with it?”

“The thought had crossed my mind.” Glenn peered at him. “Heard that things went south in your relationship, pissing you off…”

“Yeah, we broke up and it bothered me.” Beal sucked on the cigarette. “But I got over it.”

“Really?” Glenn jutted his chin. “You sure about that?”

“Look, I screwed up and Tris left me.” He sighed. “Took me a while, but I realized that we weren’t right for each other and moved on.”

Glenn wasn’t convinced of that and asked pointedly, “I need to know where you were when your ex-girlfriend was murdered.”

“I was here,” Beal replied matter-of-factly. “With my new girlfriend…” He called for her to come outside.

Glenn watched as a voluptuous twentysomething African American female with long blond box braids emerged from the house and declared, when asked, “Yeah, we’re together." She gave Beal an alibi for the time frame when Tris Lindberg was murdered and went back inside.

Giving him the benefit of the doubt until proven otherwise, Glenn asked Beal, "Did Tris ever indicate any concerns about someone who might have threatened or stalked her?"

Beal took a final drag of his cigarette, tossed the butt on the sidewalk and said thoughtfully, "Not really, but I remember one day last week following her to the bank, just to talk. We never did, but I could swear that I saw some other dude checking her out in the bank. Maybe it was just my imagination. Since we were no longer together, I didn't make a big deal out of it, only to have her accuse me of stalking her, or whatever."

"What did this guy look like?" Glenn asked attentively.

Beal shrugged. "I don't know," he responded. "Just average, I guess."

Glenn frowned. "You need to give me more than that, if you're on the level."

After contemplating, Beal said, "He was white, slender, maybe in his thirties… Oh, yeah, he was wearing a hoodie. Nothing else comes to mind."

Glenn mused about this potential new lead. "He never approached her?"

"Not that I saw."

"I may need you to speak with a sketch artist to describe this man," Glenn advised him, while also hoping that surveillance video from the bank might provide more information on the possible suspect.

"If you think it'll help, no problem." Beal ran a hand across his mouth. "Whoever killed Tris deserves to be put away…"

"That much we can agree on," Glenn said, and added,

"I'll need to narrow down the day and time frame in which you saw this person hanging around the bank—"

Beal said he would cooperate and Glenn left him on the porch stairs as he wondered if Tris Lindberg's killer had indeed been stalking her beforehand. And perhaps had done the same for the other victims in getting a handle on their routines prior to attacking them. If so, whom might the Shellview County Killer be setting his sights on now?

TISHA PLAYED WITH Jacky in the backyard after work, feeling that the retired K-9 dog seemed to have boundless energy. She imagined that, if called upon, Jacky would still be able to return to the DNR Law Enforcement Division K-9 Unit and pick up where she left off.

No way, Tisha thought firmly. She had no intention of giving up her endearing and loyal companion. She tossed a ball in the air and watched as Jacky went to fetch it, then brought it back to her on cue.

Not to say that she wouldn't mind having a human mate to fill the void—she longed for the type of affection and intimacy that were sorely missing in her life.

Someone like Glenn McElligott would do nicely, she imagined, were they to ever cross that bridge down the line.

Back inside, Tisha refilled Jacky's water bowl, and then took a shower, before sitting in an upholstered wingback chair in the living room and turning on her TV, where she caught the local news.

According to the attractive blond-haired anchor, the residents of Shellview County were on edge these days with the string of strangulation murders, the most current of which was the killing of Tris Lindberg. Tisha was surprised when her own name was brought up as the game warden who happened upon the body of the homicide victim.

Not exactly the way I want to be thought of, she told herself, even if the facts were public and the reality of a heinous death something that was unavoidable. But with Glenn and Sheriff Marjorie Pierce seriously on the case, Tisha was confident that justice was right around the corner.

On Sunday morning, she went to the Blair Bay Fitness Center on Ketchan Street for a workout with her friend and neighbor, Jeanne Rutland. Tisha spotted her on a treadmill and waved, then headed her way.

The same age and height as her, the newly divorced, green-eyed fashion designer was attractive and blond, sporting a cute shaggy haircut. More importantly, she was in great shape, as Tisha was herself. She worked hard to maintain her fitness, with group classes that included Pilates, yoga and Zumba.

"Hey," Jeanne greeted spiritedly. Her feet, in black sneakers, were moving briskly, and she was wearing a white tank top and blue joggers.

"Sorry I'm a little late," Tisha told her, knowing it was usually the opposite. "Jacky took longer than normal to relieve herself outside this morning."

"It's cool. I love your dog, so I won't fault her for going at her own pace. Kind of like I'm doing right now," she said with a laugh.

"I'd say you've got a pretty nice pace going there." Tisha smiled and stepped onto the treadmill next to hers. She was dressed in a black sports bra and gray shorts, while wearing rose-colored running shoes. Her hair was in a high ponytail.

"Back at you," Jeanne said, as Tisha had quickly gotten into a comfortable groove, while keeping up with her friend.

"Just making up for lost time," she joked.

No sooner had Tisha begun to work up a good sweat, when Jeanne commented, "I heard your name mentioned on a news update as the game warden who discovered that poor woman in the Manikeke Crossing."

"It's true," Tisha confirmed, wishing that wasn't the case. "It certainly threw me for a loop in what was supposed to be a routine data collection, more or less."

Jeanne frowned. "Must have been awful."

"Yeah, you could say that." Tisha wiped her brow with the back of her hand. "Worse is that her death has been linked to a serial killer…"

Jeanne's eyes popped wide. "The Shellview County Killer?"

"That would be the one," she said sadly.

"Scary." Jeanne caught her breath. "How long is it going to take to get this creep?"

"Your guess is as good as mine." Tisha hated to admit it. "I do know, though, that the Georgia Bureau of Investigation is working hard with the sheriff's department to solve the murders by catching the killer."

"That's good to know, anyway."

Tisha thought about Glenn in that moment. Along with the fact that as long as the unsub remained on the loose, it was anything but business as usual for everyone. "Until then, just be careful in your daily life," she warned her friend, as everyone in Shellview County should be while this was going on.

"I will," Jeanne assured her, while slowing down. "You, too."

Tisha took in the words, knowing that no one was safe from potentially becoming a victim here, with women and men targeted as if equal game for the culprit.

Not even a game warden.

GLENN LET HIS Lab run wild on the property for his daily exercise, before bringing Riley with him to a playground in

Akerston Heights on Packlin Road, where he was meeting up with fellow GBI Special Agent Kurt Stewart, to shoot some hoops on a basketball court. The two had met when both had been assigned to the Region 12 investigative office. After his divorce was finalized nearly a year ago, his ex, Dixie, had gotten custody of their two children, Kendra and Mitchell, after having lost another child, Greta, to cancer two years earlier. Kurt had transferred to the Region 6 office in Milledgeville, Georgia. It was close enough to Glenn's neck of the woods that they were able to continue getting together to play basketball, when they each had some free time.

Glenn ordered Riley to sit on the grass next to the court and the dog obeyed, ignoring its instincts to the contrary. "Good boy," he told him, and Glenn turned just in time to catch the basketball that had been thrown his way.

"You've still got the reflexes, McElligott," Kurt said with a chuckle.

"Always." Glenn gazed at the special agent who was two years older than him and maybe an inch taller on a muscular frame. His eyes were blue, and he had dark hair in a faded buzz cut and a dimpled chin. Both were wearing athletic clothing and gym shoes. He tossed the ball back at him and said amusingly, "Let's see what you've got, Stewart—"

The two engaged in some trash talking and physical play, then Kurt asked, "So what's happening with your case…?"

Glenn sighed while shooting the ball and watching as it bounced off the rim. "Still trying to dig through the evidence, or lack thereof, in coming up with a suspect and making an arrest."

Kurt ran down the errant shot. "It's never easy when you're trying to track down someone who by his very nature seems bent on killing and isn't looking to slow down by being captured."

"Tell me about it." Glenn frowned. "We'll get there, though, one way or the other."

"We always do," Kurt agreed, backing him up.

Glenn sensed that he was referring to his own current investigation into illegal gambling, as part of the GBI's commercial gambling unit. "Where are you in your investigation?"

"Making some serious headway," he responded, shooting the ball and making the shot. "I expect that we could be issuing arrest warrants at any time now."

"Good to know," Glenn said, always rooting for his fellow GBI agents, just as they always had his back.

Kurt took the ball from his hands and asked casually, "So what's happening with your love life these days? Any action? Or are you like me since my divorce, stuck in a rut?"

Glenn grinned musingly as he thought about Tisha. "Not exactly in a rut, but maybe on the right track."

"Oh, really?" Kurt's eyes lit up with curiosity. "Who's the lucky woman?"

"I think it'll be up to her to determine whether or not getting to know me is good luck or not."

"Fair enough." Kurt laughed. "Keep me posted and I'll do the same, should someone enter my orbit again…"

"You've got it," Glenn said hopefully, while thinking that the next thing he could do was invite Tisha to dinner and plan on her accepting. After all, it was his turn to pay for a meal. Cooking it as well was a fringe benefit. He scooped up the ball, placed a well-timed elbow to Kurt's chest to clear up some room, then executed a perfect jump shot and watched the ball swoosh through the net.

Chapter Five

On Monday morning, Tisha was on patrol in her F-150 truck, when her cell phone rang. She saw that the caller was Glenn, causing her heart to skip a beat. She wondered if the call was an update on the case. Or perhaps more personal in nature?

She put him on speakerphone and said cheerfully, “Hey there.”

“Hey.” He paused. “I was wondering if you’d like to come to my place tonight for dinner, if you don’t have any other plans. Or tomorrow, if that works better for you…?”

“I have no current plans for tonight’s meal,” Tisha answered quickly. “So the answer is yes, I’d love to have dinner with you.”

“Great. How does six sound?”

“Perfect.” She smiled at the thought of having someone cook dinner for her, assuming that was the plan. It was something she hadn’t experienced in recent memory, apart from her mother doing it. “Would you like me to bring wine or anything?”

“Not necessary. I think I’ll be able to cover all the bases,” Glenn assured her.

“Alright.”

“I’ll text you my address,” he said.

"Okay," she told him, and they disconnected. The idea of essentially going on a date excited Tisha, especially with someone she found herself attracted to. But she wouldn't get too carried away with it, for fear of disappointment. Best to see how it went and go from there.

As she contemplated this, a report came in of two gopher tortoises found dead under suspicious circumstances in the Manikeke Crossing WMA. She headed that way, hating the thought of deliberate harm coming to the threatened species. Moreover, she couldn't help but think of the murder victim, Tris Lindberg. Returning to the scene of the crime gave Tisha chill bumps in the middle of the summer.

Get over it, she admonished herself. Whatever ordeal Tris had been put through, her suffering was over now, for better or worse. Besides, wasn't Glenn on the case, in pursuit of justice? As was the sheriff's department. They would solve this case and give Tris and the other victims of this serial killer the lasting peace they so deserved.

When she reached her destination, Tisha found that Sherman was already there, along with another game warden. Bree McDaniels was in her late forties, medium-sized and had a light blond chin-length bob.

Tisha approached the two as they stood, as if on guard, beside the dead gopher tortoises that were lying on the bloodstained ground near a cluster of shrubs. "What have you learned about this?" she asked.

Sherman furrowed his forehead. "Looks like they've both been shot."

Tisha regarded the fallen members of the keystone species—their carapaces were brownish-black—with anger. One of the tortoises was larger than the other and appeared to have been shot at least twice, taking the brunt of the punishment. "Who would do such a horrible thing?" she moaned, knowing that the gopher tortoise had been designated the official state reptile of Georgia.

Bree wrinkled her nose and pursed her lips. "Someone—or more than one person—who was heartless and disgusting!"

"Even worse than that," Sherman grumbled. "But we'll get whoever was responsible."

"We'd better," Tisha insisted. "We can't allow someone to get away with this act, encouraging other sick people to try and emulate it."

"Don't even go there," he said, as if horrified at the thought.

"Wish I didn't have to." As it was, she knew that bad behavior often bred more bad behavior, something they had seen all too often.

Bree leaned down toward the gopher tortoises for a closer look and said, "Between the crime scene analysis, ballistics getting the info on the bullets and firearm used, and help from the public, this definitely won't end well for the perp or perps."

Tisha took that to heart as she made herself turn again toward the victims of the attack, which had come on the heels of the murder of Tris Lindberg. She wondered if there was possibly more than coincidence here.

THERE, I DID IT, Glenn thought, patting himself on the back for asking Tisha over for dinner. Better yet, she'd said yes. Now, he could only hope that it was a positive sign that something good was happening between them.

His thoughts turned to the man taken into custody by the sheriff's department as a person of interest in the murder of Tris Lindberg. Surveillance video at the Munroe Bank, where she worked, was able to zero in on the suspect, subsequently identified as thirty-six-year-old Joseph

Nicholson, who was described as a drifter and loner with a history of stalking.

"Nicholson's originally from St. Louis," Marjorie noted, as Glenn stood beside the sheriff looking at the suspect on a video monitor. "He's been in and out of trouble for much of his adult life, though nothing has risen to the level of homicidal behavior. Much less, serial murder. Still, we won't know till we know, one way or the other."

"I agree," Glenn told her. "I'll go talk to him."

She nodded. "Let's just see what Nicholson has to say for himself."

After stepping inside the interrogation room, where the suspect sat silently at a small metal table, Glenn observed him for a quick appraisal. Dressed in tattered clothing, he was slender but not skinny and had dirty and thinning straight brown hair touching his shoulders. Deep furrows were etched across his forehead, and he had wide-spaced blue eyes.

"I'm Agent McElligott," Glenn said evenly to him, while sitting across from him in a black vinyl chair. "I need to ask you a few questions."

Nicholson, who wasn't cuffed, rubbed his nose and said in a raspy voice, "Ask away, but I didn't do anything."

Not convinced on his word alone, Glenn told him, "You were picked up after being seen on a security video appearing to be studying a bank employee named Tris Lindberg."

"So what if I was," he snorted defiantly. "Is that a crime?"

"Yes, stalking is a crime," Glenn pointed out matter-of-factly. "Murder is worse."

Nicholson's eyes popped wide. "What are you trying to say?"

"Ms. Lindberg was found strangled to death Friday

morning." Glenn peered across the table. "Right now, you're our only suspect."

Nicholson muttered an expletive. "I didn't know Tris was dead," he claimed thoughtfully. "I had nothing to do with that—"

Glenn leaned forward. "Did you know Ms. Lindberg?"

He paused, then replied unevenly, "Not really… She gave me some money when passing by on the street. That's all."

"Why were you stalking her?" Glenn demanded.

"I wasn't stalking anyone. I just needed some money and followed her to the bank, hoping she would be able to give me a little when she took her break." He rubbed his nose again. "But I decided to look for some elsewhere and so I left. Never saw her again."

Glenn noted that the surveillance video supported the part of his story about leaving the bank on his own. Could he have already tracked Tris's movements, though, including following her on her day off to the Manikeke Crossing?

"What were you doing last Wednesday?" Glenn asked him, to see how he reacted when given some latitude.

Nicholson bit his lower lip. "I was at the shelter on Ninth Street," he said. "Slept most of the time. After that, I just hung out on the street, bumming money off anyone who would give it."

Glenn knew that it would be easy enough to check out the shelter. Apart from that, as much as he wished that this was the man they were looking for in the murder of the bank teller, he wasn't feeling it. Moreover, it seemed unlikely that Nicholson had the physical stamina for making his way up into the wildlife management area to commit a murder and get away with it. Same was true for pegging him as a serial killer strangling his victims, including an able-bodied male.

Still, Glenn asked the suspect about the serial crimes, anyway, before deciding to cut him loose. The sheriff agreed, believing that the real unsub was still out there, waiting to strike again.

TISHA WAS STILL grieving the loss of those poor gopher tortoises when she arrived at Glenn's house, parking in the driveway alongside his SUV. She hoped they would catch whoever was responsible. In the meantime, she welcomed an opportunity for a meal with a friendly and handsome face.

Wearing her hair down, she kept her attire simple with a blue smocked sundress and sandals. It took only one ring of the bell before the door opened.

"Hey. Right on time." Glenn grinned at her.

"Didn't want to be late," Tisha admitted. She blushed under the weight of his gaze, even while checking him out in his lime-green polo shirt, brown linen pants and black loafers.

"Come in," he said.

The moment she stepped inside the foyer, Tisha found herself practically knocked over by an excited black Lab. "And who is this?" she asked, playing with the dog, who seemed friendly enough.

"That's Riley," Glenn told her. "I can see that's he's quickly warming up to you."

"Must be that he senses that I love dogs." Tisha laughed. "I have one of my own."

"Cool." He ordered Riley to give her some breathing room and the dog obeyed the command without missing a beat.

Tisha quickly scanned the handsomely furnished, spacious interior of the house and said, "Really nice place you have here, including the property I saw when driving up."

"Thanks." Glenn seemed to downplay it. "It's enough right now for me and Riley. But if there ever need to be any additions, I'm happy to go there."

She suspected that he was referring to having a wife and family. But there would need to be a lot of children to actually outgrow the residence. "Good to know," she uttered nevertheless. As the pleasing odor of food passed to her nostrils, she asked, "Can I help with anything?"

"Nope. Got it covered. Make yourself at home."

She smiled. "I will, thanks."

"By the way, do you prefer white or red wine?" he asked curiously.

"Red would be great."

"Red, it is." He touched her arm affectionately. "Dinner will be served shortly."

"Good, as I'm starving," Tisha confessed.

He grinned and walked toward the big kitchen.

As she started to wander around the great room, Tisha spotted the acoustic guitar leaning up against a midcentury modern armchair. She picked it up and asked lightheartedly, "Do you play the guitar? Or is this only meant to impress visitors?"

"Maybe a little of both." Glenn laughed while checking a pot on the stove. "Yes, I play it from time to time as a way to keep Riley entertained. You play?"

"A little, but I'm not very good, I'm afraid, and way out of practice." Tisha strummed the guitar a little with her fingers. "I'm more at home with the piano, learning to play as a child." She had only recently sold the baby grand piano she had during her marriage, as her current residence was too small to keep it.

"Any musical talents are great to have," he told her.

"Very true," she agreed, while hoping he would play the guitar while she was there. In the meantime, Riley came up to Tisha and she petted his back and chest, which he clearly enjoyed in both instances. She imagined that the dog would get along well with Jacky, who was in need of a friendly canine companion.

When she was told it was time to wash up for dinner, Tisha went to the bathroom downstairs, while hoping to get a tour of the rest of the house, including where Glenn slept—alone, she assumed.

GLENN MARVELED AT just how stunning Tisha was as she sat across from him in a welted-back side chair at the oak dining room table. Even better was seeing her hair down. He'd love to run his fingers through it sometime.

"This is incredible," she said, breaking into his thoughts, while eating his home-cooked meal consisting of corned beef, sweet-potato pasta and lemon-flavored brussels sprouts. Along with red wine.

He smiled. "Thanks."

"Where did you learn to cook?" She gave him a curious gaze.

"Picked up pretty much everything I know about cooking from my sister, Josette. She's a few years older and a chef at an upscale restaurant, living in Anchorage with her partner."

"Cool." Tisha smiled and lifted her wineglass. "I've always wanted to visit Alaska."

"Went there once," he told her, forking some pasta. "Amazing place." He liked the idea of returning there with Tisha, whom he was certain Josette would love. "Do you have any siblings?" he asked.

"Just me, myself and I," she quipped. "My parents wanted more children, but it never happened. Guess some things aren't meant to be."

Glenn detected in her tone the regret of missing out on having children with her late husband. Maybe there was still a family in her future. And his own, for that matter.

"So how was your day?" he asked between bites, if only to break the stiffness in the air.

"Not very good, I'm afraid." Tisha frowned as she held in her fork a brussels sprout. "Someone shot and killed two gopher tortoises in the Manikeke Crossing."

"Sorry to hear that." Glenn tasted his wine. "I take it the culprit or culprits are still on the loose?"

She nodded. "Cowards and creeps."

"I couldn't agree more." He could see just how serious she took things in her job as a game warden, making him appreciate her all the more as someone who also loved nature and maintaining a healthy environment for all living species. "Had my own share of disappointment today," he remarked.

Tisha tilted her head. "What happened?"

"Thought we had a solid lead on a suspect in the murder of Tris Lindberg. A drifter had been following her, in the name of hitting her up for money. Unfortunately, it didn't add up in terms of him being her killer. Which also excluded him, more or less, from being a legitimate suspect as the Shellview County Killer."

"That's too bad." Tisha dabbed a paper napkin to her mouth. "All you can do is keep the investigation going till the right answers surface, right?"

"Right." He grinned at her. "Having you over for dinner has been right by me, in and of itself."

She showed her teeth. "For me, too."

As if he wanted in on the action, Riley barked in agreement from where he was sitting in corner observing them, then stood and came up to Tisha for some added attention.

After dinner, Glenn gave her a tour of the house, including one of the upstairs guest bedrooms that he had converted into a home office with traditional furnishings—he knew his job often required him to bring his work home with him. He gauged Tisha's reaction as she saw the spacious primary bedroom with its large windows, modern storage furniture and king-size platform bed. He was particularly interested in how she viewed the bed, imagining being in it with her, making love.

"Hmm…" she murmured. "Nice."

He smiled at her, content to leave it at that, then they went back downstairs and he showed her the grounds. She seemed equally taken with them and he found himself imagining her living there, with two dogs roaming around the property for them to chase after, like a fun-loving, energetic couple.

When they returned to the house, Tisha lifted the guitar and asked sweetly, "Will you play something for me?"

Glenn grinned, taking it from her, and responded, "I'd be happy to." He began playing the first song that came to mind, which happened to be one of the first songs he learned to play and among his favorites—"Always on Your Side."

Tisha's eyes lit up. "I love that song."

"Me, too." He smiled and was glad when she began to sing the lyrics, causing him to join in.

Afterward, they laughed like schoolchildren from the impromptu duet and Tisha looked him in the eye and asked in a sexy tone of voice, "Would it be alright if I kissed you…?"

"I would love it if you kissed me," Glenn told her without prelude.

She cupped his cheeks and laid one on his lips. Her mouth was as soft as he imagined and a good fit for his. The kiss was just long enough to make his heart race, before she pulled away.

"Sorry about that." Tisha blushed flirtatiously. "I don't know what came over me."

Glenn laughed. "Whatever it was, you won't find me complaining."

"Good to know." She laughed back. "I think I should go now."

"Okay." He wanted her to stay but didn't want to put any pressure on her. When and if she was all in, he would be ready.

"Thanks for the dinner."

"Anytime," he told her and meant it. "I'll walk you out."

Moments later, Glenn watched her drive off, as did Riley, who already acted as though he had lost his best friend. "Don't worry, boy," he told the dog optimistically. "If we play our cards right, Tisha will be back, and we can pick up where we left off."

They went back inside the house with that thought very much on Glenn's mind.

Chapter Six

Tisha drove off feeling pretty good about spending some quality time away from work with a man. Or this one, in particular.

She had actually kissed him. Imagine that. And he was clearly receptive to it, but respectful enough to not want to go too far too soon.

But there was always the next time. Or one after that.

She glanced at the ring on her finger contemplatively. It had taken her a while to get past the tragedy of losing her husband at such a young age. Maybe now, there was an opportunity to move on and find happiness again with someone.

When she arrived home, Jacky greeted Tisha excitedly and she hugged the dog endearingly. She imagined Jacky would get along well with Riley and form her own bond.

After taking a shower, Tisha slipped into a cotton chemise and headed for her bedroom, which had two large windows, handcrafted log furniture and a queen-size panel bed. She hated sleeping alone and longed for someone to hold and be held by.

Glenn flooded her thoughts in the moment before sleep overtook her.

The following day, Tisha joined other game wardens,

Bree and Sherman, and their supervisor, Sergeant Fritz Alvarez, as they zeroed in on the culprits who had killed the two gopher tortoises. The three suspects were bloodthirsty teenagers who had been discovered from a video they took of the killing, which they posted on online sites, all but bragging about their cruel actions.

"How dumb can they be?" Fritz asked. His tall and muscular frame was rigid as he peered at the trio they had tracked to a recreational area along the Chattahoochee River, hanging out as though they didn't have a care in the world. "Who does something like that, then posts it online for everyone to see—including us—and still expects to get away with it, as if they'd done nothing wrong?"

Tisha frowned and answered with indignation, "Teens who are truly sick, undisciplined and could care less about what they've done."

"Not to mention some of the other bizarre postings they put up," Bree said, "indicating a complete lack of compassion for wildlife and no appreciation for conservation."

"I'll go one step further," Sherman said thickly. "These kids are unsupervised delinquents who will have to pay the price for their actions."

"That we can agree on," Fritz stated, jutting his chin. "Let's bring them in…"

They wasted no time surrounding the three suspects—two older teen males and one petite female, who Tisha imagined couldn't have been more than fourteen or fifteen years old. They all seemed unfazed by being discovered and the seriousness of their current predicament.

"You're under arrest for what you did to those gopher tortoises," Fritz snapped at them.

As they were being handcuffed, the three were defiant, spouting off obscenities and taunts. "Get it off your chest,"

Sherman said sarcastically. "It won't do anything to get you out of the mess you've created."

Tisha seriously doubted that the suspects even cared, making it even more sad. But at least the culprits had been captured, preventing them from killing other tortoises.

They were facing charges that included the killing of threatened species, along with felony cruelty to animals—each were third-degree felonies carrying a maximum penalty of a fine totaling 10,000 dollars and as many as five years behind bars.

As far as Tisha was concerned, it was a price that needed to be paid, with protecting such species a priority. She felt the same way about holding persons accountable for human loss, as in the case of Tris Lindberg.

THAT AFTERNOON, Glenn sat at his desk and requested a video chat with his former advisor when he was a student at Georgia Southern University, Edward Kundu, an associate professor of criminology in the College of Behavioral and Social Sciences. He also happened to be a renowned criminal profiler, having written several books, with a particular interest in serial homicides. It was in this capacity that Glenn hoped to gain some insight into the elusive Shellview County Killer he was currently pursuing.

Professor Kundu accepted the invitation and appeared on the screen. An Indian American, he was in his late fifties with short gray hair and had a full salt-and-pepper beard. He touched his low-bridge eyeglasses and said with a grin, "Hi, Glenn. Nice to speak to you again."

Smiling back and almost feeling as though he was still an undergrad, Glenn responded formally, "You, too, Professor Kundu."

"Edward is fine," he reminded Glenn, as they'd become friends over the years.

"Okay." Glenn met his brown eyes fixedly. "Did you have a chance to look over the file on my serial killer investigation?"

"I did." Edward sat back in his own high-backed office chair musingly. "Well, my first thought in sizing up this Shellview County serial killer is that he's no more, no less a predator than those who have perpetrated serial murders before him. Jack the Ripper, Albert Fish, Ted Bundy, Henry Lucas, John Wayne Gacy, Gerald Gallego, Richard Ramirez, Charles Ng, Samuel Little—the list goes on. Or, in other words, there's nothing particularly special about this unsub. He's targeting people—mostly women—who have come into his crosshairs through one means or another. That being said, he's clearly chosen to strangle his victims rather than shoot, stab, hang, push off a cliff, or use some other dastardly means to kill—which, in and of itself, puts him in a certain category of serial killers. They gain some sort of perverse thrill in this mode of execution."

Glenn asked, "So apart from the murders themselves, what is the unsub gaining by killing the victims? Are we talking about doing this for sport, to see just how long he can get away with it, or what? Or is there a psychological angle here that might help me get a better fix on what we're dealing with?"

Edward touched his glasses while pondering the question, then said frankly, "There's always a psychological component to serial homicides. Most serial killers are psychopaths by their very nature, which shouldn't be confused with being certifiably insane. Quite the opposite. Few serial killers—virtually none—are so far gone so as to not be able to distinguish between right and wrong, or reality and fantasy or illusion. That notwithstanding, mental illness to some degree is nearly always a correlate of serial killing, as normal triggers fail to get the killer to stop after the first kill. Or even the second one." Edward scratched his beard. "The psychological instability is often born out of conflicts the killer is coping with internally—be it relationship, work, financial issues or something else—that he or she deals with externally by killing others to relieve the pressure. Only to have that tension rebuild time and time again. Till the killer is stopped through means other than a willingness to quit."

Glenn considered what had been laid out by the associate professor as if he was still a student. But now that he was a seasoned GBI special agent, he could interpret things differently, and said to him, "I get that the unsub has psychological issues, while also being clever enough to avoid detection. Are there any other characteristics, physical or otherwise, to look for while I'm narrowing the search for him?"

"As I'm sure you know, serial killers come in all shapes, sizes and sexes, racial and ethnic backgrounds, marital status, professions and net worth, et cetera," Edward pointed out and drew a breath. "But that doesn't mean that serial killers aren't more prone to fall into some categories than others—such as being mostly in their midtwenties to midforties, being loners in their actions, if not lifestyles. They have some proclivity to commit or have learned violence through others whether when young or older and have likely experienced some sort of familial dysfunction or childhood trauma that is a factor in the present antisocial behavior. That pretty much sums it up in terms of profiling your unsub. Whether that can make a difference in the investigation will be for you to decide. Either way, I'm always happy to be of assistance whenever I can, Glenn."

"I appreciate that," he told him, offering a nod. "And you have provided valuable insight to add to the profile of the unsub as the investigation continues and we try to nab him as soon as possible."

"Good." Edward leaned forward. "If you're unable to get the guy soon and want to try to get inside the head of a like-minded serial killer, you might consider talking to a man named Lucas Conseco. Five years ago, Conseco was convicted of strangling to death eight women in Fulton County. He's currently serving a life sentence at the Macon State Prison in Oglethorpe, Georgia."

"I'm familiar with the case," Glenn said as he pondered the matter. Lucas Conseco had murdered women named Linda or Lynda, as a warped act of revenge against his deceased mother, who had abused then abandoned him in childhood. The GBI had assisted the Fulton County Sheriff's Office and Atlanta Police Department in solving the strange case.

Edward said matter-of-factly, "I'm actually writing a book on Conseco and have interviewed him. I'd be happy to help set it up if you'd like to see what he has to say about the inner workings of a fellow serial strangler killer, if that might help your cause..."

"I don't think I need to go there," Glenn said, respectfully declining the suggestion. He winced at the thought of using one serial killer to capture another. "But I'll keep it in mind, nevertheless," he added, if only for effect.

"Alright."

Glenn ended the video chat and left the office to head down the hall and into the office of the special agent in charge, Rhianna Kingsley. She was leaning up against a black height-adjustable standing desk near a window wall, while looking at some papers, and noticed him enter.

"Hey," she said evenly. "What's going on?"

"Just spoke with a criminal profiler on the Shellview County Killer investigation," Glenn told her.

"Really?" Her eyes widened with curiosity.

He gave her a summary of the discussion and added, "Gives us something more to place into the equation in our efforts to home in on a suspect."

"Interesting." Rhianna nodded. "Whatever it takes to solve this case."

"That's how I'm working it," he stressed.

When their cell phones rang at the same time, Glenn suppressed a grin, as each responded to the calls. For him, it was Sheriff Marjorie Pierce on the line.

"There's been another murder," she told him bleakly.

"Where?" He regarded Rhianna, whose expression suggested she had received equally disturbing news.

"Kendell State Park," Marjorie replied flatly. "The death fits the pattern of the serial murders…"

"I'm on my way." Glenn disconnected and saw that Rhianna was already off the phone.

With a dour look on her face, she muttered, "Guess we received the same notification. The Shellview County Killer has apparently struck again."

Wishing he could push back against the notion, but unable to, Glenn furrowed his brow and said forlornly, "Yeah, it appears that way…"

MARJORIE WAS ANGUISHED as she conferred with her deputies at the crime scene of Kendell State Park on Rawley Road, where the victim had been found in the woods, along a trail, lying flat on her back.

Identified as Patrina Morse, a thirty-three-year-old high school teacher who was visiting from Sydney, Australia, she was staying at the Kendell State Park Lodge and had gone out for a morning run, when disaster struck in the form of a killer.

Marjorie studied the deceased white woman, who was slender with short dark brown curly hair. She was wearing a yellow tank top, dark gray leggings and white sneakers. Gazing at her neck, Marjorie could see the discoloration on it, a telltale sign that she had been strangled. Much like the four other victims that had fallen prey to ligature strangulations, perpetrated by a serial killer. Similarly, there was the clear indication of puncture wounds that likely came from a stun gun, per the unsub's modus operandi.

The fact that this one happened so soon after the murder of Tris Lindberg was troubling to Marjorie, to say the least. Did this speak of desperation on the part of the unsub? Or sheer arrogance that he could handpick any target of his choosing and operate with little fear of apprehension?

Either way, she loathed that this was happening under her watch. Along with that of GBI Agent Glenn McElligott, who had to be just as ticked off with the case and its dynamics as she was. They would either sink or swim together on this one. She was determined that it would be the latter, as Marjorie watched the special agent working his way through the crime scene tape and as he approached her.

GLENN COULD SEE the strain on Sheriff Pierce's face as she greeted him at the spot where the body was found. Not that he could blame her for feeling the pressure, just as he was. And now they had a new victim to contend with.

"What are we looking at?" he asked her routinely, even

if it was painfully obvious, as Glenn glanced at the pale and tragic homicide victim, and back to the sheriff.

Marjorie pursed her lips and replied tonelessly, “Name’s Patrina Morse. Three days ago, Ms. Morse and a female friend, Tracy Nguyen, arrived from Australia for a vacation—staying at the Kendell State Park Lodge. According to Ms. Nguyen, at approximately nine a.m. today, Ms. Morse went out for a run. She was an avid jogger. When she didn’t return by noon, Ms. Nguyen went looking for her…only to find her friend dead deep in the woods…”

“Did she happen to see anyone else before discovering the body?” Glenn asked the sheriff, wondering if the killer could have still been in the area.

“Apparently not.” Majorie hunched her shoulders. “However, as she was under duress after calling 911 and afterward, which is totally understandable, we will need to question her further on that front.”

“Good.” Glenn frowned while thinking that he needed to speak to the witness himself and see what he could gather from her. “We’ll need to access any surveillance cameras at the lodge or elsewhere in and around the park.” He was thinking that the killer could have followed the victim from the lodge, unbeknownst to her, before killing her and disappearing into the woods.

“Trust me, my department will use every angle at our disposal to try and solve this murder,” she told him.

“Of course.” He didn’t mean to step on her toes, if that was what the sheriff thought. They were all on the same page. Hell, the same book and chapter in trying to solve the murder. “Looks like our unsub is at it again.”

“I know,” Marjorie groaned. “I’m sure the medical examiner’s office will back us up on this.” She sighed. “Look at her. She didn’t deserve that while on vacation in Georgia.”

"Yeah."

Glenn gazed at the victim, imagining how this would hit her family in Australia. Being in the wrong state at the worst possible time was something her friend would have to live with for the rest of her life. But at least she would have a life to live.

Not so for Patrina Morse.

When Ned Karakawa, the associate medical examiner, and his team arrived, Glenn had already set the GBI crime scene investigators and those from the sheriff's department in motion in the collection of evidence, including photographs of the victim and surrounding area.

Karakawa wrinkled his brow as he glanced at Marjorie and then looked at Glenn and remarked humorlessly, "Wish we didn't have to keep meeting like this..."

"It does stink," Glenn muttered truthfully.

"Tell me about it," Marjorie concurred, as they stepped aside to allow him to conduct his preliminary examination of the body.

It didn't take long for Karakawa to indicate his belief that they were looking at a victim of homicide by ligature strangulation.

Glenn filled in the rest himself, as it was fairly obvious to him that this was the work of the Shellview County Killer, who seemed more than happy to rub it in their faces.

TISHA WAS GIVEN a start with the news from Glenn that an Australian woman had been murdered in Shellview County and the case was linked to the serial killer. The fact that the heinous act had taken place at Kendell State Park was even more disturbing, as it fell within her work section. *How many more people have to die?* she asked herself grimly, as she arrived at the park. It was teeming with county and state law enforcement, along with bystanders, as if they had nothing better to do than watch a murder investigation unfold.

She saw Glenn speaking with Sherman and the sheriff, and joined them. "Came as soon as I heard," Tisha told them.

"Warden Fletcher," Marjorie said, acknowledging her.

"Sheriff." Tisha met her eyes, imagining just how much she was stressing out while overseeing this investigation. "How's it going?" she asked of the investigation.

"Apart from the cold-blooded murder of a tourist, about as well as could be expected with little to go on for the time being," the sheriff responded sourly.

Tisha turned to a frowning Sherman, who muttered, "Another murder happening within our jurisdiction is not good."

"No, it isn't," she acknowledged. "But given the wide range we cover, it's not too surprising, in and of itself." Tisha twisted her lips. "The implication that it is again the work of a serial killer is another matter altogether." Differentiating those truths didn't make this go down any easier.

"True." He nodded thoughtfully and started talking to the sheriff.

Facing Glenn, Tisha said awkwardly, "Hey." The kiss they'd shared briefly yesterday crossed her mind.

"Hey." He met her gaze squarely. "Sorry about having to deal with the latest homicide."

"Me, too," she admitted. "Thanks for the heads-up, which came just before I received the news from my work section boss, Sergeant Fritz Alvarez."

"I wanted to keep you up to date on the twists and turns of this case," Glenn told her, "since you were pulled into it after the discovery of the last victim—"

Tisha winced. "So the MO in the latest murder is the same?" Not that she had any reason to believe the homicide was unrelated to the Shellview County Killer case.

"I'm afraid so." He tilted his head. "She was strangled with a ligature, with evidence that a stun gun was used on the victim."

Tisha made a face. "How horrifying."

"The autopsy will likely clear up any doubt," Glenn said. "But as it stands at the moment, the victim, Patrina Morse, was targeted by the serial killer, however she managed to fall into his crosshairs."

In that instant, they both looked to the right and watched uneasily as the decedent was being carted away by the associate medical examiner, whose work, to Tisha, would only add to the trauma inflicted upon the victim, even if they were unable to feel it on a human level.

HE WATCHED THE goings-on taking place at the Kendell State Park, keeping his distance but keenly aware that they were investigating the latest murder he had committed. Frankly, he was not too taken with the Shellview County Killer moniker the press had hoisted upon him like a badge of dishonor.

As far as he was concerned, it was totally honorable to end the lives of those whom he had sought out and extinguished like burning flames when their time had come to be snuffed out. He made no apologies for doing what needed to be done. For that matter, he had no qualms about going after others who were slated for death by his hands.

He studied the pretty game warden who was chatting amicably with the GBI special agent. Seemed as if they were more interested in one another than solving the murder of the good-looking Australian teacher he had strangled to death.

He imagined that the game warden would be easy prey, like the others, when the time was right. Maybe the GBI agent, too, if he got in his way. Much like when the IT manager who'd lost his life when he made the mistake of interfering with plans to kill the attractive girlfriend.

The Shellview County Killer remained hidden in plain view for a bit longer, relishing the attention he was getting and the ineffectiveness of the authorities to stop him. Then he quietly and calmly slipped away into the woods and farther out of reach from those who would wish to prevent him from killing again.

Chapter Seven

Kendell State Park Lodge was just miles from the Chattahoochee River and the park itself, steep in loblolly pine and red maple trees, with a waterfall and more than one trail. Glenn saw these as possible escape routes the killer of Patrina Morse had taken. He mused about this while approaching the cabin, alongside Tisha, whom he had invited to accompany him in his interview with the victim's friend and traveling companion, Tracy Nguyen.

Before they could knock, the door opened. A slim thirtysomething woman with shoulder-length brunette hair in a blunt cut stood there. Glenn met her brown eyes, reddened from crying, and asked to be sure, "Are you Tracy Nguyen?"

She nodded. "Yes."

He flashed his identification. "GBI Special Agent McElligott and this is Game Warden Fletcher. We need to ask you a few questions about Patrina Morse, as part of the investigation into her death."

Her voice shook as she responded with an accent, "Okay."

Rather than invite them inside the cabin that Glenn could see through the opening had the standard modern furnishings and some luggage, Tracy stepped out onto the porch, closing the door. With the space between cabins and relative privacy, this was fine by him as a place to talk.

He eyed Tisha then favored Tracy with an even look. He began, "I'd like to go over what you told Sheriff Pierce as to the timeline of your arrival at the lodge, up to the moment when you located Ms. Morse."

"I'm still just processing everything that happened," she cautioned, "but I'll try..."

"You're from Sydney, Australia?" he asked.

"Yes, we both lived there and taught at Blanden High School."

Tisha spoke in a friendly tone. "Long ways from home."

"It was actually my idea to travel to the States," Tracy explained, "having visited once before as a child."

"What made you choose Georgia this time around?" Glenn queried.

"Seemed like a nice place when searching online for possible states to visit. As we both love the outdoors, Kendell State Park checked all the boxes..." Her voice dropped. "Never imagined anything like this could happen—"

"I know," Tisha said sympathetically, touching her hand. "If you need a moment..."

"I'm fine." Tracy wiped tears from her eyes and looked at Glenn. "What else would you like to know?"

"Since you've been at the park, has anyone ever approached either Ms. Morse or you that was threatening in any way?" he asked her.

"Not that I can recall," she stated.

"What about nonthreatening?" Tisha regarded her. "Maybe someone you met on one of the trails. Or perhaps at the lodge's restaurant or bar?"

Tracy mulled this over for a long moment, then said, "Come to think of it, there was one man we met while sightseeing the day we arrived. He didn't really hit on us or anything, but did seem interested in the fact that we were Aussies. We talked a bit and that was pretty much it."

Or maybe there was more to this man, Glenn thought. "Can you describe him?"

"Thirties, white, dark-haired, tall and in good shape. Not bad on the eyes. Definitely American." Her brow furrowed. "Do you think he could have killed Patrina?"

"Probably not, but we need to look into every possibility," Glenn told her somewhat reassuringly. As it was, the description was, at the very least, consistent with an unidentified suspect seen on surveillance video related to the serial killer investigation. Could this be their perpetrator? "To that effect, I'd like to send over a sketch artist to speak with you, if that would be okay."

"That's fine." She wiped her nose with the back of her hand. "But just so you know, I'll be going home as soon as the sheriff gives me permission to bring Patrina back to Sydney for a proper burial."

"I understand." He nodded sympathetically, knowing they would need a day or two to complete the autopsy and any additional gathering of forensic evidence from the victim.

Tisha gazed at her and asked curiously, "With a number of trails in Kendell State Park, what made you go look for your friend on that trail, in particular?"

"We'd been on that trail every day since we've been here," Tracy said straightforwardly. "It seemed the likely route Patrina would take for her run." She sighed. "If only she had taken a different route—"

"She had no way of knowing she was running into danger," Glenn said, aware that this was little consolation for the death of her friend and colleague, very likely caused by a serial killer.

"That's the truly sad part to have to deal with." Tracy sniffled and Tisha put an arm around her to comfort her. "You will catch whoever did this, won't you?"

"We will," Tisha promised.

Glenn doubled down on this as he said firmly, "We'll do whatever it takes to bring Ms. Morse the justice she deserves."

After they had left the lodge, Glenn was behind the wheel of his Dodge Durango Pursuit, with Tisha in the passenger seat. "So what's your take on the latest homicide?" he asked her.

She waited a beat and answered, "For starters, my guess is that Patrina Morse's killer followed her to the Blakely Trail, which is one of the most popular trails at Kendell State Park, but with enough twists, turns and obscured sections to hide a predator…and probably caught her off guard when he attacked her."

"I was thinking the same thing," he said. "Whether the unsub was the same person they met as sightseers remains to be seen, but it's definitely worth checking out."

"True." Tisha gazed at him. "There should be video surveillance in enough places around the park to maybe narrow down some suspects."

"And possibly other witnesses, as well, who may have seen someone come or go that corresponds to the timeline in which the murder took place."

She drew a breath. "With all of the murders occurring within the Georgia Department of Natural Resources Region 5 Law Enforcement Division—two of which have taken place in my work sections—it leaves me wondering if there is a pattern in there somewhere that needs to be explored."

Glenn lifted an eyebrow as he glanced at her and back to the road. "You think the perp could be someone within your ranks?"

"Not necessarily," she said swiftly, "as I'd hate to go there without any rock-solid proof, but possibly someone who knows the region well and is comfortable moving around the area while being inconspicuous at the same time."

"Hmm..." he uttered contemplatively. "Makes sense. I'll pass that thought on to Sheriff Pierce and we'll look into it as part of the broader investigation."

"Okay." She paused. "I feel so sorry for Tracy. Having to end her vacation so tragically like that—"

"I know." He reached across and touched Tisha's hand. It was soft and fit into his like it was meant to be there. "The unsub won't get away with this," he promised and thought, *or any of his other killings*.

She squeezed his fingers but didn't say anything. Nor did she pull her hand away.

When he parked next to Tisha's truck, Glenn felt like this was a moment in which a display of affection was warranted. At least it felt right to him. He met her eyes squarely and said hotly, "My turn to kiss you. Are you game?"

Holding his gaze, Tisha uttered, "Yes, I'm game. Go for it!"

He did, lifting her chin and putting their mouths together. He slightly opened his, for a short kiss that became a long one. Both had to catch their breaths when he pulled away and said to her coolly, "See you later."

She touched his mouth with her fingers, smiled prettily and told him cheerfully, "Hope so. 'Bye."

With that, Tisha left his SUV and Glenn waited until she was inside her truck and headed out, before he followed briefly, his thoughts meandering between the sparks that kissing her had ignited in him like a slow-burning flame, and yet another woman being strangled by a relentless killer.

TISHA SPENT THE rest of the afternoon doing her rounds, covering more ground than usual in looking for any signs of trouble. Fortunately, she didn't find anyone suspicious lurking about to have to deal with. She touched her lips for seemingly the umpteenth time, where Glenn had kissed her, and she had kissed him back with equal ardor. There was clearly something delightful happening between them that she fully embraced, wanting nothing more than to see it through. And Tisha prayed that she might finally have a shot at happiness again that she feared might elude her forever.

But in the meantime, staying grounded was a smart thing. That included realizing that she would be competing for Glenn's time with a homicide investigation that managed to touch them both on different levels and needed to be solved for Shellview County, the victims and whatever the future may hold for her and the GBI special agent.

When she got home that day, after dropping by a fast-food restaurant for a fruit salad and coffee, Tisha put on Jacky's leash and took the dog out for a walk and to do her business. She couldn't wait for her to meet Riley and vice versa. Getting their dogs close would be a good thing in building a relationship between her and Glenn.

That night, Tisha brushed and flossed her teeth, showered and went to bed, thinking about Glenn and what they might do beneath her cotton sateen sheets. She drifted off as her thoughts turned to the ongoing serial killer investigation and the latest victim's devastating turn of events while on vacation from Australia.

GLENN STOOD AT the billiard table inside Becklyn's Bar on Flat Rock Road in Midland. On the other side was GBI Special Agent Kurt Stewart. Both were holding pool cues while they played. A nearby table held a half-filled pitcher of beer, along with their mugs. Glenn was glad to have a colleague to bounce his thoughts off regarding the current case he was assigned to, where, in all likelihood, there were now five homicide victims, with apparently a single perpetrator.

"This guy is proving to be a handful," Glenn muttered, as he lined up the cue and calmly drove a ball into the corner pocket. "I wouldn't go so far to say that he's toying with us, but the unsub has managed to spread his homicidal tendencies across Shellview County, with no signs of letting up. At least not till we can bring him in."

"He's not invincible!" Kurt asserted, creasing his brow while leaning against the table. "Far from it. The way I see things, the unsub has simply gotten the dice to roll in his favor, thus far. Not because he's some kind of genius or anything, but more that, like other serial killers he's taken advantage of the loopholes in society that can give some murderers just enough room to maneuver in killing, without getting caught. Till that happens…and eventually it will."

"I agree," Glenn said succinctly, and missed the next shot as he lost his concentration. If he hadn't known better, he would think that this had been Kurt's intention all along, to distract him just enough to lose the game. But he felt otherwise, as everything the special agent said made perfect sense. "Unfortunately, the longer this thing goes on, the more concerned I am that the unsub will take his act elsewhere, before we can slap the cuffs on, lock him up and toss the key into the river."

"That's not likely to happen." Kurt set his jaw and studied the table. "The perp is obviously someone who's at home with the outdoors and seems to know the lay of the land, making him overconfident. This will be to his detriment eventually." He drove a ball into a side pocket. "Until then, he's staying put, where he's comfortable sizing up his prey and taking action to that effect."

Glenn chuckled and tasted his beer. "Maybe we should trade places and you can take over this investigation," he quipped.

Kurt laughed. "Would if I could. As it is, the GBI's Commercial Gambling Unit would never let me go, as long as the investigation is in full steam and yielding results."

"I understand. It was worth a try," Glenn said lightheartedly. In truth, he would never turn over a case to someone else because of an inability to solve it himself. That would mean failure. Something that wasn't in his vocabulary. Or DNA.

"Doesn't mean I can't pitch in on my own time," Kurt offered. "Whatever I can do to help, just let me know."

"Will do." Glenn watched as his friend missed a shot, putting him back in control. "For now, I think that working with the Shellview County Sheriff's Department, and the DNR's Law Enforcement Division to a lesser degree, should be enough to solve this case—presumably sooner than later."

"Cool." Kurt grabbed his mug of beer and tasted. "And how are things going with your mystery woman?"

Glenn laughed. "Wouldn't exactly call her a mystery woman. Enchanting would be more like it," he admitted, recalling the effect her kisses had on him. "In fact, she's a game warden and, in answer to your question, it's still a work in progress."

"Well, just don't work too hard, McElligott," he said with a chuckle. "At least not till you see if your game warden can put the hex on you."

I think she already has, Glenn told himself truthfully, but responded contemplatively, "I'll try to remember that."

In the meantime, he called the winning shot in a corner pocket and drilled it.

Half an hour later, Glenn was at home, where he playfully wrestled with Riley for a bit and then headed up to his office and laptop to study what he knew thus far on the Shellview County Killer and where he needed to go from here.

ON WEDNESDAY AFTERNOON, Tisha put on a light blue crop top and matching leggings with her exercise sneakers and went to the Blair Bay Fitness Center, joining her friend Jeanne for a Zumba workout.

As the group class was warming up, Tisha blurted out what she had to tell someone, if only to share her excitement, "So I've met someone—"

"Oh, really?" Jeanne batted her eyelashes curiously. "Do tell?"

"He's a GBI special agent," Tisha told her thoughtfully.

"How nice." She grinned in approval.

"Glenn also happens to be the lead investigator in the Shellview County Killer case," Tisha pointed out.

Jeanne faced her. "Does that include the Aussie who was killed yesterday at Kendell State Park?"

Tisha nodded. "Afraid so."

Jeanne frowned. "How terrible for her."

"Right?" Tisha concurred and did some stretches. "Never should have happened."

"But it did. Just like the others. When will it end?"

"Wish I could answer that," Tisha responded truthfully. "I suppose it'll end when the authorities get the break they need to crack the case."

"I suppose." Jeanne drew a breath. "Anyway, it's about time you put yourself out there again."

"I was thinking the same thing." Tisha relished the thought, even if it made her a little nervous as well. She felt vulnerable to some extent in getting back into the dating game. But it needed to happen. Wherever things between her and Glenn ended up.

"Hope this works out for you, Tisha."

"Me, too."

She smiled with her teeth, and then wondered when Jeanne might also be ready to get back to meeting people now that her divorce was in the rearview mirror. Or had the bad blood between her and her ex soured her on romance for the foreseeable future?

As they began to get into the Zumba dance workout, Tisha thought about taking that next step with Glenn and what that might mean when there was no turning back. It was something she felt ready for. But was he?

Chapter Eight

On Saturday, Tisha got up the nerve to invite Glenn over for lunch. Actually, it was less about courage and more about the anticipation of seeing him again and in her own comfort zone. He didn't strike her as being the type of man who needed a comfort zone of his own, per se, when it came to socializing.

When his phone rang, her heart skipped a beat as if she had second thoughts. But she did not. She was going for it, no matter the result.

"Hey," he said amicably when answering.

"Hey." She took a moment, then said, "I was wondering if you'd like to have lunch with me today, at my house?"

"Absolutely." His voice lifted a notch. "Count me in."

"I will." Tisha chuckled while flipping her ponytail across one shoulder. "And feel free to bring Riley along. Jacky could use the company."

"Consider it done. Riley would love to develop a camaraderie with Jacky."

"Then it's a date," she spoke cheerfully. Wasn't it? "How does one o'clock work for you?"

"Like a charm," he said smoothly. "We'll be there."

"Wonderful." Tisha texted him her address. "See you in a couple of hours."

"Count on it!"

After disconnecting, Tisha tried to temper her enthusiasm as she put on a lilac knit shirt and skinny ankle jeans, and went barefoot while tidying the town house. Not that it needed much cleaning, as she was somewhat of a neat freak and Jacky was house-trained and otherwise not prone to making a mess of things. Still, after having seen Glenn's house, where seemingly nothing was out of order, Tisha felt the pressure to make him feel just as comfortable as she had felt when visiting him.

For lunch, she made marinated vegetable salad and turkey frittata, to go with peach lemonade. *Hope he likes this*, Tisha told herself in the kitchen, after admittedly being out of practice in cooking for two. Not to mention trying to measure up to Glenn's cooking, having a chef sister to learn from.

Chill, Tisha mused, realizing that they weren't in competition. Besides, she didn't necessarily agree that the key to a man's heart was his stomach. She sensed that it took more than that to win Glenn over. Was that what she was trying to do? Or was it more a desire to win each other over to see what they could both bring to the table in a potential relationship?

As she stood over the countertop, Tisha stared at the wedding ring on her finger for a moment, then removed it. She headed upstairs and put the ring in a drawer. It was time, she knew, and she wanted to embrace whatever may lie ahead with a clean slate.

When Jacky started barking, Tisha realized that company had arrived. "You must feel the positive vibes of making a new friend, don't you, girl?" she asked the dog with a chuckle, following her downstairs. Tisha slipped into some slingback flats, went to the door and opened it.

"Hey," Glenn said on the other side. He was sporting a big grin and looking great in a red button-up shirt, jeans and brown Chelsea boots. Next to him was Riley, his tail wagging with eagerness to go inside.

"Hey." Tisha smiled. "Come in, both of you." The moment they did, the dogs quickly sized each other up. "Riley, this is Jacky. Jacky, Riley." As they seemed to grow comfortable with one another, Tisha told Glenn, "Jacky is a retired K-9 with the DNR Law Enforcement Division. She still has game, but has happily left her old life behind."

"Good for her," Glenn remarked as he walked up to the dog and began to play with her naturally. He said to Jacky, in a smooth voice, "Nice to hear that you were one of us."

Jacky seemed more than amenable, easily warming up to him and the attention. As if not wanting to be left out of the loop, Riley joined in on the action. Glenn had no problem playing with both dogs for a moment, before Tisha came to his rescue and let them both out in the backyard to get to know each other better.

"Looks as if they've already become best buds," Glenn said with a laugh.

"I agree." Tisha chuckled and thought that was a good sign all the way around. "Hope you're hungry?"

"I am." He met her eyes and she nearly melted while interpreting his thoughts on the carnal side of hunger. She felt this sexual craving, too. "I like your place, by the way," he said, seemingly intent on breaking away from the moment.

"Thank you." Tisha colored. "Lunch is ready. I'll set the table, and you can wash up in the kitchen, if you like."

"Okay." He gave her a crooked grin and walked to the stainless-steel sink.

A few minutes later, they were seated at the dining room

table. Tisha waited with bated breath as Glenn dug into the turkey frittata, then declared, "It's delicious."

"Glad you approve," she told him, breathing a sigh of relief.

"How could I not?" He gazed at her from across the table. "You're gorgeous."

"I was talking about the food." Tisha giggled. "But I'll take the compliment, anyway."

"Just telling it as I see it—or you." Glenn forked some vegetable salad. "The fact that you clearly know your way around a kitchen is only a bonus, as far as I'm concerned."

She laughed. "Ditto."

He laughed, too, then said, "Guess that makes us a match."

"Oh, you think so, do you?" she teased him, while holding her glass of peach lemonade.

"Only one way to find out," he challenged her, a catch in his tone of voice.

Tisha swallowed some salad with expectation. "What exactly did you have in mind?"

Glenn got to his feet and pulled her up, close to his body. "How about this, for starters…" He planted a mouth-watering kiss on her lips, causing Tisha's knees to buckle, and unlocked their mouths just as she was really getting into it. "There's a lot more where that came from," he murmured.

"I hope so," she gushed, touching her swollen mouth.

He stared into her eyes. "I want to make love to you, Tisha."

"I want that, too." She could no longer deny her needs as a woman. Not with him. But there was still the practical side to be considered. Unplanned pregnancy. She wasn't on the pill. "What about protection?"

Glenn pulled out a condom packet from his pants.

"Thought I'd bring one along, just in case—to be on the safe side."

Tisha smiled. "Looks like you've thought of everything."

"Honestly, I've only been able to think about one thing—pushing aside my current investigation that can wait for the time being—and that's you, simply put."

"Ohh…" Her lashes fluttered with the flattery. "That's sweet." She looked up at him happily. "I think I can say the same thing about you."

He kissed her again. "Good minds think alike."

Tisha felt a surge of desire well within as she took his hand and said teasingly, "Why don't we take this up to my bedroom and whatever happens, happens…"

An eager grin played on Glenn's lips as he responded soulfully, "That sounds like a plan to me."

Me, too, Tisha thought, excited about the prospect of making love to him and whatever might come after that.

IT WASN'T LOST on Glenn that Tisha had removed her wedding ring. This told him that she was, in fact, ready to give another man a try—both in bed and in a relationship. This thrilled him, as he, too, had reached the point in his life where he wanted romance and embraced the process that started with chemistry and kisses…and had led to Tisha's primary suite.

He glanced around the room, taking in the log furniture and panel bed in particular, before he centered his gaze on Tisha. She was removing her clothes and silently beckoning him to do the same, as if to make sure they bared their souls together.

In a hurry to comply, Glenn started to unbutton his shirt while kicking off his boots at the same time. He watched, turned on, as Tisha let down her hair and quickly removed her shirt, then her bra, revealing small but full breasts, and slid the skinny jeans down and across her narrow hips and shapely legs. Then came her panties, and she stood before him in the nude.

He caught up to her, now naked, too, while tossing the condom packet on the duvet cover, and marveled at her beauty from head to toe, even as Tisha asked tentatively, "You like?"

Glenn took a breath, as if that went without saying, but said, anyway, "I definitely like!"

She showed her teeth, giving him a once-over. "I like you, too," she murmured.

He cupped her cheeks and they kissed passionately, bodies pressed together, for a long and exhilarating moment, before Glenn lifted Tisha and carried her to the bed, then climbed in next to her. He tore open the packet and slipped on the protection in one fell swoop, before moving up to her, and they resumed tasting each other's mouths.

Though he had already worked himself up to a fevered pitch, Glenn preferred to show some restraint and go the foreplay route so that this first time could be slow and rewarding. He wanted to pleasure Tisha in a way that she had no regrets whatsoever in taking this next all-important step, as he was sure that regrets in their lovemaking could never be the case with him.

He used his hands and mouth to stimulate her wherever she wanted. Tisha's reaction to his touch, along with her breaths and moans, told him when he was getting it right. So he continued to satisfy her, loving every minute. Finally, she pulled him half atop her and uttered in a yearning tone of voice, "I'm ready to have sex with you—now!"

"As you wish," Glenn said to her hungrily, not needing to be told twice.

He moved onto her the rest of the way and was inside Tisha, and they made love like it was theirs for the taking. Neither backed off an inch as their mouths and bodies, in sync and perpetual motion, worked up a sweat. Glenn fought back the urge to release his needs until Tisha experienced the high first.

As if on the same wavelength, she arched her body toward his and cried out as she had her orgasm. Only then did he let go and soon joined her, quivering from the climax. They went at it hard, riding the rapids together for one final burst of ecstasy, before things settled down and they regained their equilibrium.

Rolling off to the side, Glenn caught his breath and asked curiously, "Was it everything you hoped it would be?"

"Yes!" she said, her voice rising emphatically. "And much more, actually. How about you?"

"I enjoyed every second," he declared, as if he could ever have felt otherwise. "You were amazing. You *are* amazing," Glenn added, correcting himself.

"Good to know." Tisha laughed. "You weren't so bad yourself."

He chuckled. "Happy to be of service." *And hopefully it won't be for the last time*, he thought.

"Likewise," she promised, draping a smooth lean leg across his. "Afternoon delight can be so much fun."

Tisha giggled and Glenn admitted, "I'll say. Nights and mornings could be fun, too."

"You think?"

"Absolutely." He kissed her shoulder while assessing how she felt about the prospect of keeping this going.

"I believe they could be at that," she told him with a lilt to her voice.

Glenn almost wished he had brought along a second

condom, but he hadn't wanted to get ahead of himself. Just in case his instincts for the lunch invite and where things seemed to be headed between them had been wrong.

He would settle for another kiss for the time being and went for it. Tisha reciprocated and it gave Glenn reason to believe this really could be the start of something spectacular, beyond just sex. Great as it was, he was ready to have a real relationship with a person he was connecting with.

The momentum came to a halt as they heard the dogs barking, as though getting antsy in the backyard.

Tisha laughed. "Looks like Jacky and Riley want some of our attention to go their way."

Glenn laughed, too. "Yeah, guess they have a problem with being ignored."

"We'll have to do something about that."

He reluctantly agreed, knowing there would be more than enough other opportunities to pick up where they left off.

After getting dressed and letting Riley and Jacky back into the house, Tisha's cell phone rang. Glenn watched as she answered it. From the sound of things, the call pertained to her work. It reminded him that they both had active careers in branches of law enforcement that would be part of the equation were they to build a relationship. The fact that it gave them common ground they could both relate to was big in his mind and a positive sign for the future.

Glenn saw worry lines appear on Tisha's forehead as she said to the caller, "I'm on my way…"

"What's going on?" he asked when she disconnected.

"A little girl has gone missing," Tisha said, fear in her tone.

"Where?"

"Kendell State Park."

Without her needing to say anything more, Glenn knew it was the same park where Patrina Morse had been murdered. According to the autopsy report, her death had been ruled a homicide, and the cause was ligature strangulation. The serial killer was still at large.

It didn't take much for Glenn to assume Tisha was drawing the conclusion that the missing girl might also have been targeted by the Shellview County Killer. Though the MO didn't fit, Glenn wasn't in a position to rule anything in or out.

Not until the girl was found—hopefully, alive.

"I'm coming with you," Glenn told Tisha, wanting to do whatever he could to bring the girl home safe and sound. Beyond that, the investigation fell into his jurisdiction as well, all things considered.

"Okay," she said succinctly, her expression illustrating her unease at their cases overlapping and the real possibility of a bad outcome for the missing girl.

Glenn found himself just as unnerved on that front.

Chapter Nine

Tisha was beside herself with concern as she sped toward Kendell State Park, having quickly changed from leisure clothing into her uniform. Glenn sat in the passenger seat, wearing the same clothes he had worn to her house. They had briefly entertained bringing their dogs along to assist in the search for the missing nine-year-old girl named Rosa Bachiller, but thought better of it, believing they would only be in the way. And possibly even hinder the efforts to find the girl.

As it was, the DNR's Law Enforcement Division had already dispatched its K-9 unit to assist in the effort, along with a Special Operations Group proficient in search-and-rescue missions. The sheriff's department was using drones to aid in the search of the park and its perimeter.

Not to be left out of the mix, Glenn had requested that the GBI Investigative Division's Child Abduction Response Team join in the all-hands-on-deck effort to locate the missing child and reunite her with her family.

But Tisha feared that even these moves might not be enough—every second the girl remained missing lessened her chances of survival. Particularly in light of the recent murder of Patrina Morse at the same location.

"We'll find her, won't we?" Tisha glanced at Glenn worriedly. She sensed that they were on the same page insofar as drawing inferences between the two cases.

"Yes, we will," he insisted. "It's only been a couple of hours since she went missing. Without knowing all the details, chances are the girl got lost somehow. In a park that size with lots of places to go or hide, nooks and crannies, and twists and turns, it wouldn't be difficult to lose one's way, or get confused. We have to believe that's the most likely scenario—and not one where she's been abducted or murdered by someone..."

Tisha nodded, while reading between the lines. Though the *someone* Glenn spoke of could well be a serial killer looking for more victims in a familiar location, she didn't dismiss the possibility that the girl could have run into a child sexual predator on the prowl. Or another opportunist who may have taken her. How many children went missing each year in the country, only to never be seen or heard from again?

I can't allow myself to think of the worst-case scenario prematurely, Tisha told herself as she drove into the park. Glenn was right. Odds were that this would all end on a good note. Until proven to the contrary.

When Glenn's hand brushed against hers, Tisha couldn't help but recall the hot sex they had engaged in earlier, making her blush. He had been everything she could have imagined in bed. And then some. He seemed to feel the same way about her. Maybe she really had turned the corner and could make this work.

The musings were put on hold as Tisha's thoughts returned to the moment at hand, as they reached their destination and joined the others, including Sherman Galecki and Bree McDaniels.

Sherman regarded Tisha and said, "I imagine you're

thinking the girl's disappearance might be related to the woman who was murdered in the park?"

"Hard not to consider the possibility," she admitted, though she was trying hard to stay positive.

"Doesn't seem to fit," he argued.

"I agree," Glenn said. "But not everything fits the way it's supposed to."

Bree said, "Based on what I know about kids that age, she probably got bored and wandered off somewhere and then, before she knew it, couldn't find her way back."

"If that's so," Tisha said, "it shouldn't be too difficult to track her down."

"That's the plan," Bree told her.

Sheriff Pierce, who had set up a command post near the area where the girl had vanished, apparently wandering away from a family get-together, said equably, "We've got searchers from multiple law enforcement agencies and volunteers combing every inch of the park, the river and beyond," Marjorie stressed, "We won't stop till we find Rosa Bachiller."

Tisha took that to heart as she and Glenn spoke to the parents, Bert and Eloise Bachiller, who claimed they had only taken their eyes off Rosa for a second, before she was gone. Other families told the same story of seeing her one moment and not the next.

Now, the clock was ticking to bring the missing girl back to them.

Joining in on the search after talking with the CART, Tisha led Glenn through the woods, while trying to put herself in the head of a nine-year-old girl, in the event that she had gone off on her own. With no predator involved. Which direction would she choose? Farther into the wooded area? Or toward the river?

I'll bet she headed for the river, Tisha told herself, knowing that there was less rugged terrain there and brush that she could come upon and maybe cross without actually going into the water. At which point, she would still be in the woods, but far enough away from the original point of disappearing that it would be harder for the K-9 unit to track. Much less, other law enforcement, including drones that might not pick her up above the dense trees.

"Could *he* have taken her in broad daylight?" a wide-eyed Tisha asked Glenn, certain he understood that she was referring to the so-called Shellview County Killer.

"Anything's possible," he admitted as they worked their way through the trees. "If so, they would likely still be in the park somewhere. As I understand it, the moment the girl was reported missing—within minutes of her disappearance—action was taken right away to block the exits and begin the search. Seems doubtful that our unsub would risk this type of exposure, given his MO." Glenn took a breath. "If anyone has Rosa, the kidnapper won't get very far—"

Just as Tisha pondered his words, they heard some shuffling ahead, behind a cluster of loblolly pine trees. Instinctively, she went for the Glock pistol she carried in her waistband holster. If they were to encounter danger, she would do whatever was necessary to defend herself and Glenn, who did not have his own firearm with him.

"Come out with your hands raised!" Tisha demanded.

"She means business," Glenn barked toughly. "And so do I."

At first, Tisha was unsure if anyone would appear. Or, for that matter, if they were even dealing with a human. The forested park was home to all kinds of wildlife, including white-tailed deer, raccoons, rabbits and even black bears. Could one of these be the culprit?

Before they could consider their next move, Tisha saw a frightened girl emerge from behind the trees. She was small, with big brown eyes and short brown hair, and was wearing a red T-shirt, blue shorts and white sneakers. The clothing corresponded with what the missing girl was wearing.

"Are you Rosa Bachiller?" Tisha asked, handing Glenn her gun just in case an abductor was hiding and waiting for them to let down their guard.

She nodded. "Yeah."

"I'm Warden Fletcher and this is Agent McElligott." Tisha eyed her. "Are you okay?"

Rosa nodded again, jutting her chin. "Am I in trouble?"

"No." Glenn, who had tucked the gun in his waistband, took the liberty of responding in a soft voice. "We've been looking for you. Your parents were worried that something bad might have happened..."

"I just went for a walk," the girl explained. "And didn't realize I'd gone so far. I couldn't remember how to get back..." She rubbed her nose. "I just sat down behind the tree and waited. I knew someone would find me. Didn't mean to cause a fuss."

"We're just happy to see you safe and sound." Tisha flashed her teeth, elated to see that the girl appeared to be in good shape and unharmed.

"I'm fine," Rosa insisted and suddenly ran into Tisha's arms. "Thank you for coming."

Tisha hugged the girl, imagining someday having a daughter of her own to dote over. She regarded Glenn, who grinned at her and breathed a sigh of relief as he got out his cell phone and announced that Rosa Bachiller had been located.

ON MONDAY, Glenn paid a visit to the Western Lab's Forensic Biology section of the GBI Division of Forensic Sciences, which happened to be located in the same building where he worked. He hoped that there might be some new scientific data relevant to the latest homicide he was working on, tying it, as well, to the overall serial killer investigation.

Layla Ramaswamy, a Crime Laboratory scientist, met him at her workstation. The thirtysomething analyst, who was thin with short black hair and wore oval eyeglasses and a white lab coat, smiled and said, "Good morning, Agent McElligott."

"Morning." He glanced at her monitor and lab table, then asked, "So what do you have for me?"

Layla touched her glasses and responded, "Well, we were able to collect DNA and fingerprints from the latest victim, Patrina Morse, as well as debris found at the crime scene. Putting aside those belonging to Ms. Morse, the DNA samples were sent to CODIS and compared with known and unknown forensic profiles. Unfortunately, we weren't able to get any hits. Sorry."

So was he, though Glenn had feared this might be the case. The unsub had made it difficult for anyone to tie him to the crimes through forensic evidence. "And the prints?"

"There were a few latent prints examined. They were put into the state's Automated Fingerprint Identification System for a possible match." She sighed. "Negative. We tried the FBI's Next Generation Identification system. Same result. Could be the prints had nothing to do with the murder."

"Perhaps," Glenn said musingly, allowing that they may have come from other runners or park visitors. But he didn't discount that the unsub simply wasn't in the databases. Not yet. "What about trace evidence?"

Layla's brown eyes lit up. "I did find something there…" she hinted. "The crime scene investigators collected fibers that proved to be a match for ones the medical examiner's office pulled from Ms. Morse's neck during the autopsy. The fibers are consistent with those in a cotton cord."

"The same type of cord used to strangle the other victims," Glenn said, thinking out loud.

"Yes," she confirmed sourly. "Based on comparison, there's every reason to believe that Ms. Morse was strangled to death by either the actual cotton cord, or the same roll that led to the deaths of those murdered by the Shellview County Killer—"

Glenn had already come to the same reluctant but undeniable conclusion. Still to be determined was the identity of the unsub. And, sadly, there was a very real likelihood that he was already targeting his next victim.

That afternoon, Glenn met with Tisha for lunch at Ivanka's Food Truck on Vixon Street in downtown Blair Bay, as they both broke away from their respective duties. In fact, since becoming intimate, they had been spending more time together, getting to know one another better. He liked this part of developing a relationship and was excited to see how far it went.

As they stood beneath crape myrtle blossoms, eating chili dogs, he gave her the rundown on the latest in his investigation into the serial killer. "Same rope was used to kill Patrina Morse," he said, finishing matter-of-factly, while using a napkin to wipe chili off his chin. "Not that there was much doubt as to who strangled her to death."

"I know." Tisha frowned. "If only stopping him from killing innocent people was as predictable," she muttered.

"We'll get there," Glenn vowed, in spite of the appearance that the battle to bring the unsub in to face justice was already lost. "The sheriff is just as determined to solve this, believe me."

"I do." Tisha bit into her chili dog. "The DNR is with you every step of the way—no matter the frustration of having some of the murders occur within our work sections."

Glenn regarded her. He thought about their locating Rosa Bachiller, unharmed, in Kendell State Park, thanks in large part to Tisha's instincts and knowledge of the landscape. "How's Rosa doing, anyway, now that she's been reunited with her parents?"

"She's good." Tisha put a smile on her face. "From what I understand, all's well that ended well for all concerned."

"Great to hear." Glenn grinned at her. "You can pat yourself on the back for that one. Who knows what might have happened had she been out there all day and night."

"I was only doing my job," Tisha said, downplaying it, while dabbing a napkin to one corner of her mouth. "And maybe turning back the clock to when I pulled a similar stunt as a girl…but managed to find my way back to my parents, who scolded me and hugged me endearingly at the same time."

"Good for them." He gazed at her and said thoughtfully, "I hope to meet your folks sometime."

"I'd like that," She met his eyes. "Same here—meeting your mom, stepdad, father and sister…"

"You will," he promised, knowing that they would all be happy to get to know someone in his life that he could potentially build a serious relationship with.

It was definitely something that gave him an entirely different reason for getting up every day and looking beyond investigating horrendous criminal activity. He focused on Tisha's sweet lips and told her, "You missed a spot."

"Oh, I did…?" Color bloomed on her cheeks.

Glenn took the liberty of using a finger to wipe away the extra chili, then kissed her for good measure and said with amusement, “That’s better.”

“Yes, it is,” she said lightheartedly.

Chapter Ten

After lunch with Glenn, Tisha found the rest of her afternoon quite eventful, to say the least. First, she teamed up with other game wardens to rescue a white-tailed deer after its antlers got entangled in a tree in Shellview County. They succeeded in the endeavor and sent the befuddled deer on its way.

Then Tisha teamed up with Sherman to track down a pair of intoxicated and mischievous hunters, who decided to go on a joy ride with their Honda ATV through a farmer's crops. Lastly, she and her work section boss, Fritz Alvarez, performed a safety check of rafters and boaters along the river.

When she got home, Tisha changed clothes, fed Jacky and then checked in with her mother and father, Goretti and Victor Song. She casually mentioned to them that she had started to see someone. Though expressing surprise, they were elated that she was finally willing to put herself out there again. She felt the same way.

Tisha promised to keep them abreast on how things progressed with Glenn, knowing they were holding out hope that she would someday give them grandchildren to cherish and carry on family traditions. But before she could go there, she needed to know the man in her life was equally committed to having and raising kids as part of their commitment to each other. Was that something Glenn saw in his—or their—future?

That evening, Tisha brought Jacky over to Glenn's house at his invitation. The dogs ran free on the vast property, chasing one another playfully.

"Looks like they're having a good time," Glenn said with a laugh.

Tisha smiled. "I guess they both just needed someone to befriend and exercise with."

"Yeah, I think you're right." He faced her and lowered his chin seductively. "The dogs aren't the only ones looking for lasting friendship and exercise."

"No?" Tisha batted her lashes coquettishly and then, in trying to read him, she asked, "Is that what you're seeking out of this—long-term camaraderie and some physical activity?"

Glenn grinned coolly. "Both seem about right at this point. But, to tell you the truth, I'm hoping things can go a lot further than that over the course of time."

"Good response." Her teeth gleamed at him and Tisha's desire to be with Glenn crept up a few notches.

"I thought so, too." He ran a hand along her jawline. "What do you say, we leave the dogs by themselves for a bit, and we can do our own thing?"

"I say that works for me," she replied, tempering her enthusiasm.

They went inside the house and straight to his bedroom, kissing along the way. After quickly disrobing, Tisha climbed onto the platform bed and beneath the comforter. She watched as Glenn got naked, showing off his nice abs, before he grabbed protection from a three-drawer wooden nightstand and joined her.

Their lovemaking was thorough and demanding, as each yielded to the other's needs, exploring and being explored to their mutual pleasure. It ended with them both exhausted and contented after being victorious in the quest for sexual gratification.

"I think I can get used to this," Glenn whispered sensuously against her cheek.

"Do you really?" Tisha challenged him. "It won't cramp your style as a bachelor having me around—not to mention Jacky?"

"Not even a little." He chuckled. "Especially with Jacky on hand to keep Riley distracted, so I can focus on other things. Or one thing in particular…" He ran his hand down her smooth leg.

"Hmm." She felt a tingle from his touch. "I like the way you think."

"I think a lot about you," he said, pouring on the charm.

"Makes sense, as that works both ways." Tisha had to admit that her thoughts toward him were veering dangerously close to falling in love. Was that something he was ready to hear? Or would going out on a limb at this stage only do more harm than good?

ON TUESDAY MORNING, Glenn sat in a booth at Oliver's Coffee Shop on Quail Street, across from Rhianna Kingsley. They were discussing the latest on the Shellview County Killer investigation, along with the broader agenda for the GBI regional office. That included an ongoing probe into the sexual exploitation of children, an officer-involved shooting and a drug-trafficking case.

Though these other investigations were important in their own right, Glenn was painfully aware that his primary focus at the moment had to remain on solving the serial killer case, with five homicides to date. He understood that the special agent in charge expected no less of him.

"We're looking into every angle here," he assured her while sipping his espresso.

"I don't doubt that," Rhianna said, lifting her cup of chai latte. Her thin eyebrows knitted. "We may need to get the FBI involved," she admitted. "With our resources already stretched thin as it is and the sheriff's department relying on us to take the lead in tracking down the unsub, we could use some extra help here to get the job done."

Glenn bristled at the thought of the FBI getting in the mix and trying to pull rank on him and others from the GBI involved in the case. At the same time, though, he was no stranger to working with the Bureau in partnering on investigations. Or as part of a task force effort. His pride had to take a back seat to solving this serial killer probe.

"Whatever you say," he told her acceptingly. "I won't reject help from the FBI, if that's what it takes to stop him."

Rhianna nodded. "Good. I'll make the call." She tasted her tea. "But just so you know, it's still your case to get to the bottom of—along with the sheriff and her investigators."

"I appreciate the vote of confidence." Glenn met her eyes respectfully. "I'll try not to let you down."

She smiled. "I know that."

He felt that such a time couldn't come soon enough for both of them in representing the GBI and its role in assisting Marjorie Pierce catch the bad guy.

No sooner had that thought crossed his mind, when Glenn's cell phone rang. The caller happened to be the sheriff.

"McElligott," he answered routinely, glancing at Rhianna.

"Hey," Marjorie said, a catch in her voice. "A 911 call

just came in from a man claiming to have strangled to death his girlfriend."

"Really?" Glenn sat up.

"Yep. I'm on my way to his house, even as we speak. Might be entirely coincidental," she continued, "or it could be opening the door to a confession by the alleged Shellview County Killer."

Glenn was left with that disturbing possibility as he disconnected and relayed the information to the special agent in charge.

MARJORIE HAD BEEN making the rounds, per her role as Shellview County sheriff, when she received the call about a possible homicide by strangulation and its potential implications in a serial killer investigation. Before that, her mind had been contemplating next year's election, in which she intended to run for reelection for a third term in office.

It hadn't been an easy decision. Part of her wanted to get beyond being a county sheriff to perhaps running for the board of supervisors in Shellview County. But the fact was that she loved her job and was committed to performing it to the best of her ability. That included cleaning up the streets of illicit drugs, gangs and violent criminal activity. Such as the current case of a serial killer in their midst.

Were they about to nab the unsub? Or not?

Marjorie kept her fingers crossed. She would be happy to solve the murders herself. Short of that, she still welcomed the help of the GBI…and now the FBI, after having brought up the possibility of bringing in the Bureau earlier to Rhianna Kingsley, in wanting to do whatever it took to bring this investigation to a close.

Either way she sliced it, Marjorie was certain that this had to end sooner than later, given the work they were putting in to solve the case. She hoped it was sooner as she pulled her Ford Explorer behind one of her deputies' squad cars, outside a two-story colonial home on Steel Street.

After getting out, Marjorie walked up to the house, where she was met at the door by Deputy Dervla Haddock, a slender twentysomething woman with auburn hair in a piecey cut.

"He's in the living room…" Dervla said tonelessly. "In cuffs with Deputy Winnick keeping an eye on him."

"And the victim?" Marjorie asked.

"Upstairs on the bathroom floor."

"Anyone else inside?"

"No," Dervla told her.

Majorie nodded. "Okay."

Walking inside, she spotted her deputy, Harvey Winnick, tall and bald-headed and in his thirties, standing guard over the suspect, who was seated in a club chair with his hands behind his back. He was white, fortysomething, of medium build and blue-eyed with dark hair in a low fade military-style cut. She noted that he was wearing what looked to be an expensive navy suit and oxfords. Not too surprising, considering that the residence was located in a high-end neighborhood in town.

Marjorie glanced at the traditional furnishings in the room and back to the suspect and told him, "I'm Sheriff Pierce. And you are…?" She wanted to hear it from him directly.

"Quinn Finnegan."

She peered at him and asked bluntly, "Mr. Finnegan, you want to tell me what you've done?"

He drew a breath and replied matter-of-factly, "I killed my girlfriend."

Marjorie wrinkled her nose and said to the deputies, "Stay with him while I go up and have a look."

She scaled the staircase, went down a long hall and into a spacious and well-furnished primary bedroom, where nothing seemed particularly out of order. Laid out on top of the cane bed were women's underwear, jeans and a floral print T-shirt.

Only when she entered the en suite bathroom did Marjorie spot a naked and slender Hispanic female in her thirties, with long brunette hair, lying on the floor by the bathtub. There was a leather belt wrapped tightly around her neck.

Marjorie turned away for a moment, then looked back at the ruin of a life. As she waited for Glenn McElligott to arrive, she couldn't help but wonder if Quinn Finnegan was guilty of more than one strangulation murder.

GLENN HAD GIVEN Tisha a buzz en route to the crime scene, wanting to let her know that a person of interest had emerged in the Shellview County Killer case. He didn't want to give her false hope that they had their killer. But she also deserved to know where they were, as a witness to an earlier unsolved murder. Then there was the fact that he had grown to trust Tisha as both a confidante and someone he was starting to build a life with outside of work. Apart from their lovemaking being off the charts, they were in sync and it left him wanting more and more.

After reaching the address and going inside, Glenn flashed his identification to the deputies on duty, regarded the handcuffed suspect, who was stone-faced, and headed upstairs, where he found the sheriff in the primary suite just getting off the phone.

"Agent McElligott," she said, acknowledging him, a somber look on her face. “The victim’s in there…” She pointed to the bathroom. “It’s not a pretty sight.”

Glenn stepped into the bathroom and saw the dead woman. She was lying on her back, naked. Her brown eyes were bloodshot on an attractive face and wide open, as if forced to remain that way even in death. He took note of the leather belt that had apparently been used to strangle the victim, as it was coiled around her neck like a snake.

This differed from the type of ligature used to commit the serial murders. Furthermore, he saw no signs of a stun gun being used on the victim. Perhaps the weapon was applied to the back side of her body?

Could the unsub have changed his MO?

Or were they barking up the wrong tree in the joint investigation?

“What’s your initial take on this?” Marjorie asked, breaking into his thoughts.

Glenn examined the deceased woman again with his eyes, then responded noncommittally, “Before I answer that, I’d like to speak with the suspect…”

Forty-five minutes later, in an interrogation room at the sheriff’s department, Glenn was sitting across from Quinn Finnegan, having already discovered that he was a millionaire hedge-fund manager. The victim had been identified as Naomi Echeverría, a thirty-two-year-old cocktail waitress.

Regarding the suspect steadfastly, Glenn asked him curiously, “Why did you do it?”

Finnegan lowered his head and replied without prelude, “She was cheating on me—and didn’t even bother to deny it.”

“So you killed her for that, rather than simply man up and find someone else to date?”

“I didn’t want anyone else—don’t you get it?” he snorted.

"I was in love with Naomi. Thought she loved me, too. Guess I was wrong." His countenance contorted. "She laughed in my face." He sighed. "I just lost it..."

"And what exactly did you do in losing it?" Glenn asked for the record.

"I grabbed one of my belts and followed her into the bathroom, where she was about to take a shower...then strangled her."

"What happened next?"

"I went downstairs, calmed down and then called 911," Finnegan responded, eyes lowered as though resigned to his fate as a murderer.

Now comes the more critical part, Glenn told himself, relative to his current investigation. He rested his arms on the table separating them. "Have you made a habit of strangling women, Finnegan?" he asked him point-blank, leaving out the one male victim of the serial killer for the moment.

"Of course not," the man argued innocently. "This is the first time I've taken it to that level with someone... I never imagined I was even capable of doing that, even though I've always had a jealous streak in me."

Glenn leaned forward musingly. "In case you haven't heard, there's been a string of local ligature strangulations over the past six months. Maybe you committed these crimes, too, and added your girlfriend to the list for good measure?"

"I'm innocent of any other killings!" Finnegan insisted. "Whoever you're after, it isn't me."

He said this with such a straight face that Glenn was almost inclined to believe him. But that was hardly good enough. In spite of his reservations to the contrary, Glenn needed more to eliminate Finnegan as a suspect in the Shellview County Killer case.

"We'll need to know your whereabouts during certain days and alibis that can hold up when put to the test," he advised the suspect, while knowing that they would be able to collect his DNA and fingerprints for comparison purposes. He also needed to get a search warrant to examine his cell phone and computer for any info that might come into play.

Quinn Finnegan agreed to this, then was carted off to jail after being charged with the murder of Naomi Echeverría.

THAT EVENING, Tisha was with Glenn as they walked their dogs, held by leashes, down the sidewalk near her town house. Learning that a woman had been strangled and a man had confessed to the murder had shaken up Tisha. At the same time, she had hoped this was the break they needed to solve the serial killer case.

Unfortunately, it wasn't.

"He's definitely not responsible for any of the serial murders," Glenn told her forlornly. "Quinn Finnegan's alibis checked out. Getting beyond the fact that a different type of ligature was used by the Shellview County Killer, who hasn't been so willing to turn himself in, a preliminary exam of Naomi Echeverría by the associate medical examiner showed no signs of a stun gun being used on the victim. Though Finnegan may not have felt he needed this to overpower his girlfriend, it just doesn't stack up."

"Oh, well..." Tisha muttered, tightening her grip on the leash as Jacky sought to break free. "It wasn't meant to be. But at least Finnegan will be held accountable for killing his girlfriend."

"True, there is that," Glenn said. "And we'll keep plugging away, turning over every rock we can to catch the unsub we're looking for."

I wonder just how long that will take? she couldn't help but ask herself. Would others have to die first before the serial killer was brought to his knees?

"It's all you can do," Tisha agreed, "till he either makes a mistake or we figure out who he is beforehand."

"Yeah." Glenn rounded the corner before she did, with Riley leading the way. "I was thinking that on Saturday maybe we could barbecue some steaks and burgers on my grill, and invite my GBI buddy, Kurt, and that friend of yours you mentioned..."

"Jeanne," she told him. "Yes, that sounds like a terrific idea."

"Cool." He grinned back at her. "We'll do it."

"Should be fun." And a good way, Tisha felt, to integrate their friends into the relationship they were building with each other. If Jeanne and Kurt happened to hit it off, too, as single people, all the better.

Chapter Eleven

Glenn was happy that Tisha had agreed to the Saturday backyard barbecue idea that had popped into his head a few days ago. Seemed like a good opportunity to step away from their respective careers in law enforcement—and the Shellview County Killer investigation, in particular—for some quality time with people they cared about. Though he didn't necessarily want to try to set up his friend Kurt, who was still licking his wounds as a divorcé, the fact that Tisha's friend Jeanne was also divorced and, according to Tisha, available, seemed to Glenn to be a good enough reason for them to decide if it was worth pursuing.

He stood on the outdoor dining limestone backyard patio over a gas-and-charcoal grill combo with a smoker, using a grill spatula to turn over rib-eye steaks and burgers for his guests. Tisha had pitched in by making potato salad and homemade oatmeal-raisin cookies. Riley and Jacky were behaving themselves while seemingly trying to decide if they wanted to walk around gawking or lie down lazily on the grass.

Glenn watched as Kurt broke away from Tisha and Jeanne, who were standing near the edge of the patio in the sunshine, and walked over to him. "Looks like you have a winner in Tisha," he said, grinning, a cold beer in hand.

"You think?" Glenn grinned back, while agreeing wholeheartedly.

"Absolutely. If she's willing to put up with you, you must be doing something right. Or not so wrong."

This brought a laugh from Glenn as he flipped the meat again. "Am I that difficult to deal with?"

"Not at all, buddy." Kurt chuckled. "Seriously, I'm happy for you. All work and no play can get to be boring at times."

"You're telling me." Glenn thought about GBI work and the stress and strain it could bring. It was anything but boring with the range of investigations they dealt with.

"Sorry that it didn't pan out with the strangler you brought in the other day," Kurt said thoughtfully.

"Me, too," Glenn concurred. "Still, it's one less perp to have to contend with."

"Yeah." He put the beer bottle to his mouth.

Glenn glanced at the women and made eye contact with Tisha, who flashed her teeth and seemed eager to play matchmaker, perhaps more than him. "So what do you think of Jeanne?" he asked Kurt.

"Seems like a nice woman," he responded coolly.

"I thought so, too." Glenn smiled, glancing at the good-looking fashion designer. According to Tisha, Jeanne was pretty picky when it came to whom she dated. But maybe Kurt was up to the challenge. "See any opportunities for getting to know each other better?"

"Yeah, the possibilities are definitely there." Kurt took another swig of beer. "We'll see what happens."

"Good luck," Glenn offered supportively, as he started to put the steaks and burgers on a platter, while being more focused on where things stood with him and Tisha. He believed they were on to something and had no intentions of letting up on that front.

"TOO SOON TO TELL," Jeanne told Tisha candidly an hour later as to how she felt about Kurt, as they were clearing the wooden picnic table, while Glenn and Kurt were playing with the dogs. "Right now, I'll settle for a new friend of a friend, and go from there."

"Fair enough." Tisha had no intention of pushing her into anything Jeanne wasn't yet ready for. Each person had to move at their own pace. Or in a different direction.

"Things seem to be clicking nicely between you and Glenn," Jeanne told her.

"They are," Tisha admitted. "He's a great guy."

"And you're great, too!" Jeanne smiled. "So you can't lose."

"I suppose not." Tisha chuckled, though didn't want to be too presumptuous as to where things could go with Glenn. But that didn't mean she would shy away from trying to make it work out in having a future with him.

They joined the men and dogs, and Glenn gave Tisha a hug and kissed her affectionately, then told her, "We'll have to do these get-togethers more often."

"I'd like that," she said, touching her mouth, and gazing at Jeanne and Kurt chatting amiably.

They were about to head back inside the house when Glenn's cell phone rang. He pulled it from the back pocket of his shorts and answered. Tisha saw his expression go from joyful to one of discomfort, as he listened and then muttered, "Okay. I'll see you there—"

Tisha dreaded to ask. "What is it?"

Glenn sighed and said gloomily, "There's been another murder…"

"HER NAME'S PATRICE WHITNEY," Marjorie remarked matter-of-factly, as Glenn stared at the fully clothed body of a slender biracial female in her thirties. She was lying face up in a swamp near Loone Street in Shellview County, surrounded by an abundance of vines and bald cypress trees. Her dark hair was in a feathered mohawk around prominent features. "She was homeless and had been arrested a number of times for loitering and public intoxication," the sheriff said.

"Hmm…" Glenn muttered musingly, glancing at Tisha, who frowned, having insisted on coming with him, though she was off duty and wearing casual clothing. "Not exactly where you would expect to find a homeless person hanging out."

"Definitely not," Marjorie agreed. "Someone obviously brought her here—either while still alive, or dead—and dumped the body."

"Who discovered her?" he asked.

"A couple of hunters. Apparently, they initially thought they were looking at a mannequin." Marjorie rolled her eyes. "But upon closer inspection, realized it was an adult female. My deputies are questioning them further—"

Glenn studied the dead woman again. She was wearing a beige cap-sleeve shirt, ripped wide-leg jeans and black sneakers. He noted that there was a rosemary tattoo on her right arm and a feather tattoo on the other. Looking at her neck area, there were definite signs that she could have been a victim of strangulation.

"I wonder how long she's been here?" Tisha asked.

"Judging by the relatively good condition of the body, I'm guessing not long," Marjorie said.

"I was thinking the same thing." Tisha twisted her lips. "But assuming this is the work of the Shellview County Killer, why would she be killed elsewhere and brought here, where she might not have been discovered for a while, contrary to the other killings?"

"That's a good question," Glenn said. It certainly didn't fit the MO of the unsub serial killer. Could this be an isolated incident? Or an attempt to throw them off guard? Or hide evidence that might lead to the culprit? "I'm sure whoever did this had reasons for doing so. It'll be up to us to flush them out…"

"And we will," Marjorie said, making her intentions clear. "Whatever path that takes us down."

When the associate medical examiner and his team arrived to claim the body, Ned Karakawa wasted little time in giving his preliminary take on the decedent. He said grimly, "Appears as though this was a homicide—using a cord of some type as the ligature murder weapon of choice to strangle the victim." He drew a breath. "There are also marks on her chest that are consistent with the use of a stun gun… As of now, I'd say that death likely occurred elsewhere at some point between thirty-six to forty-eight hours ago—"

The MO is straight out of the playbook of the Shellview County Killer, Glenn told himself. He looked at the sheriff and then Tisha and could see that they had reached the same, and not too surprising, conclusion.

Glenn couldn't help but wonder whether or not this was a new trend by the unsub, in changing his style. Or was it an indication that they were getting too close for comfort in identifying him and he was trying harder to cover his tracks?

"AREN'T YOU SUPPOSED to be off today?" Fritz Alvarez questioned Tisha. He was standing alongside Sherman near the crime scene, after the DNR had been brought into the investigation by the sheriff's department with the murder occurring inside their work section.

"Yes," she told the sergeant, "but I felt I needed to be here." Even in street clothes, Tisha considered herself to be much more than an interested observer, given the stakes, which she had become part of.

Tisha glanced at Glenn, who backed her up when he said smoothly, "I agree with her. Warden Fletcher's astute insight has proven to be quite valuable in my investigation. We can always use her opinion as we try to solve this latest murder."

Fritz nodded. "That's good to know."

"We're all certainly here to lend our support," Sherman asserted. "And Tisha does have great instincts in everything she does."

She blushed. "Thanks for saying that."

He grinned. "Just speaking the truth. Like Agent McElligott."

Glenn regarded her straight-faced. "Then it's unanimous. Now, we need to get back to the hard work of solving this case—"

"I'm all for that," Tisha said evenly, preferring not to be the focal point of any of them, in terms of being a game warden. On the personal front, though, she was happy to be the center of Glenn's attention, even if she had yet to share having someone in her life with her colleagues.

"We're checking out every entry and exit of the area to see what clues the killer may have left behind," Fritz said.

"Okay," Glenn told him.

Sherman added, "And coordinating our efforts with crime scene investigators to not trip over one another as we search for evidence."

"Nearby surveillance cameras may yield some useful

information," Tisha explained, in spite of the rural nature of the landscape.

Glenn rubbed his jaw and said, "What's clear is that whoever killed Patrice Whitney did so with the intention of buying time, while keeping us guessing."

Tisha mulled that over. "I'm guessing that the unsub lured the victim away from wherever she was spending her time—perhaps by offering her food, shelter, or cash—before she realized she had been tricked. By then, it was too late to turn back the clock…"

"Which means we're left with turning the clock ahead to try and beat the unsub to the punch, so to speak, in tracking him down," Glenn stated soundly. "Before someone else has to end up in a swamp."

Tisha felt a nip in the pit of her stomach at the thought. She also saw this as another opportunity for them to close the gap between the authorities on a mission and an unrelenting serial killer at large, who was more dangerous than ever.

HE WATCHED THEM inconspicuously, reveling in being seen and invisible at the same time. This wasn't necessarily something he had planned from the outset. But then again, some things were meant to be when the circumstances called for it. He had no qualms in having the homeless woman's body found after being given ample time to cover his tracks like footprints in the sand. Quite the contrary, he was counting on the lurid discovery, if only to appease his sense of retribution.

Then there was the unexpected adrenaline rush he got with each kill. As they struggled to breathe while he twisted the cord around their pretty necks, he actually found himself counting the seconds till their breathing stopped altogether. And with each second, he savored the taste of victory and payback, to the extent possible, within his means.

He zeroed in on the good-looking game warden talking with the GBI special agent. They were no doubt discussing the homeless woman's death. And very likely, linking it to the other strangulation murders insofar as means and motive. Good luck with that. He laughed. Getting to the root of it would not be easy. He never intended it to be.

Yet there they were, conferring with each other, hoping to somehow, some way, get inside his head. Wouldn't happen. He was so much cleverer than them. Or any of the law enforcement personnel involved in trying to take him down. Including the FBI.

As it was, his mission wasn't over just yet. He gave the pretty game warden the benefit of his attention again. Soon it would be her turn to feel the life slipping away from chokingly as he wrung her neck till she was dead. And there was nothing that the special agent could do about it. Other than kick himself for not being able to save her.

He chuckled within, pleased with himself. Even while wishing on some level that it had not come to this.

But it had, and he had to live with what he had done and would still do. Till he was through.

It was time for him to leave the scene as easily as he had arrived. He calmly started to walk away. When he approached the sheriff, he gave her a friendly nod and got one in return. The same was true when encountering others who were out to get him, but were too dumb to realize that they had him within their grasp. If only they knew.

Once he was safely beyond the perimeter of the crime scene, he sucked in a deep breath of relief that he had gotten away scot-free. To live to see another day. At which time, he could pick up where he left off, without missing a beat.

That thought captured his fancy and gave him something to look forward to as he reached his vehicle and hopped in, and went on his merry way.

Chapter Twelve

On Sunday, Tisha was at Glenn's place, having spent the night and feeling very much like she belonged, with his encouragement. She was starting to seriously think that what they had was more than just a short-lived romance. Still, until they could talk more about where things stood and could go, she was determined to keep her emotions in check. She didn't want to see them torn apart, just as she had at last opened up her heart again.

They were sitting on a gray sectional sofa in the great room with the dogs resting on the floor as Glenn played his guitar. Tisha loved listening to him and dreamed of getting a piano again, to play in harmony with him.

But at the moment, she found herself thinking about the latest person believed to have become the sixth victim of the Shellview County Killer.

Patrice Whitney.

Why did the killer choose to go after her? Did they cross paths? Did something stand out that drew her to him? Or was it the other way around?

Were these dynamics the same with the other victims?

"I have a cousin named Patrice," Tisha mentioned casually.

"Really?" Glenn looked at her curiously.

"Yeah. As kids, we used to pretend to be one another, after discovering that both names were derivatives of Patricia."

"Cool." He smiled but continued to play a country music song on the guitar.

For whatever reason, the Patricia connection prompted Tisha to use her cell phone to look up online other variations of the name.

There was Pat, Patti, Patty, Pattie, Patsy, Patrina, Patrice, Patrycja, Patrizia, Trecia, Tresha, Tricia, Trish, Tris, Trisha.

On the male side was the name Patrick.

Tisha pulled up the names of the victims of the Shellview County Killer:

Patsy Dunnock.

Walt Patrick.

Patti Arnaz.

Tris Lindberg.

Patrina Morse.

Patrice Whitney.

Hmm. That's odd, Tisha told herself uncomfortably. What were the odds that all the victims would happen to have names that were offshoots, spinoffs, or whatever, of the name Patricia? Just like her own?

She looked them over again and then cast her eyes upon Glenn, who, sensing something was up, suddenly stopped playing and asked tentatively, "Something on your mind…?"

"Actually, there is," she said, hesitant to go further. "Look, this is probably going to sound ridiculous, but I think I may have found something that could connect all the Shellview County Killer victims in an odd way—"

"Okay." His eyes pinned to hers. "I'm listening."

She drew a breath. “I told you about my name and my cousin Patrice’s name being versions of the name Patricia?”

“Yeah… Go on…”

“Well, out of curiosity and maybe a gut instinct, I decided to check out other derivatives of Patricia and found that each victim of the serial killer—including the male victim—has a form of the name Patricia, leading me to think that there may be some symmetry here that goes beyond random—” She watched him contemplating this and, while doing so, showed him the names on her phone, as if he needed any help remembering them.

“Hmm… I admit this is weird,” Glenn said after a long moment. “But it does seem a bit of a stretch to think that a killer would purposely handpick victims with a range of versions of the name Patricia. And in the case of the male victim, Walt Patrick, given that Patrick is his surname, that makes it seem even more unlikely. Especially when coupled with his girlfriend, Patti Arnaz, being a victim, too. How would a serial killer even begin to have targeted two Patricia namesakes of sorts in one kill? Then there’s the fact that Patrina Morse is from Australia. How would the unsub have found her so quicky—if targeting his victims by name—given that she’d only been in Georgia for three days before being attacked?” Glenn took a breath. “The chances of making this work by lining up potential victims with the same name in Shellview County would seem to be astronomical.”

“You’ll get no argument from me there,” Tisha agreed, when thinking about it squarely. “It does appear to be unlikely for even the shrewdest serial killer to be able to orchestrate. Maybe I am way off base here,” she added, petting Jacky, who had hopped up next to her on the sectional. “But then again, who’s to say that this killer isn’t more resourceful than most in locating victims with some version of the name Patricia? Maybe this was his mother's name. The unsub could have decided to get his payback at long last after years of being abused by her as a child or something. Or maybe it's his weird way of taking revenge against a wife, girlfriend, friend, or coworker with the name while not having to own up to it. I'm just saying…"

Glenn chuckled. "Sounds like you've been watching way too many movies or reading crime novels." Before she could respond, thinking that he wasn't taking her seriously enough, even with her having second thoughts, he said levelly, "On the other hand, there may be some merit to your theory worth checking out…"

Her eyes grew with interest. "Really?"

"Yes. In fact, there was a case a few years ago in which a serial killer strangled to death eight women named Linda with an *i* or Lynda with a *y*—the latter being his mother's name—for the very reason you imagined. She'd apparently been abusing him for years, before abandoning him, giving him more reason to exact his warped revenge."

"So we could be looking at the same thing here?"

"Maybe." Glenn leaned back, thoughtful. "The two versions of Lynda would have been easier to pull off. Patricia variations as victims, not so much. But given that our unsub is still on the loose and we obviously haven't connected enough dots to expose him and bring him in, this is certainly an angle that should be looked into."

"Thanks." Tisha gave a sheepish grin. "It may be an entirely overactive imagination on my part, but this somehow entered my head as entirely plausible, when thinking about my cousin, Patrice…" Her voice lowered an octave. "Seriously, I hope the killings have nothing to do with the Patricia approach. Especially since Tisha also falls into the name variations, so it would mean that my life could well be in danger, too…" The thought hit her all of a sudden like a strong gust of wind, sending panic reverberating through Tisha.

Glenn's eyebrows joined. "Don't even go there," he scolded her. "Whatever the unsub's motivation or plans for attack, and who he may be targeting, I'm not about to let him harm you…threatening everything that's working between us—"

"Neither am I," she insisted, not wanting to see them lose momentum, either. Tisha started to regain her courage. "As a game warden who knows how to use a firearm and has taken self-defense classes, I won't go down without one hell of a fight, should I encounter the unsub."

A grin played at one corner of Glenn's mouth. "I don't doubt that for a moment." The grin went away. "Still, until we can eliminate your theory altogether, keep your eyes open and your guard up."

Tisha smiled, feeling grateful for his concern and support. "I will," she promised, putting her hand on his.

"Good." Glenn met her eyes soulfully and Tisha knew then that he was someone she could count on through thick and thin, no matter which way their romantic relationship went over the course of time.

ON MONDAY MORNING, Glenn assembled everyone in the conference room in the sheriff's department for an update, in addition to welcoming the FBI to the team. He knew that the Bureau wanted the same thing he did at the end of the day—to put the brakes on a serial monster who was plying his trade in Shellview County to the tune of six victims and counting, if the unsub had his way.

Foremost on Glenn's mind was the notion that the perp

could have borrowed a page from serial killer Lucas Conseco and targeted his victims by name. The disturbing thought of Tisha getting caught in the crosshairs of the unsub left Glenn feeling angry and petrified. Now that he had finally found someone who moved him in a way that other women hadn't, giving them both reason for being optimistic when looking ahead, losing Tisha to a serial killer was something Glenn didn't even want to fathom.

He cast his eyes upon her—she was sitting up front, exuding strength and vulnerability at the same time. Her gut instinct in establishing the possible Patricia connection in the case was both impressive and unsettling, to say the least. Yet, the better part of him still felt it was a long shot that the unsub had it in him to be so ingenious and opportunistic to orchestrate that plan successfully.

But long shots still beat the odds in society, Glenn told himself wisely. Even when it came to serial killers. In this case, he couldn't afford to turn his back on any possibility that could lead to a killer.

Using the stylus pen to control what showed up on the monitor, he showed the before-and-after images of the last two victims—Patrina Morse and thirty-four-year-old Patrice Whitney. Morse was blue-eyed and had brunette hair in a collarbone bob, while Whitney had pretty aquamarine eyes and, before the dark mohawk, pink-brown hair in a razor cut. He said equably, "They represent numbers five and six of the persons we believe were the ligature strangulation victims of an unknown serial killer. Whitney, described as occasionally homeless, was discovered on Saturday afternoon by rabbit hunters in a swamp in the county. According to the autopsy report, she was strangled to death elsewhere before being brought to the location and dumped there. The associate medical examiner has estimated that Whitney had been dead twenty-four to thirty-six hours prior to when she was found, giving the unsub ample time to hide his tracks and make a clean getaway. That being said, the autopsy showed that the victim had engaged in sexual activity before her death, and DNA has been collected. It is still to be determined as to whether or not this was left behind by her killer and if we're able to link it to the unsub…"

After going through the particulars of the Morse and Whitney murders, his obvious frustration illustrated in the dark tone of his voice, Glenn sucked in a deep breath and glanced at Tisha, then put the names of all the victims on the screen, and said evenly, "In leaving no stones unturned in this investigation, Game Warden Tisha Fletcher has presented an intriguing theory that the victims may have been chosen for their names, as all have some version of the name Patricia." Glenn paused to let that sink in, eyeing Marjorie Pierce after he had already run it by the sheriff, who was skeptical but open-minded to the possibility. "As you can see, the victims' names do lend themselves to known variations of Patricia—including Patrick, the male equivalent, as a victim's surname. While this could all be entirely happenstance—and admittedly, it would take some doing on the part of the unsub to line up the victims to fit the bill—it needs to be explored in the course of the investigation as we would any possible new leads or directions…"

Glenn put up on the screen a diagram with arrows connecting one victim to another and the final arrow leading to the unsub. "Between the GBI, FBI and sheriff's department, as a task force, we'll work overtime to do what we need to do to see if there's anything here…or if we need to continue to pursue other leads to help crack the case. As for the former, we'll investigate any possible links to anyone named Patricia in and around Shellview County, through social media, surveillance videos, cell phone records, et cetera, utilizing the Georgia Cyber Crime Center, Georgia Information Sharing and Analysis Center, GBI Polygraph Unit and supportive specialized units and resources within the sheriff's department and the Bureau—"

After finishing up, Glenn turned it over to Marjorie, who made it clear right off the bat. "We're not going to stop till the unsub's either in police custody or dead..." She then doubled down on his willingness to tackle any and all possibilities, while zeroing in on some of the more down-to-earth investigative practices, such as forensic examination of footprints and tire tracks found in and around the swamp, and victim movements prior to death, in hopes of finding the break needed to nab the killer.

"That seemed to go relatively well," Tisha commented after they had separated themselves and stepped outside, where the skies were cloudy.

"I think so," Glenn concurred.

"You think the Patricia hypothesis will resonate with others investigating the serial murders?"

"Yeah, I do—at least insofar as a willingness up and down the line to go with the flow and follow each and every lead, no matter how improbable. Believe me, no one wants to get this one wrong. The stakes are way too high."

"I'll say." She looked at him. "I just hope the stakes don't go even higher in the body count, whether those targeted have a version of the name Patricia or not."

"We're definitely on the same page there," he assured her, knowing that to feel otherwise wouldn't correspond with being in law enforcement and trying to nip any case in the bud before it spiraled dangerously out of control.

"Just *there*?" Her lashes fluttered playfully.

He chuckled. "Much more than that. The synergy between us is amazing and keeps growing."

"Good response," she told him with a little giggle.

"So, on that note, shall I swing by your place after work?"

"Sounds great." Tisha touched his arm. "Unless you'd rather I come to you?"

"Whichever." He put his hand on hers. "As long as we get to hang together."

She smiled. "See you, then, at my place. And please bring Riley along. Jacky has grown rather fond of him and gets ornery now when Riley's not around."

Glenn laughed. "In that case, we'll make sure that they get to spend as much time together as possible." In his book, that could mean a very long time, if things continued progressing the way they were between them.

"Perfect." She lifted her chin and dared him to give her a quick kiss.

He was happy to oblige, feeling comfortable to show anyone who cared to see that they were now officially a couple.

Chapter Thirteen

Glenn split from Tisha and hopped in his Dodge Durango for the drive back to his office with renewed intensity, both for solving the current case and building something special with her. Not necessarily in that order. He had always been into his career—the good, the bad, even the unexpected—but Tisha had given him a whole new reason for wanting so much more with his life. She seemed to want the same at this stage, in moving beyond being a widow living in the past, to forging ahead and embracing the bright future she could have.

When his cell phone rang, he lifted it off the seat and saw that the caller was his sister, Josette. Grinning, as he assumed she was merely checking in on him, he put her on speakerphone and placed the cell in the holder on the dashboard. "Hey, sis," he said spiritedly.

"Hey, you," she returned. "Hope I didn't catch you at a bad time?"

"You didn't." At thirty-five, Josette was only three years his senior, but Glenn had always looked up to her as being older and wiser than her years. "What's up?"

"Just wanted to make sure you were still in the land of the living, as I hadn't heard from you in a while."

"Sorry." He gave a little laugh. "I'm still here. I've been

meaning to call…" If that wasn't the lamest clichéd excuse for his neglect. She had a right to be pissed in a sisterly way.

"Yeah, right." She chuckled. "You're forgiven, Mr. Busy GBI Special Agent."

"Thanks," he said sheepishly, while watching the road. He shifted the onus on her. "So bring me up to speed on things."

He listened while she gave a short summary of being in love with her longtime girlfriend, Zoey, and dishing out some great meals as an award-winning chef. After hinting that a marriage could be forthcoming, Josette told him, "We'd love to have you visit again. There's always a room at our place with your name on it."

"I'll keep that in mind," he said agreeably, and added teasingly, "but just so you know, that room should be big enough for two…"

"You're seeing someone?" Surprise filled her voice. "Do tell?"

"Yeah. Tisha's a game warden."

"That's cool. Is it serious?"

"I think so." A grin played on his lips. "And, yes, she'd love to meet you and Zoey."

"Then we need to make it happen, little brother," Josette insisted.

"We will," Glenn promised, and they exchanged a few pleasantries about their parents before disconnecting. He recalled that Tisha had expressed an interest in visiting Alaska. Now, the opportunity was there to do just that. He looked forward to that next big step toward building bridges between their families.

When he got to his desk, Glenn called Layla Ramaswamy at the Crime Lab for an update on DNA taken from

Patrice Whitney. "Any news?" he asked when Layla picked up for a video chat.

"Actually, I was just about to contact you," she said enthusiastically. "There is news..."

"I'm listening."

"Well, we took the recovered biological evidence left on Ms. Whitney and submitted the DNA profile to CODIS, where there was a hit!"

"Really?" He gazed at her with interest. "Go on..."

"The DNA is from a Roy Gallagher," she said. "He's been in and out of jail, mostly on drug-related offenses." Layla paused. "He was definitely engaged in sex with the murdered victim shortly before she was killed—"

"Thanks, Layla," Glenn said. "I'll take it from here..."

"You're welcome." She licked her lips. "If he killed her—and the others—I hope Gallagher goes down."

"We'll see what happens."

After hanging up, Glenn immediately went to his laptop to gather as much information as he could on the suspect. He quickly learned that Roy Gallagher was a forty-year-old military veteran, who'd served in Iraq and Afghanistan, before being discharged. Never married, he'd recently been living on the streets and in homeless shelters in Shellview County. Was this how he intersected with Patrice Whitney? And killed her?

For that matter, had Gallagher somehow been able to use his lack of housing to camouflage being a serial killer?

This was something Glenn intended to find out.

THAT AFTERNOON, Tisha taught a class to educate visitors on wildlife laws and proper safety practices, along with Sherman, at the Manikeke Environmental Education Center on Dusty Springs Street in the Manikeke Crossing WMA. It was perhaps her favorite part of being a game warden—offering the public the tools needed to make the most of the rich natural environment and resources at their disposal. If that wasn't enough, it helped to take her mind off less desirable things, such as having to cope with a ruthless serial killer in their midst. Fresh thoughts rolled into her mind about discovering the body of Tris Lindberg.

During an intermission, Sherman folded his arms and asked her in an earnest tone, "So what's up with you and Agent McElligott?"

Tisha fluttered her lashes boldly. "If you're asking if Glenn and I are dating, the answer is yes." She wouldn't hide from her feelings for the man, any more than Glenn wished to do among his colleagues, such as Kurt Stewart.

"That's great." Sherman broke into a smile. "Seems like a nice guy."

"He is," she said and thought truthfully, *And so much more!*

"You're just as nice, which I'm sure he would attest to." Sherman waited a beat and said, "I wish you—and him—the best."

"Thanks." Tisha blushed. "Hope you find someone special, too."

He laughed. "Been there, done that. I'm in no hurry to go down that road at the moment."

"Understood." Only too well. She felt the same way for the longest time after Bradley's death. Then came Glenn and everything changed.

"So you really think there could be something to this serial killer using different versions of the name Patricia to target his victims?" Sherman asked, cocking an eyebrow.

"Possibly. Who knows?" Tisha tried to downplay it but couldn't shake the feeling that it might not be entirely unfounded. What were the odds that six random victims would all have some variation of the same name? But she also had to admit that the odds of being murdered at all in a single county by a serial killer were long, too. "It only entered my head because the last victim, Patrice Whitney, happened to share the first name of my cousin—an offshoot of Patricia, as is my own name." That last thought stuck in her throat like a chicken bone. "Checking out the names of the other victims, I realized that they too had variants of Patricia. Whether or not this is entirely coincidental will be up to Glenn and Sheriff Pierce to determine."

"You're right." Sherman gazed at her musingly. "You mentioned that your name also fell into the variations… Never thought of Tisha as being short for or an alternative to Patricia—"

"Now you know," she said with a thin smile.

He furrowed his brow. "You don't think you could be in any danger, do you?"

I can't rule it out, no matter how hard I try, Tisha told herself. She said to him, trying not to freak out, "I hope not. But I'll keep my guard up, just in case." She found herself unintentionally brushing her hand against the Glock pistol in her holster.

"As will I," Sherman said steadfastly. "If this unsub ever decides to come after you, Agent McElligott won't be the only one to have your back."

Tisha gave him a grateful smile for his support. "I appreciate that."

"It's what we do in the DNR," he replied matter-of-factly.

The class gathered again, only this time for some outdoor education with the sun managing to peek out from behind the clouds.

BACKED BY DEPUTIES, FBI agents and a SWAT team armed with Colt M4 carbine semiautomatic rifles, Glenn located the suspect at the Breyford Shelter on Ninth Street, which happened to be a place that Patrice Whitney had been in and out of, according to the sheriff's department.

Glenn made the decision to go in after him. If he was their unsub, there was no way they would allow Roy Gallagher to slip from their grasp. Or hurt someone inside. Or possibly take hostages.

Accompanied by FBI Special Agent Neal Montoya, fiftysomething and thickly built, with gray hair in a taper fade cut and a short beard, Glenn had already removed the SIG Sauer 9mm pistol from his holster. Montoya was holding a Springfield Armory M1911-A1 pistol, and he gave the agent the signal to move in.

As had been indicated by a female undercover sheriff's deputy, posing as a homeless woman for a sneak peek inside the shelter, Glenn found the person of interest seated in a black plastic chair at a wooden dining table against a windowless wall, drinking coffee. Wearing drab clothing and dark tennis shoes, he had a slim build and graying brown hair in a messy man bun.

They moved swiftly across the tile floor toward the suspect, and by the time he turned blue eyes at them, they already had him surrounded, guns pointed, as Glenn barked, "Roy Gallagher…?"

A look of puzzlement crossed his face, as he responded tonelessly, "Yeah, that's me. What is this…?"

"I'm GBI Special Agent McElligott." Glenn set steely eyes on the man. "We need to bring you in for questioning."

"About what?" Gallagher demanded.

"The murder of Patrice Whitney…" he told him sharply.

Montoya introduced himself coldly to the suspect and snorted, "Let's go," while helping Gallagher to his feet.

Half an hour later, Glenn had the suspect in an interrogation room to grill him about what he knew or didn't know about the case.

"Why don't we get right down to business," Glenn said without preface. He was seated across from the suspect, who was cuffed. "Let's talk about Patrice Whitney. She was strangled to death. Did you kill her?" *And ostensibly five other people, as well*, he thought, if this was their serial killer.

"No, I didn't kill her!" Gallagher shot back. "Didn't even know Patrice was dead."

"So you say." Glenn peered at him with skepticism. It didn't surprise him that the suspect was acquainted with the victim. Both had spent time at the same shelter and on the streets, so they were likely to have crossed paths more than once. Still, he had to ask… "But you knew her?"

"Yeah, I knew her," he muttered.

Glenn narrowed his eyes. "We found your DNA on Ms. Whitney's body. You want to explain that?"

Gallagher lowered his head thoughtfully. "We had sex. It was consensual," he insisted.

There had been no indication during the autopsy that the decedent had been sexually assaulted. But it hadn't been ruled out, either, giving Glenn reason to remain suspicious that the suspect could well have engaged in rape and murder. "Too bad she isn't able to verify that."

"It wasn't the first time," Gallagher asserted. "Patrice and I had an understanding."

"And just what was this understanding?" Glenn pressed.

"That we would get together whenever it felt right. I would never have hurt Patrice."

Glenn took that with a grain of salt. "Do you own a car?"

"Do I look like I have a ride?" Gallagher rolled his eyes sardonically. "That's the last thing I need in my life right now."

Glenn considered that he could have been driven to the swamp where she was murdered, but this seemed unlikely. Unless Gallagher had partnered with someone else to commit the crime.

"Someone either kidnapped or coerced Patrice Whitney into going with them, subdued her with a stun gun and strangled her to death with a cord," Glenn stated in a hard tone. "Right now, you're the only one we're looking at as a legitimate suspect. Unless you can—"

Gallagher cut him off as he stated, "You said Patrice was strangled with a cord… Well, I'm afraid that would be a real challenge for me to accomplish. After getting injured in Afghanistan during my last tour of duty, I suffered nerve damage to my right arm. It may look normal on the outside, but on the inside, I can't do much with it. Unless you're suggesting I could strangle Patrice with one hand, you're looking at the wrong dude as her killer—"

Glenn had missed this in checking out the suspect's military background. Would be easy enough to verify and, if so, would make it a tough sell to believe that Roy Gallagher was the culprit in Patrice Whitney's murder. Much less, the other killings attributed to the Shellview County Killer.

By the time he got off work, having conferred with his colleagues in the investigation, Glenn had let Gallagher off the hook for the Whitney homicide, satisfied that the military vet was not responsible for her death.

After picking up a cheese, sausage and pepperoni pizza, Glenn swung by his house and got Riley, before heading over to Tisha's place. She greeted them warmly. As did

Jacky, who seemed to like him almost as much as she did Riley.

"Thought I'd bring dinner," Glenn said sweetly, handing Tisha the pizza box.

"How nice of you." She grinned and gave him a peck on the mouth. "I'll get us some plates."

When they were at the table eating, he relayed the latest news about Roy Gallagher, and said regrettably, "Thought we might have been on to something with him, bolstered by the DNA evidence. But it didn't add up at the end of the day."

"I'm sorry, too," Tisha said, while holding a slice of pizza. "Doesn't mean it won't work out the right way the next time." She took a breath. "Has to, sooner or later—"

"You're right, it has to." Glenn bit into his own pizza slice. No matter how many setbacks they had, the investigation was hardly stalled. For one, there was still the possibility that the unsub was targeting victims with name variations of Patricia. Or perhaps some other nonrandom angle they were still missing. He grabbed another slice of pizza and grinned at Tisha as he turned his thoughts to the good feeling he had every time they were together. No matter the background noise of a homicide investigation.

Chapter Fourteen

Shortly after 11:00 a.m. on Wednesday, Tisha was at the gym on an elliptical machine. While doing her best to stay on stride and in rhythm, with a smile, she eyed the woman on the machine next to her, Carole Kitaguchi, who was thirtysomething and petite with dark hair in a topknot, and a regular at the Blair Bay Fitness Center.

Tisha took note that the elliptical on the other side of her was empty, where Jeanne was supposed to be, as they had planned to work out together. Then go for lunch afterward.

So where was she?

Tisha checked her cell phone for any messages from Jeanne. There were none. Could she have forgotten their workout was today? It even occurred to Tisha that maybe Jeanne had been out late with Kurt last night, as they seemed to be getting closer, and overslept. Or lost track of time.

Or just decided to skip the exercise, while being distracted with other things.

I'll give her a buzz after I'm through, Tisha thought, planning to playfully chide her for missing the workout. In reality, she was hoping that Jeanne's excuse was romantic in nature, knowing that her own happiness was reaching a whole new level in her relationship with Glenn. She couldn't wait to see what was in store for them, even as they continued to acclimate themselves to one another. As was true for Jacky and Riley, who were becoming almost inseparable, while ceding their individual territory to one another.

Tisha had just begun to pick up the pace when her cell phone buzzed. Sensing it was important, she stopped and pulled the phone from the back pocket of her capri leggings and saw that it was Jeanne.

Tisha put the phone to her ear and said softly, "Hey."

"Hey. Sorry I'm not there." Jeanne's voice shook. "I'm in the hospital—"

"What!" Tisha spoke louder than she had intended to, drawing the attention of those nearby in the gym. She lowered her voice and asked, "What happened?"

"I was attacked!" she exclaimed. "Someone came up behind me after I left my town house, hit me with a stun gun…and tried to strangle me…"

"I'm on my way," Tisha told her, unnerved, knowing there was only one hospital in Blair Bay.

"Okay." Jeanne's voice broke. "Can't believe this could happen to me…"

Neither can I, Tisha mused, flabbergasted as she disconnected, and turned to Carole, who had stopped exercising.

"What's going on?" she asked curiously.

"Jeanne's been attacked by someone."

Carole's mouth opened with dismay. "Is she okay?"

Tisha took a breath, then admitted dourly, "I don't know." She was so rattled that she hadn't even bothered to ask Jeanne about her physical condition after the ordeal. "I have to go…"

"I understand." Carole put her hand on Tisha's arm. "Let me know what you find out."

Tisha nodded. "I will." She took off, praying that Jeanne would get through this in relatively good shape, while eager to learn more details about the assault and whoever was behind it.

Once she reached her car, Tisha phoned Glenn with the devastating news. "Jeanne was the victim of an attack—" she told him on speakerphone.

"I know," he said somberly. "I just got word on it from Kurt. He witnessed the whole thing…"

"Really?"

"Yeah. He was meeting Jeanne at her place to accompany her to the Blair Bay Fitness Center for a workout, when Kurt saw the assailant go after her. Kurt managed to scare him off, but not before the creep used the stun gun on her and attempted to strangle her. Kurt took her to the hospital to get checked out, but it seems like she'll be alright. I was about to call you with all this when I got your call."

"I'm on my way to the hospital," Tisha told him, as she drove down Ketchan Street. She felt relieved that Jeanne was not seriously hurt. Thankfully, Kurt was on hand to prevent what could have been a tragic outcome. Still, she wanted to be there for Jeanne to offer moral support and get peace of mind on her condition.

"So am I," Glenn said. "I'll see you there."

"Okay." Disconnecting, Tisha focused on the road, even while contemplating if, in fact, Jeanne had been a victim of the Shellview County Killer. If so, it would seem to debunk her name theory for the victims of the unsub. Which still wouldn't make her feel any better that her friend had been accosted by someone who intended her bodily harm.

Ten minutes later, Tisha pulled up to Blair Bay General Hospital on Youngton Street and parked, then raced inside. It had been one of those days she dreaded, when someone she cared about had been put in harm's way. The saving grace this time was that Jeanne would apparently pull through—no thanks to the creep who assaulted her.

Tisha shuddered at the thought as she went to Jeanne's room and found her lying on the bed, with Kurt sitting beside her.

"Hey, you two," she said to them with a strained smile.

"Hey, Tisha," Kurt said, looking beat.

Jeanne sat up. "You really didn't need to cut short your exercise," she said.

"Don't be silly," Tisha replied. "After what happened, I wanted to make sure you were okay for myself, in spite of Glenn indicating as much."

"I see." Jeanne offered her a smile. "Thanks for coming. The doctor should be here any moment, but other than being a bit shaken up, I'm fine. Fortunately, no broken bones or anything."

"That's good to know."

Kurt stood and said, "Why don't I go get us some coffee?"

"Good idea," Jeanne said, and they ordered theirs black and watched him leave the room.

Tisha moved up to the bed and gave her a hug. "Toiling away on the elliptical machine wasn't the same without you," she joked.

Jeanne laughed. "Oh, really?"

"Even Carole took notice and just wasn't herself." Tisha couldn't help but giggle.

Jeanne winced. "Sorry. Guess I'm still feeling the lingering effects from the stun gun."

Tisha furrowed her brow, envisioning being made to feel disoriented and totally helpless. She sat on the bed and demanded, "Tell me everything that happened—"

NEEDLESS TO SAY, the disturbing news that Jeanne Rutland had been attacked in broad daylight, outside her town house, threw Glenn for a loop. The fact that it was just a few homes down from Tisha's place was even more unsettling. Was this coincidence or what? Could the attacker somehow have mistaken Jeanne for Tisha, in fitting in with the Patricia angle? Or had Jeanne been the intended target all along? If the unsub was their serial killer, it would indicate, more or less, that the names of the victims were coincidental and nothing more.

After arriving at the hospital, Glenn left his vehicle in the parking lot and went in, making his way to the emergency department, where Jeanne was in an exam room.

In the corridor, he ran into Kurt, who was holding a tray with three coffees, and muttered to Glenn, "Hey."

"How's she doing?" Glenn asked.

Kurt, looking grim-faced, replied, "About as well as could be expected after being attacked—" He drew a breath. "The doctor's looking her over now."

"Did you get a good look at Jeanne's attacker?"

"Not really, other than he was white, tall and wearing a blue zip hoodie with the hood over his head." Kurt set his jaw. "Honestly, the moment I saw the perp on top of her, I was mostly concerned for Jeanne's safety. I yelled at him and ran toward them. That's when he got off Jeanne and sped away on foot."

"Okay." Glenn patted him on the shoulder understandingly. "I need to talk to Jeanne."

Kurt nodded. "This way…"

Glenn followed him to the room, then stepped inside and saw Tisha standing off to the side as Jeanne sat on the bed while being examined by the doctor, a thirtysomething Hispanic female with short dark hair.

"Everything checks out," the doctor said. "Other than some soreness to your neck and a few bruises from falling to the ground, you should be fine."

Jeanne grinned. "That's good to know."

"The puncture marks from the stun gun will go away over time. Over-the-counter pain medication should relieve any discomfort, if needed."

"Thanks, Doctor Hernandez," Jeanne said.

"Always here to help," she told her, offering a smile.

Glenn introduced himself to the doctor in his professional capacity, glad that she was able to provide assistance to her patient, and watched as she left the room.

"Guess we didn't need hospital coffee after all," Kurt quipped, while handing a Styrofoam cup to Jeanne and Tisha.

"It was sweet of you to get some, nevertheless," Jeanne told him, taking a sip of coffee.

"Thanks," Tisha said, moving closer to the bed.

Glenn did the same and said, "Glad you're alright."

"You and me both." Jeanne made a face. "Never saw that coming..."

That's true with most crime victims, he told himself realistically, but said to her, "I need to ask you some questions about the attack."

"Can't that wait till she's home?" Tisha queried.

"It can," Glenn allowed, glancing at her and then Kurt, "but it's important that we get as much information as we can on the crime while it's most fresh on her mind."

"It's fine," Jeanne insisted, as she remained seated. "Let's just get this over with. I'll tell you whatever I can..."

"Okay." Glenn wanted to keep this as delicate as possible, yet could not afford to go too soft, given the stakes. Jeanne could be the first target to survive the serial predator known as the Shellview County Killer. Even then, Glenn knew that she would likely need to come in for a formal statement later. "What can you tell me about the person who attacked you, by way of description, clothing, what he may have said to you—anything that comes to mind…?"

"It all happened so fast—" Jeanne pressed her hand on the examination room bed. "Definitely an adult male, perhaps in his thirties, tall and sturdily built. He came up from behind me, seemingly out of nowhere, and zapped me with the stun gun. Couldn't really make out his face as I went down, but could tell that he had on glasses, wore a hood over dark hair and was wearing dirty jeans." She sighed. "Before I knew it, he had jumped on me and put his hands to my neck. Thought I might pass out, but he released me when Kurt showed up, and the man stormed off. I think I heard a car, but since I was disoriented from the stun gun, it could have been my imagination…"

I'll have to see if surveillance cameras picked up cars leaving the area around the time the crime occurred, Glenn told himself. He then pondered the notion of the perpetrator trying to strangle her with his bare hands rather than with a cord, as was the case for the serial killer's victims. Had the unsub chosen a different method because he'd panicked, due to the nature of the audacious attack? Or had he thrown his playbook out the window as the desire to kill intensified? Glenn also had to consider the possibility that this was an isolated attack, unrelated to the other incidents.

"Have you had any reason to believe someone might have been stalking you of late?" he asked her.

"I'm not aware of being stalked by anyone," Jeanne asserted. "But maybe the perpetrator was good enough to keep me from knowing what he was up to."

"That's often the way it works with stalkers, isn't it?" Tisha said, gazing at him.

"Yeah, they often operate surreptitiously," Glenn conceded. "This could just as easily have been an opportunistic attack," he added, considering.

Jeanne frowned. "Does that include being caught in the crosshairs of the Shellview County Killer? If so, how did I get so lucky as to come away from it alive and well, if not shaken from my experience?"

"It's less about luck and more about the timing that had you meeting up with Kurt." Glenn looked toward his fellow GBI special agent, who nodded accordingly.

"He's right," Kurt said, putting his hand on her shoulder. "I'm glad I was around to stop that monster. Just wish I'd gotten there sooner."

She smiled gratefully. "Trust me, I'm not complaining one bit!"

Glenn hated to have to be brutally honest with her, but she deserved that much. "As for the nature of the crime, there's a good chance that you were attacked by this serial killer. Some of the things fit. Others do not," he confessed, and glanced Tisha's way, wondering how she was processing this. "Whoever your assailant is, we'll do everything we can to bring the person to justice."

"That includes getting a forensic sketch artist to work with you in possibly giving us something to help identify and flush out the unsub," Kurt said firmly.

Jeanne tilted her head in his direction. "As I said, I didn't really see his face, other than the glasses—but I'll do my best."

Kurt held her hand. "That's all we can ask."

She gazed at Glenn and asked nervously, "Is he going to come after me again…?"

"I don't think so," he responded with a straight face, making eye contact with Kurt. "Now that the element of surprise has been taken away from the unsub, it's not likely he'd want to take another crack at you and risk capture." That sensible perspective gave way in Glenn's head to the other possibility. A determined serial killer—if this was one—might have an overwhelming need, along with a big ego, to want to finish what he started. They couldn't allow that to happen. "But to be on the safe side, I'll arrange with the sheriff's department's protection unit to offer you security as a witness, till your attacker is brought into custody."

Jeanne nodded. "Thank you."

"In the meantime, you're welcome to stay with me," Tisha offered sincerely.

"I've got this," Kurt told her. "I'll keep an eye on Jeanne for as long as she needs protection."

"That works for me," Jeanne said with a smile.

Glenn could see that Kurt was really into her, just as he was into Tisha. Looked as though all of them were in a good place as far as starting relationships. But first and foremost, they needed to get past the fact that someone had just tried to kill Jeanne. And that Tisha had been swept up into the case in various ways…and was still potentially a target of the killer.

"Let's get out of here," he told them, and got no arguments in leaving the hospital.

THAT EVENING, Tisha walked hand in hand beside Glenn along the beach by the river, with Jacky and Riley up ahead of them playing with each other. The dogs had gotten into a comfort zone with each other that Tisha believed paralleled the one between her and Glenn. She remained positive about where things could go between them, though still wanted to hear more from him on his take on the future.

But for the time being, spending quality time together in the midst of the dangers that seemed to be lurking around them like sharks was something she wouldn't trade for anything.

After padding across the white sand in their bare feet in for a bit, Tisha broke the silence when she asked interestedly, "Do you think the digital sketch of the unsub who attacked Jeanne will yield any results?"

"Some sketches are spot-on, leading to a quick arrest," Glenn told her. "Others may be off-center and could take longer to hit the mark—if they do at all. We're comparing it with surveillance video in the area to see if the stars can align. One can only hope for the best."

Tell me about it, Tisha thought, and said wonderingly, "I suppose that the attack on Jeanne by, presumably, the Shellview County Killer throws cold water on the culprit targeting people whose names correspond with derivatives of Patricia?"

"Not necessarily." Glenn squeezed his fingers around hers. "Assuming we are talking about the same perp—never mind the different MO from other victims and failure to complete the attempted murder—it's still possible that there was a method to his madness, so to speak."

"Such as?"

"Well, the unsub may have deliberately tried to throw us off in the investigation in feeling the heat, by changing his routine."

"I suppose." Tisha regarded him musingly. "But since the Patricia theory hasn't been made public, as far as I'm aware, how would he suspect we were onto this possible connection with the murders—if that was the reason for him shifting gears?"

"Not sure it has anything to do with the victims' names, per se," Glenn replied frankly, as Riley and Jacky circled around them. "Could be the unsub had his own reasons for targeting Jeanne, in particular. Maybe it was more about an opening that presented itself and he went for it, regardless of her first or last name. Or he could have been stalking her, unbeknownst to her, as perhaps an attempted sexual assault, robbery and homicide all tied into one." Glenn watched as Riley jumped on his leg playfully, and continued, "In any event, whether the unsub decided we were on to him or not, irrespective of public awareness of some details, it's still very much up in the air. For now, we'll have to assume that he's being driven by demons that are largely opportunity-oriented—till we find evidence contrary to that. We'll just have to wait and see where this goes…"

"Fair enough," she said, happy to be in his company in the interim.

Tisha actually hoped that the killings were not name-related, when all was said and done, as it otherwise would mean that she herself remained in the line of fire as a potential target of the unsub. Not a comfortable thought, to say the least. At the same time, she didn't want to be off the mark at the expense of Jeanne being assaulted and nearly killed.

As Jacky got her attention, apparently getting restless away from home, Tisha eyed Glenn and said, "I think the dogs are ready to go."

"Okay, if they insist," Glenn said with a grin, and they turned around and headed back up the beach.

The Shellview County Killer watched as the DNR game warden and GBI special agent walked along the beach with their dogs, oblivious to his presence. Admittedly, he had begun to warm up to the nickname he'd been given, as it did seem to fit, the more he thought about it. He was, after all, killing those he had chosen to die in Shellview County. The fact that the press had decided to supply him with a handle that was apropos was something he could live with. Even if, at the same time, others were forced to die by way of his actions.

He studied the couple again…with a particular focus on the attractive game warden named Tisha Fletcher. Like her friend Jeanne, she was ripe for the picking. It was unfortunate that the divorcée fashion designer had gotten caught up in something not of her own making, but this was how it needed to be. Some things couldn't be helped. For better or worse. To her good fortune, she had survived her brush with death.

The same would not be true for the game warden. She had to die. Just like the others. And there would be no one standing in his way. Least of all, the special agent. No matter that he had designated himself as her protector. Soon it would be time to do what needed to be done. Only then could he take a breath and appreciate what he had accomplished in exacting his revenge for reasons no one saw coming.

Except him, of course.

He watched with interest as Tisha and Glenn McElligott made their way across the beach, with the dogs now leading the way. Too bad neither animal sensed his presence, or they could have alerted their owners of the danger that was within their midst without them being privy to it.

Their loss would surely be his gain, as he observed them

until they disappeared from sight. He headed across the beach in the opposite direction, his clever mind plotting his next steps and how this would end.

The Shellview County Killer laughed to himself even as he felt anger well up inside him like hot air that needed to be released. He found solace in knowing that this would be accommodated soon enough, one way or another.

Chapter Fifteen

The following day, Glenn was in his office on the laptop, studying surveillance video in the area around Tallins Drive, near the town house where Jeanne was attacked. Not to mention, it was uncomfortably close to Tisha's place, giving him more cause for concern and making Glenn even more determined to get to the bottom of this attempted murder.

He was relieved that he wasn't reading another autopsy report on a strangulation victim of the Shellview County Killer. Apart from that meaning someone else had to die, it would also have further emboldened the unsub into thinking he was invincible while looking to add more victims to his list.

Beyond that, Glenn hated the thought of Tisha's friend being killed, just as Jeanne and Kurt seemed to be on track for a romantic success story. *Just like me and Tisha*, Glenn told himself satisfyingly, as he continued to pore over the footage. *We have something really special, no doubt about it*. They, too, deserved happiness, considering that both had fallen short in their previous relationships.

When he spotted a vehicle that sped off on Judson Drive, which ran parallel to Tallins Drive, one street over, it got

Glenn's attention. Especially since it occurred shortly after the attack, when the unsub had run off, and in that direction.

Glenn rewound the video and paused on the car, zooming closer. It was a blue GMC Acadia midsize SUV. He couldn't make out the driver, but it appeared to be a male. Turning to the back of the car, Glenn was able to see the license plate clearly enough. He ran the plates and, shortly thereafter, was surprised to see that the vehicle was registered to a Sherman D. Galecki.

As in Game Warden Sherman Galecki? Glenn asked himself. What the hell was he doing in that area at the time Jeanne was attacked, given that his home address had him living miles away in Akerston Heights? Coincidence? Though the description of the unsub was sketchy at best, Galecki seemed to at least fit the general physical characteristics of the man who tried to strangle Jeanne to death.

Glenn couldn't help but think back to a conversation with Tisha in which she tossed out the possibility that the serial killer could be someone inside the DNR. If not the Region 5 Law Enforcement Division itself. Had she been given reason to suspect Galecki?

Had that been true, would Tisha have kept it to herself? He seriously doubted that.

As it was, they had looked into the possibilities in that regard, and there had been no red flags pointing toward anyone in particular at the DNR.

Had they missed the boat here?

I'll refrain from jumping to any conclusions yet, Glenn thought, though his suspicion radar was off the charts. Especially after documenting that a digital license-plate scanner had picked up the SUV moving rapidly away from the area several streets over during the same time frame.

Lifting his cell phone, he rang Tisha for a video chat.

Momentarily, her lovely face appeared on the screen. "Hey," he said.

"Hey." She flashed a thin smile. "What's up?"

"What can you tell me about Warden Sherman Galecki?"

"Sherman?" Tisha frowned curiously. "Well, for starters, last year he was named by the DNR as Game Warden of the Year."

"Is that so?" Glenn was admittedly impressed. But that still didn't give him a free pass from being capable of committing murder. "What else?"

"Let's see…" She mused. "He's obviously good at what he does. Was in a long-term relationship till recently. Keeps mostly to himself on the job, but is still friendly toward others when he wants to be."

"I see." Glenn let that sink in. Seemed like a stand-up kind of guy. Didn't mean there wasn't a very dark layer beneath the facade.

Her eyes widened suspiciously. "Why are you asking about Sherman?"

Glenn paused and thought, *How do I put this without indicting her colleague prematurely?* "Galecki's personal vehicle was spotted leaving the area around the time Jeanne was attacked," he said bluntly.

"Really?" Tisha's voice rose with incredulity. "Hmm…"

"I'm sure Galecki has a legitimate reason for being there," Glenn offered politely, "but like me, he lives in Akerston Heights. Do you know if he knows anyone in your neck of the woods, besides you?"

"Not that I'm aware of," she admitted thoughtfully. "But we aren't really that close or anything, so I couldn't tell you why he was in Blair Bay at that time." She made a face. "I'm sure he can explain himself."

"I hope so." Glenn still wondered about the game warden

and if he could possibly be doubling as a would-be killer and serial killer all at once. "When you discovered the body of Tris Lindberg, did Galecki appear genuinely surprised?"

Tisha pondered his question, then answered, "Yes, it seemed so." She paused. "Do you really suspect Sherman of having something to do with her death? Or attacking Jeanne…as a serial killer?"

"I'm not pointing any fingers at this point," he told her candidly. "But we have to look at everything and everyone that manifests itself in the investigation. As it is, Galecki had access to and knowledge of most—if not all—the places where the serial murders occurred. Now, a car registered to him happens to be fleeing the scene shortly after Jeanne was attacked. This may be totally coincidental, but it certainly gives me pause. Only Galecki can clear this up."

"When do you plan to talk to him?" Tisha asked.

"This morning," Glenn said matter-of-factly. "I'll ask Galecki to meet me at the sheriff's department for routine feedback on the investigation as a game warden, so he'll have his guard down, just in case things go south along the way."

"Okay." She was thoughtful. "I'd like to be there. If Sherman could really be this horrible creature, I want to see him fess up. Also, my presence could defuse the situation, if it should come to that."

"I understand. You're more than welcome to come. If this is a nothing burger, all the better. It would just be a short hiccup." Glenn narrowed his eyes. "But if Galecki has something sinister to hide, he'll need to be held accountable."

"I agree," she said evenly.

Though he wasn't entirely comfortable with her being anywhere near Galecki if he was guilty of assaulting

Jeanne—as well as committing multiple homicides—Glenn understood Tisha's point of view as his colleague. *I'll make sure she's kept at a safe distance while he's being interrogated*, Glenn told himself.

After they disconnected, he ran this by the special agent in charge and Rhianna agreed that they needed to jump on it. He then called the sheriff, explaining the circumstances, and Marjorie was also on board and ready to do whatever was needed in the investigation.

HONESTLY, TISHA WASN'T quite sure what to expect as she watched on the video monitor alongside Sheriff Pierce as Sherman entered the interrogation room under the guise of a friendly conversation about assisting with the investigation. Only it was far more than that, unfortunately, with greater implications for him. Jeanne's vague description of the unsub had hardly described Sherman as her assailant. Nor had Kurt seen enough of his face to describe him accurately.

But the general description of the attacker did not exclude Sherman. To this, Tisha was left to wonder if someone she worked with could possibly have been a serial killer, right under her nose. Had he actually known in advance where Tris Lindberg would be found in the Manikeke Crossing and was merely putting up a good front as a law enforcement game warden? Was the same true for the other murders attributed to the so-called Shellview County Killer?

Why would he have gone after Jeanne, who didn't fit the Patricia-named derivatives of the other victims? And was the attempted strangulation with his hands, rather than a ligature, meant to throw off the investigation? Or was it a sign of desperation by someone intent on killing by any means necessary?

That still brought it all back to whether or not Sherman was the unsub, hidden in plain view. Till now.

Guess I'm about to find out, Tisha told herself, as she watched Glenn step into the room in what could well be the break they had been looking for in the case. Or a misdirection that was playing into the hands of the real culprit.

GLENN KEPT HIS cool as he shook Sherman Galecki's hand, while trying to keep an open mind about the man. Per standard procedure, Galecki had to temporarily give up his service firearm while in the sheriff's department.

"Thanks for coming in," Glenn told him as he sat across from him at the table.

Sherman looked frazzled as he touched his glasses and said, "No problem. How can I help?"

"We're looking into the attempted murder of a woman that occurred yesterday morning in Blair Bay on Tallins Drive."

The game warden cocked an eyebrow. "Are we talking about Tisha?"

"No, thankfully," Glenn happily reported, while verifying that Galecki was well aware of where Tisha's residence was located. "She does know the victim, though..."

Sherman seemed relieved. "Okay...?"

"As of now, the perp is still at large," Glenn pointed out. He opened the laptop on the table and turned the screen toward him.

"What am I looking at?" Sherman asked, as if clueless.

"Surveillance video picked up this blue GMC Acadia SUV speeding away on a parallel street shortly after the attack on the victim. The suspect was seen running in that direction beforehand." Glenn peered at him. "I ran the plates and discovered that the car belongs to you, Warden Galecki."

"Not sure I like where this is going." Sherman narrowed his eyes and said, "Just what are you asking me, Agent McElligott?"

Might as well get to the nitty-gritty, Glenn thought, and responded straightforwardly, "I need to know why you were in the area at that time. And why you were in such a hurry to get away…"

Sherman sucked in a deep breath and sat back. "It's not what you think."

"Hope you're right," Glenn retorted. "Since the unsub tried to strangle the victim, it has me thinking that it could be the same person we believe has strangled to death six individuals, thus far. If you're innocent, you'll need to convince me here and now. Otherwise, this is not going to end well for you…"

Glenn realized that they had no hard evidence to link Galecki to the attack of Jeanne. Much less, the serial murders. And he deserved the benefit of the doubt. But at this point, there was little room for error. Or second-guessing. For the game warden's sake—and maybe even Tisha's peace of mind as she watched from another room—it was best to play hardball and see which way the pendulum swung.

"Yeah, I was in the area at that time," Sherman admitted, "as the surveillance footage indicates. But it was only coincidental. I had no idea that someone was being attacked one street over." He sucked in a deep breath. "I was visiting a woman I'd been dating off and on. Name's Emily Vanasse. She's a registered nurse at Blair Bay General Hospital. We had a disagreement about where things were going between us. She wanted more of a commitment, I wanted less of one. We broke things off and, feeling flustered, I left her house in a huff. Guess I drove away faster than I should have. I'm sure Emily will vouch for everything I've just said—including providing video from her security system that shows me leaving her place and getting into my SUV and driving off."

"We'll check out your story," Glenn told him, feeling it seemed credible enough. In truth, he was hopeful that someone Tisha worked with daily would not be doing double duty as an attempted murderer and serial killer. But that remained to be seen.

Sherman nodded. "Am I free to go?"

"Yeah, you're free to go," he allowed, knowing they couldn't hold him without just cause. "Just don't go very far till your alibi is verified." Glenn stopped short of demanding that he accounted for his whereabouts during the serial killings. The evidence as yet did not support that the game warden was guilty of anything. Especially if it was proven that he played no part in Jeanne's victimization, with Kurt as an eyewitness to the attack, and neither able to finger Sherman as the unsub.

TISHA FELT SORRY for Sherman, having listened as he defended himself. She had no idea that he'd been seeing someone and that it didn't work out. Not that he owed her an account of his love life. Even if he knew about hers.

Mainly, she just wanted him to be cleared of any wrongdoing against Jeanne. The thought that Sherman would try to hurt—or actually murder—her friend was one that Tisha would just as soon not have. Same was true of the notion that he could be a serial killer. Presumably, the investigation would now move in a different direction.

When they awkwardly ran into each other in the hallway

of the sheriff's department, Sherman, who looked like a wounded puppy, muttered, "Sorry to hear about your friend being attacked."

"Me, too."

"I had nothing to do with it."

"I believe you," she told him, trusting her instincts even before verification of his alibi.

Sherman nodded. "Better get out of here before they find another lame excuse for interrogating me."

Tisha smiled thinly. "Catch you later."

She watched him walk away and then went to find Glenn—who was conferring with the sheriff and other investigators—to check on the state of the investigation, now that it appeared Sherman would no longer be the focal point of Jeanne's ordeal.

More troubling to Tisha at the moment was how Jeanne's attack figured into the serial killer case. Could one have absolutely nothing to do with the other? If so, did this keep alive the possibility that her theory on the murders was not so far-fetched after all?

It would mean that a potential target still remained on her back as someone who fit the unsub's warped philosophy in killing, whatever the actual motivation or reasoning may be for his deadly actions.

Chapter Sixteen

In spite of having a feeling that Sherman was likely on the level with his claims of innocence in the attack on Jeanne—to say nothing for his possible role in the serial slayings affecting Shellview County like the plague—Glenn still needed to verify his alibi, in order to eliminate him as a suspect.

He walked down the corridor at Blair Bay General Hospital and approached the curvy nurse in her late twenties with curly chin-length crimson hair, and asked what he already knew the answer to, "Emily Vanasse?"

She looked up at him and responded, "That's me."

"GBI Special Agent McElligott." He showed his identification. "I wonder if I can have a word with you?"

"Sure..." she said tentatively. "Did I do something wrong?"

"No. It's regarding Sherman Galecki."

"Sherman?" She frowned. "What's he done...since I last saw him?"

"Hopefully nothing," Glenn stressed. "Just need you to clear up a couple of things."

"Okay."

"Why don't we step over here?" He indicated an area apart from traffic in the hall. Once there, Glenn regarded her and said straightforwardly, "I'm investigating an attack of a woman on Wednesday morning in Blair Bay. The perpetrator got away. The incident happened to occur shortly before the time in which a vehicle that was driven by Warden Galecki sped off on the next street over."

Emily's eyes widened. "You think Sherman had something to do with the attack?"

"Not necessarily," Glenn suggested, trying to allay Emily's fear for the moment. "Just a routine part of the investigation." He paused. "According to Galecki, he was at your house when the assault occurred—he says he left after you had an argument, and drove off in a hurry. Can you vouch for that?"

"Yes, of course." Her nostrils flared musingly. "We had a fight over his commitment issues and broke up. That's it. He's a jerk and I'm probably better off without him, but Sherman would never intentionally harm a woman…or anyone else, for that matter."

That's good enough for me...almost, Glenn told himself. "When it's convenient, I'll arrange for a sheriff's deputy to drop by your house to check your security video to verify the time."

"Sure, no problem," she agreed. "My shift ends at seven and I can be home by seven thirty."

"Great." He smiled at her. "I'll let you get back to it. Thanks for your time."

She nodded and said, "Whoever attacked her, I hope you find them."

"So do I," he assured her and walked away, feeling as though Galecki had just dodged a bullet.

Meaning that Jeanne's assailant, who was likely a serial killer, was still at large and becoming more brazen than ever.

ON FRIDAY, Glenn got word that another suspect had emerged, with Sherman Galecki off the hook. Surveillance video showed a man matching the physical and clothing description of Jeanne's attacker running into an alleyway close to the time of the attack. This corresponded shortly thereafter with a reported stolen late model Mitsubishi Outlander, believed to have been taken by the unsub. Using facial-recognition technology, the Shellview County Sheriff's Department identified Jimmy McPhail, a forty-two-year-old ex-con, as a person of interest. A BOLO alert was issued for the car and McPhail.

When the car was found abandoned near a convenience store on Kellem Road in a rural part of the county, GBI crime scene investigators processed it for evidence. Latent prints were retrieved and put into the automated fingerprint identification system, leading to a positive identification of McPhail.

"He couldn't have gone far," Glenn told Sheriff Pierce after they had joined other investigators at the scene, in what was believed to be a positive development in both the attempted murder of Jeanne Rutland and the overall Shellview County Killer investigation.

"I agree," Marjorie said, having dispatched the department's drone unit to scour the region, along with having a SWAT team and a crisis negotiation unit on hand to deal with the situation. "We'll find him."

To Glenn, this pretty much went without saying. If McPhail was their unsub, allowing him to slip through their fingers wasn't an option. With the close call for Jeanne and the likelihood that it was tied to the serial murders of six other individuals, it was imperative that they bring the suspect in before more harm could come to others.

When it came across the radio that a body, believed to be

that of Jimmy McPhail, had been located behind a nearby abandoned farmhouse, Glenn wasted little time hopping in his Dodge Durango Pursuit and following the sheriff's Ford Explorer toward the address on Lyman Road. The last thing he had wanted was for the suspect to die before being interrogated.

After arriving at the scene, Glenn made his way past deputies and other law enforcement personnel, overgrown weeds and the dilapidated farmhouse, to the backyard, where he spotted the corpse of a tall and muscular man in his early forties lying on his back on brown grass. A pool of blood encircled his short black hair and there was a cut on his chin. He was wearing glasses, a blue zip hoodie, dirty jeans and dark-colored tennis shoes. The clothing corresponded with Jeanne's description of what her attacker was wearing.

Glenn noted the subcompact 9mm handgun lying by his side, the dead man's thick fingers clutching it, as Marjorie stated presumptively, "Looks like McPhail chose to check out, rather than turn himself in."

"Yeah." Glenn sighed. "Too bad. There's still a lot of unanswered questions he's taken to the grave with him."

"We'll try to get as many of those questions answered as possible," the sheriff remarked, "once we can get a look at his cell phone, computer and residence to gather evidence..."

"Can hardly wait," Glenn muttered humorlessly. He happened to spot something beneath the dead man that caught his eye, prompting him to don a pair of disposable nitrile gloves to check it out. He squatted down and carefully pulled out a mini stun gun that must have fallen out of the suspect's pocket upon impact. "This might answer one question in connecting the dots between McPhail, Jeanne and the other victims of a serial killer…"

"Indeed." Marjorie nodded, then opened a plastic evidence bag for him to drop the stun gun in. "We'll get this processed right away, along with what looks like a ghost gun."

"I think you're right," Glenn concurred, gazing at the firearm again, knowing that privately made firearms, or PMFs, were hard to trace and therefore popular among offenders.

As crime scene investigators moved in and a team from the medical examiner's office arrived, Glenn stepped away, along with Marjorie, to assess the situation and what looked to be the biggest break yet in the case.

With the deceased positively identified as Jimmy McPhail, Glenn and other authorities, armed with a search warrant, raided a second-story apartment on Twenty-third Street in Baldwin County, Georgia, where McPhail lived. Potential evidence confiscated from the modestly furnished one-bedroom unit included a roll of twine cotton cord. There was also crack cocaine, fentanyl, heroin and drug paraphernalia recovered, as part of the dark picture being painted of the man believed to be the Shellview County Killer.

"LOOKS LIKE WE'VE identified the perp responsible for attacking Jeanne and strangling to death six people," Glenn told Tisha later that day, as they were walking the dogs.

"Really?" She eyed him interestedly as he held Riley's leash steady. It was music to her ears and would be to Jeanne's as well, no doubt, as someone who had managed to survive the killer, against the odds.

"The pieces have come together to support that contention," he told her. "Jimmy McPhail had a stun gun that was apparently the one used on Jeanne and the other victims. The GBI Crime Laboratory revealed that the roll of cotton cord found at McPhail's apartment was consistent with fibers collected from around the necks of the victims and their clothing. Then there's surveillance video at various locations that showed someone fitting McPhail's description lurking around, coming or going." Glenn took a breath. "It appears that McPhail, took his own life as we were closing in on him, rather than be a man and face justice," he said with dissatisfaction. "We ran the ghost gun he used through the ATF's National Tracing Center and National Integrated Ballistic Information Network, from which we learned that the firearm had been used to commit crimes in Georgia, South Dakota and Michigan."

"Wow!" Tisha was relieved that McPhail hadn't used the gun to shoot Jeanne. She may never have recovered. "Thank goodness he'll no longer be able to terrorize Shellview County, whatever his rationale was for the killings," she added, realizing that they might never know if there was any merit to the Patricia perspective. *Probably just the luck of the name draw*, she decided, given that Jeanne's name did not correspond with that theory.

"I was thinking the same thing." Glenn grinned at her, as though reading Tisha's mind.

"Hmm..." She looked at the man she had fallen in love with and wondered if he felt the same way about her. His body language may have said one thing. But until the words came from his mouth, she wouldn't presume to speak for him. Instead, she said awkwardly, "So where do we go from here...?"

He seemed to give that a long moment of consideration, then responded in an ambiguous way, "Wherever our hearts desire…"

She couldn't let him off that easily. "What does your heart desire?" she asked directly, ignoring Jacky pulling on the leash to get her attention.

Glenn gazed at her as he answered smoothly, "You and only you, Tisha."

She couldn't help but blush at his earnest response. Though she would have liked to hear more on his feelings, Tisha didn't want to press the issue. Right now, she took delight in knowing he seemed totally committed to her and what they were developing between them.

At the moment, that would have to do.

IT WAS OBVIOUS to Glenn that he was in love with Tisha. How could he not be? She had everything he could possibly want in a woman, partner and best friend—all rolled into one stunning and talented beauty. But he wanted to express this in words when he popped the question. Was she ready to jump back into marriage again? With him?

I sure hope so, as nothing would make me happier than to be her husband with an entire future ahead of us, Glenn told himself, as they went back to his place and kissed affectionately.

Later, Glenn and Tisha joined some of their colleagues at the Penton Club, a popular law enforcement bar on Twelfth Street and Romeo Drive, a few blocks away from the sheriff's department. Sitting around the table and sharing pitchers of beer were Sherman Galecki, Marjorie Pierce, Rhianna Kingsley and Fritz Alvarez, to celebrate solving the Shellview County Killer murders, now that Jimmy McPhail was dead.

Glenn, for one, wasn't necessarily in a celebratory mood.

Not with six victims dead and buried ahead of their time. They happened to come into the viewfinder of a stone-cold killer and paid the ultimate price. Fortunately, Jeanne had escaped the same fate. As had Tisha, who might have been a victim at some point, had her theory on the unsub held up.

He grinned at her and said candidly, not even wanting to think about losing the woman of his dreams, "Glad this is over."

"So am I," she told him, flashing her teeth nicely. "Hopefully, everyone can take a breath now and move on."

"Amen to that." He lifted his mug of beer and clinked hers. After what he construed as the cold shoulder from Sherman, Glenn felt a bit guilty. He tasted his beer, got the game warden's attention and said, "It was nothing personal. Just doing my job."

Sherman shrugged. "It's cool." He sipped his beer and grinned. "No harm, no foul, right?"

"My sentiments exactly," Glenn agreed.

"Yeah." Tisha patted Sherman on the shoulder supportively. "Let bygones be bygones, as the saying goes," she stated.

"Hey, we're all on the same page here," Fritz commented. "Getting to the heart of the issue was all that mattered."

"And we did at that," Marjorie declared. "Jimmy McPhail will no longer be a thorn in our sides and that's definitely a good thing."

"I'll drink to that!" Rhianna said triumphantly, putting the mug to her mouth.

Everyone did just that, Glenn included, and then they lifted their glasses in a group toast. Though he certainly shared the satisfaction that McPhail's days as a maniacal serial killer were over and done with, Glenn couldn't help but believe that something was still missing in the equation.

What was it that was gnawing at him like a splitting headache?

Chapter Seventeen

On Monday morning, Glenn still felt something was off as it related to the Shellview County Killer investigation. Though Jimmy McPhail was presumed to be the serial killer who strangled to death six individuals and tried to murder a seventh person, it didn't quite sit right.

Yes, the indicators pointed toward McPhail, by and large, and he hadn't done himself any favors by taking his own life before being interrogated if he was really innocent. But what if he'd been made a fall guy and had actually been murdered, even if there was no solid evidence to contradict the suicide theory?

Glenn knew this type of thinking was reckless at best and downright dangerous at worst. There was no need to go against the grain in a case that had already fallen back, more or less, under the jurisdiction of the sheriff's department, where Marjorie Pierce could take much of the credit for solving the serial murders under her watch.

But I can't turn my back on gut feelings that tell me this isn't adding up, Glenn told himself, as he stood in Rhianna Kingsley's office, where he was supposed to be listening to her give him a new assignment. He didn't need to be a mathematician to know that two plus two didn't equal five or ten. How had McPhail managed to pull off multiple murders without being caught? Or identified till he risked a broad daylight attack that failed, then stole a car that was amateurish by the standards of the Shellview County Killer up to that point?

Then there was the sudden shift in the serial killer's MO, when he decided to go after Jeanne. Was this just sloppiness? A clever maneuver to throw off the investigation?

Or an indication that they were, in fact, talking about two different perps?

Could Tisha have been on to something about the link between the victims having names that derived from the name Patricia? Glenn considered the Lynda/Linda inspiration for a serial killer that criminology professor Edward Kundu was writing a book on and had brought to his attention. Convicted killer Lucas Conseco had gone after and successfully strangled eight women fatally, as his way of punishing an abusive mother named Lynda.

Had history found a way of repeating itself?

Or had it been helped to do so in the modern era?

Maybe Conseco could explain the ways and means of his homicidal tendencies, Glenn told himself. And how he was able to track, locate and kill the victims that fit the bill.

"Are you with me, McElligott?" Rhianna snapped, breaking his musing.

Glenn gazed at the special agent in charge, who was hovering over her standing desk, which was situated among other black office furniture. He was vague on the details but had picked up the gist of what she was saying. "Yeah," he muttered. "I'll be working with the GBI Human Exploitation and Trafficking Unit for my next case…going after child sex traffickers and rescuing trafficking victims…"

"Okay." Her eyes narrowed at him, as she still seemed dissatisfied. "So what's going on with you?"

Glenn sucked in a deep breath, then replied, "Something's come up."

"Care to share?" she asked.

He wanted to, but decided it was best to wait until he had more to go on, if anything at all. "Let's just say I need to tie up some loose ends..."

"On your last investigation?"

"Yeah, afraid so." Glenn met her hard gaze. "As soon as I get what I'm looking for, you'll be the first to know."

Surprisingly, she accepted this at face value and allowed him to be on his way. The rest was up to him in what would be an unusual path to take, but one that he sensed might yield some fruit.

Glenn went to his own office, where he phoned Edward Kundu, his former criminology professor. "Hey, Edward," he said, before getting right to the crux of the call. "Thought I'd take you up on your offer to help me get a face-to-face meeting with Lucas Conseco..."

"Of course, I can arrange that," the professor said. "Is this regarding your serial killer case?"

"Yes," he said flatly.

"Thought I'd heard that had been put to rest with the perpetrator's suicide?"

"I thought so, too..." Glenn leaned back in his chair. "Except for the fact that I still have a gut feeling something is off. The last attempted murder by Jimmy McPhail, the purported serial killer, deviates just enough from the other crimes attributed to the Shellview County Killer to have me second-guessing whether McPhail truly is responsible for all the deaths."

"I see." Edward paused. "But what makes you think that Conseco can be of assistance in reopening the investigation?" he asked curiously. "Or do you simply want to compare notes on one strangulation serial killer to another?"

"The latter is partly correct," Glenn confessed. "But it goes beyond that—" He explained Tisha's hypothesis on variations of the name Patricia linked killings.

"Interesting," Edward murmured.

"Assuming it is legit, with Conseco also having this in common with the Shellview County Killer, I figured it was worth a shot to see if he'll talk to me about his process of tracking down victims," Glenn said. "Maybe he can give me some insight that can either put this case to bed for good…or point me in a different direction—"

"Understood. Knowing Conseco as I've come to, I'm sure he'll be happy to explain his rationale and methods."

"Good."

"When would you like to see him?"

"This afternoon would be great," Glenn responded equably. "I can be at the prison in about an hour."

"Shouldn't be a problem," Edward said. "It's not like Conseco has something better to do with his time."

"Great."

"Good luck."

"Thanks." Glenn hung up, while believing that he didn't need luck in questioning the inmate, but rather uncovering anything that could tell him he was going on a wild-goose chase.

Or an indication to the contrary.

TISHA TEAMED UP with Sherman to give out two BUIs at Lake Oliver, then responded to the ranger hotline, where a tipster reported a poacher in a forested area of the county.

While searching for the unsub, who was thought to be hunting illegally, Tisha broke the silence between them, feeling a chill in the summertime air, as she said in a friendly voice, "So I didn't realize you'd been seeing someone..."

Sherman snorted, and responded sarcastically, "Was that before or after your boyfriend practically accused me of attempted murder?"

Tisha narrowed her eyes at him. "I thought you understood that Glenn was only doing his job in questioning you, given your proximity to the crime at the time it occurred?"

"I did—I do," he said humbly. "Agent McElligott was obligated to follow every lead. I get that." Sherman ran a hand across his brow. "Guess it still hurts a little that someone in my position with the DNR should be suspected—even for a moment—of trying to strangle a friend of yours. With the greater insinuation of being a serial strangler and murderer."

"It hurt me, too," she stressed honestly, as they made their way through tall pine trees. "For the record, I never believed you would hurt Jeanne. Much less, led a double life as the Shellview County Killer."

"That's good to hear." He offered her a crooked grin. "Anyway, it's over now and the bad guy is dead."

"True." Tisha smiled back at him, feeling as if a load had been lifted off all their shoulders with Jimmy McPhail's suicide. It made making arrests for boating under the influence or poaching pale in comparison to dealing with a callous serial killer.

"Regarding Emily, the woman I was dating, it just didn't work out," Sherman muttered. "We didn't see eye-to-eye on what we wanted out of the relationship. So I bailed. I admit, I probably could've and should've handled things a bit differently than I did."

"You're human," she said, giving him an out. "Maybe you'll fare better with the next person you date."

"I won't hold my breath on that." He snickered. "Not everyone can be so fortunate to find someone again that fits, as you have with Glenn McElligott. Could be I'm just not cut out for commitment to any one person." He shrugged. "Or maybe I am, but still searching for the woman who can win me over…"

"You just never know." Tisha flashed her teeth, pulling for him on whatever made her fellow game warden happy. At least they seemed back on track as friendly colleagues. Meanwhile, she was definitely counting her blessings in finding Glenn and being found by him, wherever this path took them.

GLENN DROVE DOWN GA-540 while wondering if speaking with the convicted serial killer would produce any results. Or if it would just be a big waste of time. It was the second option that kept him from sharing this with Tisha just yet.

Now that she had reconciled herself with McPhail being responsible for the attack on Jeanne and the serial homicides, there was no reason to throw cold water on it for the time being. Certainly as it related to intimating to Tisha that her theory on the killings had not been eliminated entirely. As of now.

I'll be happy to share what I learn, if there's anything to it that warrants further investigation of the serial murders…beyond McPhail's supposed guilt, Glenn told himself, as he turned right on GA-240 South.

A few miles later, he reached Macon State Prison on Highway 49 South, in Oglethorpe, parked in the designated area and, after locking his firearm away in the glove compartment, headed inside.

Once he got through the procedure as a GBI special agent, Glenn went to an interrogation room and waited for the inmate to show up.

Momentarily, Lucas Conseco walked through the door, wearing a khaki jumpsuit and in handcuffs. In his late thirties, he was a lean man around Glenn's height, bald-headed and clean-shaven with a noticeable scar on his right cheek.

Glenn pretended not to notice as he said tonelessly, "I'm GBI Special Agent McElligott."

Conseco peered at him with brown eyes and said, "Yeah, I know. Ed Kundu told me you were coming." The prisoner sat in a wooden chair on the opposite side of a metal table from Glenn. "But he didn't say what this was about." His brow creased. "So why don't you fill me in on why I should waste my time talking to you?"

Looks like he intends to make this more difficult than it has to be, Glenn thought, but wasn't about to be deterred or intimidated. "I'm investigating a serial killer case that's similar to yours," he told the inmate.

"How do you figure…?"

"Apart from strangling his victims, the killer has apparently targeted victims that had some variation of the name Patricia," Glenn said, and could see that this sparked an interest in him. "Given that you went after women named Lynda, I thought you might provide some insight into not so much his motivation, but how he might have gone about finding victims that were suitable for killing…"

Conseco jutted his chin. "Patricia, huh?" He pondered this for a long moment. "I like Lynda better, for obvious reasons… As for this other killer and locating the ones he wanted to find, it's not as difficult as you think—"

"Why don't you enlighten me," Glenn said, prompting him to proceed.

"Alright." Conseco took a deep breath. "Just asking around can get people talking," he said. "Next thing you know, there were more Lyndas in the vicinity than met the eye—giving me choices to pick and choose whoever I wanted. If that failed, there's always social media, where people love giving you info about themselves and how to find them, starting with their names..." He gave a little laugh. "When all that went nowhere, there was always running into a Lynda at a store, in a bar, at the hospital...or even by chance sometimes. I was patient enough to wait it out till the right person came along. Maybe this dude did it the same way," he said, speculating.

Glenn absorbed his thought-provoking take on what he did and how he did it. Perhaps the Shellview County Killer did operate the same way. He asked the convict, "Would you have ever gone after someone not named Lynda with a *y* or Linda with an *i*...maybe to try to throw the police off?"

"Nah." Conseco shook his head adamantly. "Why would I? That's not what it was all about. Wasn't in it to play games with the police, for sport, or to change my strategy just for the hell of it!"

That certainly fits with conventional wisdom, at least among criminal profilers, Glenn told himself. He also knew there were no absolutes when it came to serial killers. Was his latest case an anomaly of sorts? Or a deliberate case of diversion?

Glenn cast his eyes at the inmate and asked out of morbid curiosity, "So was it worth it—killing all those women? And for what...to spend the rest of your life behind bars?"

Conseco stared at him with a frown. "Yeah, it was worth it," he claimed. "After being betrayed by my mother over and over again, this was the ultimate payback, even if she was already dead..." He took a breath. "You wouldn't understand."

"You're right, I don't," Glenn had to admit unapologetically, "and never will. Guess it's something you'll have to live with."

"Yeah, I guess so," Conseco said defiantly. "Are we done?"

"We're done." Glenn saw no further reason to waste any more time. He wasn't sure he got what he came for. Or maybe he did in that there might not be any definitive answers that demanded the Shellview County Killer case be given another hard look. He stood up. "Thanks for the chat," he said sardonically.

"Anytime." Conseco's voice rang with equal contempt. He rose, regarded Glenn inquiringly, and said, "So what's with you special agents, anyway? Why am I so special compared to other serial killers? Or do you hound them, too?"

"You've lost me." Glenn cocked an eyebrow. "I don't follow—"

"You're the second special agent I've talked to."

"Really?" Glenn locked eyes with him. "Who was the first?"

Conseco seemed to wrack his brain and then replied, "Special Agent Kurt Stewart, I believe he called himself. Had the ID to back him up..."

Kurt? Why the hell would he have come to see him? Glenn wondered. "When was this?"

"About six months ago," the prisoner said matter-of-factly.

"What did Agent Stewart want?"

"Like you, he wanted to know all about me killing women bearing the name of my mommy dearest," he said wryly. "Why I killed them, how I found them, how difficult was it to locate them. How I managed to get away. Same old, same old." Conseco licked his lips. "Seemed just as interested in what I had to say as you, if not more."

"I see." Glenn rubbed his nose. "I suppose your unusual tale has captured the fancy of both law enforcement and true crime writers alike," he said musingly.

"Yeah, right." Conseco left the room without looking back.

Glenn's mind was racing like a thoroughbred. It wasn't lost on him that Kurt came to visit the convicted serial killer around the same time that the Shellview County Killer got started in his ligature strangulations. Why? Coincidence? Professional curiosity? Just what was Kurt up to?

Glenn didn't like at all what he was thinking as he left the prison.

Chapter Eighteen

When Glenn got home, he let Riley and his active new buddy, Jacky, run around on the property. It was his turn to take the dogs, giving Tisha a breather. This was also another example of the comfort zone they had established with one another, extending to even their furry companions. As far as he was concerned, they were all now part of one happy family. They only needed to make it official.

But at the moment, Glenn's attention was still on Kurt Stewart and what drew the special agent to pay serial killer Lucas Conseco a visit six months ago. Was his interest in Conseco related to the job? Or was his intent much more sinister?

What am I missing here? Glenn asked himself as he headed up to his office and sat at the desk. Something, like a perfectly logical explanation? *I sure as hell hope so*, he thought. He needed to find out—and soon.

Getting on his laptop, he requested a video chat with the special agent in charge of the GBI Region 6 Investigative Office, Freda Nanouk, where Kurt was currently assigned. Freda had been the special agent in charge of the Region 12 office when Glenn was working there at the same time as Kurt.

When Freda appeared on the screen, she said, "Hey,

stranger," and gave Glenn a warm smile, assuming, no doubt, that the call was more for catching up for old times' sake than something business-related.

"Hey." He smiled back softly at the fortysomething Native American, who had brown eyes and straight brunette hair in a shoulder cut, and quickly lost the smile, as Glenn said, "I need some info…"

"Okay." She gazed at him. "How can I help you?"

Glenn hated to have to go to her regarding a current special agent, but she put integrity above all else, including agent loyalty. Especially if there was any chance that the agent had gone off the rails. "I need to know if there was any reason, in particular, for Kurt Stewart to have paid a visit to a serial killer named Lucas Conseco at Macon State Prison around six months ago?"

"Hmm…" Freda was thoughtful. "No reason that I can think of pertaining to an investigation or anything. Why the interest?"

Again, Glenn hesitated, not wanting to jump the gun in accusing one of their own of wrongdoing. He explained the Patricia theory and possible connection between his latest investigation and the serial murders perpetrated by Conseco, and concluded, "Though the Shellview County Killer case has been linked to a man who killed himself, I'm not convinced that there isn't more to this story that bears looking into—"

Her brow creased. "And you think Agent Stewart could be involved…as a copycat killer…?"

Glenn sucked in a deep breath, then said in a level tone, "Until I'm convinced otherwise, I can't rule it out."

"Well, you did the right thing in bringing this to my attention, Agent McElligott," she told him squarely. "I'll certainly look into it—discreetly, of course—before pointing any fingers."

"I understand." Glenn realized she needed to go through the proper channels and procedure when it came to potentially dirty GBI agents. Unfortunately, he wasn't afforded the time for a lengthy process. Not when a serial killer could still be on the loose. And aiming to add more victims to his list of strangulation kills. Another thought occurred to Glenn. He regarded the special agent in charge and asked curiously, "Did Kurt happen to be involved in any way with Jimmy McPhail, the suspected serial killer who committed suicide as the walls began to close in around him?"

Freda's eyes widened. "McPhail was a CI in our ongoing probe into illegal gambling in the state," she responded, ill-at-ease. "So, yes, Agent Stewart would almost certainly have crossed paths with McPhail in the scheme of things..."

I was afraid of that, Glenn told himself, as he pondered this new development in connecting dots that he wished he hadn't. If Kurt was indeed a serial killer, he surely was more than capable of having made his confidential informant a scapegoat, and could have set up McPhail to escape justice himself for homicidal crimes that Kurt was guilty of.

But what Glenn couldn't figure out was the Patricia angle in lining up victims with a variation of that name. No one named Patricia came to mind that existed in Kurt's orbit, as far as he knew. So why would Kurt go through such trouble, in patterning himself after Lucas Conseco?

Had this been merely a convenient justification for the murders? Or was there some symmetry in Kurt's head to justify the murders of six innocent individuals? Not to mention the attempted murder of Jeanne, someone Kurt was supposed to care for and had been a witness to her attack.

Now, Glenn had to seriously wonder if the entire thing

had been a charade on Kurt's part, with him having orchestrated the entire assault on Jeanne. And he possibly used his acumen to murder McPhail and make it appear as a suicide?

"What are you thinking?" Freda asked, snapping Glenn from his thoughts.

"That things are beginning to line up against Kurt," he told her bluntly.

"Hmm..." she murmured contemplatively.

Glenn asked, "Do you know where Kurt is now?"

"He's on an assignment," Freda answered confidently.

"Good." While still trying to put the pieces together, Glenn wanted to know that the special agent was at least temporarily preoccupied, so as to not be able to cause more trouble, if he was indeed a killer at large. Glenn leaned forward and requested, "I'd like to reach out to Kurt's ex-wife, Dixie. She may have some info relevant to the investigation—"

"Okay." The special agent in charge gave him Dixie Stewart's contact information, while he promised to keep Freda informed on where things went from there.

After ending the conversation, Glenn wasted no time in calling Kurt's former wife. He had gotten together with them a couple of times when things were still going good in the relationship. Dixie struck Glenn as a loving mother who seemed to have given it her all to keep the marriage together. Especially after they had lost their five-year-old daughter so tragically. It was Kurt who let things fall apart, with the marriage ending in divorce.

When Dixie answered the phone cheerfully with "Hi, Glenn," in seeing the caller ID, he instantly envisioned her the way he remembered the thirtysomething veterinarian as good-looking with big blue eyes behind cat-eye glasses and mounds of wavy burgundy hair, parted in the middle.

"Hey, Dixie." He tried to sound pleasant but knew that wouldn't last. "Look, this may sound like a strange question, but do you or Kurt happen to know anyone named Patricia or someone with any variation of the name?" Glenn felt this was the best way to approach the subject, without outright accusing her ex-husband of being a possible cold-blooded serial killer, who fed off a convicted serial killer to orchestrate his deeds.

"Um… Well, our late daughter's middle name was Patricia," Dixie informed him.

"Really?" Glenn was attentive. "Greta, right?" he recalled.

"Yes, Greta. But Kurt always liked to call her Pat for short, and simply because it was his special way of relating to her." Dixie paused. "Why are you asking this?"

How do I respond to that without tipping my hand? Glenn asked himself. He didn't want to get ahead of himself. Or do wrong by her by suggesting that her dead daughter may have been connected to a string of homicides in Shellview County.

"Just out of curiosity," he replied. "It was mentioned offhandedly that one of our special agents may have known someone named Patricia, similar to a name that came up during an investigation. I've been asking around, considering the irony." *I know that sounds lame and she'll probably see right through it*, Glenn thought guiltily.

"Oh." Dixie took a breath. "Greta was our little darling," she said maudlinly. "When she died, suffering the way she did, Kurt took it particularly hard. He seemed to want to blame anyone and everyone, including me." She sniffled. "Our relationship seemed to go downhill from there," she pointed out. "I gave it my best shot, but realized there was no turning back. Kurt became a no-show, both mentally and physically, for me and our other two kids. He really left me no choice but to want out of the marriage, for the sake of my family..." She stopped herself abruptly. "TMI... I'm sorry—"

"It's fine," Glenn told her sympathetically, while knowing her words carried more weight than she realized. She had unwittingly given Glenn a possible motive for Kurt turning into a killer—as bizarre as the connection seemed to Patricia. But the shoes seemed to fit, insofar as Kurt's ability to move around in plain view, his knowing the lay of the land where the homicides and attempted murder of Jeanne had occurred, and his connection to both Jimmy McPhail and Lucas Conseco. Was this enough though to make Kurt guilty? Much less, charge him and bring him in? "I wish you and Kurt had been able to work it out," he said to Dixie sincerely.

"Believe me, so do I." She waited a beat. "But it is what it is and we've both moved on, while hopefully holding on to the memories that count most—"

"Yeah," Glenn concurred. No sooner had he disconnected when a call came in from Freda Nanouk. "Hey," he answered nervously.

"I wanted you to know that Agent Stewart is not where I thought he was..."

"He isn't?"

"Looks like he called in sick, so he never showed up."

"That's a real problem," Glenn said straightforwardly, feeling his heart pounding as he passed along to her what he'd learned from Dixie Stewart about her dead daughter and how it had impacted Kurt's psyche.

When all the pieces were added together, Glenn knew

that the GBI special agent had suddenly become a clear and certainly present danger.

With Tisha—another Patricia variant—in possible and probable peril.

FOLLOWING THE ARREST of the burly poacher, caught red-handed, Tisha had separated from Sherman and driven to the Manikeke Crossing, where she did some work on her computer, before heading out to track bird migration. These included hooded warblers, northern Parulas, prothonotary warblers and wood ducks, among others. She loved tracking their movements as part of the conservation aspect of being a DNR game warden.

The fact that Glenn loved nature, too, and spending time with her and their dogs, gave Tisha that much more to find satisfaction in. She loved the man and decided it was high time she conveyed this to him and let the chips fall where they may. She hoped they'd fall right into his lap with a quid pro quo admission.

As she moved farther up into the wildlife management area, Tisha suddenly had a sense that she was being watched. But by whom? A curious animal? A hunter, taking a break while quietly observing a game warden at work?

Or none of the above?

Was this her usual overcharged imagination playing tricks on her yet once again?

Maybe, she decided, and continued with her work. No use allowing a dead serial killer to haunt her from the grave. Was there?

Jimmy McPhail was no longer a threat to her or anyone else in Shellview County. He had seen to that by taking the coward's way out of facing true justice for his horrendous actions. This came too late to save Tris Lindberg and the other poor victims from dying by his wicked hands.

But Jeanne had been spared from a similar fate. Thanks in large part to Kurt coming to her rescue, just in the nick of time. How fortunate it was that he happened to have made plans to meet up with Jeanne at the very time that McPhail decided she was an easy target.

Could McPhail have been that dense or desperate so as to suddenly decide to go after Jeanne randomly in a much more visible setting than with his other victims? Even to the point of trying to strangle her with his bare hands, in a distinct change of course?

How was that even possible?

Especially given the craftiness the perp had exhibited when handpicking his other victims for his signature ligature strangulation. And before managing to get away without detection, much less being taken into custody.

Yet this was apparently exactly what happened.

Tisha wanted to question this. But to do so would mean that the case had come to a close prematurely. That the killer was still out there. And on the prowl for victims, just as they let their guard down.

Just stop it, Tisha admonished herself, as she moved deeper into the woods. She didn't want to look for trouble that wasn't there. Not when there were so many positive things in her life right now that she should be focusing on.

When her cell phone rang, Tisha removed it from her uniform pocket, and smiled when she saw that it was Glenn calling. No doubt to make dinner plans for the evening. Or even breakfast in the morning.

But before she could respond to the call, Tisha heard some footsteps from behind her, and a familiar voice that commanded, "I wouldn't answer that if I were you, Tisha—"

She turned around and her heart skipped a beat as Tisha saw Kurt Stewart standing there, glaring at her. In his hands was what she recognized to be a Ruger-built Marlin Model 336 Classic .30-30 lever-action rifle, and he was aiming it at directly and menacingly at her.

Chapter Nineteen

Glenn was disturbed that Tisha failed to pick up her phone when he called to warn her about Kurt and her being a possible target of the special agent, now suspected of being a serial killer.

Had she been prevented from doing so? Or was she otherwise too preoccupied to answer her cell phone?

Sensing it was more likely than not the former set Glenn into near panic mode. The thought that Kurt would go after Tisha was worrying, to say the least. All things considered, he sure as hell wasn't about to leave it to chance that Kurt's thirst for death had ended with the ligature strangulation of Patrice Whitney.

And possibly the murder of Jimmy McPhail.

Not in a million years.

Or even a trillion years.

Not when Tisha means everything to me, and so much more, Glenn told himself. He loved her. Dearly. Losing Tisha would rock his world and destroy everything they were heading toward as a couple. Including starting a family. He couldn't allow this to be taken away from them.

After getting the dogs, Glenn loaded Riley and Jacky into the back of his SUV, before the three of them headed out. With his cell phone on the dashboard mount, he put it on speakerphone as he called Sherman Galecki.

Sherman answered immediately. “Agent McElligott…” he said tentatively.

“Hey,” Glenn began, realizing that there were still some tender feelings there after interrogating the game warden as a suspect in the attack on Jeanne. “I need to find Tisha. Do you know where she is right now?”

“Yeah. She’s in the Manikeke Crossing, tracking bird migration.” Sherman paused, then asked instinctively, “What’s going on…?”

“Tisha could be in danger,” he told him without prelude, while heading toward the WMA. “I think the Shellview County Killer is still alive.”

“What?” Sherman’s tone rose with shock. “But I thought Jimmy McPhail had been identified as the killer…?”

“I thought so, too.” Glenn peered at the road. “It looks like McPhail may only be guilty of attacking Jeanne Rutland.”

“So who are we talking about here as the serial killer culprit?” Sherman’s voice broke as if the finger was again pointed at him.

“I strongly suspect that GBI Special Agent Kurt Stewart is the killer,” Glenn told him straightforwardly.

“Seriously?” Sherman muttered an expletive. “I remember talking to Agent Stewart at one of the crime scenes. I thought he seemed smug, but never imagined this.”

“Trust me, neither did I.” Glenn sighed. “Can’t really go into the details right now. I just need to make sure that Tisha is safe. I’ve been unable to reach her by phone. Maybe you can try?”

“Of course. If I can’t connect with her, I’ll alert the work section sergeant, Fritz Alvarez, to send out a search party to the Manikeke Crossing."

"Alright."

"We'll find her," Sherman said, trying to reassure him.

"We'd better," Glenn snapped with more force than intended as he disconnected, then put on the speed, fearing that every second counted if he were to save Tisha.

TISHA NEEDED A moment to come to grips with the situation she found herself in, as she stared down the barrel of a rifle that Kurt aimed at her while wearing black gloves. It obviously wasn't good. "What is this…?" she demanded of the special agent, who was wearing an orange hunting vest over a flannel shirt and jeans.

"Just what it looks like, Tisha," he said, stone-faced. "I'm holding you at gunpoint." He jutted his chin. "Now, why don't you ditch the phone for starters, please…"

She hesitated, knowing it was her lifeline to the outside world. To Glenn, in particular, who had called and would know she didn't—or couldn't—pick up to respond.

"Do it!" Kurt demanded sharply, then warned her, "And don't even think about turning your body cam on!" He glared at her threateningly. "Toss your phone my way—"

After she threw the cell phone to the ground near his feet, Tisha watched as he slammed his hiking boot onto it several times, rendering it inoperable, while never taking his eyes off her.

"Now, the gun, Tisha," he ordered. "Remove it slowly with your left hand and drop it—"

Tisha wanted desperately to reach for her Glock pistol, secure in its holster. Not to do as he wanted. But to use it to defend herself. Should she give it a go? Was she quick enough to hit him before he could shoot her?

"I know what you're thinking..." Kurt chuckled daringly. "I don't doubt that you know how to use that firearm. But in this instance, I'd advise you to not even try. I can assure you that in a battle to see who's quicker to the trigger, you'll lose. So do as I tell you, or die trying, right now!"

Unwilling to hedge her bets in putting this to the test, Tisha again did as she was told in using her left hand to remove the gun and placed it on the ground.

"Now, back up," he ordered her, which she did, and he moved forward and grabbed her firearm with one gloved hand, while keeping the other aiming the rifle at Tisha squarely.

As Kurt tucked her firearm in the front of his jeans, she glared at him unnervingly and stated, "Never took you for a what...kidnapper, rapist, or—"

"Try serial killer," Kurt boasted, watching her stunned reaction. He added, "Or shall I use the tried-and-true familiar moniker, the Shellview County Killer..."

Tisha's eyes widened as what he was indicating registered. "You?"

"Afraid so," he said gloatingly. "The cat's out of the bag, so to speak—at least for you."

"And why is that?" Tisha asked, even as she processed what he was saying and what the big reveal meant for her getting out of this alive. If that was even possible, with him holding all the cards.

"Heard through the grapevine that you'd figured out the Patricia connection to the killer," Kurt pointed out. "Patricia was actually the middle name of my dead daughter, Greta. For the record, though, my special nickname for her was Pat. I don't mind telling you, seeing that you'll never get to reveal this to another living soul."

Tisha was shocked to learn that there was a link to the

name variations after all. Had Glenn been able to piece it together somehow? Did he even have a clue that she was now a prisoner of his fellow special agent friend, who clearly intended to kill her, too?

"You killed six innocent people because of your late daughter?" she asked, in trying to make sense of this.

"Yeah," he confessed. "I went after them in honor of my little Pat, who never got the opportunity to grow up to live the lives they did. As far as locating suitable victims, it wasn't all that difficult to find some with other versions of her middle name. In the case of Walt Patrick, it was entirely coincidental that his surname happened to be a male form of Patricia, as it was actually his girlfriend, Patti Arnaz, that I targeted. And in case you're curious about how I managed to kill an Australian with a version of Patricia as her name, well, Patrina Morse introduced herself to me during a hike, which proved to be quite fortunate for me and not so much for her."

"That's sick!" The words spurted out of Tisha's mouth, in spite of being at a disadvantage to the killer. "How could you, as a member of law enforcement, do such a thing?" She recalled that Sherman had once been in the same situation, only to prove himself innocent. That obviously wouldn't happen here.

Kurt laughed, while keeping the rifle steady in front of him. "You'd be surprised just what law enforcement personnel are capable of, should the circumstances warrant bad behavior. This was such an occasion. But that doesn't mean I was willing to cut my own throat. I planned this, without making it too obvious, so as to ruin my own life any more than it already had been ruined—with Pat's death, ending my marriage, and losing custody of my other kids. The way I saw it, why should these other females get to grow up and enjoy adulthood when Pat couldn't? So unfair—"

And so insane, Tisha told herself, hating to think that Jeanne had gotten involved with a homicidal maniac. He had clearly succeeded in pulling the wool over Glenn's eyes, too, in wanting to set them up. If only they had been able to see through Kurt for the monster he truly was. Had Jeanne begun to see the light, even after he appeared to be her savior?

Kurt's jaw set as he said musingly, "I'm sure you're wondering where Jeanne fit into the equation as a victim. Well, she was only meant to be a distraction—to throw off the investigation and any notion that the victims were connected by their names. I coerced my confidential informant, Jimmy McPhail, to attack Jeanne, but not hurt her badly. He was supposed to use all my tricks of the trade, including the stun gun and cord, to pretend to strangle her. Unfortunately, the idiot forgot to bring the cord and had to rely on his hands to put around her neck…before I conveniently came to Jeanne's rescue."

Tisha wrinkled her nose and snorted, "You're unbelievable." She knew that he was truly much worse than that. Jeanne deserved so much better than to have aligned herself with a fraud and killer.

"Maybe I am." Kurt gave a humorless laugh. "But for what it's worth, I actually like Jeanne and intend to continue seeing her, once you're out of the picture, Tisha, as one final offshoot of Patricia in my daughter's memory."

Tisha recoiled at the thought of meeting the same fate as his other victims. Even if he was changing his methods for the kill. Being shot to death instead of strangled was hardly a picnic that she wanted any part of. So how could she fight back, before there was no fight left in her?

"Start walking," he demanded, using the rifle to point deeper into the forest. When she hesitated, he said coldly, "Or you can die, here and now, and that will be it. Your choice."

Knowing that there was only one choice—give herself a fighting chance—Tisha complied with his order. She began to head toward the trees, where sounds became muffled, and one could easily get lost to the point of disappearing entirely. Was that his intention?

"Did McPhail really kill himself?" she asked out of curiosity and to buy her precious time.

"In a manner of speaking." Kurt chuckled. "He signed his own death warrant by botching the job, giving Glenn reason to believe it might not be the same perp that killed the others. Truthfully, McPhail had to go, any way you sliced it, as someone who could tie me to the attack on Jeanne. And, by extension, the Shellview County Killer. So I lured him to a spot, where I used a ghost gun I'd confiscated from a crime scene, shot him with it, then planted the weapon in McPhail's hand." He snickered. "Worked like a charm, if I say so myself!"

What a jerk, as well as psychopath, Tisha told herself, more than a little worried that he would be successful in his dastardly plans for her. She turned her head, while continuing to walk into the woods, and growled, "You're never going to get away with this."

"You think?" Kurt asked, mocking her. "Watch me. You'll be shot accidentally by a hunter, who will never be found. Since the Shellview County Killer case was already resolved with the death of Jimmy McPhail, your death will be entirely unconnected to the serial killer investigation. While I commiserate with Glenn over his loss, over a beer or while playing basketball, I'll be home free. So, yes, I'm pretty confident that I will get away with ending your life, Tisha, with Jeanne by my side all the way."

He laughed sardonically, as though believing himself to be untouchable and able to continue hiding his maniacal character from everyone.

Though Tisha would like nothing better than to wipe that smug grin off his face, trouble was, she wasn't exactly in a position to wrest that rifle away from him, while they were further apart than arm's length to try and grab the barrel. Not without the real risk of getting shot, and probably never being able to show her love for Glenn and the amazing life they could have together.

And so she waited for the slightest crack in the rugged armor of the GBI special agent turned serial killing fiend that would allow her to fight for her life…without necessarily dying while trying. With the clock ticking, one second at a time.

DURING THE DRIVE, Glenn phoned the sheriff and said, "There's been a new development in the Shellview County Killer case—"

"Really?" Marjorie responded.

He relayed to her what he suspected about Kurt, providing just enough specifics to make his case, and listened as she gasped with incredulity, before Glenn said abruptly, "On the off chance that Stewart actually took a legitimate sick day, you should work with the Baldwin County Sheriff's Office and send deputies to his house in Milledgeville."

"Count on it," she assured him. "We'll get a search warrant as well. If Agent Stewart truly is our serial killer, he's likely to have kept evidence in his safe space."

"I agree." Glenn also requested and was promised

backup as he neared the Manikeke Crossing, not wanting to leave anything on the table in locating Tisha.

Lastly, he called Rhianna, filling her in on everything, knowing the special agent in charge should have been the person he brought this to first. Except for the fact that with time being of the essence, he needed to kick things into gear as quickly as possible in achieving the best results.

Rhianna, who was understandably distraught with the news that a GBI special agent had become the primary suspect as a serial killer, promised her full support in bringing this to a close, however it went down.

"Bring Agent Stewart in," she commanded unflinchingly.

"I fully intend to," Glenn told her determinedly. "One way or the other."

Upon reaching his destination, he let the dogs out and rendezvoused with Sherman, who was standing in the parking lot near Tisha's empty Ford F-150. "Help is on the way," he told Glenn reassuringly.

Though happy to hear that, it wasn't nearly soon enough for Glenn's comfort. "Can't wait around while Tisha is out there, perhaps injured…" He couldn't bring himself to say dead. "Which direction is she likely to have gone to track the bird migration?"

Sherman contemplated this and answered, "My guess is that she would have headed toward Harlin's Creek—" he pointed in that direction "—where they're most active at this time of year."

"I'll check it out with the dogs," Glenn told him. "We should split up to cover more ground, till others arrive—"

"I agree." Sherman met his eyes. "I want to find Tisha safe and sound as much as you do."

"Thanks." Glenn nodded, appreciating his fondness for

her as a great game warden. He headed out, and said urgently to the dogs, "Let's go find Tisha—"

With Riley and Jacky leading the way, Glenn made his way through trees, shrubbery and streams, while hoping against hope that he could reach Tisha in time, if she was in harm's way…but then he noticed that the dogs were circling something on the ground. He caught up to them, and asked curiously, "What you have there?"

He saw that the red-colored object in question was a cell phone, and picked it up, recognizing it.

Tisha's phone.

It had obviously been damaged beyond repair, and not likely by Tisha.

Kurt must have her, Glenn told himself. Or hurt her. His heartstrings pulled at the thought, as he surveyed the landscape in search of Tisha.

Just then, Jacky and Riley bolted, as if picking up Tisha's scent. Glenn followed them, struggling to keep up, while removing his SIG Sauer handgun.

When he caught sight of Tisha—still alive, thankfully—being forced to move through the woods by Kurt, who was holding a rifle on her, Glenn knew that this was crunch time. He needed to distract Kurt in order to prevent him from shooting Tisha, before taking down the crooked special agent.

Without a second to spare, Glenn told the dogs, who were already on the move, "Get him!"

As they raced to protect Tisha from a very bad guy, Glenn took aim at Kurt, knowing that in this instant, there was no room for failure.

"THAT'S FAR ENOUGH," Kurt told her snippily, once they were deep enough into the wooded area to satisfy him.

Tisha turned around tensely to face the serial killer, who was still aiming his rifle at her. "I hope you rot in hell!" she snapped, meant mainly to get a reaction, before she made a desperate attempt to come out of this alive.

He laughed at her mockingly. "I'm sure I will. Too bad you won't be around to spit on my grave."

As she contemplated his ominous threat and saw her life flashing before her eyes, Tisha saw Jacky and Riley racing through the woods to get to her—and him—before it was too late, with Glenn in hot pursuit. Though she tried to avert her gaze, Kurt caught her eye movement and looked in that direction.

He turned the rifle toward the dogs. Knowing she couldn't let him shoot Jacky or Riley, in a split second, Tisha lunged at Kurt, forcing the barrel of the rifle down as a shot went off and hit the ground.

Putting into practice the self-defense techniques she'd learned, Tisha used her knee to hit him as hard as she could in the groin, while simultaneously striking the killer in the throat with the palm of her hand. As Kurt doubled over in pain, but still managed to hold on to the rifle, Jacky flew up in the air and clamped her teeth around his wrist. As Kurt howled, he let go of the rifle, just in time for Riley to jump on him, propelling both to the ground.

The serial killer was kept at bay until Glenn arrived and pitched in with a solid blow to Kurt's jaw, then slapped cuffs on the man. "Did he hurt you?" he asked Tisha, concern in his eyes, as Jacky licked her cheeks affectionately after coming to her rescue with Riley.

Tisha glanced at her bloodied, moaning assailant and answered comically, "I think it's more the other way around."

Glenn chuckled as he looked at the fallen foe. "Yeah, seems that way."

"With a little help from my furry family," she added, as Jacky and Riley circled her, clearly proud of their efforts to avert disaster.

"It seemed like a good idea to bring them along while searching for you, and let them have at him when push came to shove."

"How thoughtful of you." Tisha smiled gratefully. "Didn't hurt the cause any for you to contribute a nice crushing blow as well in putting a stop to Kurt's deadly intentions toward me."

Glenn acknowledged this, as he stated, "Happy to help. Believe me." He then glared at Kurt and asked with asperity, "Just tell me why all this? And why go after Tisha, in particular?"

As he struggled to maintain consciousness, Kurt sighed and responded callously, "They all had to die as versions of Patricia, because with my daughter Pat's illness, she never had the chance to reach adulthood to be like them someday..." He cast a wicked gaze at Tisha, and hissed, "She had the misfortune of also having a name variation of Patricia—so she had to die. You have to know that it was nothing personal toward you, Glenn..."

"That's where you're dead wrong, Kurt," he growled. "It was very personal to me. Maybe someday you'll come to realize that while you spend the rest of your miserable life behind bars!"

Kurt grumbled before passing out as Sherman came upon the scene. He approached them, eyeing Tisha. "You okay?"

"Yeah." She smiled thinly, glanced at Kurt and back. "Have to admit, though, for a while there, it was pretty much touch-and-go. Agent Stewart fully intended to do me in and make it look like a hunting accident. Or a stray bullet that just happened to have my name on it."

Sherman wrinkled his brow. "That wasn't going to happen," he argued. "Agent McElligott had your back every step of the way. So did I." He gazed at the dogs. "Guess they did, too."

Tisha watched as Jacky and Riley stared intently at him, clearly still in defense mode. "Thanks, Sherman," she told him with a sheepish grin.

"Just glad you're all right." Sherman regarded Kurt, who was coming around, then turned to Glenn and said, "Sorry it had to be a GBI special agent who went rogue."

"No more than I am." Glenn glared at Kurt. "But he'll be held fully accountable for everything he did, as would anyone else in society who broke the law as a serial killer and—" Glenn met Tisha's eyes endearingly "—attempted murderer."

Sherman nodded. "Good to know."

Tisha concurred, casting her eyes from Sherman to Glenn. "The important thing is that this seems to finally be over, for all of us and Shellview County—"

Almost on cue, deputies and other law enforcement personnel arrived and Kurt Stewart was placed under arrest and led away from Tisha and Glenn, and the crime scene of a planned attempted execution.

Glenn moved to Tisha and the dogs, who still seemed very protective of her, and said regretfully, "I wish we'd been able to figure out his madness and menace sooner."

"Me, too." She wrapped her arms around Glenn's rigid waist. "But it's truly over now. Kurt confessed to it all, and his warped sense of honoring his daughter's memory as a serial killer. Including setting up Jimmy McPhail to attack

Jeanne and take the fall as the Shellview County Killer; before killing him and making it seem like suicide."

"I'd gathered as much," Glenn told her, holding her close to his body. "Kurt was inspired by the serial killer I told you about, Lucas Conseco. I paid him a visit earlier today at Macon State Prison, and he enlightened me about receiving a visit six months ago from Kurt and giving him the skinny on his modus operandi and means for tracking down his victims."

"Wow." Tisha's brow creased. "Definitely two peas in a pod."

Glenn laughed humorlessly. "Yeah, that's one way of looking at it. Now, Kurt will have the opportunity to join Conseco in prison, where they both belong."

"You'll get no argument from me there," she assured him, pulling away and standing on her tiptoes to give Glenn a kiss. "For a minute there," she admitted, "I wasn't sure I'd get the chance to do that again."

"The thought crossed my mind once or twice, too," he confessed. "But together, we made sure that wasn't the case. Instead, we'll have plenty of time to enjoy each other's kisses."

"Promise?" Tisha gazed lovingly into his gray eyes.

"With a cherry on top!" Glenn said amusingly, and kissed her again, then said, "Let's get out of here."

"I'm all for that. And so are Jacky and Riley." The dogs barked simultaneously to that effect.

Tisha felt Glenn's fingers interlock with hers on one hand and, looking beyond her official statement on her ordeal to give to the DNR, GBI and the sheriff's department, welcomed the opportunity to spend precious time with those she cared about most.

Epilogue

A week later, Glenn was still counting his blessings that Tisha had been unharmed physically during her dangerous encounter with Kurt Stewart at the Manikeke Crossing. Knowing that the deranged, at least in some respects, serial killer had set his sights on Tisha as the supposed final victim of Kurt's rage against society in losing his daughter made Glenn all the more grateful that Tisha had lived to see another day.

If he had anything to do with it, that would stretch into many, many days, months, weeks and years, where he could cherish her with everything he had. And if he could get back even half as much, it would definitely make him one extremely happy man.

They were sitting on the couch in Tisha's living room, eating takeout Chinese chicken chow mein with bamboo chopsticks, with the dogs dining on their own food, when Tisha broke into Glenn's thoughts, as she asked, "So what do you suppose Kurt's ultimate fate will be? Will a good lawyer with the help of a capable psychiatrist be able to use some sort of insanity defense to try and get him an eventual get-out-of-jail-free card?"

Glenn weighed this for a moment or two, while eating, then he replied, "My guess is that any attempts to somehow mitigate his guilt will fall flat. Courts these days tend to frown upon defense strategies based on the perpetrator unable to distinguish right from wrong in justifying heinous actions. One need not look any further than Kurt's mentor, if you will, in Lucas Conseco. Beyond that, given the ball of cotton rope found at Kurt's place that corresponded with strands found on the victims—not to mention a DNA match with one of the victims found on a section of rope that he apparently used to strangle her and failed to dispose of—and a treasure trove of circumstantial evidence found on Kurt's laptop, it's pretty clear that there was willful intent on his part to commit the murders, while concealing his guilt. Hardly what you would call someone not playing with a full deck."

She nodded agreeably above her chopsticks. "You know, I was thinking the same thing. Crazy behavior can only go so far when choosing to end lives for some convoluted rationale."

"Right?" Glenn agreed thoughtfully. "I just hate that Kurt's ex-wife and children will have to bear the burden for his homicidal actions and the dead bodies left in his wake."

"Me, too." Tisha scooped up some noodles. "Also, it's so sad that Jeanne thought she had a potential keeper in Kurt. Only to find out that he was anything but someone she wanted to start a romance with."

"At least she lived to talk about it," Glenn pointed out. "Though Kurt had Jimmy McPhail do his dirty work for him—with a little more pressure around her neck or the stun gun being applied to the wrong part of Jeanne's body, the result could have been far worse for her."

"I know." Tisha ate food ponderingly. "I'm pretty sure there's someone out there for Jeanne, worthy of however long it takes for her to want to go back down that road."

"Yeah, definitely." Glenn met Tisha's eyes solidly. "Just like there's someone in here for me…and you—"

She fluttered her lashes boldly. "Oh, really?"

"Absolutely."

"Well, I have to admit, I think you're wonderful, Glenn."

"Is that so?" He smiled askance. "Right back at you, Tisha…and then some."

"Hmm…"

Glenn took that moment and said to her, "Uh, I think you've got a little bit of chow mein on your chin—" Just as she was about to wipe it away with the back of her hand, he checked her, and said smoothly, "Allow me."

He leaned over and kissed her perfect chin, following this with a kiss on the lips, then declared, "All better now."

"Nice to know. So clumsy of me." Tisha blushed and puckered her lips. "Shall we try that cute trick to kiss me again…?"

"Got me." Glenn laughed guiltily. "Absolutely. Let's go for it."

"You'll get no disagreement from me," she promised.

As they went for a longer, tastier kiss, Glenn found himself wanting more than ever to finally tell Tisha how he truly felt about her. Yet he held back, knowing he needed only a few more days to be able to make the announcement perfect for what it meant toward their future. He only hoped they were in sync in that regard.

For now, he was happy to settle for running his hand through Tisha's long hair and kissing the most gorgeous, sexy and on-top-of-her-game woman in the world.

ON SATURDAY, Tisha sat on Glenn's deck, beside him, as he played his guitar. Jacky and Riley were lying there lazily, liking the soft music, and perhaps the satisfaction of having their owners together, enjoying each other's company.

Tisha had hoped that by now Glenn would have expressed his feelings more for her in words, though his adorable actions were quite affectionate. She decided that now might be a good time to tell him exactly how she felt about him and what she wanted more than anything—a second chance at love and to be his wife and the mother of his children. Would this pull them closer together? Or push them apart?

As she contemplated this, Tisha took note that Glenn had started to play and sing at the same time, the 1920s classic romantic tune, "It Had to Be You," recorded by such artists as Billie Holiday, Frank Sinatra and Harry Connick Jr.

Mesmerized by the words, Tisha flashed her teeth and wondered where this was leading as Glenn stopped midway through, put the guitar down, took her hands and uttered soulfully, "It has to be you for me, and only you, Tisha."

Her heart nearly melted. "Really?"

"One hundred percent." He peered into her eyes. "I've been sitting on this knowledge for a while now, waiting for the right time to tell you how I felt about you… I'm totally and deeply in love with you, Tisha—and I want you to be my wife…" Glenn released one of her hands and pulled out from behind him a yellow double halo 1.2 carat diamond engagement ring, wrapped in platinum. After falling on one knee, he slipped the ring onto her finger, and it fit perfectly, then he asked, "Will you marry me, Tisha Fletcher, and make this GBI special agent the happiest man on the planet? Not to mention, Riley would love to have you as his adopted mother…and hopefully we'll have some human kids to add to the family down the line…"

"Yes, yes, yes, and as many yeses as it takes," she blurted

with glee, while admiring the ring and then the handsome man himself. "I love you, too, and will marry you, Glenn McElligott! And I'd be honored to adopt Riley and give Jacky a canine sibling to have fun with for a lifetime." Tisha chuckled as Jacky barked, in giving her wholehearted approval. "And as for children, I love the thought of being a mother, with you as their doting father."

"Thank you!" Glenn beamed as he straightened back up. "I can hardly wait to make this a reality," he declared.

Her eyes lit. "Neither can I."

"How do you feel about honeymooning in Alaska?" he asked expectantly. "My sister would love that and they'd give us an amazing place to bring our families together. Or if you'd rather have a honeymoon in Hawaii, Europe, Asia, or the Caribbean—"

"I'd love to have our honeymoon in Alaska," Tisha insisted. "That would be so incredible! There will always be other occasions to vacation in Hawaii, Asia, Europe, the Caribbean, or anywhere else we choose to visit."

"Very true. Anywhere at any time. As long as we're together—forever!"

"Absolutely," she replied, seconding his words enthusiastically.

A big grin played on Glenn's handsome face, as he cupped her cheeks and planted the biggest kiss on Tisha's mouth. She reciprocated in kind, as she loved kissing him every chance she got, while knowing there would be much more of this to look forward to for years to come.

* * * * *

COLTON'S DEADLY TRAP

PATRICIA SARGEANT

To My Dream Team:

My sister, Bernadette, for giving me the dream.
My husband, Michael, for supporting the dream.
My brother Richard for believing in the dream.
My brother Gideon for encouraging the dream.
And to Mom and Dad, always with love.

Chapter One

"Excuse me. I'm sorry." Maxwell Powell III stepped back from Mariposa Resort & Spa's reservations desk late Friday afternoon. He pulled his ringing cell phone from the front right pocket of his pale gray Dockers and held it aloft. "This might be my family."

The young clerk on the other side of the counter wore a name tag that read Clarissa. She inclined her head with a smile.

Max took another step back as he looked at his screen. The caller wasn't a relative. "Sarah? Is something wrong?"

Sarah Harris was his administrative assistant for *Cooking for Friends*, his streaming channel show. She was the first person he'd ever hired who wasn't connected to one of his two restaurants. Why was she calling him? He'd told her—and his agent—that he would be on vacation for six weeks. In fact, this trip had been his agent's idea after his New York apartment had been broken into the second time.

"Max, I'm so glad I caught you." Sarah's voice was breathy with relief. "I know you're leaving for vacation today."

"I'm checking into the resort now." He glanced back at Clarissa. She was welcoming another guest. He was relieved the clerk wasn't waiting for him but still uncomfortable with the personal call. Max turned his back to the reservations desk and stepped farther away. "Is there something I can help you with?"

"No, nothing's wrong. Well, actually something's wrong. I'm calling to let you know I'm in Arizona. I'm staying with relatives in Sedona for a while."

Sedona? Surprise rooted Max in place. Sarah was here? "I hadn't realized you had family in Arizona."

He didn't want to tell Sarah that, coincidentally, he also was in Sedona. One of his motivations for coming to the resort was to get away from everything and everyone who could distract him from creating the new recipes for his cookbook. Sorry, family. The other reason was to catch up with his college buddy Adam Colton, whom he hadn't seen in person for years. Adam co-owned Mariposa with two of his younger siblings, Laura and Joshua.

"You didn't know about my relatives here because I haven't told many people. But I'm comfortable telling you." Sarah's soft laugh carried across their connection, which wasn't as far as he'd hoped. "I needed to get away from New York for a while. Luckily, my relatives invited me to stay with them. I wanted you to know where I am in case you needed my help for anything like your book or your show. Whatever."

"Thank you for telling me." Max was already shifting his thoughts back to checking into his bungalow, assuring his family he'd arrived safely and taking a nap, although not necessarily in that order. "I'd better—"

"I'm getting a divorce." Sarah's announcement was stark and startling.

"I'm so sorry, Sarah." In a dark, dusty corner of his mind, Max remembered Sarah had told him she and her husband had been childhood sweethearts.

Sarah's sigh was nervous and unsettled. "Thank you, Max. I really need the time away to deal with…all of it. I guess I should have seen it coming. Steve's very jealous of you."

He stiffened. "Of me? Why?"

"He's convinced we're having an affair." Sarah's giggle seemed inappropriate.

"What?" Max glanced around as he lowered his voice. "Why would he think that?"

He had never, nor would he ever, pursue a woman who was in a relationship. That went double for married women. He had too much respect for the institution of marriage. He hoped to join it one day soon.

"Because of all those late nights we worked together at the studio." She sighed. "He *really* lost it when you bought me that bracelet."

"Did you tell him I'd bought bracelets as Christmas presents for *all* the women on the show?" He'd bought tie pins for his male employees. His younger sister, Melanie, designed jewelry. The gifts were a way to support her craft without seeming like he was humoring her and show appreciation for his team. They worked hard, put in long hours and did great work without ever complaining.

Max heard traffic noises on Sarah's end of the line, passing cars, squealing brakes and screaming horns. He imagined his young, redheaded assistant behind the wheel of a rental car. He hoped she was paying attention to the traffic.

Sarah made a rude noise. "He should've known better. He should've trusted me. Instead, he accused me of being unfaithful and threatened me with divorce. I called his bluff and told him *I'd* file for it myself."

Translation: no, Sarah hadn't told her husband there was nothing personal between them. Now somewhere out there was a very jealous man who was convinced Max had been sleeping with this wife. Max rubbed the frown lines forming between his eyebrows. Terrific.

"Sarah, I agree your husband should've trusted you, but I wish you'd told him the truth."

Sarah grunted. "If he could think so little of me, he doesn't deserve the truth."

Jeez.

He didn't like the idea of people believing he was the kind of person who'd sleep with a married woman. However, it wouldn't be wise to set the record straight with Steve himself. In fact, that would be stupid.

Just let it go.

Max closed his eyes, battling fatigue and exasperation. "Sarah—"

She interrupted. "Now I just need some time away to deal with the fact that my marriage is over. Steve and I were only married for seven years but we'd been together since I was fifteen. I'm about to be single for the first time in seventeen years."

Max was torn. On the one hand, he didn't want to tell Sarah he was in Sedona. He'd looked forward to taking a break from the show and everything related to it so he could focus on his book. On the other hand, she sounded like she needed someone to talk with.

He unclenched his teeth. "Sarah, I'm in Sedona also—"

"Really?" Her voice rose several octaves. "Where in Sedona?"

"I'm pretty tired right now. After I get some rest, I'll call you and we can set a date to catch up. I've got to go. I'll call you."

"I'd really like that, Max." Her sigh sounded like gratitude. "Thank you."

Max ended the call—and immediately started second-guessing himself. He and Sarah weren't friends. They were colleagues. She worked for him. He shouldn't blur the lines between their personal and professional relationships, especially since her husband suspected they already had. But it sounded like she needed support. He couldn't turn his back on her. With a mental shrug, Max returned his cell to his front pants pocket. He'd done the right thing.

Returning to the reservation desk, Max gave Clarissa an apologetic look. "I'm sorry. It was a colleague."

Clarissa gave him a bright smile. "No explanations necessary, Mr. Powell. It won't take long to get you checked in."

She was right. Within minutes, Clarissa was handing him the keys to his bungalow and a map of the property.

"And, finally, Mr. Powell, there's a package for you." Clarissa handed Max a square box roughly the size of a personal double-layer birthday cake.

"I wasn't expecting anything." He automatically accepted the parcel. It was as light as a dinner plate. A wide, plain white label listed his name, sent in care of Mariposa Resort & Spa with its physical address. There was no return address or postmark. "Do you know who sent it?"

Max's mind was still mushy from the morning's eight-hour flight from New York City's LaGuardia Airport to Flagstaff Pulliam Airport with a layover in Dallas. Pulliam was the nearest airport to the resort. And then there was the helicopter trip that carried him to Mariposa. The two-hour time difference wasn't helping, either.

"I'm afraid I don't know the sender's identity." Clarissa's bright smile faded. A puzzled frown marred her smooth white brow. "The Mailroom staff received it and asked Reservations to give it to you when you arrived."

"Thank you." Max turned the box over to examine it from all sides.

It was wrapped in nondescript brown paper and secured with large pieces of transparent tape. But who was the sender? His family, his parents and two sisters, were the only people who knew where he was. Had one—or perhaps all—of them sent him a surprise for his vacation? Why wouldn't they have included their return address? Unless that was part of the surprise. What was the surprise for? It wasn't his birthday, and they'd already celebrated his book contract and wrapping the first season of his show. He was impatient to see what was in the box.

"Of course, Mr. Powell." Clarissa's smile returned, sweeping the frown from her round features. "I'll ask Aaron to help you with your suitcases."

He set the package on the counter and stifled a yawn behind his fist. Those sleepless nights were catching up with him, too. The stress of waiting to learn whether his show would have a second season, pitching his first-ever cookbook and having his home broken into multiple times had given him temporary insomnia. Max was looking forward to hiding in the resort's kitchen and experimenting with new recipes.

"The two-hour time difference can hit you hard." The rich, warm female voice flowed over Max like the soft, warm waters of a healing spa. He caught the faint scent of wildflowers before he turned to the speaker.

Max was face-to-face with one of the most beautiful women he'd ever seen. His heart stopped. His breath caught. Time stood still. Everything around them—sounds, sights and smells—faded into the background. She was the only thing he was conscious of.

Long-lidded hazel brown eyes sparkled up at him from

a warm brown diamond-shaped face. She'd swept thick raven tresses into a bun at the nape of her neck, emphasizing her high cheekbones. Full, heart-shaped lips curved and parted to display perfect white teeth. Two-inch nude pumps boosted her average height to his chin. Her dark bronze blazer dress silhouetted her trim, athletic build and highlighted the gold undertones of her skin.

Suddenly wide awake, Max smiled in anticipation of a light flirtation with an attractive woman. And then he saw her name tag: Alexis Reed, Senior Concierge. The lovely lady wasn't flirting; she was welcoming him to the resort. And he recognized her name. *Thank you, Adam.*

She offered him her right hand. "Mr. Powell, welcome to Mariposa Resort & Spa. I'm Alexis Reed. I look forward to assisting you during your stay."

Max wrapped his long fingers around her much smaller, much softer ones. A current of awareness shot up his arm. Alexis didn't seem affected by it. Was this another symptom of sleep deprivation? He hadn't been able to get comfortable on the flight over. He was looking forward to taking a nap before meeting Adam for dinner.

"Thank you." Max couldn't believe his good fortune. "It's a pleasure to meet you, Ms. Reed. Adam mentioned you. Please call me Max."

Alexis inclined her head as she reclaimed her hand. "Thank you, Max. And I'm Alexis." She glanced behind her as a young man stationed a large scarlet-cloth-and-silver-metal baggage cart beside his suitcases. "I'll accompany you and Aaron to your bungalow."

Aaron tossed a friendly grin toward Alexis as he started loading the cart. Max's cheeks heated with embarrassment as the wiry young man stacked his three large dark gray cloth suitcases on the conveyor.

"Thanks, Aaron." Max returned the porter's smile as he searched for a way to justify having so much luggage. "I'm known for packing light for vacations, just a small suitcase or maybe a small suitcase and a knapsack." He adjusted his navy-blue-and-silver knapsack on his left shoulder and tucked his surprise package in the crook of his left arm. "But I'm staying at the resort for quite a while."

Alexis's captivating eyes were unreadable as she waited for him to stumble through his defense. "Adam said you'd be with us for six weeks."

There was no judgment in her tone. She turned to lead him to the parking lot at the back of the building. Aaron brought up the rear.

"That's right." Max's shoulder muscles relaxed. "Hence the uncharacteristic number of suitcases."

Alexis's nonverbal hum left him uncertain. She held the door open for him, Aaron and his luggage before leading him to a Mariposa Resort & Spa-branded minivan. It was pale yellow, drawing from the resort's pale-yellow-and-burnt-umber butterfly logo. Max sat beside her on the rear seat, setting the box on his lap and his knapsack between his feet. Aaron loaded his three suitcases into the cargo space in back before climbing in behind the vehicle's steering wheel. As they pulled away from the parking space, Max took in the view.

Sedona had fewer than ten thousand residents. The cozy desert town was dotted with diverse pines and cacti, and ringed by sheer canyon walls and majestic red rock buttes. Mariposa Resort & Spa sat on twenty-four acres along a ridge that backed up to Red Rock State Park. Adam and his siblings had assumed operation of the resort almost ten years ago, shortly after he and Max had graduated from New York University. The three Coltons had turned the property into an ultra-exclusive luxury resort with a five-star restaurant and private bungalows. According to reviews, their wealthy guests were happy to pay for the complete privacy—there weren't any cameras on the property—and tight security the resort offered.

A variety of cacti, grasses and wildflowers featured in the landscaping following the paths that wound throughout the resort. The public buildings and guest bungalows were contemporary structures with clean lines and large tinted windows. Their red-orange facades blended with the red-orange earth and stark, impressive mountains that rose all around them. Max's tension eased as his eyes followed the lines of the mountain ridge up to the cerulean blue sky dotted with whiffs of white clouds. Stunning.

"The resort is beautiful." This was Max's first trip to his friend's property. Why hadn't he visited sooner? Oh, right. Work.

"Yes, it is." Alexis's voice was quiet pride. "I've lived in this area all my life. The views never get old."

Max's eyes were drawn to her. She seemed serene and happy as she stared into the distance toward the soaring mountains. "Do you have family here?"

Her eyes widened with surprise. She must not have expected the personal question. "Yes. My mother."

The ride to the bungalow assigned to him was over far too soon. He could have spent hours looking at Alexis and getting to know her. But he'd have to be more aware of the woman and the vibes he was sending out. The one question he'd managed to ask during the drive may have been a little stalkerish. All work and no play had rusted out whatever skills in flirtation he may have once had.

They'd stopped in front of a bungalow that must have the best view in the resort. He needed to get Adam something great for his birthday. Max got out of the van, extending his hand to help Alexis step out after him. There it was again, that pulse of electricity that warmed his arm and jolted his heart when she touched him. She slipped free of his hold and stood beside him.

"Wow." All Max could do was stare at the bungalow.

Similar to the other buildings, the bungalow's red-orange stucco facade blended almost seamlessly with the soil in front of them and the mountains in the distance, making it appear to be part of the landscape rather than an addition to it. The foliage highlighting its perimeter was subtle and alluring. Max wasn't a botanist, but he recognized some of the plants, including the bouquets of warm gold brittlebush, deep blue desert chia, brilliant yellow desert marigolds, hedgehog cacti, prickly pears and, of course, saguaro, the cactus plant that appeared in every Western he'd ever seen.

Alexis tossed him a smile. Her eyes sparkled with pleasure. "Let's show you your home for the next six weeks."

She led him up the paved walkway. Max gripped his knapsack in his left hand and balanced the mystery box in the crook of his right arm. Aaron followed behind, wheeling two of Max's suitcases.

Alexis opened the door and stepped aside so he could enter his accommodations first. The bungalow was bright, open and spacious. The last remnants of his tension drained away. The natural light pouring in through the sliding glass doors to the balcony drew him across the room. The threshold framed the view of the mountain ridge just beyond his bungalow. Max dropped his knapsack beside one of the bamboo chairs.

"I'm glad I arrived early enough to appreciate this scene." Max turned, shifting the package to his left palm. He surveyed the room. It was comfortably cool. "I've stayed at several high-end resorts. This one puts them all to shame. Those Colton siblings know how to impress."

"I'm pleased you think so." Alexis stood near the center of the room. She looked good in it.

The bungalow's decor was minimalistic and tasteful. Both the floor and ceiling were made from bamboo. The off-white walls were bare, which was good. Max wasn't a fan of the generic paintings resorts usually displayed in their rooms. Instead, Mariposa let its surroundings, visible through the large windows, satisfy their guests' need for beauty. Vases of vibrant desert wildflowers were placed around the sitting area, providing color and adding a soft, clean fragrance to the air.

Aaron pulled his suitcases through a door to Max's left, probably the bedroom. He reemerged, sending Max another quick, polite smile. Although still professional, his expression warmed when he and Alexis exchanged looks. Alexis gave the younger man an approving nod.

Max drew his eyes from her and set the box on a chair beside the glass doors. He ran his hand over the chair's smooth bamboo back before wandering the bungalow. The bathroom was across from the bedroom. The spacious area included a burnt-umber-and-white-marble tub and frosted-glass shower.

Alexis gestured toward the glass doors. "There's a small golf cart parked behind your bungalow that you can use to get around the resort."

Max returned to the doors, angling his body to see the side of the patio past the hot tub. The vehicle was a two-seat white cart with the Mariposa butterfly logo. "That's convenient."

Another quick glance around his immediate surroundings confirmed his suspicion. There weren't any electronics in his room: clocks, radios, TVs. Luckily, he'd brought his laptop. He wasn't about to miss March Madness, the National Collegiate Athletic Association's basketball championship series. He could stream the games on his computer. He had a watch to keep track of time. As for music, he was still rebuilding his playlist, which he'd stored on his older cell phone. That device had been stolen during the second break-in two weeks ago.

Aaron returned with Max's final suitcase. He pulled it into the bedroom, then returned to the sitting area. "I'll wait for you at the van, Alexis."

Max started unwrapping the package he'd received from the reception desk. It gave him something to do with his hands. At the moment, he was more restless than curious. He would see Alexis again. She was going to help him purchase the fresh ingredients he'd need for his cookbook recipes. But for today, he wanted a little more time with her.

"Thanks, Aaron." Alexis waited for the porter to leave before continuing to enumerate the resort's features. "The paths back to L Building, which is our main building, and S Building, which houses our spa and gym, as well as our hiking trails and other amenities, are all marked."

She highlighted the resort's offerings, including horseback riding, swimming pools and fine dining at Annabeth, the resort's five-star restaurant, which was named for Adam's mother. Its menu included a champagne breakfast that sounded very tempting. Max set down the half-opened box and strolled the sitting area again. He focused more on Alexis's voice than her words. The warm, husky notes were at the same time soothing and stirring. It brought to mind images of champagne, canapés, cozy fireplaces and rumpled sheets.

Max had experienced an instant interest in attractive

women before. But he'd never felt such a strong, immediate connection. It was a restless need to be near her, to learn everything about her. Did she feel this way, too? How would she react if he asked her to spend time outside of work with him?

"If I can." Alexis's words startled him.

He turned to her. She stood in the center of the sitting area. Her patient eyes were fixed on him as she waited for him to respond.

"Excuse me?" For a split second, Max was afraid he'd spoken his private musings out loud.

Alexis's polite smile remained in place. "I said I'd be happy to answer any question you may have about the resort at this time, if I can."

Max sent her a self-conscious grin. "Oh. No, I don't have any questions right now. Thank you."

Good grief. How did he recover from this embarrassment? He found himself back beside the chair on which he'd left the package. He picked it up.

"All right, but if you think of anything, please don't hesitate to ask. Anyone at Mariposa would be happy to assist you."

Max's hands stilled on the box as he shifted his attention to Alexis. "Thank you. I don't know whether I'll have a lot of time to take advantage of all the resort's offerings. I have a lot of work to do."

"I thought this was at least partly a vacation." There was humor in her voice.

"I'm sure I'll have some downtime." He responded with a slow smile. "But it's more of a busman's holiday."

Alexis took a step toward him. "Would you like to discuss that now? Laura asked me to acquire the ingredients you'll need for your recipes."

"That's right and I appreciate your willingness to help me." His discomfort eased as he thought about the adventure of creating new dishes. "I'm adding a Southwestern twist to several of my dishes that I want to include in my book."

Her smile brightened into a grin. "Congratulations. It's all very impressive, your restaurants, your show and now your cookbook."

"Thank you." His eyes roamed her face, taking in her delicate features and the sparkles in her eyes. "I'll need fresh, high-quality ingredients, spices, fruits, vegetables, fish and poultries."

"You're in luck." Once again, Max heard the pride in her voice. "We have an excellent farmers market not far from the resort. It's open Sundays and Mondays from seven a.m. to noon. They have great fruits, vegetables, juices and condiments. They've also recently started selling poultry. I'll have to go to a separate market for fish, though, if you'd like me to pick that up for you."

Max shook his head. "I'll be coming with you."

He felt a surge of happiness at the thought of spending that time alone with her. Based on the surprise she quickly masked, Alexis didn't have the same reaction.

She lifted her palms. "There's no need for you to take the time and trouble to come with me. I'm happy to do the shopping for you." She lowered her hands. "You can just make a list of everything you'll need, and we can add those items to your final billing."

Max considered her professional demeanor. Her expression was calm and friendly, but he sensed she really didn't want him to do the shopping with her. Why not? A never-before-recognized imp of contrariness prompted him to dig in his heels.

"Well, you mentioned the market opens at seven a.m. That's pretty early." He spoke slowly as though he was considering his options. "And I'm not much of a morning person." Max saw the light of relief in her eyes. "However, this is really important to me, so I'll make the effort. In fact, we should get there before the market opens to make sure we get the best, freshest picks. After all, a great meal starts with great ingredients."

Alexis spread her arms. "I realize you're the expert, but I assure you, I'm capable of grocery shopping for you."

"*Grocery* shopping?" Max's eyes widened with surprise and disbelief. This time, his reaction wasn't feigned. "This isn't *grocery* shopping. It's much more than that. The produce has to be fresh and unblemished. The poultry and fish cuts have to be lean and perfect. I'm very particular. It would be best if I came with you."

Alexis considered him. Max sensed her sizing him up and going over his explanation. "Of course, Max. You're the expert and the guest."

Victory! He did a mental fist bump.

And, bonus, Max finally got the box open. His smile vanished. His body froze. His mind went blank. Inside the box were the two items that had been stolen from his condo during the break-ins: his old cell phone on which he'd saved his playlist and his deodorant. There was also a note, "Enjoy your stay at Mariposa Resort & Spa."

"Max?" Alexis's hand was warm against his bare forearm. She'd moved to stand beside him without his noticing. "Is something wrong?"

He raised his eyes to hers. "I'm being stalked."

Chapter Two

Alexis didn't need to hear another word. She urged Max onto the chair behind him before hurrying out to the van. She went to the driver's side, where Aaron was waiting for her behind the wheel. "We have an urgent situation. Could you please meet Roland in the L's lobby? I'll let him know you're on the way."

Aaron started the engine. His face was creased with concern, but he recognized this wasn't the time for questions. "Sure thing."

Alexis watched the young man speed away as she tapped Roland's number into her cell.

The director of security answered before the first ring ended. "Alexis, what can I do for you?"

Like her, Roland didn't believe in small talk. One of the many things she appreciated about him. "We have a situation at 11." She referenced Max's bungalow. "A suspicious package was delivered to the guest. Aaron's on his way to the L. Could you meet him in the lobby?"

"On my way." He ended the call.

Alexis returned to Max, leaving his front door open in anticipation of Aaron and Roland's arrival. He'd stood from the chair and put the box on the small bamboo end table beside it. He stood with his back to the room, staring out the rear glass doors. His arms were crossed. Alexis took this moment to do what she'd wanted to do since they'd met: admire his appearance.

In her mind's eye, she pictured his dreamy, deep-set eyes in chiseled, sienna features. They were the color of milk chocolate and reflected a quick, sharp wit. A deep dimple had creased his right cheek each time he'd teased her with his sexy grin.

Her eyes traveled from his close-cropped, dark brown hair to the casual rust-colored shirt that stretched across his broad shoulders. The short sleeves hugged his biceps. For a chef, he was built like an amateur athlete. Runner? Swimmer? Cyclist? Perhaps all the above. He was tall, at least a couple of inches above six feet. Warm brown slacks covered long legs and exceptional glutes.

He turned toward her suddenly as though he'd sensed her presence.

Alexis's eyes leaped to his. Her cheeks burned. "Aaron's getting Roland Hargreaves, our director of security. You should give him as much information as you can about your suspicions regarding this package." She forced herself to stop babbling.

"Thank you. It caught me off guard." His baritone carried a hint of New York City. It made her hungry to hear more.

"That's understandable." Alexis turned to the mini-fridge hidden in the credenza in the dining area. She selected one of the twelve-ounce bottles of water and offered it to him. His long sienna fingers brushed hers as he took it. His warmth spread up her arm.

"Thank you." He spoke softly.

"Afternoon, Alexis." Roland's gruff voice came from behind her.

She turned to find him just inside Max's bungalow. Alexis didn't want to think about the speed with which Aaron had driven to return to the bungalow so quickly—but she was grateful.

A former Oklahoma State University football linebacker, Roland made Aaron seem even slighter. He was a capable and comforting figure in his security director's uniform: cider-brown suit, white shirt and burnt-umber tie. The Mariposa Resort & Spa logo was embroidered on his jacket's upper-left breast pocket with the word "Security" underneath.

"That was fast. Thank you, Aaron." Alexis gestured from Roland to Max. "Roland Hargreaves, director of security, this is Max Powell III. He's just arrived." She pointed to the box on the small table near the rear glass doors. "That package was waiting for him. It had been shipped to his attention, care of the resort. I haven't touched anything. We've been waiting for you."

Roland stepped forward, offering Max his large right hand. "Mr. Powell, welcome to Mariposa Resort & Spa. I'm sorry your arrival has been marred by this experience."

Max released the older man's hand. "I appreciate your coming so quickly. Please call me Max."

"Roland." The middle-aged man pulled on protective gloves before handling the box. He examined each side as though checking for markings before looking at the contents. "What's the story here?"

Max drew a deep breath, further expanding his broad chest. "About six weeks ago, someone broke into my condo. The strange thing is, it's as though they had a key. The locks weren't damaged."

Roland's perpetual frown deepened. "Then how do you know it was a break-in?"

Max rubbed the back of his neck as he paced away from the glass doors. His footsteps were muffled as he crossed the warm-gold-and-burnt-umber area rug. "Because they tossed the place. They went through my stuff—the kitchen, the bathrooms, everywhere. They slept in my bed. And they took an old cell phone."

Roland jerked his square chin toward the inside of the box. "Is that the cell phone?"

"Yes." Max looked over his shoulder. "My deodorant went missing after the second break-in about a month ago."

"Were those the only items taken?" Roland looked around the room before crossing to the coffee table.

"Yes." Max watched Roland examine the paper in which the stalker had wrapped the box. "The NYPD believe it may be an obsessed fan, but I don't know how they're getting through the building's security, much less into my home."

Alexis wrapped her arms around her waist. Her blood chilled at the thought of someone being so obsessed with the celebrity chef that they'd break into his home, sleep in his bed and steal his deodorant.

Creepy.

She glanced at Aaron beside her. His eyes were wide with disbelief as he listened to Max's recount.

Alexis stepped closer to him and lowered her voice. "Aaron, please remember not to discuss anything you hear about our guests with anyone. Not one single person. Everything that happens at the resort is confidential."

Aaron closed his gaping mouth and offered Alexis a weak smile. "I promise. I won't tell a soul. But this is just so...*cray*, right?"

Shrugging her eyebrows in silent agreement, Alexis returned her attention to Roland and Max. Mariposa's guests—actors, musicians, public servants, athletes—had

had their share of wild encounters with fans, nonfans and the media. That was the number one reason so many of their guests checked into the resort. It wasn't just the exemplary menu from their Annabeth restaurant, the relaxation offered by the myriad spa services, the stunning views from their hiking trails or the pampering they received from their accommodations and the staff. It also was the ability to be anonymous at the resort. The respect for their privacy. The seclusion of the high-security, ultra-exclusive grounds.

But Aaron was right. Max's situation was super creepy.

Roland scanned the brief ominous note that had been included with the mailing. "Have you received any other strange messages or phone calls?"

Max shook his head. "No, this is the first time anyone has contacted me."

Alexis shivered again. She wished none of this had happened. That no one had broken into Max's home, that the package had never arrived, that the note had never been written.

Roland looked at him from over his shoulder. "Does the NYPD have any leads?"

Max dragged a hand over his close-cropped hair. "None."

Roland put the single sheet of plain white paper back into the box. "I'll look into this package with our mailroom and our post office contact. And I'll keep both of you apprised of what I learn." His look included Alexis. "Sorry, Aaron." The security director's stern look eased a little as he broke into one of his rare smiles.

Aaron waved both hands. "It's all good. I get it."

Roland's muscle memory returned his features to their usual serious setting. He pulled his wallet from the inside pocket of his uniform jacket. "In the meantime, I'd encourage you to update the NYPD on this development."

Max inclined his head. "I'll do that."

Roland handed Max his business card. "Here's my contact information, in case they have questions for me."

Max took the cream card and examined it. "I appreciate your help."

Roland turned to leave. "I'll brief my staff and let them know about the possible threat. We'll keep an eye on you—without being intrusive. And we'll keep you updated whether we discover anything or not."

"Thank you." Max sounded relieved and grateful.

Alexis approached him. "Max, if there's nothing else, we'll leave you to update the NYPD and settle in. If you do decide to get some rest before dinner, I recommend turning the Do Not Disturb switch on your phone."

Those dreamy milk chocolate eyes caught hers. "Thank you for everything, Alexis. You've helped to put my mind at ease."

The pulse at the base of her throat fluttered. "Of course." She swallowed. "We take our guests' safety very seriously."

Even those without dreamy eyes and New York accents. In addition to keeping Max safe, Alexis was keenly aware that a threat to one guest could affect the well-being of others at the resort—clients as well as staff.

"WE'RE SO GLAD you arrived safely." Max's mother, Erika Ross-Powell, spoke on a sigh of relief.

"We thought we'd hear from you hours ago." Maxwell Powell II spoke at the same time.

Max had called his mother after Alexis, Roland and Aaron had left late Friday afternoon. Erika had put him on speaker so his father could join the conversation. As usual, they talked over each other. Max mentally shrugged. It was a family trait. He and his sisters did the same thing.

Erika admonished her husband. "MJ, he's calling us now."

"MJ" was short for Maxwell Junior, which was his father's designation before Max's birth.

Max sat on the edge of the mattress and surveyed the bedroom as he spoke with his parents. Its decor was similar to the sitting area: bamboo flooring, ceiling and furniture. Instead of artwork, the north-facing wall had a large picture window that framed the mountain ridge. The scent of wildflowers came from the three vases placed around the room, one on the dressing table facing the bed and one on each nightstand.

"Sorry I didn't call sooner." He absently stared at the colorful area rug beneath his loafers. It was identical to the ones in the sitting area. "I met the resort's senior concierge. We discussed some of the tasks I'll need help with while I'm here."

And he'd had a suspicious package to deal with. He didn't want to get into that, at least not with his parents. Not now. He wasn't withholding information. He didn't have anything to share. In fact, he had more questions than answers. How had the stalker known where he would be or when he would arrive? Had the thief planned to return his stolen items all along? Most importantly, who was harassing him and what did they want? He'd keep the incident to himself for now. His parents would only worry, which would increase his stress.

"How beautiful is the resort?" Erika's question replaced his troubled thoughts.

Max imagined his mother holding the phone between herself and his father, her eyes wide with excitement. "It's very beautiful." He rose from the mattress and crossed to the window. Once again, the view stole his breath. "Adam and his siblings have a lot to be proud of."

"Try to find time to relax and unwind." Erika was in full-on Mom Mode. "You've been under a lot of stress and working so hard for so long. You deserve to have at least a little fun."

"Your mother's right. You're there." MJ paused as though he was sipping a beverage. Was it coffee? His father was addicted to the stuff, but probably not. It was after seven over there. His mother cut off his supply after 4 p.m. "You might as well enjoy yourself."

"It was nice of Adam to invite you to the resort and give you a discounted rate, but you're still paying something." Erika's tone was gentle persuasion. "Make the most of it."

An image of Alexis appeared in Max's thoughts. "I promise to try."

Max wandered the room. He ran the tips of his fingers over the bamboo dressing table as he eyed the matching nightstand. The design was calming and intriguing.

"How are you feeling?" Erika asked.

Max could almost hear her concerned frown. He sensed her grip on the phone as though she was wrapping her arms around him.

"I'm fine." He hesitated. "A little tired." By not telling them about the mailing, he'd already lied by omission. He wouldn't add another sin to the list.

"Couldn't you sleep on the plane?" MJ sounded surprised. "I know it was a long flight."

"You know he's never been able to sleep on a plane." Erika laughed. "It used to drive me nuts. Miri and Melly would fall asleep as soon as the plane took off. But not Max. He'd stay awake the whole time, which meant one of *us* had to be alert the whole time."

Those family trips were great—once they got off the

plane. Max still envied his sisters' ability to sleep during the flights.

"Have you heard anything more from the police about those break-ins at your condo?" MJ's abrupt change of subject caught Max off guard.

"No, they don't have any updates." Before calling his parents, Max had spoken with the officers assigned to his case about the package. They'd told him they didn't have any new information on the investigation. Somehow Max didn't think his outdated cell phone or used deodorant stick was a priority for them. "I've asked the building manager and a neighbor to keep an eye on my condo until I get home."

"The attractive young woman who lives across the hall?" Erika's sly tone hinted at the ulterior motive for her question.

His mother was anxious for all her offspring to give her grandchildren. His older sister, Miriam, was the only one married. She worked with their mother, who was a casting director. Miri and her husband, Odell, weren't in a hurry to have kids. Neither Max nor his younger sister, Melanie, were in a relationship. In addition to designing jewelry, Mel was an up-and-coming actress. Like Max, her focus was on building her career. Her dedication was paying off. She'd landed a supporting role as an FBI agent in a new crime drama. With the success of their first season, the show had been renewed for two more seasons. Max was as excited as if he were in the cast.

MJ had wanted Max to join his production company, but Max's first love had always been cooking. Owning a restaurant had been his dream. MJ had finally accepted that, giving him ideas and suggestions along the way. His father had been thrilled when a studio had offered Max his own cooking show. MJ had declared they were now a show-business family.

Max shook his head, more amused than exasperated. "That's right, Mom. My very attractive neighbor—who's happily engaged and planning her wedding to someone else—is keeping an eye on my condo."

"Son, I've been giving some thought to the second season of your show." MJ offered another drastic subject change. Max braced himself for his father's input. "You should tape the show in front of a live audience."

All at once, the fatigue of the travel, time zone change and weeks of restless nights crashed into him. Max's body was heavy with it. His eyes struggled to stay open. "Dad, I'm not really up to talking about plans for next season right now. I'm pretty—"

MJ's enthusiasm couldn't be stopped. "What do you think of the idea? It's a good one, right?"

Max rolled his shoulders to ease his tension. "Dad, you have years of experience in both television and film production. You know opening a show's production to a live audience would be expensive. We'd have to double our security, add bathrooms and offer audience members at least water if not snacks."

"You could recoup all those costs by charging for the tickets. People would pay good money to watch you cook in person."

Oh, boy.

"Why would anyone pay to watch me cook in person when they could attend tapings of late-night talk shows for free?" Max returned to sit on the edge of the bed. "And what if no one came?"

"It's worth the risk, son." MJ's tone brushed aside all Max's concerns. "Having a live studio audience would add energy to the show. Trust me. I know this. As you said, I have a lot more years of experience in the TV and film industries than you do."

Those words put Max's back up. "I know, Dad, and I respect your experience. But the show has been successful. Our viewing audience has consistently put us in the top ten ratings."

"Yes, and that's wonderful. But that was only the first season. Don't you want a long-running program?"

"Yes, of course, but—"

"*Non*-celebrity cooking shows are beating you in the ratings." MJ paused again as though taking another sip from a beverage. Maybe it was coffee. His father sounded overcaffeinated. "Historically, they do better anyway. You have to beat them at their own game. That's why you have to return your show to the people. Put them in the center of your program."

"You want me to change the format of the show?" The muscles at the back of his neck were knotting. Why didn't his father have more faith in his ideas? What was he doing wrong? What could he do better? What more could he possibly do to prove himself to his parent?

Erika intervened. "MJ, let Max get some sleep. First your own restaurants, then the cooking show and now a publishing contract. No wonder you're tired. We're so proud of you, hon."

"Of course we're proud of him." MJ sounded like he was only half listening. "But think about the idea, son. You're doing great! But you could do even better. There's room to grow."

Max had been hearing those words all his life. They were his motivation—and his burden. When would success be "good enough"?

"I don't think the show's producers would want to break the bank on adding a live audience, Dad. The show's not a comedy." At least it wasn't intended to be.

MJ tsked. "If they give you any pushback, just remind them they have to spend money to make money."

"Let him rest, MJ." Erika's tone was firmer this time. "Hon, we'll let your sisters know you landed safely. That way, they won't text you while you're trying to sleep."

"Thanks, Mom." He loved being part of a close-knit family. It was great knowing there were people who were always looking out for you—except when that concern prevented his sleep.

"Your mother's right. Get some rest, son. We'll talk more about the studio audience idea after you've had a chance to rest."

"All right, Dad." Max appreciated the warning.

"YOU'VE BEEN SCAMMING our guests." Alexis stared across the rectangular blond wood conference table at Mark Bower late Friday afternoon. The twenty-something-year-old was the newest addition to her concierge team.

Leticia Bailey sat between them at the head of the table. The tall, slender personnel director wore a striking mustard pantsuit with an ebony shell blouse. Long thin dark brown braids framed her diamond-shaped brown face.

Mark's round glass-green eyes flared wide with surprise. He obviously hadn't seen this coming. Alexis clenched her teeth. How long had he expected his clandestine operation to last? She relaxed her jaw and once again thanked the good fortune that had allowed her to uncover his dealings before they'd gone any further.

He shot a panicked look at Leticia before answering Alexis. "No, I haven't."

Alexis heard the fear in his words. Her muscles trembled with outrage. She wanted to shout at Mark that he was a liar. But he'd already damaged her professional reputation and caused her to question her own judgment. She wouldn't let him take her self-control, too.

She drew a long breath of the cool, citrus-scented air and tightened her grip on her temper. "I heard you speaking with the Elliots at the paddocks."

The horse paddocks were in the northern part of the resort. Earlier in the week, Alexis had taken one of her exploratory late-morning walks around Mariposa, checking on guests and waving at coworkers. That's when she'd overheard Mark speaking with the Elliot family. Mr. Elliot was a famous television star. He'd come to the resort with his wife and their four preteen children.

"You were spying on me?" Mark's shaggy sandy-blond hair swung forward as he leaned into the table. At least part of his anger seemed manufactured to put her on the defensive. He failed.

Alexis's voice was tight. "The Elliots sounded so happy that you were able to get their event tickets. It's such a nice feeling when guests appreciate our work. Then I heard you tell them that as usual, you'd added the cost of the tickets to their resort bill, but you were invoicing them separately for the service fee to reduce their tax burden. Imagine my surprise. As you know, we don't have a service fee."

Leticia tapped the manual on the table in front of her. Her chunky bronze earrings, a match to her necklace, swung as she turned her head toward Mark. "You signed a statement attesting to your having read the employee handbook. The handbook explicitly states staff are not permitted to accept any type of gratuity related to or in the course of employment."

The Coltons' legal counsel insisted on that specific language to ensure that clause encompassed bribes from the media and paparazzi.

Mark's prominent Adam's apple bobbed. "Well, yeah. I… I read it."

"And you went to all the new employee orientation seminars." Leticia flipped through several sheets of paper. "Your signature appears on each of these attendance certifications, confirming you attended and understood the policies, benefits and conditions of employment covered during the sessions. So you are aware soliciting and/or accepting gratuities in any form is cause for immediate dismissal."

"That policy exists for many reasons." Alexis clenched her hands together on the table, entwining her fingers. "First, this is an all-inclusive resort. Our guests have prepaid for every service, meal and activity available to them at the resort. Second, we don't want employees to be tempted to do anything inappropriate in exchange for a bribe. This is another way we protect our guests' privacy."

Mark spread his thin arms. "But I didn't do anything inappropriate." His voice rose several octaves.

Leticia didn't bat an eye. "You violated personnel policies. Policies you acknowledged receiving and understanding. Therefore, your actions were very inappropriate."

Inappropriate in every way. And Alexis had to admit to Laura Colton—her friend, direct supervisor and co-owner of Mariposa—the mistake she'd made in hiring Mark.

Alexis's skin burned at the unpleasant memory. "We also know this wasn't a one-time mistake or oversight. I spoke with several of the guests who'd been assigned to you." She pressed her palm on top of the documents that stood in a tidy stack in front of her. "They all signed these statements, attesting they'd paid you several so-called service fees for event tickets and restaurant reservations you'd made for them."

Mark interrupted. "They gave me those tips to thank me for my trouble. Some of those tickets and stuff weren't easy to get, you know."

Alexis's face burned with anger at his continued lies. "Every one of their statements makes it clear you told them they had to pay you a service fee."

"Alexis is right." Leticia gestured toward her. "But even if your clients had offered you a gratuity of their own will, you were required according to our employee handbook to decline the gift. Your response should have been some version of, 'Thank you, but the resort's policy prohibits me from accepting gifts.'"

Alexis was grateful for Leticia's support and her further clarification of Mariposa's policy, but she sensed Mark wasn't ready to admit his guilt.

He divided his scowl between her and Leticia. "But I'm still on probation."

"All the more reason to expect you to know and respect the rules." Leticia shifted on her chair to face Mark. "If you're willing to so blatantly disregard the rules at this stage of your employment, how much worse could your actions become?"

"That's not a chance I'm prepared to take." The possible answers to Leticia's rhetorical question could cause Alexis's head to explode. "Mark, your services are no longer needed. You can pack your belongings. Security will escort you out."

His jaw dropped. "You're firing me?"

Alexis's eyes never wavered. "That's right." Her words dropped into the thick silence.

Her sense of failure was complete. She'd hired someone who'd repeatedly flouted Mariposa's employee policies.

Alexis's eyes drifted toward the view outside the room's floor-to-ceiling tinted windows. The timing couldn't have been worse. The resort's event manager was getting ready to retire. Alexis had applied for the position. It would be a promotion, which she believed she was capable of and ready for. But after this experience, would Laura, Adam and Joshua agree? Would they ever trust her judgment again?

"It was one mistake." Mark's lips tightened.

Alexis returned her attention to him. "And you made it repeatedly."

Mark's wiry frame stiffened with outrage. "You've always resented me."

Alexis narrowed her eyes at his change in tactic. He'd gone from defense to attacking her directly. "What makes you say that?"

"You've felt threatened by me from the day I entered your department two months ago." He jabbed a finger toward her. His eyes were hard with anger and resentment. "You knew I was a better concierge than you could ever be."

She would have laughed if she hadn't been so angry. "I hired you because I thought you would be a good addition to our team. I realize now I made a mistake."

"You're lying." His voice shook. Was it anger or anxiety? "You resent me. You treat me differently from other people in the department. I'm not the only person who's noticed it, either. Everyone else has, too."

Alexis's anger was giving way to disgust. "That's not true, Mark. You're making up these allegations to strike back at me, but it won't work."

"No, I'm not." He stabbed a finger toward her. "I want to file a complaint against my manager."

Leticia looked confused. "Mark, you no longer have a manager. You no longer work for the resort."

Shock wiped all expression from his thin, pale features. "What?"

Leticia stood and crossed the room. Opening the door, she invited the two young security guards who waited in the hall to join her before turning back to Mark. "Please remember you signed a nondisclosure agreement, stating you wouldn't share information about Mariposa's guests. That agreement is legally binding and enforceable even after your employment ends."

Mark stood. His eyes were dark with hatred as he stared down at Alexis. "You haven't won."

"You still don't understand." Alexis rose, straightening her shoulders. "This isn't about winning and losing. This is about right and wrong. What you did was wrong. The fact you have the nerve to lie about your actions proves you know that."

He glared at her for several moments more before turning to leave. His movements were stiff as he approached the door without looking back. Leticia and the two guards followed him out.

As they disappeared beyond the doorway, Alexis braced both hands on the smooth, cool table and shook her head. Laura may not fault her for hiring Mark, but Alexis blamed herself. How could she have missed the signs that Mark was a grifter?

"How are you feeling?" The question startled her.

She looked up to find Roland standing just inside the room. She found a smile for the older man. "What are you doing here?"

"Checking on you. I know how upset you are about this business with Bower."

Her smile faded. “Can you blame me?” She stopped beside the director of resort security. “Fortunately, the guests didn’t seem upset or resentful. It probably helped that we reimbursed them for the fraud. But we can’t be certain whether they’ve forgiven us unless they come back.”

“Don’t be so hard on yourself.” Roland stood back so Alexis could precede him from the room. “He’s only been here two months. You caught him and now he’s gone.”

“I hope he hasn’t done lasting damage to Mariposa.” Alexis looked up at her coworker. “How long will we have to deal with the fallout from this situation?”

Chapter Three

Max drifted out of a half-remembered dream. Far in the distance but lurching ever closer was an inescapable force that sounded like a ringing phone. Groaning, Max rolled toward the disturbance and lifted his eyelids just enough to locate the device.

With an effort, he stretched out his left arm to clutch the receiver. He croaked into the phone, "Hello?"

There was a brief pause almost like a gasp before a young woman spoke. "Mr. Powell, this is Clarissa at the front desk. I'm so sorry to disturb you."

Max cleared his throat. "It's all right, Clarissa. Alexis suggested I turn on my Do Not Disturb switch. I must've forgotten. What can I do for you?"

A relieved sigh proceeded Clarissa's next words. "You have a visitor, Sarah Harris."

Max was still groggy. Had he misunderstood? "Sarah? She's here?"

"Yes, sir. She's waiting for you at the front desk." Clarissa sounded determinedly upbeat.

Max rolled onto his back. Oh, for the love of everything holy. For a second, he considered asking Clarissa to tell Sarah he'd checked out of the resort and returned to New York. That way, he could go back to bed. But then his annoyance turned inward. Sarah was upset. Her marriage was ending. She was probably looking for someone other than family to whom she could just vent. He shouldn't be churlish. Surely, he could spare a few minutes—or even an hour—for a colleague in need.

He tossed off the bed's soft gold coverlet. "I'll be right there. Thank you, Clarissa."

"You're very welcome, Mr. Powell." Relief was evident in her young voice before she ended the call.

What time is it?

Max retrieved his watch from beside the resort's landline and blinked until the LED numbers came into focus. It was a few minutes after five o'clock Friday evening. He'd slept for less than an hour. Swinging his legs off the side of the bed, Max canceled the alarm he'd programmed on his phone. He'd set it for six o'clock, which would have given him enough time to get ready to meet Adam for dinner later this evening. He climbed out of bed and into black slacks, a white shirt and a slate gray jacket. That attire would be suitable for both his meeting with Sarah and dinner at the resort's fancy restaurant.

The golf cart was fun to operate and, as Alexis had promised, the directional signs leading him from his bungalow back to the L Building were frequent, well-lit in the waning daylight and easy to follow. Max was walking into the building within minutes of leaving his bungalow.

"Max!" Sarah ran forward, then launched herself at him.

He caught his breath and a lungful of her jasmine-and-lemon perfume. Max withdrew Sarah's arms from around his neck and stepped back, putting an arm's length of space between them. What had gotten into her? They had a professional relationship. Why had she leaped into his arms as though they shared something much more personal?

"Hello, Sarah." Max took another step back as he looked uneasily around the lobby. His eyes connected with Alexis's. *Perfect.*

She inclined her head with cool professionalism before returning her attention to the older woman standing beside her. The stranger looked like wealth and influence. There was something familiar about her. Max narrowed his eyes. She reminded him of Glenna Bennett Colton, Adam's stepmother. He'd seen photos of her.

Max pulled his eyes from Alexis and looked down at Sarah. She was frowning in Alexis's direction. "Sarah, what are you doing here?"

His administrative assistant turned her back to Alexis and beamed up at him. Her brown eyes glowed in her round porcelain face. "I'm here to collect on that drink you promised me, silly."

Max searched his memory. He was certain drinks had not been discussed in their earlier conversation.

He scanned their surroundings, careful to avoid attracting Alexis's attention. From what he'd seen so far, this main building was the largest on the property. Like his bungalow, this one-story structure had bamboo flooring and ceilings. Nature featured as its main decor. Vases of fresh flowers had been placed around the reception and lobby areas, and large square windows displayed mesmerizing views to the resort's east, west and south.

Max turned away from the bar on his right and gestured toward the open-air lobby opposite it. "Let's sit down."

Sarah raised her right arm as though preparing to point out the bar beside them. But something in Max's set features must have convinced her to join him in the lobby. She led him to a cozy bamboo love seat. Max swallowed a sigh. He would've preferred the individual armchairs but at least they weren't on the barstools.

His administrative assistant looked like a different person. She'd freed her shoulder-length red hair from the clips that usually kept it off her face. Tonight, her tresses were styled into a blowout. Heavy makeup emphasized her round brown eyes and turned her pink lips cherry red. Her crimson minidress looked more like a negligee. Had her divorce rattled her more than she was letting on?

Max angled himself to face her. His back was to Alexis. Was she still in the lobby? "Sarah, how did you know where I was staying?"

She shrugged her shoulders, which were bare except for thin red spaghetti straps. "You said you were staying at a resort in Sedona. I took a chance that it was this one." She took his right hand from his knee and cupped it between hers. "Where else would someone with your celebrity status stay?"

He took his hand back. Max's eyes dropped to the sterling silver bead bracelet he'd given her—and the other women on his production team—for Christmas. It was an understated design.

Max ignored her reference to his celebrity. "Sarah, I'm sorry you and Steve are getting a divorce. Are you sure the two of you can't work things out? Do you want me to speak with him, let him know you and I aren't involved in any way outside of work?"

Irritation flickered briefly in her eyes before she masked her emotions. "I'm done with Steve. If he doesn't trust me, that's his problem." Sarah stood, offering him her hand. "Let's get a drink and toast my soon-to-be-single status."

"I don't think that would be a good idea." Max wondered if she'd already had a glass or two.

Sarah laughed, pointing toward the bar across the lobby in front of her. "What do you mean, silly? The bar's right there. You won't even have to drive home after."

"But you will." Max came slowly to his feet. Before he could continue, Alexis's voice came from behind him.

"Excuse me." Her soft, husky syllables commanded his attention and made his knees shake. "I'm sorry to interrupt—"

Sarah shoved her right hand onto her hip. "Then why are you?"

The aggression in her voice surprised and embarrassed Max. "Sarah—"

Unfazed, Alexis continued. "The resort's amenities are for guests only. I'm afraid people who aren't guests of the resort can't enter beyond the L Building's lobby. I'm sorry."

Sarah gave the resort's senior concierge a stony stare. "Why not?"

Max swallowed a sigh. "Sarah, the resort's rules—"

Alexis interrupted him. "It's all right, Mr. Powell. It's a fair question."

Max narrowed his eyes at Alexis. *Mr. Powell?* Earlier, they'd been Max and Alexis. What had changed?

She turned back to Sarah. "Ms. Harris, non-guests aren't permitted on resort grounds or to avail themselves of resort amenities, including our bar and restaurant, because they aren't clients. It wouldn't be fair to our registered guests to allow visitors to take advantage of services they're paying for. I hope you can appreciate that."

"No, I can't. Your rules are ridiculous." Sarah raised her voice. She flung a hand toward Max, barely missing striking him. "Do you even know who this is? This is *Maxwell Powell III* of the *New York* Powells."

If mortification was fatal, Max would be a corpse on

the ground at Alexis's sexy nude pumps. "Sarah, you're making a scene."

"I don't care." Nevertheless, she lowered her voice. "They need to give you the deference you deserve. Is this a resort or some sort of cult camp?"

At Sarah's insult, fury flashed in Alexis's champagne-hued eyes. Max felt a stirring of anger as well. His friend put a lot of time, effort and talent into transforming the once-modest hotel into an exclusive getaway for the rich and famous. He was proud of Adam's accomplishments and didn't appreciate Sarah's denigrating comments.

He faced Alexis. "Thank you for making us aware of the resort's rules. Of course, we'll respect them." The temper in Alexis's eyes drained and was replaced by gratitude. He wanted to keep looking into them. But with an effort, he shifted his attention to Sarah. "I'll take you to your car."

Sarah's jaw dropped. "But—"

Max took her arm and walked with her to the entrance. He felt the eyes of other guests following them across the lobby. This was not how he'd wanted to start his working vacation. He'd come to the resort to relax. Instead, drama had followed him.

He pushed through the glass doors. "Are you all right to drive or should I call you a cab?"

"I'm not drunk, Max." Sarah's voice was tight. She looked over her shoulder back toward the L Building. "You should file a complaint against that woman."

"She was doing her job. *We* were the ones in the wrong." A mild breeze snuck under Max's sports jacket. It would have been calming if it weren't for the waves of aggression rolling off Sarah and the responding irritation scratching under his skin. "I wish you'd told me you were coming, Sarah."

"I wanted to surprise you." She lowered her voice. "I wanted to see you."

"I'm sorry you're upset about your divorce, but I can't meet with you today." He retained his hold on her arm as she led them to her car. "I have another engagement."

Sarah scowled. "Well, I'm not sure how long I'll be in Arizona." She stopped beside an older-model white Toyota Corolla hatchback. "I mean, I have an open invitation from my relatives to stay as long as I'd like, but I've been thinking of taking a real vacation. Maybe to Hawaii."

Max released her arm. "I think that would be a good idea. Being away from familiar people and places might help you put things in perspective."

Sarah pouted. She put her hand on his chest and gazed up at him. "No, Max. What I need right now is a friend. That's what you've always been to me. A friend."

Something in her voice, in her touch, made him uncomfortable. No, they'd never been friends. She worked for him. He didn't want to blur those lines.

Max stepped back, breaking Sarah's connection. "Drive safely, Sarah." He turned to leave.

"Call me, Max." Her voice carried to him as he walked away.

Seriously, what had gotten into her?

MAX WALKED BACK to the L Building Friday evening in a cloud of confusion. The only explanation for Sarah's uncharacteristic behavior was her divorce. Steve's accusations must have hurt her much more than she was letting on—maybe even more than she admitted to herself. For him to accuse her of cheating on him must have felt like the biggest betrayal. His lips tightened, thinking about the attack against *his* honor. He didn't appreciate it and he certainly didn't deserve it.

"Excuse me." A female voice scattered his thoughts.

He looked up to see Glenna Bennett Colton emerge from the main building. She gave him a tight smile as she walked past him toward the main parking lot.

"Pardon me." Their exchange pulled him out of his fog.

From the corner of his eye, Max caught a glimpse of a bronze skirt suit. Alexis was walking across the parking lot.

"Alexis." Max hurried to catch up with her.

She turned to him, a polite smile fixed in place. "Hello again, Mr. Powell. Is your bungalow comfortable?"

He stopped a little more than an arm's length from her, watching a cool breeze tease wayward strands of her raven hair forward. He curled his fingers into his palm to keep from brushing them back.

Max offered her a curious smile. "It's Max. Remember?"

Her bright eyes danced with mischief. "That's a relief. Maxwell Powell III is a mouthful."

Max's cheeks warmed with embarrassment. Why had Sarah made such a public display of his identity as though anyone would—or should—care?

"Trust me. I know." He straightened his shoulders and held her eyes. "I apologize for Sarah's rudeness. She's been under a lot of stress but that doesn't excuse the way she acted toward you."

"I appreciate that." Alexis pulled her black purse farther onto her shoulder. "But you aren't responsible for her behavior."

"I feel responsible, though, since she works for me." Max gestured toward the lot. "May I escort you to your car?" It wasn't dark yet, but the sun was starting to set, and the shadows were growing longer.

"You may." Alexis turned.

"May I take your briefcase?" He offered her his hand.

Alexis blinked. She handed him the accessory. "Thank you."

Max glanced at Alexis from the corner of his eye as they walked across the asphalt parking area. He was thirteen again, experiencing the same anxious and excited feelings he'd had when he'd walked a girl he'd liked home from school.

Just breathe, Powell. "I had the impression you were aware of Sarah before you joined us. You addressed her by her last name without an introduction."

Alexis's lips twitched as though she struggled against a smile. "Clarissa, the front desk agent who processed your registration, called me. She was concerned Sarah might not appreciate all the resort's rules."

A weight pressed down on Max's shoulders. He didn't want to imagine what Sarah had done to raise Clarissa's concerns. "I'm sorry about that."

"Apologizing again?" The teasing glint in her eyes brushed the responsibility from his shoulders.

Max spread his arms. "I know I'm not responsible for Sarah, but everyone at the resort—you, Clarissa, Aaron, Roland—you've all been so welcoming. You don't deserve Sarah's rudeness."

"I'm glad we've made a good impression on you." Alexis stopped beside an older-model silver compact sedan. "In light of the suspicious package you received, we have to be even more aware of the resort's security rules and your safety. Frankly, we have to be extra careful about the welfare of everyone at Mariposa—our guests and our team. If someone has malicious intentions toward you, they could endanger everyone on the property."

"I hadn't considered the effect the threat would have on other people." Max stared across the lot, picturing a shadowy figure romping around his bungalow and stealing his stuff. He'd carry that burden for the rest of his life if anyone came to harm because of this stalker.

"Roland spoke with everyone who'd handled the package since it was delivered to our mailroom." Alexis extended her hand for her briefcase. Max reluctantly gave it to her. "There wasn't anything unusual about its arrival. Our postal carrier doesn't have any additional information on it."

Max didn't think they would. "I appreciate Roland's checking. He's very thorough." He tucked his hands into the front pockets of his black pants. "The NYPD's investigation is stalled. I appreciate your concern, and everything you and Roland are doing to solve this mystery."

This was much more than a mystery. He wasn't searching for misdirected mail or lost keys. It was a threat. Someone was following him. Who and why?

"Of course." Alexis again adjusted her purse strap on her shoulder. "The resort has exceptional security. We take our guests' safety very seriously. If you have any concerns or if there's anything you need, just let us know. Everyone here wants to make sure you enjoy your Mariposa experience."

Max heard the sincerity in her voice. "I appreciate that. And I'll make arrangements away from the resort to meet with Sarah. I'll abide by the resort's rules."

"Even though you're *the* Maxwell Powell III?"

"I'm just Max." He liked the way her eyes twinkled like stars when she teased him.

Alexis's chuckle strummed the muscles in his lower abdomen. She deactivated her car locks, then turned to set her briefcase and purse on the front passenger seat. Alexis closed the door before circling the car's hood as she moved to the driver's side. "I'll see you bright and early Monday, Max."

"I'm looking forward to it." Was his grin as goofy as it felt? "The project, I mean. I'm looking forward to getting started on the project."

Alexis waved before disappearing inside her vehicle. Max backed away from her sedan. He watched her pull out of her parking space and drive away.

Although he loved his career, this was the first time in a long time he was looking forward to a Monday.

Try having a vacation during your vacation.

Max received the text from his older sister, Miri, on his way to the resort's restaurant Friday evening. She'd copied their youngest sibling, Mel. Miri was the last person to get on his case about relaxing. Max paused to respond to her message.

When was the last time you & Odell took a break? Oh. Right. Your honeymoon 4 yrs ago. Farmers market tomorrow. Should be fun.

Miri responded with the eye-rolling emoji. Sounds like work.

Max chuckled, then put his cell on Mute before dropping it in his front pants pocket. He continued to the restaurant, Annabeth, where he was meeting Adam for dinner. Despite their demanding careers, they'd stayed close after graduation through calls, videoconferencing, emails, texts and occasional greeting cards. But it had been too many years since they'd seen each other in person.

He walked into the five-star restaurant and took a moment to enjoy the image of the vast, free-form pool with the stunning mountain ridge beyond. Every view of the mountains from the resort was gorgeous. He believed Alexis when she said the sights never got old.

The restaurant was quiet and classy with low lighting and white linens. As with the rest of the resort, the decor was tasteful and minimalistic with bamboo ceilings and flooring. The area was spacious but gave a sense of intimacy.

The kitchen was also in this building. Adam had told him it prepared the meals for the restaurant, pool service and any private meals guests might request be delivered to their bungalows, including the resort's signature champagne breakfast. Curiosity drove Max forward, eager to get a glimpse of the kitchen. A large hand caught his upper arm, stopping him in his tracks.

Adam's voice was thick with amusement. "I promise to give you a personal tour of the kitchen. But would you mind if we ate first? I'm really hungry."

"Adam, it's good to see you." Max returned his friend's embrace. "It's been too long."

"Yes, it has." Adam gave him a chiding look. "And I don't want to make it even longer by having to search for you in the kitchen."

"I don't know what you're talking about." Max stepped back to get a better look at his former college roommate. "The video chats aren't as good as speaking face-to-face. You're aging well."

In his tan business suit, Adam looked as fit as he'd been in college. A couple of inches shorter than Max, Adam was broad-shouldered but lanky. His deep blue eyes and tousled blond hair had attracted a lot of attention around NYU, but he'd only had eyes for his college sweetheart, Paige Barnes.

Adam briefly squeezed Max's shoulder. "You look *exactly* the same."

Max saw beyond the smile and worried about the fatigue and strain on Adam's tanned features. "You look stressed and hungry. Let's eat, then you can tell me what's on your mind."

Adam's broad brow creased. "I'm fine."

Max arched an eyebrow. "Try that on someone who hasn't known you for almost two decades. We roomed together for four of those years. I can read the signs."

Their host appeared. After greeting them, he led them to a window booth toward the center of the room. From that position, they could see the entire restaurant. Max wondered whether this was Adam's regular table.

After settling into his seat, Adam opened the menu but didn't look at it. "One of my concerns is the threatening message that came with the unmarked package that was waiting for you at the registration desk."

Max shouldn't have been surprised that Adam had been apprised of the situation. He looked up from his menu. "Roland told you?"

"He and Alexis." Adam's frown deepened. "You'd told me about the break-ins, but you didn't tell me the thief was stalking you. Should you hire security until this person's caught?"

"I live in a supposedly secure building." Max laid his menu down. "I was going to move before this trip, but my family thought I should take some time to relax first since moving is stressful."

"They're right." Adam hesitated. "I'll have one of our security guards accompany you when you're off-site."

Max started shaking his head before Adam finished speaking. "We don't have to go that far. This is a working vacation. The only time I'll be off-site is when I go to the farmers market. The rest of the time, I plan to be in your resort's kitchen."

"Are you sure?" Adam didn't seem sold on the plan.

"Yes. But if I change my mind, I'll let you know."

Their server arrived to take their drink orders. They both asked for iced teas.

"Now tell me what else is on your mind." Max lowered his voice. "Is it your mother's remembrance?"

Annabeth Colton had died seventeen years ago this coming Sunday. Adam had been fourteen. Since he was the oldest, he had the clearest recollections of Annabeth and did his best to share them with his siblings to help keep her spirit alive.

Annabeth had been buried in a secluded section of Mariposa Resort & Spa. She'd loved the resort and had helped create wonderful memories here for her children. During the Colton siblings' remembrance ceremony, they went to her grave site together and placed bouquets of mariposas, their mother's favorite flower, on her grave.

Adam's shoulders rose and fell as he drew a deep breath. "This time of year is always difficult for Laura, Josh and me. And somehow my father always manages to find a way to make it even harder."

"What do you mean?" Max braced himself for the bad news.

Adam hesitated as though gathering his thoughts. "My father's lost all his money. He's trying to raise cash by taking the resort away from us."

Max's eyes widened with shock. He hadn't expected any of that. He reeled from the news that Clive Colton was broke. But the fact he would try to take away the legacy his children's mother had left for them made his skin burn with anger.

He struggled to clear his mind. "How could your father do that? I thought your mother specifically entrusted you, Laura and Joshua with the resort?"

"She did." Anger simmered in Adam's blue eyes. He masked it when their server arrived with their drinks and took their orders.

Max had been looking forward to the meal from this five-star restaurant but now he'd be satisfied with a sandwich—made with fresh bread. He was much more interested in what Adam had to say and with what was going on with the resort, his friend's first love. Adam had started making plans for Mariposa's future while they were still in college. Maybe before that.

Shortly after they'd graduated, Adam had relocated to Sedona and taken legal control of the resort—at the cost of his personal life, including a future with Paige. He'd become general manager in addition to equal partner with Laura and Joshua. Laura was the resort's assistant manager and Joshua was the activities director.

Adam had dedicated his life to Mariposa. He'd put business before pleasure time and time again. His efforts and sacrifices had paid off spectacularly. Mariposa's unique location, stellar reputation and spectacular security allowed for a very private and highly sought-after experience for its wealthy clientele. And Clive wanted to take it away from him and his siblings.

Adam continued. "My father's the head of Colton Textiles."

"I remember. It's an elite importer."

Adam took a sip of his drink. "He's run his business into the ground. He can't pay the bills. He's laid off almost a third of his staff but even that hasn't helped his bottom line. The company's on the verge of bankruptcy. The only thing that might save Colton Textiles—or at least delay the inevitable—is a large influx of cash."

Max swallowed some of his iced tea, hoping to dislodge the knot of anger from his throat. "Is that where you, Laura and Joshua come in?"

"Yes." Adam ran the tips of his fingers over his glass. "My father came to me about a month ago to ask for a loan."

When Adam paused again, Max prompted, "But you knew if you gave him a *loan*, you'd never see that money again. And, even more importantly, he'd keep coming back for future *loans*."

Hence Adam's reference to Clive's cash influx only staving off the inevitable. Max had heard rumors in the business industry that Clive's father-in-law and his deceased wife had been the real geniuses behind the fabric import company.

Adam took a drink of his iced tea. "You're right. That's exactly what I'm afraid would happen. But when I refused to give him money—let's call it what it is—he showed me the land ownership papers for Mariposa. The land our resort is built on is held in trust by none other than Colton Textiles."

"Then whoever owns the company owns the land." Max watched Adam's nod of agreement. "How is that possible? Your mother wouldn't leave the property to your father, at least not without telling you."

Adam grunted. "I don't think she knew. My father admitted to sneaking the provision into paperwork my mother had signed while she was ill. Even then, seventeen years ago, he'd known he'd need money to help save his company."

"That was low." Max modified his language. His friend

was already hurting. He didn't want to pile onto Adam's pain with the string of obscenities pounding against his skull.

"That's one way of describing it." Adam stared into his glass.

Max rubbed the tension from the frown between his eyebrows. "Can you buy him out?" He knew it was a futile question. If the Colton siblings were in a position to buy the land from their father, his friend would have led with that.

Adam shook his head, confirming Max's suspicions. "We can't afford the price he's named. It's a huge amount and he's not negotiating. Our only hope is to go into partnership with another business. Laura, Josh and I are looking for a company capable of purchasing half ownership of the resort. This will give us the cash we need to buy the property from my father. But we want a company that will still allow us to have control of the resort."

"A silent partner." Max shook his head, heartbroken for his friend. "I'm so sorry, Adam."

"So am I." Adam sighed. "The situation's not ideal. It's not what we want or what we ever imagined happening, but it's better than losing the resort, which is what would happen because Clive is definitely not playing fair."

An understatement. Max leaned into the table. "How can I help?"

Chapter Four

"Suz and I have been to Out with Friends during our trips to New York a few years ago." Alexis's mother's voice swung with enthusiasm. "We didn't see Max, though. Such a pity. We're planning another trip to New York in the fall. Maybe we'll see him then. What's he like?"

Alexis and her mother, Catherine Allen-Reed, were clearing the dishes after their regular Sunday dinner at her mother's home.

Catherine's question tugged Alexis from her thoughts. Today was March 16, the anniversary of Annabeth Colton's death. Laura had been twelve years old when her mother had died of pancreatic cancer seventeen years ago. Laura, Adam and Joshua would have held their annual private remembrance ceremony for their mother that morning. Today was the only day of the year the three siblings took off from work. How were they?

A ridiculous question. Alexis's father had died from cancer when she was seven. Her sister had been killed by a distracted driver a year after that. Their deaths were hurts that never went away. But loved ones made the pain a little easier to bear.

Alexis gave Catherine an indulgent smile. Her mother was a huge fan of the celebrity chef. "Mom, you know I can't talk about the resort's guests. In fact, I shouldn't have told you Max was staying at Mariposa."

Her mother looked much younger than her sixty years. A couple of times, they'd been mistaken for sisters. They were about the same height. Catherine managed to look both stylish and casual in a loose-fitting pale rose blouse and slim black jeans. Her mother's active lifestyle kept her fit and strong. Her still-dark raven hair was styled in a simple bob that framed her smooth, delicate golden-brown features.

"Don't worry. I haven't told anyone else, not even Suz." Catherine waved a slender dismissive hand. Her bright hazel eyes, which Alexis had inherited, sparkled. "But surely, you can tell me just a little bit. Is he nice? Polite? Does he have a good sense of humor?"

Suzanne Moore was her mother's best friend. They'd been close all Alexis's life. Suz had been a rock for her and her mother during her father's long illness and death. The two women had become inseparable after Alexis's older sister, Kaitlin, and Aunt Suz's husband had died. Suzanne's only child, Jacob, was one of Alexis's best friends.

"He's very nice." Alexis remembered his touch as he'd helped her out of the van. "And very polite. His parents raised him well."

She stiffened at the memory of the threatening note. She wouldn't tell her mother about that, though. It would be an invasion of Max's privacy, which was taboo at the resort. The Colton siblings as well as their employees signed nondisclosure agreements to secure their guests' confidentiality.

"Ah." Catherine started the dishwasher. "That's encouraging. He seems polite on his show but one never knows whether it's just an act. You know I've never missed an episode of *Cooking for Friends*."

Cooking for Friends was the only cooking show her mother watched and she was obsessed. Although she recorded each episode, she still arranged her schedule to avoid conflicts with the live viewing. On more than one occasion, she and Aunt Suz had hosted watch parties and invited their friends. Alexis couldn't think of a single program that inspired as much commitment from her parent.

"I know, Mom." Alexis dried the last pan and stored it in the cabinet under the sink. "You talk about Max's show all the time. How could I *not* know? You're such a foodie. But why don't you ever try his recipes during our Sunday dinners?"

"Because sadly, they would be wasted on you." Catherine sniffed. "Your idea of fine dining is thin-crust pizza."

"I love the way you know me." Alexis wrapped her right arm around her mother's slim waist to give her a quick hug. "I much prefer your home cooking or a basket of burger and fries to a spoonful of tiny food I can't pronounce."

"Where did I go wrong?" Catherine led Alexis into her living room. They settled next to each other on the off-white, fluffy sofa. "Now you know why I save the fancy cooking for my dinner parties with Suz and the other ladies."

Once a month, her mother, Suz and four other women, all foodie friends from church, took turns hosting a dinner party. The ladies had been getting together for decades. The events gave these like-minded single mothers an opportunity to try elaborate recipes and share investment advice, career guidance, retirement strategies and parenting tips.

"You know, Suz and I will be eligible for early retirement in a couple of years." Catherine's cautious tone and change of subject put Alexis on alert. It was unusual for her blunt-speaking mother to weigh her words.

"That's exciting, Mom. I'm happy for both of you." She searched Catherine's expression for a hint of the direction this conversation would take. "You'll have a lot more time for your trips. Maybe you could travel abroad, too."

"That's true. You know how much I love to travel." There it was again, that hesitation in Catherine's voice. "And international trips would be exciting. We were also considering possibly relocating."

"Relocating?" Alexis blinked. "You and Aunt Suz are thinking of leaving Sedona? When? Why? Does Jake know?" If Jake knew and hadn't told her, the two of them would have to have words.

"It's just a possibility, Lexi. Nothing's definite." Catherine took Alexis's hands in her own. "Suz and I wanted both of you to have plenty of notice that this was something we're thinking about doing."

She held her mother's hands a little tighter. "But why would you leave Sedona?"

Her family's roots grew deep in Sedona. Her parents had been born and raised here. They'd gotten married and started a family here. Alexis and her mother had buried her father and then her sister here. This was home.

Catherine gave her a gentle smile. The expression showed she understood how difficult change was for her daughter. "I agree Sedona is lovely. Suz and I have enjoyed raising our children here. But there are a lot of places that are just as lovely. A few are even lovelier and have more to offer. Some of them are close to the water. We want to allow ourselves the freedom to at least consider moving to one of those other places."

Alexis released her mother's hands and leaned into her embrace. "You're right, Mom. You and Aunt Suz deserve the freedom to pursue whatever makes you happy—as long as it's within the law."

Catherine chuckled, just as Alexis had intended.

She kissed her mother's cheek. "Thanks for giving me the heads-up."

Catherine gave Alexis a big hug before letting go. "Of course, dear."

Her mother's condo had an open floor plan with an abundance of natural light. As the sun set, Alexis rose to help her mother close the faux blond wood blinds around the living and dining rooms.

"You should experience Max's restaurant at least once." Catherine spoke over her shoulder as she closed the blinds behind the sofa. "He and his staff create dishes that bring foodies from all over the world to his upscale restaurants in Manhattan and Fort Lauderdale. And that was before he started his cooking show on that streaming channel."

Alexis closed the blinds near the fireplace. "It's probably even harder to get a table now."

"I'm sure it is." Catherine sounded as cheerful as though she benefited from Max's success. "His show has developed into almost a cult favorite. He has so much energy and enthusiasm."

"Really?" Alexis wondered whether she should start tuning in. She usually found cooking shows boring with a capital *B*. Maybe Max would change her mind. Or maybe she was making excuses to look at him without his being aware of it.

Did that sound creepy? Maybe a bit.

Her mother was still talking. "He's been getting a lot of traffic on the internet. And he's made appearances on talk shows and morning news programs. His cookbook's going to fly off the shelves. I can't wait to preorder it."

"How do you know about his internet traffic?" Was her mother tracking him, too?

Catherine either didn't hear Alexis's question or she chose to ignore it. "There's a lot of gossip about his personal life. Columnists and celebrity watchers are trying to start rumors about who he's dating but they haven't been able to connect him with anyone. There was a brief mention of perhaps something going on between him and his assistant, but I don't think those rumors lasted even a day."

A frown tightened Alexis's brow. She swallowed the denial in her throat. "There were rumors about a relationship between Max and Sarah Harris?"

Catherine's eyes widened with surprise. "How do you know Max's assistant?"

Alexis shook her head to clear her thoughts. "It's resort stuff, Mom. I can't talk about it."

"I understand, Lexi. The resort's guests pay a lot for their privacy. Although sometimes I wonder whether you work for some national spy agency." Catherine rolled her eyes as she returned to the sofa. "At the end of last year, an anonymous source had started a rumor that Max was involved in a *very personal* relationship with Sarah, who's a married woman, by the way. There wasn't anything to substantiate the gossip, no photos of the two of them together in public. There weren't any photos of the two of them working together, either. So as quickly as the rumors started, *poof*, they also died down." She snapped her fingers.

Alexis sat on the sofa, shifting to face her mother. "Perhaps someone from Max's organization tracked the source of the rumors and put an end to them."

She'd heard of the rich and famous having the resources to do that sort of thing. Thinking about Max's encounter with Sarah at the L, she was certain there wasn't anything romantic between them. Sarah had thrown herself—literally—into Max's arms when she'd seen him, but he'd quickly untangled himself from her embrace. According to Clarissa, he hadn't sounded pleased at Sarah's arrival, either. That was the reason the registration desk clerk had contacted Alexis about the situation. She'd wanted backup in case Sarah became disruptive, which she had. Kudos to Clarissa for planning ahead.

"It's possible Max had someone shut down the rumors." Catherine shrugged a negligent shoulder. "But I've read on the internet that Max's fame has brought *a lot* of gossip and fans who have very little respect for his personal boundaries."

Was Max's increasing celebrity the reason the stalker had latched onto him? It made sense. She and the rest of the resort staff would have to be aware of that possibility. They'd hosted high-profile guests before but, to her knowledge, they'd never had a stalker follow that guest or contact them at the resort. Fortunately, their security was tight. Although there weren't any security cameras on the grounds—again for the benefit of their guests' treasured privacy—Mariposa had guards on duty 24/7/365.

They'd have to remain vigilant for Max's sake—as well as the rest of their guests.

"MAX? MAX! I thought that was you."

The familiar female voice commanded Alexis's attention as she and Max crossed a four-lane street in downtown Sedona early Monday morning. She located Sarah Harris, waving at them from the curb they were approaching. Behind Sarah was the entrance to the Sedona Family and Community Farmers Market. Alexis's heart sank but her professionalism kept her shoulders squared and her brow smooth.

Today, Sarah's bright red hair fell in large, loopy curls to her chin. A slight breeze teased it. A knee-length old gold dress hugged her full figure. Max stepped up to the curb. Immediately, Sarah wrapped her arms around his neck.

Alexis's eyes widened in surprise. She stepped to the side to give them a semblance of privacy.

Max gently freed himself from her embrace. He circled Sarah and put an arm's length between them. He looked uncomfortable as he adjusted his dark sunglasses and black ball cap. "Sarah, hi. This is a surprise."

"I know, right?" Sarah stood with her back to the street. She held on to his hands. "Although I should've guessed you'd be here since you'd need to buy ingredients for your recipes."

Max tugged his hands free and gestured toward Alexis. "You remember Alexis Reed, the senior concierge with Mariposa."

Alexis could have done without Max drawing the other woman's attention to her.

Sarah's expression went from open and friendly to closed and hostile in a New York minute. "Of course."

Alexis inclined her head. "Good morning, Ms.—"

Sarah turned back to Max, effectively cutting Alexis off. Her pale, round face glowed with warmth and admiration. "Since we're both here together, I'll help you collect the ingredients you need. It'll be fun."

Alexis struggled not to let her temper at Sarah's dismissal show. It wasn't easy. If she strained a muscle during the effort, she'd file a worker's compensation claim.

"That's not necessary." Max inclined his head toward

Alexis. His eyes were masked behind his shades' dark lenses. "Alexis is helping me."

Through her own sunglasses, Alexis watched a frown roll quickly across Sarah's face. It disappeared like a computer glitch. In contrast, it was hard to read Max's expression since his ball cap and shades obstructed his features. Did the celebrity chef realize Sarah had a crush on him?

"Nonsense." Sarah's laughter was forced. Alexis was sure of it. "*I'm* your assistant. Of course *I'll* assist you. It's *my* job."

Alexis expected Max to acquiesce to Sarah. She was preparing to be sent back to Mariposa. Disappointment tightened the muscles in her back and shoulders. Was it resentment at the thought of being set aside like damaged luggage after she'd gone to the trouble of adjusting her schedule to accommodate Max's needs? Or could it be envy at the thought of the other woman spending time with Max? She tried to deny it to herself, but the truth was part of her had spent the weekend looking forward to showing Max around the market this morning. She stepped toward the crosswalk, ready to make as gracious an exit as possible.

Max's words stopped her. "The show's on hiatus, Sarah. I've made other arrangements for my needs but thank you for your offer." He stepped closer to Alexis, lightly resting his hand on the small of her back. "Please excuse us."

Apparently, Sarah wasn't one to take no for an answer, at least not the first time. Instead, she moved to block them. She put her hand on Max's shoulder. "If you're working on recipes for the show, I'd like to be a part of that, Max. Please. Don't shut me out. Working with you while we're both here will be good for me. It will help keep my mind off the other issue I'm dealing with."

Her last statement caught Alexis's attention. Max had

told her Sarah was going through a difficult time. Alexis should make a greater effort to be more patient and understanding toward the other woman.

Max stepped back, startling Alexis from her thoughts and breaking his connection with both her and Sarah. "Spend time with your family, Sarah. That's why you're here. At a time like this, you need their support."

Sarah rolled her eyes. Frustration poured off her. "My family's getting on my nerves. What I need is some time away from them." She fixed a pretty smile on her face. "You promised me a drink. When are we going to get together?"

Alexis's head was spinning from Sarah's rapid mood swings. She'd moved briskly through flirtatious, wheedling and frustration all while anger simmered right beneath the surface.

Max sighed. "I'll call you once I have a better idea of my schedule. In the meantime, get some rest, Sarah. You need to take care of yourself."

Sarah split a look between Alexis and Max. Her eyes were dark with resentment. After a brief pause, she nodded. "All right. I'll wait for your call, but don't make me wait too long." She gave him a tight smile before moving to the corner. Her gait was stiff.

Max's warm hand settled again on the small of Alexis's back. "I'm sorry to have taken up so much of your time with those negotiations. Sarah means well."

Alexis shook her head. "Please don't worry about it. It was nice of Sarah to offer to help you. Have the two of you worked together long?"

Max walked with her toward the collection of temporary booths, tables and tents that comprised the farmers market.

"For a little more than two years. I hired her as my assistant for the show. She helped us get the project up and running."

"That's wonderful." From his tone, Alexis was certain he had no idea of his assistant's personal interest in him. It was so obvious, though. How could he miss it?

They entered the main market area. As always, Alexis was transported by the sights, sounds and smells of the vendors' products. It was crowded today, although not as packed as it had been yesterday when she and her mother had bought produce for the week.

At one of the vendor booths, Alexis lifted a packet of strawberries. She held it close to her face. The sweet, juicy fragrance filled her senses. She closed her eyes and allowed herself a moment to enjoy the experience.

She didn't have her mother's love of fussy little meals served on ridiculously large plates for exorbitant amounts of money, but she did share Catherine's love of fresh, organic fruits and vegetables. Alexis breathed the ripe clementines and grapefruits that surrounded her. Scallions, garlic, chili and cayenne woke her senses. The crisp, clean scents of broccoli and carrots made her mouth water.

"From your glowing expression and the bounce in your step, I have the feeling you've been here a time or two before." Max's gentle teasing was like a hug.

Alexis laughed to cover her discomfort. She hadn't meant to let her professional mask slip so far. "My mother and I come here every week in season. We love it. What do you think of it?"

Max wore a plain black T-shirt and smoke-gray shorts. Alexis wondered if he thought those clothes, in addition to his sunglasses and ball cap, would allow him to blend into the crowd. If so, he was mistaken. The simple clothes drew attention to his tall, leanly muscled physique. Nearby shoppers were giving him second and even third looks. Max either hadn't noticed or he was pretending not to.

"I think produce that elicits a reaction like yours must be worth its weight in gold." He tossed her a smile and extended his hand. "May I get those strawberries for you?"

Alexis's fingertips itched to trace the deep dimple in his right cheek. His teeth were perfect. His deep voice wrapped itself around her, inviting her to… What had he asked her?

Alexis stepped back to clear her thoughts. Her laughter was even more nervous and embarrassed this time. "Thank you but I can handle the strawberries. I'm here to help with your cookbook recipes. Remember? What can I help you look for?"

Stop mooning over the man!

This wasn't a social outing. Mariposa's general manager himself had assigned her to help one of their many high-profile guests with a work project. Completing this task satisfactorily would provide another example of the exceptional service she offered the resort's guests and would be one more step toward proving herself deserving of a promotion to a management position, specifically the event manager's job.

Besides, Mariposa had hosted plenty of attractive celebrities: actors, models, singers, athletes. Alexis had never lost focus before. What made this guest different?

Her eyes moved from his clean, chiseled features to his long, lean physique.

Exactly.

Max shifted to face the produce. His stance brought him closer to her. Alexis recognized his fresh-mint scent above the smells of the fruits and vegetables. Was it his cologne, aftershave, deodorant, soap?

"This cookbook is the first in a series I've proposed, putting regional twists on fine-dining favorites, sort of like Manhattan clam chowder and New England clam chowder, or the one thousand and one ways to make mac 'n' cheese."

"That sounds interesting." Alexis approached the produce vendor and paid with cash for the strawberries.

"Thanks. I hope it will be." Max paused in front of a display of limes. He lifted one from the basket and gently squeezed it.

Alexis studied his sharp sienna features softened by full lips and wished she could draw.

Max turned and met her eyes. "Think fast."

Alexis gasped as a small lime cut through the short distance between them, flying toward her face. She caught it inches from her nose with both hands. Max burst into laughter.

She gaped at the celebrity chef. "Suppose I'd dropped it?" She sent the vendor an apologetic look. He forgave them with a wave.

"I'd have been embarrassed for you, but I would've paid for it." Still chuckling, he turned back to the produce. "Luckily, you have good reflexes." He selected more limes and added asparagus, a red onion and herbs. He handled the onion while giving her a considering look. "Think—"

"Don't." Alexis held up her left index finger.

Max shrugged, but his eyes twinkled with mischief. He paid for his items before leading her to another spice vendor. "And we're off."

Alexis's muscles remained on high alert. She hadn't expected this playful side to the soon-to-be published author. Was this his personality or were the scents of the farmers market making him giddy? She was beginning to suspect the sweet aromas of the fruit and the tangy scents of the vegetable were having an effect on her—although she never felt this way when she came to the market with her mother.

She watched Max touch and feel the coriander leaves. "What are you making?"

His lips curved into a smile. The teasing lilt in his voice invited her to join his game. "It's a secret."

That was disappointing. "Could I at least have a hint?"

He handed the herb vendor a credit card to pay for the cumin, mustard and coriander. "Nope."

She was more deflated than she'd thought she'd be. "All right, Chef. What about protein? Do we need the fish or meat market? Or both?"

Max took his purchases and his credit card receipt, then allowed Alexis to lead him from the table. "The Annabeth chef said she'd buy extra meats for me. I asked her to add whatever I use to my bill."

Alexis led Max out of the consumer pedestrian traffic before facing him. "Then I guess we're done."

Max patted her shoulder as he shook his head. "No, young padawan, we've only just begun."

Alexis arched an eyebrow. "Was that a *Star Wars* reference?"

He smiled with pleasure. "Yes, it was."

Shaking her head, Alexis walked past him and toward the crosswalk. With her back to Max, she freed the grin she'd been holding back since they'd started shopping. What a nerd. She could understand why Sarah had fallen for him.

LESS THAN HALF an hour later, Alexis pulled into the parking lot in front of the L. Max wanted to get right to work on the recipe he was creating for his cookbook. Alexis felt the excitement shimmering around him as he sat on the passenger seat of her silver four-door sedan. He hadn't told her anything about the dish. Instead, they'd talked about Sedona and Mariposa. She'd described the advantages of the resort's proximity to Red Rock State Park, which was on the outskirts of the city. The park was close enough to allow Mariposa to benefit from its bird-watching and hiking trails. For those guests who occasionally wanted to venture off the property, Sedona was renowned for its New Age shops and its vibrant arts community, which supported a number of wonderful art galleries.

As Alexis pulled into a parking space near the front of the lot, she locked eyes with Mark Bower, the resort's recently fired concierge. He stood to the right of the L's entrance. Alexis suspected he was waiting to confront her. Her suspicion was confirmed when he straightened away from the building as she and Max emerged from her car.

Mark strode toward her. His steps were long and determined. The late Monday morning sun touched his sandy-blond hair. "Alexis, I want to talk to you."

Beside her, Max stiffened at Mark's aggressive tone. She turned to him. "I'm sorry, but may I ask you to wait for me in the lobby? I won't be long."

Max stared at Mark as though memorizing his description for a police report before facing Alexis. He'd taken off his shades. His beautiful brown eyes were dark with concern. "I can stay."

Mark frowned at Max's words. "This is a private conversation."

Ignoring Mark, Max repeated his offer. "Do you want me to stay?"

He was offering her a choice, which was empowering. She chose to let Mark know she didn't regret her actions. "No, but thank you. I won't be long."

Max took a moment, searching her expression. Alexis gave him a confident smile. She didn't have anything to worry about. She wouldn't speak for Mark.

Max finally nodded his acceptance of her decision. He gave Mark a deliberate look as he stepped past the other man. But instead of entering L, Max stationed himself three stingy strides from Mark. He was far enough to give them privacy but close enough to intervene, if necessary.

Alexis returned her attention to Mark. "Why are you here?"

Anger snapped in his green eyes. "Why do you think? I want my job back."

Mariposa paid generous salaries. It wasn't a surprise Mark wanted to return to his position with the resort. He'd realized he wouldn't be able to get another job in hospitality that paid nearly as well.

Alexis strained to keep her voice even. "You're no longer eligible to work at Mariposa. I removed you from your position on Friday for cause."

"You mean you fired me." A flush filled his thin, fair features. He flicked his right index finger straight up. "I made *one* mistake, and you fired me. Just *one*."

Alexis's mind still reeled when she considered what she'd found during her investigation into Mark's transgressions. Her body shook with something stronger than fury. "You made that *one* mistake over and over and over again. If I hadn't overheard you, you would have continued to make it."

It had been Alexis's responsibility to tell Laura that someone Alexis had hired had scammed their guests. Her skin burned with embarrassment. Laura had commended her on the way she'd handled the situation, but Alexis still felt guilty. There never should have been a situation to handle.

"I told you I wouldn't do it again." He stood several inches above her. "It's not as though anyone got hurt."

Alexis's eyes widened with disbelief. He still hadn't digested the magnitude of his betrayal even after she'd laid it out for him in painstaking detail during their meeting with the personnel director Friday afternoon.

She unclenched her teeth. "Mark, you violated the trust our guests put in us. You broke the trust the resort put in you. You've lost my trust completely."

"But—"

Alexis was too angry to listen. "Your job was to get tickets to events, concerts and shows for our guests. You were supposed to make reservations for them at restaurants and theaters. Simple. Straightforward." She fisted her hands to keep her body from shaking apart with anger. "You receive a salary way above the industry average to provide those simple and straightforward tasks for our guests. But you decided on your own to upcharge them directly for your services."

Mark's nostrils flared. "They didn't seem to mind."

Alexis saw red. "You took advantage of our guests. As Leticia and I reminded you Friday, during your orientation, you were told such actions were grounds for immediate termination. It's also in your employee handbook."

"I want my job back." Mark stepped forward, shouting at Alexis. "Now."

Alexis didn't back down. But before she could respond, Max's back appeared in front of her.

"Back. Off." The chef's impossibly broad shoulders blocked Mark from her view.

"You need to mind your business." Mark sounded less than certain.

"You need to mind your manners." Max's body radiated the heat from his temper.

Alexis stepped out from behind him. "Mark, I've made myself clear. The Coltons signed off on your dismissal. HR processed your termination. You're no longer employed by this resort. You're not welcome on this property. Leave. Now."

Mark looked from Max to Alexis. "We're not done."

"Yes." Alexis held his eyes. "We are." She took a breath to clear her head. "If you're seen on these grounds again, security will escort you off and I'll file the police report for trespassing myself."

She watched Mark turn and stomp his way across the parking lot to a cherry red pickup truck. It looked fully loaded. What were the payments on that thing? No wonder he was agitated about losing his job. Her muscles were still shaking with anger as she watched Mark climb into the truck's cab and drive off at a speed way above the limit.

"Are you all right?" Max's question refocused her attention.

She faced him. "I appreciate your concern, Max. But there was no need for you to intervene. I can take care of myself."

His frown eased. "I'm sure you can. That doesn't mean I'm going to stand by and do nothing when I see someone being attacked by a bully. What's his issue? He doesn't seem like an ex-boyfriend."

Alexis's eyes stretched wide with incredulity. "He's not. He's an ex-employee who wants his job back. You heard me. That's not going to happen."

Max nodded. "I see. What did he do?"

Alexis turned to lead him into the L. "It's a resort issue."

"I understand." He offered her a smile. "I admire your discretion. I'm sure all your guests do." Max sobered. "But, Alexis, he's furious and he's threatened you. Promise me you'll be careful."

His concern touched her heart. Alexis nodded. "I promise."

Max shook his head as he matched his strides to hers. "First, I receive a threat and less than a week later, you receive one, too. What are the odds?"

Alexis shivered with foreboding. She would think those odds would be slim to none.

Chapter Five

"Lunch is served." Max's voice rang out from Alexis's office doorway early Monday afternoon.

She looked up from her paperwork. Max had covered his black T-shirt with a navy blue chef's smock. The color warmed the sienna tones of his skin. Her eyes dropped to the food trolley he'd wheeled across her threshold. It held two place settings.

"Wait. What's all this?" Alexis suspected she already knew the answer to that question. Beneath those silver domes were the meals Max had created using his new recipes.

"Your lunch." He removed the first cloche with a flourish. "Dry-rub chicken breast with grilled asparagus." Bright lights danced in his eyes.

Alexis pulled her attention from the chef and switched it to their lunch. A row of thinly sliced grilled chicken breasts were beautifully arranged in the center of the very large plain white porcelain plate. Asparagus spears, seasoned and grilled, lay across their width. The steam billowing up from the plate filled Alexis's office with the scents of chili, cilantro and mustard.

The meal smelled wonderful and looked tempting. It seemed moist, well-seasoned and hot. But Alexis's mind brought an image of her homemade Italian sub on whole grain bread served with a dill pickle spear and a bag of barbecue potato chips. She'd made the lunch with the fresh ingredients she'd bought from the farmers market yesterday. That had to count for something.

She stood from her desk. "Oh, wow. Thank you so much." She gestured toward the plate. "Your presentation is so beautiful. I'm really impressed."

"Thank you." Max grinned. "I hope you enjoy the meal." He gestured over his shoulder toward the small Plexiglas-and-sterling-silver conversation table behind him. "Do you mind if I set up over there?"

Alexis blinked. He was going to eat with her. Of course he was. There were two settings. *Duh.*

She placed her palms flat on her desktop to keep from wringing her hands. "I didn't realize you were cooking for me."

"Of course. We're in this together." Max transferred the place settings to her table without waiting for her reply. "I want your feedback on the recipes before I finalize them for the cookbook."

He what? Oh, my. Adam hadn't said anything about that.

Alexis hurried around her desk toward him. Her palm landed on the back of his hand as he reached for the second plate. The heat from his body rose up her arm and settled in her chest. Alexis couldn't move. She couldn't speak. Max stilled and lifted his eyes to hers. Seconds felt like minutes. She took an awkward step back, breaking their contact.

Her voice was husky to her ears. "The thing is, I'm not really into fancy foods. I'm more of a tacos-and-chips kind of person. Perhaps Laura would make a better taste tester for your recipes."

Max straightened, shaking his head. His eyes were full

of questions she didn't want to read. "You've lived in this area all your life. I trust your feedback to help me with the regional flavors in my recipes."

Alexis couldn't think of an excuse that wouldn't make her seem churlish. Accepting defeat, she settled into the chair beside her. "All right. But I'll have you know, I eat meals that aren't specifically regional, too. In fact, I brought an Italian sub and barbecue chips for lunch."

"That's good to know. It shows you enjoy variety." Max spread the white linen napkin across his lap.

Alexis did the same, then sliced into the chicken breast. The knife slipped through the poultry as though it were cutting melted butter. It freed more spices: peppers, paprika and brown sugar. She took a bite. Cayenne, garlic and kosher salt teased her taste buds. The chicken melted in her mouth.

She closed her eyes in delight. "Mmm. Delicious."

"Really?" He sounded skeptical. He cut a slice of the chicken.

Alexis's eyes popped open. "Really." But she could tell he didn't believe her. "My mother's a big fan of your cooking. She's been to your restaurant in New York and has watched every episode of your show at least twice. She and her friends try your recipes during their monthly dinner parties."

"Alexis." He gently interrupted her nervous chatter. "What's wrong with the food? I can tell you're holding back. This cookbook is very important to me. I'd appreciate your honest reaction no matter how hard it might be to hear."

Alexis sighed and set down her silverware. "There isn't anything *wrong* with your food. It's just that, if you're going for a Southwestern style, you're not quite there. Yet."

"All right." Max leaned into the table. "How far off am I and what do I have to do to hit the target?"

Alexis selected an asparagus spear with her fork and held it up. "First, your choice of side. Asparagus doesn't really say 'Southwest.' It says 'California' or 'Washington.' Maybe 'New York.' In any case, it's more reminiscent of the coasts than the Southwest. You may be trying to add a twist to your recipe with the seasonings and the style of cooking, but when I see asparagus spears with a Southwestern meal, I think the chef hasn't made a connection with the region. It's like cosplay on a plate."

"That's a good point." Max inclined his head. "What else?"

Alexis saw the intensity in his gaze. Being the focus of his attention made her restless. "The seasonings. You're giving me a sample of the heat, but Southwestern cooking packs more of a punch. You need to really pour it on."

"This is great feedback. Exactly what I need to know. I'll go back to the drawing board and try again." Max picked up his knife and fork, and sliced more of the chicken breast.

"Please, not on my behalf." Alexis looked at him in dismay. "I'm not the audience you're cooking for."

"You're exactly the audience I want—people who love Southwestern cooking."

Alexis studied the entrée. It looked wonderful, smelled delicious and tasted great. She just wasn't into fancy meals and expensive restaurants. She preferred taco shacks and bar food, places where she didn't have to wonder which fork to use or wine to choose. Give her a highly caffeinated, carbonated beverage and she was good to go. She returned her attention to Max. She enjoyed visiting his world, but she preferred living in hers.

She lowered her silverware with a sigh. "Let's be honest, Max. With all due respect, I would probably never go to your restaurant."

Max cocked his head, giving her a curious half smile. "Why not?"

Alexis used her hands to illustrate her points. "In my experience, upscale restaurants serve you a little bit of food." She held her hands inches apart. "Then present you with a great big bill." She increased the distance between her palms. "If I'm going to spend that much money on a meal, I want to leave feeling full."

Max chuckled. "We'll have to agree to disagree."

"If we disagree, why do you want me to be your recipe tester?"

"Because you've presented me with a challenge, and I can never back down from one." The look in his dark eyes made her pulse skip.

Max was referring to his cooking, but Alexis was awakening to a challenge of her own. Her growing attraction to her client.

MAX LEFT HIS bungalow late Friday afternoon and went in search of Alexis. He'd seen her around the L during the week as he contrived to take breaks from his work that might coincide with her arrival to her office, her lunch breaks or her leaving work for the day. But he hadn't spoken with her since Tuesday afternoon when he'd served her his second attempt at a Southwest-inspired chicken dish. He'd incorporated her feedback, but he still hadn't won her over. Max hadn't worked this hard to impress someone with his cooking since he'd first started in his career. Alexis was shoving him out of his comfort zone. That realization brought him up short. Had he been taking the praise and rave reviews for granted? Had he lost his edge?

Arriving at her office, Max squared his shoulders, then knocked softly on her open door. Her eyes widened in surprise when she saw him. She seemed to relax when she realized he'd left the food trolley behind.

"Come in." Alexis gave him a welcoming smile. "How can I help you today?"

Max sat on the burnt-umber guest chair closest to the window in front of her white modular desk. "What are you doing tomorrow morning?"

She tilted her head. "Why?"

"I thought we could go hiking on the trails you'd told me about Monday." *I really want to spend time getting to know you.* "Consider it a thank-you for helping me with my work and giving me so much of your time."

Alexis grinned. Her full, bow-shaped lips parted over bright white teeth. "I thought the lunches you made for me Monday and Tuesday were your way of saying thank you."

Max leaned back against his seat, balancing his left ankle on his right knee. "I mean a non-work-related thank-you."

Alexis's brow furrowed but her bright eyes twinkled with amusement. "You want to thank me for giving you my time by taking up more of my time?"

This wasn't going the way he'd imagined. "Do you have other plans?"

"Actually, I do." Her bright eyes teased him as though saying, *Come strong or don't bother.*

Challenge accepted. "Let me rephrase that. Do you have other plans that can't be moved so you can go hiking with me tomorrow morning?"

"No, I don't."

"Then come hiking with me."

She still hesitated. "Max, Mariposa employees are not supposed to fraternize with our guests."

"We're not fraternizing. You're going above and beyond helping me with my work. I want to thank you. It's just a friendly hike out in the open. It'll be fun."

"All right, Max." Alexis's smile was uncertain. "A friendly hike on the open trail. I'll see you tomorrow morning."

"Great. I look forward to it." Max stood to leave before she could change her mind.

But not before he realized she'd added another challenge to his list. How was he going to get to know Alexis if spending time with her was against the rules?

"I DON'T KNOW whether it's the hike or the scenery that's taking my breath away." *Or the woman I'm hiking with.*

Max stopped beside Alexis at an overlook just off the hiking path early Saturday morning. From their vantage point, he enjoyed the majesty of their surroundings. Rich red earth covered the hiking trails and the mountains circling them. Wisps of bright white clouds streaked the wide blue sky.

"It's the scenery." Alexis moved away from him and closer to the guardrail that bordered the edge of the overlook. She shoved her hands into the front pockets of her black hiking shorts, which hugged her slim hips and displayed her long dancer's legs. Her lemon yellow T-shirt highlighted her skin's warm gold undertones. "It always takes my breath away."

Max drew a deep breath, catching the woodsy, cedar scents of the nearby foliage, which Alexis had identified as manzanita and juniper trees. They were beautiful. "You were right. I could never get tired of this view."

Alexis beamed at him from over her shoulder. Her eyes sparkled like stars. Max could gaze into them all day. A cream tennis cap helped protect her skin from the sun's rays. She'd gathered her shoulder-length raven tresses in a ponytail that waved in the mild breeze. The style emphasized her classic features, which were free of makeup. This moment would make such a beautiful photo, especially with the mountains in the distance behind her. Max had a feeling Alexis would object to having her picture taken, though, and he didn't want to make her uncomfortable.

She turned back to the overlook. Pulling her right hand from her pocket, she pointed straight ahead. "Red Rock State Park. Oak Creek cuts through it. You should visit while you're here."

He exhaled, feeling more relaxed than he had in years. "This view is therapeutic. I can better appreciate why my family's always after me to take a vacation. They were happy last night after I texted them that I was going on this hike with you this morning."

Alexis turned toward him. "You've mentioned your family's concern about your not making time to relax before. When was the last time you went on vacation?"

"It's been a while." Max rubbed the back of his neck as he tried to calculate the passage of time. "A few years, perhaps. Between the restaurant and the show and now the book contract, I've been a little busy."

Alexis tilted her head with curiosity. "Why open restaurants and do the show? It seems like just one of those enterprises would be a lot of work. You're doing both. Why not focus on just one?"

Max let his right arm drop back to his side. "I think Jay-Z put it best. I'm not a businessman. I'm a business, man."

Alexis rolled her eyes. "Still, while you're here, you should at least take a few hours each day to enjoy the resort's amenities—the spa, pool, horseback riding. It would be a waste if you didn't."

"All right." Max raised his hands in surrender. "Which ones would you recommend?"

Feigning offense, Alexis gasped, pressing her right hand to her chest. "*All* of them. As the senior concierge, I've used all the amenities so I could personally recommend them to our guests."

Max grinned at her playacting. "How long have you worked at the resort?"

"Seven years." Alexis exhaled. "I love it here. I love what the Coltons have built and I'm proud of the role I've had in it."

His senses drank in her expression. It was more than contentment. It was happiness radiating from the inside out. "My mother always repeats the maxim, 'If you do what you love, you never work a day in your life.'"

"It's true." She held his eyes. "Do you love what you do, Max?"

He didn't have to think about it. "Yes, I do. I'm exactly where I want to be, doing exactly what I want to do."

"I feel the same. But whenever I feel stressed, all I have to do is look out a window." Alexis faced the overlook. "Who could be stressed with a view like this?" She set her forearms on the guardrail.

Then everything happened so fast. Max saw the guardrail collapse beneath Alexis's touch. He saw her throw up her arms as her body tipped forward.

He heard her scream.

Before he could think—before he could breathe—he leaped forward. Max caught Alexis's wrist as she fell over the edge. He tightened his grip as he landed on the ground, coughing as he inhaled the soil.

His heart was in his throat. He swallowed it down. "I've got you." His voice was breathless.

"Oh. Oh." She was panting. Max stretched forward to get a better view of her. Alexis tipped her head back. "Don't let go." Her voice was thin with fear.

"I won't." Max's mouth went dry. Beneath Alexis was a sheer drop of several feet onto a pile of large, sharp rocks. He extended his right arm. "Give me your hand. I'll pull you up."

Her eyes widened with fear. "I don't want to pull you over."

Max forced a confident smile. "My luggage weighs more than you do. Give me your other hand."

She offered her hand. He took her wrist. He felt the tremors of fear racing up her arms. Max closed his eyes and prayed for her safety and his strength. Alexis steadied herself with her feet on the side of the hill, using her legs to push herself up as Max pulled her.

Max rocked his hips to draw himself backward. "I've got you. You're doing great."

Undergrowth dug into his thighs and torso. Rocks cut into his flesh. His shoulder muscles burned. He gritted his teeth and carried on. Her breaths were amplified in his ears.

"Just a little farther. We're almost there." *God, please don't let anything happen to her.*

Suddenly her weight was lifted from his arms. Max looked up and saw Alexis crawling toward him. He released her wrists and rose onto his knees, drawing her to him. She was shaking so hard, he thought she'd fly apart. Or maybe they were both shaking. He tightened his arms around her. Now that they were on solid ground, Max could admit—to himself at least—that he'd never been more afraid in his life.

He squeezed his eyes shut. "You're going to be all right. I've got you. You're going to be all right." He crooned the words against her ears. He didn't want to let her go.

Alexis leaned back to look up at him. Her eyes were wide. Her pupils were dilated with fear. "You saved my life." She pressed her face against his chest and tightened her arms around him.

He kissed the top of her head and held her until they both stopped shaking. Max took a deep breath, filling his senses with the faint wildflower fragrance of her perfume. He exhaled as he helped her to stand with him. Max looked her over. There were several thin scratches on her right cheek. Deeper scrapes on her right thigh, both of her knees and shins were bleeding. He saw the bruises that were starting to form on her wrists and his heart clenched.

He brushed his left hand over the marks. They were roughly the size of his fingers. "I'm so sorry."

Alexis bent her head to catch Max's eyes. "You saved my life. I can't thank you enough." Her voice quavered. She looked down at his legs. "You're hurt, too."

Max looked down at his wounds. "It's nothing. Let's get you back to the resort." He offered his left arm to steady her. "I believe the brochure says there's a medical clinic on-site."

"You're right. It's in the L." Alexis took a step forward. With a sharp hiss, she tightened her hold on his bicep.

Max glanced down at her legs. "Is it your ankle?"

"I think I twisted it." She gingerly rotated her left foot. "Yes, it feels tender."

"I'll carry you back to the car." Max bent to lift her.

Alexis stopped him with a hand on his shoulder. "I can walk, if you let me lean on you a little."

"Of course." Max wrapped his left arm around her lithe waist. "We need to get you to urgent care."

Alexis reached up to put her arm on his shoulder. She nodded her agreement but didn't look happy about it. He couldn't blame her. This wasn't the way he'd seen their day together ending. This certainly wasn't the way he'd hoped to get her into his arms.

MOVING SLOWLY IN deference to Alexis's injury, it felt like it took twice as long to get back to the L late Saturday morning as it had hiking the trail to the overlook. When Max finally pushed through the main building's entrance, near pandemonium broke out. Resort employees from the reservations desk, the concierge counter, the bar and other areas hurried toward Alexis. Their eyes were wide with shock. Their brows were creased with concern.

"Alexis, are you all right?"

"What happened?"

"Are you okay?"

Alexis stiffened against him. She drew her hand from his shoulder. Her smile seemed stiff. "I care about all of you and appreciate your concern but, please, let's not agitate our guests."

Clarissa rested her hand lightly on Alexis's left shoulder. "But what happened?"

Alexis glanced at Max before answering. "I fell during our hike."

Max felt the eyes of the guests in the lobby area on them. He sensed Alexis's rising tension and knew she didn't want to be the center of this distraction.

He shared a smile with the small group of caring coworkers around them. "Ladies and gentlemen, thank you for your concern. I'll help Alexis to the clinic now. We can talk later."

Alexis gave him a grateful look. He helped her past her colleagues, across the lobby and down the hall toward the clinic.

She braced her arm on his shoulder again. "I should've gone home and taken care of these scrapes and wrapped my ankle myself."

Max's arm reflexively tightened around her waist. "After a fall like that, it's better to have a professional examine you to make sure you're okay."

She gave him a side-eyed stare. "Then they should check you out, too."

Max frowned as they reached the blond wood door to the little clinic. "I suppose that's only fair."

The clinic was the last office in the administrative hall. The cozy space was cheerful and bright with homey touches. According to the resort's website, it had a small staff, which included physician's assistants, nurses and nurses' aides. They were available 24/7/365 to assist guests as well as employees in the event of a sudden illness or injury. Max admired the forethought Adam and his siblings had in offering these services on-site. He just hadn't imagined needing to use them.

A middle-aged woman at the front desk sprang from her seat as soon as Max assisted Alexis across the bamboo threshold. Her dark brown eyes widened. Her thin brown face cleared of all expression as she rushed toward them.

"Alexis, honey, what happened?" She was several inches shorter than Alexis. Her slight accent tagged her as a Southern transplant.

Alexis's smile seemed more natural this time. "Nurse Zoe Morgan, this is—"

"Chef Max Powell. I love your show." Zoe's eyes dropped to Max's legs. She hissed in empathy. "You're pretty banged up, too, Chef."

Max could imagine he and Alexis looked like they'd limped away from a terrible accident, which they had. "We fell during our hike."

Zoe motioned them to nearby visitors' chairs. "That must've been some fall." She waited for Max to assist Alexis onto one of the chairs before she knelt in front of them. With a gentle touch, she examined first Alexis's legs, then Max's. With a sympathetic wince and a sigh, Zoe pushed herself to her feet. "Since Alexis looks a little worse for wear, I'll bandage her up first, then I'll come back for you." She waved Max back to his seat when he started to rise. "I'll help our friend into the exam room. I'm stronger than I look."

Max watched Zoe assist Alexis across the reception area, ready to lend a hand, if they needed one. They didn't. As Zoe closed the door behind them, his cell phone rang. It was Adam. Strange. He'd been about to call his friend.

"Hey, I—"

Adam interrupted. His voice was tense. "Where are you?"

Max frowned. "I'm at your clinic. Why?"

"We're on our way."

Max's confusion doubled. "Who's we?" But Adam had hung up.

Minutes later Adam, Laura and Joshua arrived at the clinic. They wore almost identical expressions of concern and dismay. Max stood in time to catch Laura as she flung herself against him.

"Thank you for saving my friend." Her voice shook with emotion. She hugged him tightly before stepping back.

Adam's eyes were on Max's wounded legs. "For crying out loud, Max, you and Alexis could've been killed."

"How did you know about the accident? I was about to call you." Max shifted his attention from Adam to his siblings.

There was a strong family resemblance among the Coltons. Laura, the middle child, stood a step behind Adam. She was a tall, blue-eyed blonde. Her pale pink skirt suit emphasized her peaches-and-cream complexion. Beside her, Joshua, the youngest, was the same height as Adam but he wore his dark blond hair longer. He was the only sibling not wearing a business suit. His lanky form was clothed in khaki, knee-length shorts and a mud-brown polo shirt tagged with the Mariposa Resort & Spa logo.

Joshua tapped his cell phone screen before turning it toward Max. A video played with an off-screen voice narrating the events. The caption read, "Celebrity Chef's Heroic Rescue."

Max stiffened with surprise. "How could they have posted the footage so quickly? Is that from a drone?" He hadn't noticed one near them. But then, he hadn't been aware of anything but Alexis and their efforts to get her to safety.

His eyes stretched wide as one of the most frightening experiences he'd ever had replayed on some internet entertainment news site. Max's blood turned to ice as he watched himself leap across the screen like a professional football receiver going after an impossible pass. He saw himself securing his hold on Alexis and helping her to safety before they collapsed in each other's arms. Max locked his knees to keep from collapsing back onto the chair behind him. The video ended with Alexis and him limping back down the trail.

"I think so." Joshua glanced at his phone screen. "What happened to the guardrail?"

Max met the younger man's wide blue eyes. "It collapsed when Alexis leaned against it."

The blood drained under Joshua's healthy tan. "How's that possible? I checked it just last night. I checked all of them. They were solid."

"I believe you." Alexis's simple words came from across the room. Zoe had bandaged her deeper cuts and wrapped her ankle. Alexis held a cane in her right hand. Zoe stood beside her with a first aid kit.

Laura led the group to her. She rested her hands on Alexis's shoulder. "How are you?"

"I'm fine." Alexis managed a smile.

Zoe snorted. "She'll need to stay off her ankle for a day or two." She dragged a seat to Max and waved him toward the chair behind him. "Let's get you cleaned up now."

Max took the seat Zoe indicated, then rested his legs on the one she'd pulled over. Zoe sat beside him to tend his injuries. The iodine stung. Max gritted his teeth and tried not to flinch. He looked up and caught the empathy in Alexis's eyes. This must have been what she'd gone through.

Alexis nodded toward Joshua's cell. Her voice was stiff with dread. "Is there a video of the accident?"

Joshua returned his cell phone to the front right pocket of his shorts. "I'm afraid so. We've been able to prevent drone operators from flying their machines directly over the resort. But this one looks like it was over Red Rock State Park, which is illegal. I'll file a report about it."

Alexis rubbed her eyes before looking back to Max. "I'm so sorry for this invasion of your privacy."

Max could feel her frustration and anger from across the room. "All that matters is that you're safe."

"I'm glad you're both going to be okay." Joshua took a step back, jerking a finger over his left shoulder. "I need to repair that guardrail and check the others before there are any more accidents."

Max watched the youngest Colton stride from the room. Joshua had said the guardrail had been secure when he'd checked it last night. Like Alexis, Max believed him. Then why had it broken free of its restraints and fallen down the hill so easily?

"You're good to go, Chef Max." Zoe's pronouncement broke his train of thought. She packed up her first aid kit.

"Thank you very much, Nurse Zoe." Max tossed her a smile before switching his attention to Alexis and her cane. "If you don't mind my driving your car, I'd be happy to take you home."

Alexis balanced her cane as she rotated her left ankle. "I'll be fine but thank you for offering. I should get going. I need to warn my mother about the video before she learns about it from someone else."

Laura stopped Alexis with a hand on her left forearm. She looked at Max. "I think you should let Max drive you home, Alexis. You're injured and you've had a horrible scare. I'd feel better if he was with you."

"So would I." Adam shoved his hands into the front pockets of his pale suit pants. "We want to make sure you get home safely."

Max looked between the two Colton siblings. He heard the sincerity in their voices. They were serious about their concern for Alexis's well-being. Then why did he also have the feeling they were trying to play matchmaker?

"Sorry, Alexis." Zoe crossed to the exam room doorway where Alexis still stood. "It's four to one. And I'm sure it would be five to one if Joshua were still here."

Alexis shook her head with a smile. "All right. I surrender." She turned that powerful smile on Max. "I don't mind your driving my car, if your offer still stands. But you'd have to pick me up for work Monday morning."

Laura frowned. "But Zoe said you need to stay off your foot for a few days."

Alexis tilted her head. "And I'll be able to do that at work. I have a desk job, remember?"

Laura turned to the nurse. "Zoe, what do you think?"

Zoe snorted. "You know how stubborn Alexis can be. I think we should take the win with her agreeing to let Max drive her home." She pinned Alexis with a look. "As long as you promise that the only walking you'll do is to the bathroom and back to your desk."

Alexis's eyes widened in what Max could only describe as indecision. "I can only promise to try my very best."

Zoe sighed, shaking her head as she disappeared into the exam room.

Max stood. "I'll take you home."

Those words made him almost lightheaded with longing. He hoped it wouldn't make him unsafe to drive. He'd had more than enough excitement for the weekend.

Chapter Six

"Chef Max is driving me home." In his peripheral vision, Max saw Alexis hold the phone away from her ear as a scream emerged from the mic. "Yes, Mom. He's in my car with me now."

Max chuckled. He hadn't expected that information to prompt such an extreme reaction from Alexis's mother, or anyone's mother, for that matter.

"Mom, please don't call Aunt Suz." Alexis rubbed her eyes with the thumb and two fingers of her left hand. She listened in silence to the voice Max could just make out through her cell phone. "Because there's no reason to worry her. Just as there's no reason for you to worry. I only called because I didn't want you to be caught off guard if you saw the video before we had a chance to talk."

Alexis tapped Max's right arm, then signaled for him to get into the left-turn lane. He followed her instructions. She'd been using hand motions to direct him to her condo since she'd called her mother after they'd pulled out of the resort parking lot. Max didn't mean to eavesdrop on her call, but the one-sided exchange made him smile. It reminded him so much of his conversations with his family.

"No, Mom. I'm sorry. I didn't mean to imply you wouldn't have the right to freak out over the video. Of course you would." More silence. The voice on the other end of the line came across as a high-pitched murmur. "Yes, please, let's have Sunday dinner at my house this weekend. I'd like that." While Alexis listened to her mother, she pulled an electronic door opener from her purse. "No, please don't call Aunt Suz. I mean it, Mom." A shorter pause. "Because Aunt Suz will want to call to check on me and I'd really like to get some rest."

Alexis tapped his arm again, then pointed to a condo on the right side of the street. She depressed the device to raise the garage door.

"Thank you, Mom. I really appreciate that. Okay. Bye. Yes, I'm home now. B—" Alexis paused again. "I will. Bye." She disconnected the call. "My mother thanks you for driving me home."

"Please tell your mother she's very welcome." Max parked Alexis's car in her attached garage.

As she depressed the button to lower the unit's automatic door, Max hustled to the passenger side to assist her from the seat. He feared she'd hurt herself trying to get out on her own. As he suspected, she was already trying to manage with the help of her cane. He'd only known her eight days, but he'd already picked up that she was determined not to lean on anyone, ever.

He offered her his right hand. "Let me help you."

"I'm usually a lot more graceful." Alexis lightly took his hand. She steadied her cane before pushing herself up and out of the seat.

Max searched her quietly determined expression. "You're doing fine. Better than fine."

"I also apologize for being on the phone with my mother during the entire drive over here. I feel so rude."

"You weren't rude. I understand. My parents are the same way."

With his hand on the small of her back, Max escorted her across the threshold of the garage entry door. It opened into her kitchen. One could tell a lot about a person from their kitchen. Alexis's was spotless. It had updated blond wood cabinetry and flooring, granite kitchen countertops and stainless-steel appliances. But the space was short and narrow.

Her refrigerator was dotted with magnets in the shapes of colorful fruits, vegetables and wildflowers. Potted herbs sat on the window ledge and measuring spoons stood in a container near the stove. Max smiled to himself. He suspected Alexis enjoyed cooking but didn't entertain a lot.

He followed her from the kitchen. Alexis moved cautiously, perhaps because she was still getting used to the cane. He was ready to catch her if she stumbled. They walked through the dining area and into her family room. Max was struck by the amount of natural light filling Alexis's townhome. The open floor plan welcomed the early afternoon sunlight. Rays danced against the blond wood flooring and spun back to the warm cream walls and pale tan furnishings. Red, orange and grape accents drew his eyes to the curtains, rugs and throw pillows that beckoned him farther into the space.

"Your home is so welcoming." Max's eyes swept the photos arranged on the mantel on the opposite wall. There were several of her with a woman who looked a lot like her. Her mother?

"Thank you." Alexis's cheeks pinkened with pleasure. "The few hours I do get to spend at home, I want to feel as relaxed as possible."

"I can relate to what you're saying. You want your home

to be a sanctuary." That was one of the things that bothered him the most about the break-ins. The thief had intruded on a space he'd considered his retreat.

Max shoved his hands into the front pockets of his shorts. His eyes dropped to the wounds on Alexis's legs. "Alexis, I'm so sorry about the accident and your injuries, about the entire experience. I feel responsible. Hiking had been my idea. If I hadn't talked you into it, none of this would have happened."

Alexis held out her hand, palm out. "That's ridiculous. This was an accident. Nothing more. None of this is your fault, and I'd agreed to go hiking with you."

Max ran a shaking hand over his close-cropped hair. "I've never been as scared as I felt when I saw you falling over the edge of that cliff."

Alexis's knuckles turned white with her grip on her cane. She began to visibly shake. Max rushed forward to catch her as she started to crumble. He helped her to the tan cloth couch beside her.

"I'm sorry." She repeated the words in a voice as thin as a spider's web.

Drawing her into his embrace, Max pressed her head to his shoulder and stroked her right arm. "Don't. You have nothing to be sorry for. I'm the one who put you in danger. I should be apologizing to you."

Alexis pulled back to meet his eyes. "No, none of this is your fault. It's just… If one small thing had been different, I could've died today. If I'd been hiking alone. Or if you hadn't been able to catch me. Or if you hadn't been able to hold me." A violent tremor rolled through her.

Max held her more tightly. "But you weren't alone. And you were able to help pull yourself by climbing up the side of the hill. You were strong and calm the whole time. Your courage helped me keep it together."

Alexis took a shuddering breath. Her muscles were taut. "I may have seemed calm on the outside, but I was quietly having a meltdown on the inside." She held his eyes. "Thank you so very much for saving my life."

The look in her bright eyes was more than gratitude, more than caring. It was hypnotic. Max felt himself leaning closer. Alexis's eyes darkened. They dropped to his lips. Max's pulse leaped once. He pressed his lips to hers. They felt warm and soft. He stroked his tongue across her lips. Their taste was sweet, intoxicating. Alexis's body softened in his arms. She parted her lips to let him in. Max's body warmed in response. He swept his tongue inside her mouth. She caressed it with her own. The muscles in his lower abdomen quivered. Her arms wrapped around him. The scent of her perfume filled his head. He heard the pulse drumming in his ears.

Or was it a fist pounding on Alexis's door?

The doorbell chimed incessantly, accompanied by a demanding male voice. "Lex. Lex. Let me in."

Alexis started in his arms, then pulled back. Her eyes seemed dazed as she looked at him. She licked her lips and his muscles ached. "Excuse me. I should get that."

He stood with her. He cupped her left elbow, providing some small support as he accompanied her to the front door. Whoever had come to see her wasn't letting up on the noise. The wannabe guest continued pressing the bell and calling her name.

Alexis's scowl grew ominous. She started speaking before she opened the door. "Jake, what is wrong with you—"

A tall, broad-shouldered man strode forward. He enveloped Alexis in a bear hug, rocking her from side to side. "Lex! Thank goodness you're safe."

Max's eyes widened. His jaw dropped. He let his arm fall to his side and stepped back.

Who was this?

THE TALL, GOOD-LOOKING man finally gave Alexis some breathing room, but Max noticed he kept an arm around her shoulders.

The new arrival was about Max's height, six foot two, lean, with fair skin and coal black eyes. His thick, tight, black curls were shaped into a trendy fade.

"Max, I'd like you to meet Dr. Jacob Moore. He's an accounting professor at Northern Arizona University in Flagstaff and a dear friend." The warm smile Alexis gave the other man filled Max with envy. "Jake, this is Maxwell Powell. He's a chef and host of *Cooking for Friends*. He's also a guest at Mariposa."

Jake's balanced features brightened with a huge grin. His perfect white teeth were gleaming testaments to the benefits of good oral hygiene. "You're the dude who saved my girl." He pulled Max into a bear hug. "Thank you so much, man. From the bottom of my heart."

My girl?

Max patted Jake's shoulders before stepping back. "Of course."

Disappointment drained the oxygen from the room. Why hadn't he considered that Alexis—beautiful, brilliant, charming and funny Alexis—would be in a relationship? Why hadn't that possibility occurred to him before he'd kissed her? But… She'd kissed him back. He turned his attention to Alexis. She was still looking at Jake.

"Did my mother call you?" she asked.

Why was she acting like nothing had happened? She'd kissed him back, knowing she had a boyfriend. Apparently, that didn't matter to her. Had he misjudged her?

Jake locked her front door before maneuvering himself between Max and Alexis to help Alexis back to the sofa. "Your mother called my mother, who called me."

"I specifically asked Mom not to call your mother." Alexis looked to Max. "You heard me ask her not to call Aunt Suz, didn't you?"

"I did." What was happening right now?

Jake continued. "I promised Mom I'd check on you, but you know she's going to call you later." He propped the cane against the side of the sofa and positioned one of the pillows on the coffee table. Max gritted his teeth as he watched Jake lift both of Alexis's legs onto the pillow, then kneel beside her. He stared at her bandages. "Lex, your legs are a mess."

"Thanks." Her tone was dry.

Jake didn't seem to hear her. "I thought I was going to have a heart attack watching that video."

A part of Max wondered if he should excuse himself. A larger part wanted answers to a myriad of questions, starting with why had Alexis kissed him back?

Alexis sat up on the sofa. "You didn't send the video to my mother, did you?"

Jake gave her a sarcastic look. "Of course not. That video should come with an H rating for being hazardous to your health." He pushed himself to his feet. "Do you need anything before we leave?"

We? Max glanced at the other man. Who said *we* were leaving?

Alexis swung her legs off the pillows and reclaimed her cane. "No, I'll be fine." She pushed herself to her feet. "Max was going to use my car to get back to Mariposa, though."

That's right. Her car keys were still in his pocket. Max started to assure her that he'd take good care of her vehicle, but Jake spoke first.

"I'll run you back to the resort." Jake jerked his thumb toward the front door.

Max stiffened. He didn't want to accept a ride from Alexis's boyfriend, especially not with Alexis's taste still on his lips. He turned to her, but her serene expression seemed to approve of Jake's plan.

He searched his mind for an excuse out of the situation. "I don't want to leave you stranded. How will you get to work Monday?"

Alexis waved a dismissive hand. "I'll be fine to drive myself by Monday."

Max frowned. Was she really that unbothered by the fact that they'd exchanged a passionate kiss while she was in a relationship with another man? What was he to think of this?

"Max has a good point." Jake tipped his head toward Max beside him. "I'll swing by and drive you to work Monday morning. We'll have to leave a little early, though, so I can get to my office on time."

Alexis rolled her eyes. "Fine. You both can stop playing nursemaid now."

Defeated, Max returned Alexis's car keys. "I hope you're feeling much better by Monday."

"Thank you." Alexis dropped her keys into her shorts pocket and glanced at his wounded calves. "I hope you are, too."

She smiled at him, but her eyes seemed wary with curiosity. It was as though she sensed something was bothering him but didn't know what it was. How could she miss it? The six-foot-two-inch source of his problems was literally standing between them.

Max followed Jake to the door. On impulse he turned back to Alexis before leaving. "If you need anything, please call me."

She smiled again. "I promise."

Max nodded, then turned away. But how could he trust someone who would kiss him the way Alexis had when she was already involved with someone else?

MAX WALKED INTO his bungalow after bidding goodbye to Jake. Within five minutes of being in the car with the other man, he found it hard not to like him. He was good-natured, intelligent and interesting. He could understand why Alexis would be with him. Max bit off a curse. He threw his knapsack to the ground and marched across the great room to stare at the mountainscape through the sliding glass doors.

But why had she kissed him back? He wasn't mistaken about that. He could still feel her tongue on his. He couldn't be wrong about her. Alexis wasn't the type of person to make out with one person when she was dating another.

Why did this hurt so much? He'd only known her eight calendar days.

The knock on his door rescued him from his thoughts. Max checked the spyhole, recognizing Joshua on his doorstep. Another man was with him. The stranger was tall and muscular, and carried what looked like a black gym bag. His white face was covered by a full brown beard and moustache. Piercing green eyes locked onto the spyhole as though the stranger could see him. Who was he? Max opened the door to find out.

"Noah Steele. Max Powell." Joshua tossed him a poor

imitation of the usual charming Colton smile as he crossed the threshold. “Do you have a minute?”

This was Laura’s boyfriend, the homicide detective. He wore straight-legged black jeans and a loose black T-shirt. Adam had filled him in on the murder investigation in which his sister had been involved. He didn’t think Adam had recovered from the scare, but he knew his friend had been impressed by the detective. He also was pleased his sister was happy and in love.

“Sure. Have a seat.” Max locked up before joining the two men. They’d taken seats at the dining table just inside the bungalow. He sat beside Joshua. “What did you learn about the guardrail?”

Joshua sighed. His frown was still in place. “Tell us exactly what happened.”

Max looked from Joshua to Noah and back. “You saw the video. Alexis turned toward the guardrail. She rested her forearms on it—barely—and it crumbled like pieces of a jigsaw puzzle.” He briefly closed his eyes. “She started to go over the edge.”

“And you caught her.” Noah’s voice was reassuring. “She’ll be all right.”

Max nodded. “Yes, she will. But what happened? What caused the railing to fall apart?”

Noah glanced at Joshua before responding. “Sometime between six o’clock yesterday evening when Joshua last checked the rails and nine this morning when you and Alexis went on your hike, someone shaved the rods. They shortened them just enough so that they weren’t actually fitted together. They just looked like they were. They did the same thing to several other guardrails on that path.”

Max’s brow knitted with confusion. “Someone sabotaged the rails?”

Noah unzipped the gym bag he'd set beside his chair and pulled out a large evidence bag. Max glanced at the tattoos on his arms and the side of his neck before turning his attention to the bag. It contained one of the rails.

Noah pointed to it. "You can see where the rod was shaved. The edges are uneven."

Looking closely, Max could see what Noah described. He looked between the two men. "Were all the rails tampered with like this?"

"I'm afraid so." Joshua's voice was tight with anger.

"Who knew you were going hiking?" Noah asked.

Max gestured to Joshua beside him. "Joshua and Alexis. I mentioned it to my family but they're in New York." He shifted his attention back to Noah. "But anyone could have been on that trail. What makes you think whoever tampered with the rail was targeting Alexis and me?"

Joshua nodded toward the detective sitting across from them. "I gave Noah the suspicious package that was waiting for you when you arrived. Because of that note, we don't believe the guardrail was a coincidence."

Max had his doubts. "The person who sent the box is probably connected to the break-ins at my condo in New York. But no one has threatened me."

Noah held his eyes. "The threats could be escalating, meaning the break-ins could have been the start. I'm going to dust the package for prints and compare them against a national database."

Max went cold. "And Alexis could be hurt the same way she was today." He stood to pace the great room. His strides carried him toward the wall beside the sliding glass doors. "But how could the stalker have gotten into Mariposa? The property's secure."

Joshua sighed. “I haven’t figured that out yet, but I’m on it. No one in our employ would provide access to people who don’t work here or who aren’t guests.”

Max turned to pace back to the table. “If someone’s targeting me, I need to leave the resort.” He shoved his fists into the front pockets of his shorts. “I don’t want to put Alexis—or anyone else—in danger.”

Noah stood. “I understand your concern, Mr. Powell—”

Max shook his head. “Max, please.”

Noah nodded. “Max. But I think you should stay at the resort. If someone is trying to harm you, we have a better chance of catching that person here.”

Max continued pacing. “If this attack is connected to the break-ins, then the danger started in New York.” He turned when he reached the front door.

“But it escalated here.” Noah crossed his arms over his chest. “I can contact the detectives assigned to the case in New York and keep them apprised of our progress. They’re welcome to come lend a hand, if they want to. But what happens in Sedona gets handled in Sedona.”

“I agree with Noah.” Joshua spread his hands. “Besides, where are you going to go? If you return to New York, you’ll be putting your family in danger. If you go somewhere else, you won’t have any backup.”

Max rubbed the tense muscles in his neck. “You have a point. There aren’t any good solutions.”

Joshua stood from the table. “If someone’s after you, Max, leaving Mariposa will only prolong the situation. Noah’s already opened a case. We can keep you safe here. And if Alexis is in danger, we’ll bring her into the resort, too, until the case is solved.”

Alexis's safety was all that mattered. If they could guarantee that, then he would stay. "All right."

"WHY AM I not surprised to find you here?" Laura's question preceded her as she walked into Alexis's office before 8:00 a.m. Monday. Her light blond bob swung just above her shoulders. Her azure coatdress made her eyes seem bluer.

"Maybe because you know I work here?" Alexis watched her friend and direct supervisor settle into one of the two visitors' chairs in front of her desk.

Laura coupled her sigh with a long-suffering look. "Do you want me to ask the nurse on duty to take a look at your ankle?"

"No, thank you." Alexis angled her head to check her injured joint. She'd propped it on a tall, empty box she'd found in the supply room. "It feels better. I'll go to the clinic if I have any pain." She wished Zoe was in today, but she was sure the nurse had left detailed notes in case someone needed to follow up while she was out of the office.

Laura pointed to her. "I'll hold you to that."

"I offered to arrange for another concierge to accompany Max to the farmers market this morning, but he said the chef was going to get his ingredients for him." Which meant she wouldn't be seeing Max today. She shouldn't feel so disappointed. It was inappropriate. Max was a guest at the resort and her client. They weren't friends—or anything more. Although after their kiss, the boundary lines had never seemed so blurry.

Alexis gave her friend a searching look. "So, I'm fine, but I can tell you're not. Something else is on your mind. I can hear it in your voice."

Laura sighed. "Noah believes the guardrail collapsing wasn't an accident. He's concerned the person who sent the package to the resort for Max tampered with the rail, intending for him to fall over the cliff."

Alexis's hand flew to her mouth as she gasped. "Oh, no. That's horrible. Max didn't mention any of this to me when I spoke with him this morning. What are we going to do?"

"Max was thinking of returning to New York, but Noah convinced him to stay at Mariposa. We have twenty-four-hour security and Noah's already started investigating." Laura held Alexis's eyes. "We also prepared a bungalow for you. We're concerned whoever's targeting Max may also go after you since you've been spending time with him."

"I don't think I'm in danger." Alexis shook her head even as a chill seeped under her skin. "I didn't have any strange or threatening events this weekend. But I agree with Noah. Max will be safer here."

"Alexis, one weekend isn't a good test of your safety." Laura leaned forward in her seat as though trying to emphasize the urgency of the situation. "And why should we take the risk? Everyone agrees you should stay here for however long it takes to find Max's stalker. If it makes you feel better, think of it as saving time on your commute to work."

Everyone? How many people had the Coltons told about the incident? Although with the video circulating the news channels and the internet, they probably wouldn't have had to tell anyone. Alexis believed it was the video that had put her in the position of having to field questions from her neighbors, church congregation and everyone she'd walked past on her way to her office this morning.

"All right. I'll accept your offer of staying in the bungalow until the stalker's found. Thank you." Alexis tilted her head to the side, giving Laura a thoughtful look. "What else is on your mind?"

Laura stiffened as though in surprise. Then she relaxed

back into her seat. "Your perception is one of the many reasons I love our friendship." She sighed. "My brothers and I just learned Clive owns the land Mariposa is on."

"What?" Alexis's lips parted in shock. "I thought your mother left the resort to the three of you. Why would she have left the land it sits on to your father?" It was disconcerting that Laura referred to her father by his first name, but considering she and her brothers didn't have much of a relationship with their sole surviving parent, it made sense.

Laura's peaches-and-cream features tightened with temper. "We think Clive tricked our mother into signing the land ownership papers to him while she was sick. Her chemo treatments really sapped her energy. She wouldn't have been able to read the documents clearly."

Alexis shook her head in disgust. "That's reprehensible."

"That's Clive." Laura's voice dripped with contempt. "He offered to sell the land to us, but he's asking for more than we could afford—and more than the land is worth. But if we don't give him the money, he's threatening to sell the land to someone else."

Alexis went cold as she realized what Laura wasn't saying. If Clive Colton sold the land on which Mariposa was built, the Colton siblings would become tenants of the new property owners. Such a drastic change for the business would inevitably change the resort's operating structure.

Her head was spinning. "Why is your father doing this?"

Laura drew a breath. "Clive is broke."

Another stunning revelation. Alexis winced, briefly closing her eyes. Clive owned half of Colton Textiles, a fine fabrics importer based in Los Angeles that he'd inherited from his father-in-law. The Colton siblings owned the other half.

Laura continued. "Colton Textiles is on the verge of

bankruptcy. Clive's run the company into the ground. Now he needs a huge influx of cash just to keep it open. And he's decided that, if we don't give him money, he's going to take Mariposa from us."

The resort was named after Annabeth Colton's favorite flower, for crying out loud. The idea of Mariposa being stripped away from her children was obscene.

"Is there any way you could reason with him?" Alexis spread her arms to encompass the resort. "Mariposa was his deceased wife's dream. This is where they spent their honeymoon. It's where your mother has been laid to rest. Doesn't that mean anything to him?"

"Not at all." Laura shrugged. The jerky gesture was anything but casual. "None of that matters to Clive. All he cares about—all he's ever cared about—is money."

Alexis believed Laura. Still, she had trouble imagining a parent who would be so uncaring of their children's feelings and well-being. What kind of parent would deliberately destroy the legacy their children had inherited from their mother rather than support their offsprings' success? Apparently, the answer was a parent like Clive Colton.

"What are you and your brothers going to do?" Alexis's heart broke as she watched sorrow and distress settle like a mask over her friend's features.

Laura's eyes drifted away from Alexis. "We're thinking about going into partnership with another company."

The other woman made it sound like that plan would be their last option. Alexis could understand why. "You're considering giving another business part ownership of Mariposa?"

"We may not have a choice." Laura sighed. "If we sold a portion of Mariposa, we'd have the money to buy the land from Clive and we'd still be in a position to run the resort as we see fit."

Although not ideal, that strategy seemed to make the most sense. The bottom line was Laura, Adam and Joshua wanted to hold on to the legacy and the vision their mother had passed on to them. Laura had told her how much her late mother had loved the resort. She'd even shared some of the wonderful childhood memories she and her siblings had of the time they'd spent together on the property. The siblings had sacrificed everything, including personal lives, to build the resort into what it was today. They'd even built their homes on the property.

Together, Laura, Adam and Joshua had grown what was once a small hotel into an exclusive getaway for the wealthy and famous. The Coltons and their resort had built a stellar reputation, which they worked hard to preserve. Now their father had put them in an untenable situation that threatened everything—and everyone.

The Coltons treated their staff like an extended family, which had earned them loyalty and respect. If Clive sold the property, all their jobs would be on the line. Alexis didn't want to lose the resort.

She made Laura a promise. "I will do everything I can to help you and your brothers hold on to Mariposa."

To ensure the property was as appealing as possible to prospective partners, she'd have to help prevent any further scandals. The video of Max saving her from falling over the cliff came to mind. Well, no one said this would be easy.

Chapter Seven

"Lunch is served." Max's voice preceded him into Alexis's office early Monday afternoon. He wore his navy blue chef's smock with bronze pants.

Alexis looked up from her desk to find Max wheeling in a food trolley with two place settings, including large highball glasses of ice water. It was déjà vu all over again. "I didn't realize this was going to become a weekly appointment." She eyed the silver cloches covering the plates with a twinge of panic. What were they hiding today?

"People don't usually look so distressed when I cook for them." Max didn't sound offended. Thank goodness. Instead, he seemed amused. Alexis started to make an excuse. Max forestalled her by holding up a hand palm outward. "Honesty. Remember? My ego can take it."

Alexis gave him a crooked smile. "I'm sure it can."

"I need an ego if we're going to be friends." His brown eyes twinkled with disarming mischief.

Friends. Isn't that what she wanted them to be? But, oh, that kiss. Alexis kept her smile in place.

Max removed one of the cloches. "Portobello mushroom renello with black beans." He sounded so proud of himself.

A plume of steam wafted toward her. It carried the scents of cilantro, jalapeno peppers, onions, garlic and tomatoes.

Delicious. The stuffed mushroom was topped with guacamole. It looked fresh and succulent. Max had garnished the plate with cilantro leaves and lime slices, which helped it look less empty.

Where was the rest of the food? "It looks wonderful."

Alexis pulled her purse from her desk's top left-hand drawer. She retrieved the greeting card in the hot pink envelope from the bag's center pouch, then stood to join Max at the conversation table. She moved with barely a limp.

"Thank you. I've passed the first test." Max watched her closely as he held the chair for her. "It was a good idea to wear sneakers today. How's your ankle?"

Alexis had felt awkward about wearing the black tennis shoes to work but they were much more comfortable than her pumps. And they almost disappeared beneath the hem of her black wide-legged pants.

"It's much stronger. Thank you." She settled into the seat closest to the door, then spread the napkin on her lap. "What about your injuries?"

"They look a lot worse than they feel." Max circled the table and took the seat opposite her.

"This is from my mother." Alexis offered him the card. "It's a thank-you-for-saving-my-daughter's-life card."

Max's eyebrows rose in surprise as he accepted the envelope. "That's so nice of her." As he read the message, his smile grew into a grin. "Your mother's very kind and very welcome." He set the card beside his plate.

"I'll let her know you appreciated it." She took a deep breath. The scent of the peppers, onions and cilantro made her stomach growl. She pressed a hand to her torso. "Excuse me."

"Bon appétit." Max waited for her to sample the meal.

Alexis's cheeks warmed under his scrutiny. She cut into

the stuffed portobello mushroom and chewed. It was warm and spicy, but still not spicy enough. "You're getting there. It's delicious, but you have a little room to add more seasoning. And it needs cheese."

"It's still too bland?" Max looked and sounded disappointed.

"Food should be seasoned with abandon. And don't forget the cheese."

"Cheese. I'll make a note of that." The twinkle returned to Max's eyes. "Thank you for your candor, Alexis. You've been very helpful. Tell me, what's the most exotic meal you've ever had?"

Alexis eyed the black beans as she cut into the mushroom again. "Ever had or ever enjoyed?" His chuckle strummed the muscles in her lower abdomen. She caught her breath.

"All right. The most exotic meal you've ever enjoyed." He swallowed a forkful of the mushroom.

Alexis sipped her water as she considered his question. "That's easy—bacon and guac cheeseburger with seasoned fries."

Max watched her with a blank expression. "Are you kidding?"

"I'm totally serious." Alexis gestured toward her plate. "I mean, look at this plate. It looks like art, not food. You've got this ginormous plate and this itty-bitty food. Where's the rest of it?"

"That's called 'presentation.'" Max spread his hands. "Part of the enjoyment of dining is the way the food is arranged on your plate."

Alexis shrugged her eyebrows. "I understand that. But could you present across a larger part of the plate? If I have to work half a day or more to pay for one meal, I want to leave feeling full." She tried the black beans. They were delicious but could use a bit more salt.

"Point taken." Max inclined his head. "But remember, when you're dining out, you're not just paying for the food. You're paying for an entire experience—the quality of the service, the ambience of the establishment as well as the freshness of the ingredients and the chef's training."

Alexis fought back a smile. She was enjoying this banter with him, perhaps too much. "You sound like my mother. I'll tell you what I always say to her. If I want an experience, I'll grab a couple of friends and a burger to watch a movie on a streaming service."

Max laughed. "You're a hard woman to convince but as I've told you before, I can't resist a challenge."

Alexis swallowed another forkful of the beans. "Is that the reason you're involved in so many projects—your restaurants, show and now a book?"

Max drank his water before responding. "My fifteen minutes of fame is almost over. Unlike Julia Child and Wolfgang Puck, most chefs won't be household names forever. I understand that. At the end of the day, everything goes back to the restaurants. They're my first loves. While the spotlight's on me, I want to make sure I'm doing everything I can to ensure their success for the long term."

"That's a solid plan." Alexis bent her head, pretending to focus on her meal, but her lunch companion was a major distraction.

Kind, courageous, attractive and smart. How was a person supposed to resist the full package that was Maxwell Powell III?

Max's voice interrupted her thoughts. "Laura told me you'd agreed to move into one of the bungalows until the stalker is caught. I'm glad." He held her eyes. "I'm sorry you've been pulled into this, though."

Alexis lowered her knife and fork. "I'm sorry someone's trying to hurt you. Do you have any idea who could be behind these acts?"

"No, I don't, and I don't know what I could've done to make someone so angry." Temper hardened Max's eyes. "And to think they've involved you in this… Saying sorry doesn't seem like enough. Have you told Jake you're going to be staying at Mariposa for a while?"

Alexis sensed Max's tension and wondered at its source. "No, but I told my mother. She's relieved I've accepted Laura's offer. I'm sure she'll tell Jake and Aunt Suz."

Max took another drink of water. "Jake seems like a nice person." Was he deliberately avoiding her eyes?

"He is." Alexis didn't date much, but every man who'd been interested in her had also wondered about Jake. She'd never lied about their relationship, and she never would. "He's like a brother to me. Our mothers have been best friends for decades. We grew up together."

Max's tension drained away and Alexis returned to her lunch. Their comfortable silence was broken by the occasional questions about their plans for the rest of the day, amenities at Mariposa, and Laura and Adam.

Alexis set her silverware on her empty plate. "Max, there's something we should discuss." His sudden stillness made her even more uncomfortable, but she steeled herself to continue. With Mariposa's uncertain future, Alexis couldn't risk having a relationship with a guest. If the media found out, the resort would be in the center of even more salacious gossip. And it would be all her fault. "You're a guest at Mariposa. You're also one of my clients. As much as I enjoyed our kiss, a romantic relationship between us is against the rules. It also would be inappropriate."

Max gave her his crooked smile. "I'll admit to being disappointed. I enjoy your company, Alexis, and I want to get to know you better. But of course, I'll respect your decision. Besides, my home is in New York and you live here. I've heard long-distance relationships can be brutal."

The regret in his dark eyes reflected the pain in her heart. Alexis clenched her hands under the table. She desperately wanted to change her mind.

Just kidding! Forget everything I said! Backsies!

Alexis looked away and rose from the table. "I've heard the same thing about long-distance romances."

Max stood with her. "So we'll settle for friendship?"

Alexis swallowed the lump of regret in her throat. *No! I want more.* "I'd like that."

"Good." Max returned their place settings to the trolley. "I meant what I said about your feedback on the recipes. Your honesty is invaluable, and I'm enjoying the challenge of trying to impress you." He chuckled. "See you later, Alexis."

"Have a good day, Max." She watched him disappear beyond her doorway before returning to her desk.

Her office felt so empty without him. Alexis dropped onto her black wheeled desk chair. She'd have to fill the void with work as she always did. The problem was that plan wasn't as appealing as it had been before she met Max.

"I'M SURPRISED YOU'VE come in today." The cool, indifferent notes of Glenna Bennett Colton's voice made the hair on the back of Alexis's neck vibrate like an early warning system. In the back of her mind, the scene music for the *Wizard of Oz*'s Wicked Witch of the West played.

Alexis gave Clarissa an apologetic smile before cutting their meeting update short Monday evening. The reservations desk clerk returned the smile with a sympathetic look.

Straightening her posture, Alexis faced Laura's stepmother. "Good afternoon, Ms. Bennett Colton. Why are you surprised to see me?"

Glenna was a few inches taller than Alexis. Her blood-red, straight-legged pantsuit made a statement—not a friendly one. She briefly dropped her cool green eyes to Alexis's feet. "You don't usually wear sneakers to the office. I heard about your *accident*."

"You have? From whom?" Alexis couldn't read Glenna's pale features. How did Clive Colton's second wife feel about his plans to take Mariposa away from Laura, Adam and Joshua? She imagined Glenna supported Clive's decision.

"I'm sure you know the video's all over the news." Glenna's narrow shoulders shrugged beneath her cap-sleeved jacket. She wore it with a cream V-neck shell blouse.

"Yes, I've seen it." The memory of the recording made her mouth dry. One of the most terrifying experiences of her life had been captured on video.

Alexis had the uncomfortable sensation Glenna was trying to get information from her. The Coltons' stepmother had been spending a lot of time at the resort. What was she after?

Glenna swept back an imaginary strand of her bone-straight, bleach-blond hair from her face. "You seem awfully calm. You're very lucky Maxwell Powell III was with you. The incident could have ended in tragedy. You could have been killed."

Alexis shivered despite the comfortable temperatures

maintained in the L. "Luckily, I wasn't. That's not something I want to dwell on."

"I'm sure you don't. I'm sure Josh wants to put the *accident* behind him, too. It doesn't reflect well on the resort."

"What do you mean by that?" Something in Glenna's tone made Alexis's back and shoulders tighten.

She gave a short, scornful laugh. "What do you think I mean? Last month, there was a murder investigation. This month, there was a near-fatal accident caused by negligence. Do you think these events put Mariposa in a *good* light? If I were you, I would demand Josh be fired. I don't know why you aren't."

Alexis unclenched her teeth. "The accident was in no way Joshua's fault."

Glenna arched a skeptical eyebrow. "Then whose fault was it? *He's* the activities director. As such, he's responsible for the safe conditions of all the activities—pools, saunas, *trails*."

A deeper voice flavored with a New York accent joined their conversation. "Yes, he is. And he's excellent at his job."

Alexis turned to see Max come to a stop beside her. He was wearing the bronze pants from when he'd served her lunch. The sleeves of his wine-red polo shirt hugged his well-defined biceps jealously.

She gestured toward him, fighting back a smile. "Maxwell Powell III, this is Glenna Bennett Colton."

The twinkle in Max's eyes promised retribution.

Glenna offered him her right hand. "I know who you are, Mr. Powell. I've seen the video of your heroic rescue of Alexis several times. Before that, I've had the pleasure of dining at your restaurant in Fort Lauderdale a number of times. Each was a transformative experience."

"Thank you. I appreciate that." Max released her hand. "Just as I appreciate Joshua's conscientiousness toward the well-being of Mariposa's guests."

Glenna's lips curved into a thin, condescending smile. "With all due respect, Mr. Powell, how could you possibly know whether Josh is conscientious? Your misperception of his abilities allows him to escape responsibility."

The corners of Max's eyes crinkled with amusement. "I've been at the resort for well over a week. I've observed Joshua at work. I also know how dedicated Adam, Laura and Joshua are to their mother's legacy."

Glenna's smile stiffened at the reference to Annabeth. "I wasn't aware Josh had so many champions."

Alexis inclined her head. "He's earned it. Joshua isn't to blame for the accident. That's a fact."

Glenna's sigh signaled the other woman was nearing the end of her patience. "On what are you basing that?"

Alexis glanced at Max. "We're not at liberty to say. If you want additional information, you should speak with Joshua."

Glenna scoffed. "Of course he would come up with some story to cover his negligence."

Alexis clenched her hands. "We're serious, Ms. Bennett Colton. Speak with Joshua. Or you could ask Laura and Adam. But as I said, neither Max nor I are at liberty to say."

Max inclined his head. "Alexis is right. If you have questions about the accident, speak with Adam, Laura or Joshua. Otherwise, it isn't fair of you to spread false rumors about Joshua."

Glenna split a considering look between Alexis and Max. "I see. Josh and his siblings are very fortunate to have such loyal friends and employees."

Alexis didn't respond. Neither did Max. Without another word, Glenna pivoted on her four-inch stiletto heels and walked past them toward the administrative offices. Alexis hoped she was taking their advice about speaking with Laura, Adam or Joshua. Or all three of them.

She drew her attention from Glenna and turned to Max. "Thank you for everything you said about Joshua. You're right. He takes his responsibilities seriously. He's very dedicated to Mariposa and our guests. It made me angry to hear Glenna disparage him as though he were a recalcitrant child."

Max raised his eyebrows. "I could tell. I was afraid for Glenna." He glanced over his shoulder in the direction Glenna had disappeared. "Joshua's a good guy. He doesn't deserve to have Glenna smear him, especially since she has no idea what happened or of the other events that are going on."

Alexis frowned, tilting her head. "Doesn't she?"

Max's eyes flew back to hers. "What are you saying?" He searched her features as though looking for the answer to his question.

Alexis regretted her words. "Nothing. Never mind." She lowered her voice. "It's just that Glenna was quick to say Joshua should be fired. She said if she were me, she'd demand it. That really made me angry."

Max frowned. "She has no right to say that. She doesn't have any authority over Mariposa."

Yet.

Alexis considered Max, standing beside her. Had Adam confided in him about Clive Colton's money problems and his intentions toward Mariposa the way Laura had confided in her? She wasn't going to bring it up, just in case.

She adjusted her purse strap on her shoulder and glanced toward the hallway again. "Glenna has her own agenda and

I'm certain whatever that agenda is, it doesn't bode well for Mariposa."

"I agree."

Alexis faced him, arching an eyebrow. "Did you just happen to be walking by just now?"

"No, I was looking for you. I thought you might be leaving for the day." Max gestured toward her briefcase. "May I take that for you?"

"Yes, you may. Thank you." Alexis gave him her briefcase, then fell into step with him as he escorted her to her car.

Max tossed her a smile that revealed the deep dimple in his right cheek. "'Maxwell Powell III'? You had to use my full name for the introduction to Glenna?"

Alexis swallowed a chuckle. "No, I didn't have to, but I really enjoyed it."

Max held the door open for her and she led him outside the building. "Are you moving into your bungalow tonight?"

Alexis's amusement vanished. "Yes, I am. But it's not my bungalow. It's a temporary living arrangement."

Max stopped beside the building's entrance and turned to face her. "I'm glad you accepted the Coltons' offer and that you're moving into your temporary living arrangement tonight." He hesitated. "There's an unknown threat out there. We don't know whether it's connected to my stalker or if it was an unfortunate coincidence. I feel much better knowing you're here with round-the-clock security at least until we can get those answers."

"So am I." It was unnerving hearing it in those terms. She forced her lips into a smile as she started walking again. "And so is my mother. But who could have sabotaged the guardrail?"

Max paced beside her. "It could be someone who wants to damage the resort's reputation. Or maybe someone who wants to hurt the Coltons personally."

An intonation in Max's voice made Alexis wonder whether he knew more than he was letting on. She was searching for a way to ask him when she caught a movement in her peripheral vision.

Mark Bower stepped out of his truck and into their path. "I see you brought your knight in shining armor." He turned to Max, gesturing back to Alexis. "I don't suppose it would do any good for me to ask you to let us talk privately."

Max gave the other man a stony stare. "No, it wouldn't."

"Why are you here, Mark?" Alexis was certain Max understood she didn't need a knight in shining armor. He knew she could take care of herself, but he was too much of a protector to step aside a second time.

Mark returned his attention to Alexis. "I want you to know I've hired a lawyer to get my job back."

She suspected her former staffer was bluffing. Although the resort paid very well, between legal and living expenses, it would undoubtedly cost Mark more to sue to get his job back than it would for him to find another suitable position. But since he'd turned this into a legal situation, she had to be careful how she responded.

Alexis adjusted her purse strap on her shoulder. "Thank you for letting me know. I'll brief Mariposa's legal counsel."

Mark's eyes shifted as though she'd given him a response he hadn't expected. "We can take care of this without our lawyers. I'd be willing to return to Mariposa on a probationary status. After a couple of months, you can reassess my performance."

Alexis had to bite her tongue to keep from saying anything that could be used against the resort if Mark's suit made it to court. She decided to repeat herself. Her earlier response was innocuous enough. "Thank you for letting me know."

Mark's jaw flexed as though he was grinding his teeth. She sensed his tension and his anger. Alexis held his gaze without expression.

Finally, he nodded. "Good. You and your bosses can respond to my lawyer when you get her message." Mark turned and climbed back into his truck.

Max walked with Alexis past Mark's vehicle on their way to her car. "Do you think he's telling the truth about retaining a lawyer?"

Alexis was reluctant to discuss resort matters with a guest. But Max had been standing right there and he was Adam's best friend. She could trust him to be discreet with this matter. "I don't think so, but I could be wrong. I'll call Laura when I get home." She wanted to update her manager before she packed for her temporary relocation to the bungalow. "One thing I am certain of is that I can't trust him. Even if his performance is stellar during his probationary period, he violated our employee standards many times, and I couldn't be confident he wouldn't revert to that same behavior."

Max stopped beside her compact sedan. "Do you think Mark is upset enough over being fired that he'd try to take revenge against you or Mariposa?"

A chill raced through Alexis like a cold, foreboding wind. "Are you asking whether I think he could be capable of destroying the guardrail?"

Max flexed his shoulders. "He's a disgruntled ex-employee. I think it's worth discussing him with Noah."

"Yes, and Roland as well." She looked over her shoulder, catching sight of Mark's truck's taillights as he swung out of the parking lot. "But how would he have known you and I would be hiking Saturday?"

"Perhaps the guardrail wasn't tampered with as a way to hurt one of us. If Mark were responsible, it might have been an attack aimed at the resort as revenge for his being fired."

It was a chilling thought, but a possibility they had to face. If Max's theory was correct, too many lives were at stake.

Chapter Eight

Laura entered Alexis's office early Tuesday morning, carrying two mugs of coffee. "Have you settled in okay at the bungalow?"

After placing one of the mugs on Alexis's desk, Laura took the visitor's chair closest to the office door. Her deep pink coatdress warmed her pale skin and highlighted her light blond bob.

Alexis hit a couple of keys on her laptop to save the document she'd been working on before spinning her black wheeled executive seat to face Laura.

Gesturing with the mug, Alexis smiled. "Thank you." She breathed in the dark roast coffee before taking a deep drink. The burnt-umber porcelain was warm against her palms. The caffeine gave her system a jolt. "And yes, the bungalow is very comfortable. Thank you. I can see why we have such a high percentage of repeat guests. And the work commute is a dream."

"Thank you for saying that about the bungalow. I'm glad you're enjoying it." Laura's blue eyes gleamed with pride over the rim of her mug. "How's your ankle healing?"

"I'm almost one hundred percent." Alexis was wearing her black tennis shoes again today. "Tomorrow will be the real test. I'm resuming my morning runs."

"Ooh. Ambitious." Laura gave her a narrow-eyed, skeptical look. "Try not to push yourself beyond what you're comfortable with."

"I promise, Dr. Colton." Alexis teased her as only old friends could. She lifted her mug, drawing Laura's attention to it. "For you to bring me a cup of joe means we have a lot to go over this morning. Where would you like to start?"

"We know each other too well." Laura settled back against her seat. "Thank you for calling me about Mark last night. I can't believe he's going to try to fight his dismissal. You have records of everything and so does HR. We have his signature on the orientation attendance sheets and the form asserting he'd read his employee handbook. We also have statements from several of the guests he upcharged for his services."

Alexis set her mug on her desk before clenching the arms of her chair. "As you know, I didn't want to fire him. But we can't have employees running cons on our guests." She was still outraged over Mark's behavior. His repeated demands to be rehired only made the situation worse.

"No, we can't." Angry color stained Laura's cheekbones. She lowered her mug. "Mariposa's brand is trust. Our guests trust us to ensure their privacy and security, to provide them with an all-inclusive vacation getaway and to not rip them off. Mark's scamming our customers betrayed that trust."

"Which is exactly what I told him." Alexis turned her attention to the window beside her conversation table. Red rock mountains circled the resort, but in her mind's eye, Alexis saw an image of Mark's expression when he'd told her he'd retained legal counsel. "I don't think he's hired a lawyer but it's better to be prepared in case he has."

Laura nodded her agreement. "I called Greg last night to brief him."

Alexis smiled with pleasure. "How is he?"

Greg Sumpter was the Colton family's private attorney. He also handled legal issues for the resort. Alexis always looked forward to his visits. He didn't in any way resemble her mental image of a high-powered lawyer. Unless high-powered lawyers wore cargo shorts and Hawaiian shirts. Really loud Hawaiian shirts.

"He's well." Laura gave her a conspiratorial grin. "He asked about Tallulah."

Rumor had it that Greg had a long-time crush on Tallulah Deschine, head of housekeeping for Mariposa.

Alexis's eyebrows stretched toward her hairline. "Of course he did." Her smile faded as she changed the subject. "Did you mention my concern about Mark to Noah? Actually, Max thought of it first. It was his idea." *Stop babbling.*

Laura's eyes twinkled briefly with amusement. Alexis could almost read her friend's mind. She was filing Alexis's awkward rambling for future reference.

"Yes, I did. He thought it was a good lead. He's going to question Mark and let us know what he learns." Laura shook her head. "Although I can't believe we have to worry about an angry ex-employee trying to damage the resort in addition to Clive's threats to take Mariposa from us."

Alexis's eyes dropped to Laura's hands wrapped around the mug. Her knuckles showed white. "It's a lot. I know. But our suspicion about Mark is just a theory. We could be wrong. Either way, I'm certain Noah will get to the bottom of this quickly."

Laura nodded. "You're right. Noah's very good at what he does."

"Yes, he is." Alexis knew Laura wasn't biased by the fact she and Noah were dating. Noah was a great detective. He was going to track down every viable lead.

"None of this has anything to do with the main reason I'm here, however." Laura crossed her right leg over her left and leaned forward on her chair. "I got a call from Valerie last night."

"Your phone got quite the workout yesterday between me, Greg, Noah and Valerie." Alexis pictured the redheaded, full-figured young woman who served as their daytime bartender.

"That's true. It was a long but very productive day." Laura sighed. "Valerie said she needed to take a few days off immediately—as in she's already gone. She has a family emergency."

"Oh, no." Startled and concerned, Alexis leaned forward into her desk. "I hope everyone's all right."

"So do I." Laura's thin, dark blond eyebrows knitted. "She didn't share any details, though, and I really didn't want to pry. I just wanted you to know she's taking time off."

Alexis sat back, searching her memory for her past conversations with Valerie. She didn't know much about the other woman.

"I understand." She waved a dismissive hand. "I wouldn't have pried, either. If she wants us to know what's going on, she'll tell us. I don't know anything about her family. Do you?"

Laura shook her head. "No, I don't know how many relatives she has or where they live. But I need to find a replacement for her yesterday." She gave a humorless laugh. "I wasn't going to deny her request for time off to help her family. I know how important families are."

"Of course." Alexis thought of her mother. She loved her Aunt Suz and Jake, but Catherine was her only living relative.

Laura continued. "Valerie didn't give me many details, like how long she'll be gone. She said she'd contact me when she has more information about her situation. In the meantime, we're short a bartender. I've found someone to cover her shift for a few days, but we need a backup in case she needs to be away longer."

Alexis realized this was another chance to prove she was ready for the promotion to event manager. She wanted to be promoted based on merit and not because Laura was her friend. This situation would give her the opportunity to demonstrate that she'd developed connections and had resources in the community. Those connections and resources would benefit the resort and support her in her role as event manager, if she was promoted.

She held Laura's eyes. "Let me take care of that. I have a couple of ideas."

Laura was shaking her head before Alexis finished speaking. "Alexis, I wasn't asking for your help. I can take care of it. You already have so much on your plate between working with Max and being short a concierge on your team. And you're injured."

"Really, Laura. I can handle this. It won't take long."

Laura spread her arms. "Alexis, I know you're interested in the event manager's position when Cheryl retires, but you don't have anything to prove."

Alexis sighed, trying to ease her impatience. "Laura, I'm serious. I can take care of this. I already have a lead."

Laura frowned. "You do? All right, if you're sure."

"I'm sure." A surge of excitement rushed through her. She was one step closer to her goal.

MAX WAS TORN. He stared at his ringing cell phone Tuesday afternoon. Should he answer Sarah's call? It was almost time for his daily accidentally on-purpose bumping into Alexis during her afternoon stroll through the L's lobby. He admired the efforts she made to stay connected with the resort's guests as well as her coworkers. It showed the pride she took in her work.

He picked up Sarah's call on the third ring. He'd keep their conversation short. "Sarah. How are you?"

"Max! It seems like you've been having a lot of fun at the resort." Her voice was sulky. "Have you forgotten about me?"

His brow creased in confusion. His eyes moved to the view of the mountain ridge framed by the French doors at the back of his bungalow. "How do you know what I've been doing?"

"Are you kidding?" Sarah sounded amused. "Ever since the video of you saving Alexis Reed's life, the paparazzi can't get enough of the two of you together at the resort."

Max's lips parted in shock. *Oh, no.*

Alexis was going to be irritated. Max clenched his left fist so tightly it hurt. Anything that threatened the safety and privacy of Mariposa's guests stirred her temper. He could imagine her reaction when she learned the media was recording drone footage of the two of them around the property. Would she insist they not spend any more time together in an effort to stop drawing attention to Mariposa?

Max rubbed his eyes with the fingers of his left hand. "Thank you for letting me know." How was he going to fix this?

"I'm surprised you haven't seen them." Beneath Sarah's voice, Max could hear traffic noise. Was she driving while using her phone again?

He turned away from the French doors and wandered the great room. The scents of the wildflowers were soothing. They reminded him of Alexis. He drew a deeper breath.

"You usually handle those types of things for me." Max knew the importance of using social media to build his brand and increase his audience, but he didn't enjoy coming up with content for those platforms. Sarah, on the other hand, was addicted to hashtags, views, likes and algorithms—whatever those things were. "Listen, Sarah, I'm sorry but I need to get back to work so—"

"When would you like to get together for that drink you promised me?"

Max briefly closed his eyes. He couldn't keep putting her off. "Why don't we meet for lunch Sunday?"

"That sounds great." There was a smile in her voice. "Where and when?"

Max glanced at his watch. "Where would you recommend?"

He needed to get moving if he were to have any chance of "bumping into" Alexis. He wanted to see her. Needed to see her. Even if it was a smile and wave from across the lobby, perhaps catch a trace of her perfume.

"Hmm." Sarah's hesitation spiked Max's impatience. "I'll ask my relatives for a recommendation."

"Great." He crossed to his front door. "Text me the time and place, and I'll meet you Sunday."

"I'll look forward to it." Her farewell sang in his ears as he ended the call.

Within minutes, Max was jumping out of his golf cart and hurrying into the L. To his relief, Alexis was speaking with Clarissa at the reception desk. He made his way to her.

She looked up as he approached and gave him the smile

he'd been craving. Her black sneakers looked like they'd been made for her wide-legged slate gray pantsuit.

Alexis shifted to face him. "Hi, Max. How was your morning?"

Max greeted Clarissa before responding to Alexis. "Can I speak with you?"

Her smile dimmed. "Of course. Let's talk in my office." Alexis said goodbye to Clarissa before leading him down the hallway. She lowered her voice. "Do you have more information on the accident or your stalker?"

Her limp was barely noticeable. His wounds were healing, too. He should be able to go back to wearing shorts in a day or two.

"No, but this is about something else." Max followed her into her office and closed the door. He waited for her to sit behind her desk, then took the visitor's seat near the door.

"This must be pretty serious." Alexis glanced toward the closed door. "What is it?"

Max braced himself. "There are videos of us together at the resort on the internet."

Her reaction wasn't what he'd expected. She sat back against her chair and frowned at him as though she didn't understand the words he was speaking. "Someone posted videos of the resort itself to the internet?"

Max nodded. "It's probably drone footage like the video of our accident."

"That's impossible." She straightened, spinning her chair toward her laptop. Rapid clicks sounded as her fingers flew across her keyboard. She shifted the monitor to face him. "My search brought back only the video of my fall and the ones from our own website. I've set up internet alerts to notify me when people post anything connected to Mariposa to the web. What made you think there were videos of us at the resort?"

Max stood, leaning over her desk to get a closer look at her monitor. "Sarah told me she'd seen them."

Had he misunderstood what his assistant had said? No, he was sure he hadn't. He felt like such a fool. Why hadn't he done a search for the videos himself? Because he'd been impatient to see Alexis, to be near her as he was now. He breathed in her soft wildflower scent.

Alexis waved a hand toward her laptop. "As I've said before, our guests' security and privacy are vitally important to us. How safe and secure would you feel if there were drones flying all over the property, recording your every move? Besides, drone recordings of private property violate the FAA's privacy guidelines. Our legal counsel would take care of that."

She looked up at him from over her shoulder. Her eyes hypnotized him. Her scent embraced him. Time slipped away. Her eyes dropped to his lips. Max stiffened. What would she do next?

Alexis looked away, breaking their connection. "Sarah was mistaken." She kept her eyes on her desk. "Other than the hiking footage, there aren't any unauthorized videos of the resort on the net."

Max felt empty as he returned to his seat. "Why are drones able to record footage from the hiking trail but not from any other part of the resort?"

"Legally, drone operators aren't allowed to operate on either property." She shrugged. "However, there are always people who are willing to take the risk, believing they won't get caught. Although our legal council eventually tracks them down, the violators just move their footage to another website."

Max set his right ankle on his left knee. "Maybe I misunderstood what Sarah said." Although he didn't think so. "I'll ask her about it when I see her Sunday."

Alexis gave him a quick glance, then tapped some computer keys. Her screen returned to her internet homepage. "You're meeting Sarah Sunday?"

"Yes, we're having lunch. Could you recommend a nearby restaurant?" He considered her delicate features. Was she avoiding his eyes? Why?

"It depends on what kind of ambience you want." She reached for some papers from a tidy stack on her desk. "If you're looking for something casual, I can recommend Tipsy Tacos. It's a Mexican cantina. A mariachi band plays there every Sunday evening."

Max watched Alexis rifle through the printouts on her desk. "That sounds appealing. We'd miss the band, though, since we're having lunch."

"There's also The Cloisters. It's a high-end restaurant and bar. I'm going there Thursday night."

Max stilled. "Alone?"

"Yes." Alexis stopped fidgeting and finally looked at him. "We need a bartender to fill in for one of our day shifts. I read about a talented, engaging bartender who works at The Cloisters. I'm going to check her out as a possible fill-in until our regular bartender returns."

Max heard the excitement in her voice. He scowled. "Do you think that's a good idea? Whoever's behind sabotaging the guardrail could still be after one or both of us. Under the circumstances, I don't think you should go off the resort alone."

Alexis's body seemed to relax. "There are always plenty of people at The Cloisters. I'll be fine."

Max spread his hands. "There may be a crowd at the bar,

but what about when you're traveling to and from it? It's a bad idea for you to go alone. I'll go with you."

Alexis's eyes widened with surprise. For a second, Max thought she'd argue against his decision. Alexis Reed had a very strong, very stubborn independent streak.

But then she smiled. "All right. I don't think it's necessary, but you're welcome to join me. As a restaurateur, I'd appreciate having your opinion of the bartender."

"Great." Max rose to his feet. That hadn't been so hard. And he'd gotten a date out of it. Alexis may not call it that, but he would. "I'd be happy to give you my feedback. I should let you get back to work."

He sketched a goodbye wave as he turned to leave. His steps were much lighter now than when he'd first arrived. Thursday couldn't come fast enough.

Chapter Nine

"Between our losing Allison and your meeting Noah, I was half afraid our ladies' nights would come to an end." Alexis sipped her frozen margarita as she and Laura waited for their vegan tacos late Tuesday evening.

Laura drank her house margarita. "I'd never give up our ladies' nights. I don't think Allison would want us to, either."

Allison Brewer had been one of the yoga instructors at Mariposa. In the time she'd worked at the resort, Allison, Alexis and Laura had become very close friends. Her death earlier this year had left Alexis and Laura shattered and struggling to cope. Their grief had been magnified when they'd learned Allison had been murdered. Her body had been found in one of the empty pool cabanas as though the killer had just discarded her. Noah, who was Allison's foster brother, had gotten involved with the homicide investigation. Laura had helped him, which had scared Alexis almost out of her mind.

"You're right. Allison would've wanted us to continue this tradition. She looked forward to these evenings. So do I." Alexis raised her glass. "To Allison."

"To Allison." Laura touched her glass to Alexis's.

Alexis sipped her drink as she took in their surroundings. Taco Tuesday at the Tipsy Tacos. As usual the place was packed. Boisterous laughter and lively conversations covered the dining room. The rustic decor was fitting for a Mexican cantina. Wood carvings in vibrant colors decorated the stone walls. The floors and furnishings were built from aged brown wood. Sporting events, game shows and local news programs played on the televisions mounted around the restaurant.

The aromas of spicy salsas, melted cheeses and seasoned meats made Alexis's stomach growl. What would Max think of this place?

"I look forward to these dinners, too." Laura sighed. "For the longest time, our friendship was the only thing that kept me from being swallowed up by work." Her eyes flew up to meet Alexis's. "Don't get me wrong, the resort is very important to me. But now that Noah's in my life, I have more of a balance between my personal and professional lives. It's helped me with my work. Adam and Josh need to make that adjustment, too, especially Adam." A twinkle sparkled in her eyes. "So do you, maybe with Max?"

Alexis shook her head with a smile. "I knew you were up to something with your suggestion that I move into one of the bungalows."

"Oh, no." Laura held up her right hand, palm out. "I asked you to stay at the resort out of concern for your safety. Adam, Josh and Noah agreed with me. We don't know who destroyed the guardrail or why, or who the intended target was, you or Max or someone else at the resort."

Alexis inclined her head. "I appreciate your concern and I promise to be careful."

"Thank you." Laura's smile was soft with relief.

"In fact, Max is coming with me to The Cloisters Thursday night to observe the bartender I told you about. He didn't think I should go alone. He's also going to give me his opinion of her."

"Oh! I should have thought of that." Laura's hand flew to her mouth. Her eyes were wide with dismay. "I'm a horrible friend."

"You're one of my best friends."

"What was I thinking?" Her voice was muffled behind her palm. "Obviously, I wasn't thinking. I'm so sorry."

"Laura, stop." Alexis held up both of her hands. "I didn't think about the stalker, either. This is a new experience for both of us. But luckily Max did remember and offered to be my wingman." She struggled not to squirm under the speculative look in Laura's eyes.

"Now, if your staying at the bungalow gives you more time with Max, that wouldn't be such a bad thing. Would it?"

Alexis remembered their kiss and the pulse at the base of her throat leaped. "Max is great. He's kind, intelligent, ambitious, funny." She cut the list of his attributes short before she started sounding like a besotted heroine in a rom-com.

Laura nodded. "And very attractive."

"Yes, he is." Understatement. "He also lives in New York, twenty-four hundred miles away. Approximately." She'd looked it up.

Their server arrived with their entrées, putting a pause on their conversation. Alexis thanked the young man before sampling one of the hot corn-shell tacos. They were filled with seasoned shredded chicken, tomatoes, lettuce, red onions, cheese, jalapeño peppers and black olives.

She searched her mind for a change of topic. Before she could think of one, Laura picked up their conversation where they'd left off.

"Fortunately, Max isn't in New York now. He's here."

Laura had the air of a defense attorney, giving her closing argument.

Alexis had a few objections. "Exactly. Not only is he a guest, he's also my client. A relationship with him wouldn't be appropriate."

Laura giggled around another bite of her barbacoa taco. She swallowed before responding. "Alexis, you're people, not robots. We don't choose when, where or how we meet our soul mates." She hesitated. "I certainly didn't imagine myself finding Noah during the murder investigation of one of my best friends."

No one could have imagined that happening. "I don't know that Max is my soul mate." Her body warmed at the thought, though.

"How will you know if you don't give a relationship with him a chance?" Laura arched an eyebrow as she sipped her drink. She obviously thought she was winning this debate.

Alexis wished it were that simple. "Max and I are from different worlds, Laura. He was born and raised in New York City. His father is a film producer, and his mother is a casting director. I was raised in Sedona by a single mother who works for the state of Arizona. He's a celebrated chef who owns two fine-dining restaurants. I'm a concierge who lives on burgers and fries."

"First, stop putting yourself down." Temper darkened Laura's sky-blue eyes. "It doesn't matter where you came from. What matters is where you're going. My father's proof of that. Everything he has was given to him and he's on the verge of losing it all. Second, Max isn't a snob. Adam wouldn't be friends with someone like that."

"Points taken." Alexis considered it a good sign that Max and Adam were such good friends.

Like Laura, Adam was a good boss. All the Coltons

were. They never hesitated to roll up their sleeves and pitch in wherever and whenever help was needed. Their attitude helped inspire loyalty and commitment among Mariposa's staff.

Laura leaned into the table and lowered her voice. "What are you afraid of?"

Alexis stiffened. She placed her taco on her plate. "What makes you think I'm afraid?"

Laura cocked her head. "I know you. Come on. Spill."

Alexis's shoulders rose and fell with her sigh. "The men I've dated in the past haven't understood my career ambitions."

Another understatement. They'd resented the long hours she'd worked, and they'd tried to talk her out of going back to school for her MBA. Rather than giving up her goals, she'd ended those relationships.

"I remember." Laura nodded. "Their loss. But, Alexis, you don't know that Max will be like those other guys. He's ambitious, too."

"I know. That's not what I'm afraid of." She held Laura's eyes. "Suppose my feelings for Max make me give up my professional goals? If there comes a time when I have to choose between Max and my goals, which choice would I make and what would it say about me?"

"Seriously?" Laura smiled as though Alexis was teasing. She sobered when Alexis didn't smile back. "Alexis, you've never given up your dreams before. What makes you think you would this time?"

Alexis sat back with a sigh. "Because I've never felt this way before."

THE CLOISTERS WAS CROWDED Thursday evening. Max wasn't surprised. The parking lot had been packed. Alexis had been lucky to find a spot toward the far end of the lot near some hedges under a lamp. He took a firm hold of her hand, drawing her close to his side to keep from losing her amid the masses. She looked up at him. Her bright eyes were wide with surprise and curiosity. Staring into them, Max could barely breathe.

She was so beautiful. Her wavy raven hair was thick and loose around her shoulders. His fingers itched with the urge to bury themselves into the heavy mass. Her little black dress skimmed her firm, toned figure. The scooped neckline gave only a hint of her cleavage. The long, wide sleeves billowed around her arms. The knee-length hem showed off her long, shapely calves. Her low-heeled pumps boosted her height to his chin.

Max gave her a reassuring smile, then set a course for the bar. As he cleared a path for them, he scanned the posh interior. They were surrounded by polished white oak wood, shiny bronze fixtures and soft black leather furnishings. The air was redolent with well-aged liquors, seasoned, high-quality hors d'oeuvres and money. The ambience telegraphed wealth and prestige. It was so different from Mariposa's warm, friendly environment. Could they find a bartender in this upmarket establishment who would fit into the resort's culture?

"Let's find seats at the bar." Alexis leaned against him to be heard above the instrumental music and murmurs of conversation.

Max felt her warmth against his back and a shiver went through him. Unable to form a response, he nodded. Was his palm sweating against hers? He found two seats together at the bar. Max could see his reflection in the gleaming, rectangular wood surface. Beneath the cylindrical bronze fittings, bottles of liquors and mixes arranged against the mirror on the back wall sparkled in the light. The action was happening at the center of the bar where a young woman moved briskly in the open space, taking requests and mixing drinks.

"Is that her?" Max held the back of Alexis's black leather barstool as she settled into the seat. She pushed her purse into the space on the seat beside her.

"Yes. That's Kelli Iona." Alexis watched her subject closely. "I recognize her from the photo in the magazine interview."

The young woman appeared to be in her mid-twenties. She was tall, perhaps five seven or five eight, and physically fit. She wore a double-breasted black vest over a crisp white oxford service shirt and what looked like black stretch service chinos. Her long, wavy brown hair was gathered into a ponytail holder that swung from shoulder to shoulder as she attended to her customers.

As though she had eyes in the back of her head, Kelli looked over her right shoulder toward Max and Alexis at the other end of the bar. "Welcome to The Cloisters! I'll be right with you. There are two customers ahead of you." Her smile was warm as though they were next-door neighbors, the good kind.

Max made himself comfortable on the barstool beside Alexis. "Take your time."

Maybe they could find a suitable bartender for Mariposa at this upscale bar after all. He should've known better than to have doubted Alexis.

"That was a good sign." Alexis folded her hands on the bar's smooth surface. "She acknowledged us as soon as we sat down."

"Yes, that's good customer service." And she'd greeted

them with a smile. Max shifted to face Alexis. "How did you find her?"

Alexis glanced at him before returning her attention to Kelli. "She was profiled in an e-zine that covers local restaurants, bars and events. Her interview was very charming and personable. She started bartending after high school. She just recently moved to Sedona."

Max was impressed. "She must be good at her job, otherwise The Cloisters wouldn't have hired her."

He watched Kelli mix an order for one of the customers ahead of him. Her flair commanded her customers' attention. She selected a napkin from the top of a nearby pile, spun it in the air with a flick of her wrist, then tapped it onto the bar. Holding a bottle in each hand by their long necks, she free-poured the liquors into a silver mixer, then brought the bottles down and around to stop their flow. She added a few more ingredients, mixing them together with a quick stir. She transferred the contents into a highball glass and set the glass on the napkin.

"Very impressive. And quick." Alexis sounded like she was mentally applauding the bartender. "So far so good. She has one more customer before she gets to us. Do you have your drink order ready?" Alexis had asked him to request a complicated mixed drink to test Kelli's ability.

"Do you have one?" He lowered his voice and leaned closer. The pretense gave him an excuse to breathe in her perfume. He felt her warmth in the comfortably cool bar.

"Yes." She flashed a smile that dazzled him. "I had to look one up, though. I usually drink white wine. Or if I'm in an adventurous mood, a margarita."

"So you're experimenting tonight?" Max chuckled. "I may need to drive us home, then."

Alexis laughed. "Don't worry. I'll cut myself off if I start feeling tipsy."

Kelli appeared before them. Max sensed her energy. Her big brown eyes sparkled with excitement as though she was inviting them on an adventure. "Thank you both so much for your patience. What can I get for you?"

"You didn't keep us waiting long at all." Alexis returned the bartender's smile. "May I have an Aviation, please?"

Kelli raised her eyebrows. Her eyes glinted at the challenge. "A very good choice for the lady." She spun a napkin in front of Alexis, then turned to Max. "And what can I mix for the gentleman?"

"I'd like a Dark and Stormy, please."

Kelli's eyes widened with pleasure. She swung her right index finger between Alexis and Max. "I like these choices." She did her signature napkin spin for Max. "Ladies first."

Max watched Kelli collect the bottles of gin, maraschino liqueur, crème de violette and lemon juice. She free-poured the liquids into the silver mixer with a balance of deft precision and captivating flourish. She poured the mixture into a cordial glass, added fruit and floral garnish, then presented the glass to Alexis.

"Thank you." Alexis looked delighted.

"My pleasure." Kelli winked at her. She pointed at Max. "And now for your Dark and Stormy."

Max liked the drink but he'd only had it a few times. The last time had been years ago while training with a chef in the Caribbean. The drink only had two ingredients—dark rum and ginger beer—but finding the right balance of spicy and sweet was complicated. He watched her brisk, sharp movements as she made the beverage.

Kelli poured his drink into a cognac balloon glass and placed it in front of him. “What do you think?”

Max took a sip. His eyes widened in surprise. “Perfect.”

“Yes.” Kelli pumped her fist. “Thank you.” She turned to Alexis. “How do you like your drink?”

Alexis nodded. “It’s also perfect. Thank you.”

Kelli’s face glowed with pride and pleasure. “Thank you both.”

Max slipped Kelli his credit card to pay for their drinks. The young bartender inclined her head before bouncing away. He watched as she stopped to check on another customer near the opposite end of the bar. An older gentleman sat back on his seat, revealing the guest Kelli was speaking with.

Max stiffened in surprise. “Isn’t that Joshua?”

“Where?” Alexis followed his gaze. “You’re right.”

The youngest Colton was generous with his smiles as he chatted with the attractive bartender. She laughed at something he said before continuing to process Max’s card and print his receipt.

Kelli returned to their side of the bar with Max’s credit card and gave him his receipt. “I’ll stop by to check on you, but if you need anything else before then, just give me a wave.” With a wink and a smile, she turned away to check on her other guests. Max noticed she lingered a little longer with Joshua.

He took another sip of his drink. It was really good. “Does it look to you as though Kelli and Joshua have known each other for a while? It doesn’t look as though they just met today. They’re pretty comfortable with each other.”

“You could be right.” Alexis seemed to be nursing her drink, paying more attention to Kelli and her interactions with her customers. “She’s very talented. This drink is delicious, and she has a great attitude. She seems to connect easily with her guests, and not just the male ones. I'm going to recommend Laura bring her in for an interview."

Alexis was right. More women than men sat around the bar and the women were just as comfortable with her. Kelli would be a wonderful addition for Mariposa, even for the temporary position. Max's only hesitation was Joshua.

He watched the younger man's interaction with Kelli. Other men tried to monopolize the bartender's time beyond ordering a drink. She put them off firmly but politely. However, she always had a few extra moments for Joshua. Did Joshua come to The Cloisters to see Kelli or was seeing the bartender an added bonus of the venue?

Max took another drink. "Joshua's attracted to her."

Alexis glanced down the bar. She must have seen what he saw. "It does appear that way."

"Doesn't he have a rule against dating employees?"

"That's what Laura told me." She returned her attention to Max. "You're not suggesting I tell Laura not to hire Kelli because her brother may have a crush on her, are you?"

Was he? "I think that's another consideration. Suppose there's something building between them. But because she comes to work at Mariposa, they have to pump the brakes on whatever that is. Is that something we're comfortable with?"

Alexis looked at him as though she questioned his sanity. "What I'm *not* comfortable with is not offering Kelli this chance just because of what may or may not be growing between her and Joshua. Kelli should decide whether she wants to accept this career opportunity."

Max raised his hands, palms out. He was embarrassed by how badly he'd misspoken. "You're right. It's her choice. But maybe you should tell Joshua you're recommending her for the fill-in position."

"I'll leave that to Laura. She's the assistant manager." Alexis still sounded more than a little perturbed by Max's suggestion. "I'll let her know we saw—"

"Max. Alexis. It's great to see you guys." Joshua's voice startled Max. Had the other man heard what he and Alexis were saying? Joshua's tone grew somber. "Have you both recovered from the accident?"

Alexis's eyes lit up. "Yes, thank you for asking. I've even started jogging again. My ankle's a little tender, but otherwise fine."

Joshua chuckled. "Of course you're running again. Nothing keeps you down, at least not for long." He glanced toward Kelli at the other end of the bar before addressing Max. "How're you, Max? I've heard Noah has a suspect who's not connected to that stuff in New York."

"I appreciate his looking into it." Max glanced toward Alexis. Her expression was tense. Was that because of Joshua's sudden appearance or their topic of discussion? "I know we're all looking forward to solving this mystery so we can put it behind us."

"Yes, we are." Joshua's eyes drifted back to Kelli as though he couldn't help himself. Max could empathize. He felt the same way when Alexis was nearby. "I hope you both have a good evening."

Max joined Alexis in wishing Joshua well before returning to their conversation. "Joshua couldn't keep his eyes off Kelli. But you're right. Kelli deserves the opportunity at Mariposa. She's an excellent bartender and the resort would be lucky to have her."

"I know." Alexis shook her head. "You're a hopeless romantic."

"I prefer to think of myself as a *hopeful* romantic." Max

had more of his drink. It didn't pack as much of a punch as Alexis's laughter.

"Fortunately for Kelli, you're not the one making the referral. I am."

"Are you hopeless or hopeful?" Max held his breath.

Alexis took a moment to answer. "I prefer to think of myself as practical."

What does that mean? He exhaled. "Haven't you ever met someone who made you want to flush *practical* down the drain and follow your heart?"

Alexis shook her head. "Have you?"

I have now. "I haven't lost hope." Max cleared his throat. "Since we're here, would you like to get dinner?"

She smiled. "I'd love that."

And he'd love it if the night never ended. But for now, he'd hold on to *practical* with both hands and hope his heart could stand the wait.

THE HOST LED them to a table not far from the bar. With her decision about the fill-in bartender's position made, Alexis checked her evaluation of Kelli off her to-do list and focused on dinner with Max. That was definitely not a hardship.

The celebrity chef looked camera-ready in a casual brown suit. His black vintage shirt had a standing collar. He'd left the top button undone. The fabric stretched across his muscled chest. It featured a leaf embroidered pattern she'd dearly love to trace. Alexis curled her fingers under the table to resist the urge. His clean mint cologne was a distraction. So was his charm; the way he took her hand, held her chair, rested his palm on the small of her back. He made her feel like part of a couple. She hadn't realized how much she'd missed that. It was nice.

It also was scary. As she'd told Laura last evening, even if she decided to pursue a relationship with the charming chef, what would happen in three weeks when he returned to New York, leaving her behind? For tonight, she pushed the worry to the back of her mind.

They both chose the blackened salmon entrée. Descriptions of their days and their plans for the rest of the week carried them almost to the end of their meal.

"Where does love stand on your list of priorities?" Max's question caught her by surprise. Were they back to the hopeless romantic versus practical relationship debate?

A forkful of salmon found its way into Alexis's windpipe. She covered her mouth with her right hand and cleared it with a cough. That bought her a little time. "Excuse me?"

"Are you okay?" Max put his hand on hers where it rested on the table. His eyes were dark with concern.

"Yes, thank you." Alexis took a steadying breath. The scents of cayenne, thyme and oregano wafted up from her salmon. "Um, well, I've never really thought about where my love life was on my list of priorities." *Not until recently.*

His lips curved with amusement. "I think that answers the question of where it stands on your list. So, you and Jake have never dated?"

Alexis thought his tone was too casual. "No, we haven't."

"You've never been tempted?"

"I told you. Jake's like a brother to me and he thinks of me as his sister. Dating would be too weird. Although our mothers, who are both crazy impatient for grandchildren, have brought it up more than once."

Max smiled as he sipped his drink. "My mother wants grandkids, too. Mel and I have thrown Miri under the bus. She's the only one who's married."

Alexis's shoulders shook with amusement. "Oh, I'm sure

she appreciated that. Well, Jake and I refuse to get married—especially to each other—just to satisfy our mothers' need to spoil our as-yet-unborn children."

Max lifted his glass in a mock toast. "Mel and I salute you."

Alexis arched an eyebrow. "So what about *your* love life? Where is it on your list of priorities?"

"The same." Max pierced his last piece of salmon. "I've been too busy building my restaurants to spend much time pursuing a relationship."

"I know what you mean." Alexis hesitated as she watched Max put the forkful of salmon between his lips. The act seemed so intimate. She dropped her eyes and forced her thoughts into a semblance of order. "With all of your projects, I'm surprised you have time to sleep." She braced herself to meet his eyes again. "A relationship would probably put you over the edge."

His myriad business pursuits were additional reasons a relationship between them wouldn't work. She was building a career, but he was building an empire.

"My restaurants are my first love." Max nudged his nearly empty plate to the side. He folded his arms on the white cloth that covered their table. "I want people to think of Out with Friends as a place to go for a great meal and a good time."

"That's how my mother described it." Alexis admired people with a plan. She wiped the corners of her mouth with her linen napkin, then slid it and her plate to the side.

"My father had wanted me to join his production company, supporting documentaries and feature films that educated as well as entertained." Max stared at his glass of water, but Alexis suspected he saw a different image in his head. "I'm very proud of the company he built, but my first love has always been cooking. I hated disappointing him, but I didn't want to go into TV and film production."

"I seriously doubt your father's disappointed in you." Alexis paused as their server came to collect their plates and deliver their bill.

Max claimed the black leather check holder before Alexis could even move. He glanced at the receipt, then returned it to their server with his credit card.

He waited until the young man disappeared again before continuing. "My father's motto is, 'You can do better.' He's said that to me and my sisters all my life."

Alexis's eyes widened with surprise. "That's kind of harsh."

"Tell me about it." Max gave a humorless laugh. "My sisters and I think he's trying to encourage or maybe motivate us. I think he'd be surprised to know it's having the opposite effect." He sat back against his chair. "We've finally decided one of us should tell him. I think it should be my sister, Miri. She's the eldest."

"Or maybe the three of you should tell him together."

Max cocked his head. "Wouldn't that feel as though we're ganging up on him?"

"Not if you make it clear that your words are coming from a place of love."

"That's a good idea." Max's eyebrows knitted as he seemed to consider her advice. "I'll discuss it with them. Thank you."

"You're welcome." Alexis sipped her Aviator. She was alternating between it and ice water.

"What about you?" Max asked. "Where do you want your career to take you?"

"That's an interesting way to put it." She considered his

questions. "Lately, I've started to feel as though I'm running in place."

"I can relate to that."

His understanding encouraged her to confide even more. "I've worked at Mariposa since I was in college. I started at the reception desk like Clarissa, then moved up to concierge. Now I'm the senior concierge. It's a supervisory position, but I'm ready to move into management."

Max's eyes gleamed with admiration. "Do you have a position in mind?"

Alexis nodded. "One of our event managers is retiring at the end of the month. I would love to be promoted into that position."

"Does Laura know you're interested in it?"

"We've discussed it." Alexis winced when she recalled the awkward conversation. "One of the drawbacks of having a best friend who's also your boss is the impression that perhaps my promotions were handed to me."

"What do you care what other people think?" Max shrugged his powerful shoulders.

"I know it shouldn't bother me, but I don't want other people's suspicions to undermine my position at the resort. I told Laura that, if I get the job, I don't want there to be any doubt that I earned it."

Max nodded his approval. "What do you need to do to earn it?"

"It's a matter of proving my project management and customer service skills." She gestured toward Max. "That's one of the reasons I was so happy when Adam trusted me to work with you on your recipes. It shows he believes I can provide you with satisfactory customer service."

"You've been better than satisfactory. Your feedback on the entrées has been critical to the success of my recipes."

Alexis shook her head. "You're being too kind."

"No, I'm not."

She ignored his interruption and continued. "I have to show I can coordinate with outside vendors." Alexis jerked her head toward the bar. "I'm hoping being able to refer Kelli Iona will score me some points with Laura."

"Your awareness of a talented bartender like Kelli has impressed me."

Alexis laughed. "You're good for my ego. I also have to bring my projects in at or under budget. To plan whole events at the resort or even *for* the resort would be so exciting. Weddings, anniversaries, family reunions." Her body vibrated with excitement. "I don't want to change the feel or flavor of the resort. But I would love for more people to experience it."

Max leaned into the table. His eyes darkened with an exciting emotion. He lowered his voice. "I love the sound of your voice when you're excited. The way your enthusiasm brings a sparkle to your eyes and a flush to your cheeks." He brushed the backs of his long, warm fingers across the side of her face.

Alexis felt a delicious shiver roll down her spine. "We agreed we should just be friends." Was that husky sound really her voice?

A ghost of a smile played with Max's full lips. He let his hand drop away from her face as he leaned against his chair. "We can still be friends."

Not if he kept looking at her like that. The heat in his eyes could make her forget her common sense.

Alexis cleared her throat and pushed away from the table. "We should get back to Mariposa."

Without another word, Max stood with her. He placed his hand lightly on the small of her back and escorted her to the parking lot. Alexis's steps were heavy with regret. The evening was coming to an end. It was better they said good-night sooner rather than later—before she did something she might regret.

Wasn't it?

Chapter Ten

Another beautiful night in Sedona. As Alexis walked beside Max, she filled her lungs with the cool night air. Beneath the scents of rich sauces, spicy poultries and fish, Alexis detected the fragrance of pines and juniper. In the clear, mid-March sky, the stars appeared like small diamonds scattered across blue velvet. A soft breeze threaded through her hair. The setting was too romantic.

Did Max feel it, too? Alexis slid him a look from the corner of her eye.

"Thank you again for coming with me." She stopped beside her car, which stood under a lamp in the back of the bar's rear parking lot. "You're great comp—" An object glinting in the bushes beneath the lamp distracted her.

Loud pops, two of them at first, rang out across the parking lot quickly followed by the screams and shouts of the people in the area behind them. Max grabbed her, using his body to shield her as he pushed her away from the car.

"Stay down." His words were curt and loud.

Alexis heard more popping. More and more. It seemed like the popping would never end.

They ran back to the bar, sticking close to the other parked cars. They stayed low, as low as possible. Their romantic surroundings had become a threat. The air smelled like gun smoke. The stars were too bright. Alexis feared they'd give away their position. Each gentle breeze was the shooter's breath on the back of her neck. Alexis gritted her teeth. She prayed she and Max would make it back inside the bar without being shot. The establishment's entrance came into view. Max clasped her hand and sprinted beside her. She was torn between gratitude for his selfless protection and fear for the danger in which he was putting himself.

Behind The Cloisters' solid front doors, Alexis breathed again. But they still weren't out of danger. She pulled her cell phone from her purse and called for help.

"Nine-one-one. What is your emergency?" The dispatcher's voice was like air to a suffocating person.

Alexis gulped down her panic. "Someone's shooting at us."

"NOAH." ALEXIS FELT a rush of relief to see a familiar face in the midst of an unfamiliar and terrifying situation. The detective was walking across the lot toward her and Max. "I'm so glad to see you."

"So am I." Max's hand kept up a steady rhythm as he rubbed Alexis's upper arm. Was he aware he was doing that? Was he comforting her, himself or both of them?

"I heard the dispatch report over the radio that you'd called in a shooting." Noah came to a stop in front of them. He wore baggy blue jeans, a tight black T-shirt and a faded gray hooded jacket. "Laura would never have forgiven me if I didn't check it out. And she'll expect a full report when I see her."

He was probably right.

"I would be the same way." She was still shaking. Max

tightened his arm around her waist, offering her comfort as well as support.

Alexis's eyes scanned the parking lot. She was struggling to make sense of all they'd been through. Uniformed officers were searching the immediate area. She'd overheard them discussing the fact that they'd found seventeen bullet casings. *Seventeen.* So many. And how had they not been hit by at least one?

While she'd called emergency services, Max had warned Kelli and the manager on duty about the shooting. They'd discreetly asked those guests who'd been preparing to leave to wait until after the police had secured their surroundings. Now dozens of their customers were cautiously stepping outside like penguins checking the water for sharks.

Alexis shifted her stance to take some of her weight off her left foot. Now that her adrenaline rush was over, she could feel her ankle throbbing. She'd run as fast as she could with Max back to the bar to escape the shooter. She hadn't given any thought to the injury she'd sustained during the previous attempt on her and Max's lives.

Noah shared a look between Alexis and Max. "Can you walk me through what happened?"

"Max and I got back to my car." She pointed toward her vehicle, which still stood under the lamp in the rear of the parking lot. "I noticed the light from the lamp glinting on something in the bushes. That's when I heard a popping sound."

Max picked up the recount. "Even as we ran back to the bar, I could still hear the gun firing."

Noah stepped back to get a better look at them. "Neither of you were hurt?"

Max squeezed Alexis's shoulders. "We're fine, fortunately."

"I'm fine, thanks to you again." Alexis's eyes lingered on Max.

Noah dragged his fingers through his thick brown hair. "It doesn't sound like an attempted mugging."

"It didn't feel like one, either." Max's voice was dry.

"Nothing was taken and your car's still there." The detective shook his head in amazement. "You're both lucky. Seventeen bullets. Someone emptied their gun at you. That's a lot of hostility."

"Hostility toward us?" Alexis took a steadying breath. "We can't be certain this was personal to Max and me. It could have been a mass shooter."

"I don't think that's what this was." Max's tone was pensive. "This was personal. The shooter was hiding in the bushes beside your car. They were aiming at us. At you. Then they left."

"I agree with Max. Although, since you two were together again, there's no way to tell which one of you the shooter was after. They could have been after both of you." Noah addressed Alexis. "What brought you to The Cloisters?"

Alexis glanced at the establishment over her shoulder. "We need someone to fill in at L bar temporarily for one of our regulars. I told Laura I'd check out one of the bartenders here to see if we should invite her for an interview."

Noah frowned. "Did you tell anyone besides Laura that you were coming here tonight?"

Alexis shook her head. "Just Max. There wasn't any reason to tell anyone else."

The detective addressed Max. "Did you mention it to anyone?"

Max also shook his head. "Only Adam and my family in New York."

Noah stared at the ground. Alexis could feel his thoughts churning. "Someone could have followed you from the resort. But they would've had to have been parked outside the grounds on the off chance that one or both of you would be going out."

Alexis heard the skepticism in the detective's voice. She wasn't buying that theory, either. "Have you spoken with Mark Bower?"

"Yeah." Noah shoved his hands into the back pockets of his jeans. "His alibi's weak. He claims the night the guardrails were tampered with, he was at the laundromat. There aren't any cameras at the one he used. He could've come and gone without anyone noticing. And we don't know what time the rails were cut."

"So he's still on the list." Alexis glanced up at Max. "I can't think of anyone else with a motive to do something like this. I don't want to think it could be Mark, either. I'm the one who recommended hiring him."

Noah turned to Max. "Have you thought any more about who your stalker could be?"

"I have no idea why someone would want to kill me." Max rubbed his jaw with his left hand. "And if that's their plan, why didn't they do it in New York? Why follow me to Sedona?"

"How are they tracking your movements?" Alexis spread her arms. "For that matter, how is Mark tracking my movements?"

"All right. I'll add this to our case file." Noah walked with them to Alexis's car. "In the meantime, I'll see how the search is progressing. Are you two okay to get back to the resort on your own?"

Max nodded. "We'll be fine. Thanks."

"Good." Noah's eyes scanned their surroundings again

before he returned his attention to them. "Listen, I appreciate that you both have work to do but maybe think about staying on the resort until we find whoever's behind these attacks."

"That's good advice." Max lowered his eyes to meet Alexis's.

"I promise to be careful." She stopped beside her car and looked cautiously behind it. Max and Noah circled the vehicle. No one noticed anyone lurking in the bushes. She offered Noah a smile. "Thanks again. I'm glad you were here."

"I'm sorry this happened." Noah shook their hands. "It's a horrible experience. But please know I'm giving your case my full attention. Hopefully, nothing else will happen, but if it does, call me directly. And be careful driving home."

Alexis felt much better after his assurances. "Thank you for everything, Noah. Good night."

"Thank you." Max looked at Alexis. "Do you want me to drive?"

"No, thank you." Alexis engaged the keyless entry as she turned toward the driver's side door. "I can manage."

With a final wave goodbye to Noah, Alexis pulled out of the lot. She wasn't shaking any more, but her muscles were tight. Seventeen bullets had been shot in her direction. If Max hadn't pulled her away, would one of them have struck her?

Max broke the tense silence. "Noah's right. We shouldn't leave the safety of the resort anymore. At least not until this stalker is caught."

"I agree. When the guardrails were sabotaged, it was easier to think we weren't really the intended target. We were in the wrong place at the wrong time." Alexis released a shaky breath. “Having a loaded gun unloaded at me cleared up any confusion.”

The rustling sound from the passenger seat indicated Max had shifted to face her. “I’m sorry you had this experience.”

“I wasn’t the only one running from bullets. I’m sorry this happened to you, too.” She checked the traffic before merging into the left-turn lane. She stopped at the red light. “I wish we knew who’s targeting us and what they want.”

“So do I.”

Alexis looked at the night sky and the mountains in the distance. The evening shouldn’t have ended this way. She gripped the steering wheel and beat back the feelings of fear that were trying to take hold of her again. “Would you mind if we stopped by my condo so I could pack a few more things for my stay at the resort?”

“I don’t mind at all.”

“Thank you.” When the traffic light turned green, Alexis pulled out of the turn lane and through the intersection.

Conversation was stiff and sporadic during the twenty-minute drive to her condo community. Alexis had the sense they were both still processing their terrifying experience. She pulled into her attached one-car garage and welcomed Max into her home again.

She was suddenly very tired. Was it the long day, the alcohol—or the shooting? “I could really use a cup of coffee. Would you like some?”

“Yes, please. If it’s not too much trouble.”

“It isn’t.” Alexis moved toward the coffee maker on the marble counter. “Why don’t you have a seat. This shouldn’t take long.”

Behind her, Alexis heard Max cross to her dining table

and pull out a chair. His steps seemed slow as though he was fatigued as well.

She was on autopilot as she moved around her kitchen, collecting the mugs from the cupboard and filling the carafe with water. Her fingers were clumsy as she tried to separate the coffee filters.

She laid her hands flat on the counter and stretched them before trying again. "Someone shot at us. I don't understand why." Her patience frayed, Alexis gave up and stuffed two or three of the thin white papers into the brew basket.

"I can't apologize enough." Max's words were heavy with regret. "It's my fault your life's in danger."

Alexis spun to face him. "No, it's not." That maneuver had taken its toll. Her knees were shaking again. She leaned heavily against the counter behind her. "The creep who's been following us around is entirely to blame. Besides, as Noah pointed out, we don't know whether that attack was directed at you, me or both of us."

"Do you really think Mark Bower would shoot you for firing him?" From his dubious tone, Alexis sensed Max didn't agree with that theory.

She found it hard to believe, too. Still… "I don't know."

Alexis fumbled for the tub of grounds she stored in the cupboard above the coffee maker. Her hand trembled as she measured the first teaspoon. She drew a breath to steady herself and caught the light, nutty aroma of the breakfast blend. The relaxation technique failed. The grounds were leaping from the teaspoon. Her breathing became more ragged. She needed to calm down.

Two large hands took hold of her shoulders. Alexis jumped and the coffee grounds scattered across her counter.

Max's voice came from behind her. "Lean on me. Just lean on me. I'm here for you."

She turned in his arms and stared up at him in amazement. "You aren't rattled?"

Max hesitated. "I'm a lot of things. Anxious, angry and chilled to the core." His eyes delved into hers. "Maybe I need to lean on you. Maybe I think we need to lean on each other."

"I was so scared." Alexis wrapped her arms around his shoulders and leaned into him. She tasted the tears she hadn't realized were falling.

"I know, sweetheart. I was scared, too." Max rubbed her back. His shirt was soft under her cheek. He'd hung his jacket on his chair. "I'm so sorry you went through that."

"I wasn't scared for myself. I was frightened out of my *mind* for you."

"For *me*? Why?"

Alexis leaned back in the circle of his arms. Swiping the tears from her cheeks with the back of her right hand, Alexis glared up at his handsome, puzzled face. "Do you think you're bulletproof?" How could he be so brilliant, capable and creative about so many complicated things yet so silly about this? "You put your body between me and an active shooter." Her voice quavered. "If anything had happened to you, I would have lost my mind."

Max framed her face with his large palms. "If anything had happened to you, I would've lost mine."

He lowered his mouth to hers. Alexis's eyes drifted shut. She nibbled at his firm, full lips and shivered as those lips teased her own. Max stroked his tongue across the seam of her mouth. Alexis sighed as she sent her tongue to play with his.

From the moment she'd picked him up at the L Building and he'd strode toward her in his brown suit and black shirt, it had been hard for Alexis to remember the evening wasn't a date. They were friends and he'd offered to help her with a work project. Her mind was aware of those boundaries. But her body kept reacting to the sound of his voice, the dimple in his smile and the pull of his scent. Deep in her fantasies, she'd wanted the evening to end like this. Not with them racing away from gunshots.

Alexis parted her lips. Max deepened their kiss. He pressed her against him, molding her body to his. His tongue swept inside. Alexis shivered under the intimate caress. Her skin heated. Her pulse raced. Her body grew restless. She moaned deep in her throat. The pulse was loud in her head.

"I love the way you feel against me." Alexis spoke on a breath. She lifted on her toes to fit her body even closer to his. She opened her mouth wider and sucked his tongue inside her.

A BALL OF heat burst into flames inside Max. Pleasure, sweet and sharp, pierced him.

"And I love the way you feel in my arms." He slid his hands down Alexis's back, cupping her hips and lifting her from her feet.

"Wrap your legs around me, sweetheart." His words were a whisper. Max pressed his lips against the curve of her neck. He breathed in her soft scent.

Without hesitation, Alexis wrapped her long, toned legs around him. She trailed kisses down his neck. Max shivered when she dragged her teeth lightly against his skin.

Four strides carried him into her dining area. Max lowered her onto the table. Her legs dropped away from him. Alexis pulled his shirt free of his pants and stroked her palms up and over his torso. Max's body burned. He drew a deep breath.

Reaching behind Alexis, Max released the zipper of her dress. He straightened and watched her bodice pool around her waist. The curves of her breasts rose above her demi-cup black lace bra. Max stopped breathing. He remembered the condom in his wallet and his palms dampened.

He also remembered Alexis racing away from gunshots, trembling in his arms, sobbing against his chest. She looked up at him. Her bright eyes were hot with need. Did she need *him*—or did she need to forget? The answer mattered. Very much. It would mean the difference between waking up to rejoice—or to regret. Max briefly closed his eyes. He gritted his teeth as he bit back a sigh.

Max wrapped his arms around her. He kissed her lips softly as he zipped her dress. It was one of the hardest things he'd had to do. His heart pounded against his chest as though in protest of his actions.

He spoke against her lips. "Why don't you pack your things, sweetheart? I'll make the coffee." He forced himself to let her go. Stepping back, he met her eyes. The heat in them was cooling. Confusion and disappointment took its place.

Alexis frowned. "I don't understand. What's wrong?" The uncertainty in her voice was like a gut punch.

He needed to have his head checked. Alexis wanted him. He was sure of that. And he wanted her so much more than he could express. Then why was he just standing there?

Max took a breath. "Alexis, someone tried to kill us tonight. It's unsettled us more than we probably realize. I don't think it would be a good idea for us to take such an important step in our relationship now, not after the shock we've had."

Alexis's lips parted in surprise. Max offered her his hand

to help her off the table. She ignored him and stepped down on her own.

"Are you sure that's the only reason?" She adjusted her dress as she circled him.

"What do you mean?" Max turned to keep her in sight.

Alexis marched toward what he thought was her bedroom. Her movements were stiff and jerky. "I realize you're used to dating women in your same social circles. Is that the real reason you've decided not to get involved with me after all?"

Was she kidding? He wanted her so badly he could barely walk.

Max forced himself to follow her into the other room. That probably wasn't the best idea, but he wasn't going to let her accusation go unchallenged. "That's false and unfair. You're the one who wanted to just be friends."

"And you're the one who suddenly doesn't want anything to do with me." She pulled a large suitcase from the closet and started indiscriminately throwing clothes into it.

"Wrong again." He stood in the doorway, far from the bed. "But when we do make love, I don't want you to wake up with regrets."

Alexis stiffened at his words. She straightened from the suitcase and turned to him. "What makes you think I'd have regrets tonight?"

Max crossed his arms over his chest. "Like I said, too much has happened tonight. I don't want our first night together to be remembered as the night we had to run for our lives."

Her eyes moved over him as though she was imagining him naked. Max's groin stiffened even more. He bit back a groan.

Finally, she met his eyes. "You're right. Looking down

the barrel of a gun affected me in ways I hadn't expected. I'm sorry I took my anger out on you and accused you of being a snob. I know you're not. I'm sorry."

Max didn't hesitate. "Apology accepted." He jerked a thumb over his shoulder. "While you pack, I'll make the coffee."

What he really needed was a cold shower. A long one.

ALEXIS HURRIED TO the L lobby early Friday morning. Clarissa had called to tell her Jake was waiting at the registration desk. What was he doing here? He had class at the university on Fridays. Had something happened to her mother? To Aunt Suz?

She'd been stuck in auto-panic because of the shooting at The Cloisters last night. Alexis stumbled over nothing. Thank goodness she hadn't tripped last night. That could have made the difference between life and death. She had a flashback of gripping Max's hand as they'd raced across the parking lot. She'd run so fast, she'd felt like she was flying.

And now Jake was here unexpectedly. Alexis's palms were sweating. Her breath came in gasps. Her pulse was jackhammering at the base of her throat. She'd continue this way until he told her everyone was okay.

Jake stood beside the wall opposite the registration desk. His hands were in the front pockets of his gunmetal-gray slacks. In his navy sports jacket, gray tie and conservative cream shirt, he looked like a men's cologne model masquerading as a university professor.

As she reached him, Jake's tension slammed against her like an invisible truck. Her heart in her throat, Alexis stopped in her tracks an arm's length from him. The strain in his chiseled features eased as his coal black eyes examined her.

His voice was barely audible. "You look well—for someone who was shot at last night."

How did he know?

Alexis swallowed. First things first. "Are Mom and Aunt Suz all right?"

"For now." He took his hands from his pockets. "We need to talk."

Some of Alexis's anxiety eased. Their mothers were okay. Her pulse went back to normal, and she breathed again. It would take a minute for her palms to dry.

She led Jake to her office and closed the door. "How did you find out about the shooting?"

"Not from you." Jake stood behind the nearest visitor's chair. He'd shoved his hands into his pockets again. "A friend texted me this morning. He and his fiancée had had dinner at The Cloisters and were excited to have seen Chef Max there with an attractive woman. They'd enjoyed the evening—until the shooting in the parking lot. Seems that's not a regular occurrence at The Cloisters. Why didn't you tell us?"

Alexis's eyes widened with fear and dread. Us? "Did you tell our mothers?"

"Really?" Jake gave her a sarcastic look. "If I'd told our mothers, you would have heard from them by now. But stop changing the subject. How are you? What happened? And why didn't you tell us?"

"I'm fine," Alexis lied. She circled her desk to take her seat before her knees gave out. Seeming to take pity on her, Jake sat, too. "I was going to call Mom as soon as I figured out how to explain to her what happened. I'm still not sure how to approach it. Everything happened so fast. One second, I'm getting into my car. The next, there are these popping sounds and Max is pulling me to safety."

Jake closed his eyes and dropped his head. "Thank God." His voice carried a wealth of fear, relief and fear.

"We ran back to the bar and called the police. Noah Steele arrived with them."

"Noah? Laura's homicide detective?" His phrasing made Alexis smile. She really needed that levity, no matter how brief.

Alexis nodded. "He said they'd recovered about seventeen bullet casings beside my car."

"Seventeen?" The blood drained from Jake's face. He leaned forward in his chair. His voice was muffled behind his hands. "We could have lost you."

Alexis left her chair to kneel beside his. "But you didn't, thanks in large part to Max."

Jake straightened. His eyes were cloudy with fear. "I have to thank him. Although I would've preferred he'd talked you out of leaving the resort."

"He tried." Alexis returned to her seat. "The compromise was his coming with me."

Jake shook his head in exasperation, then straightened in his seat. "The shooter emptied their gun all in the same spot. Do the police think they were trying to kill you or scare you?"

"They don't know yet."

"Is this connected to the threats against Max?"

Alexis nervously patted the bun at the nape of her neck. "The threats aren't just against Max. I recently had to fire an employee. He threatened me."

"Alexis!" Jake sprang from his chair. "And you're only now telling me this? This drip, drip, drip of information is torture."

"I'm sorry."

"Does Aunt Cat know?"

"Not exactly." Alexis held up her hands in surrender. "But in fairness, we don't know who's behind these threats. It could be someone associated with Max. It could be someone connected to me. Or it could be someone who wants to damage Mariposa's reputation."

"By shooting at you? I don't know, Lex. That sounds a little personal to me." Jake served his sarcasm as he paced her office.

Alexis let his reaction slide. She understood where he was coming from. If their roles were reversed, she'd be freaking out, too. "The police are investigating. We know Noah's an excellent detective. And as I told you, I'm safe here at the resort. They have security checking the grounds 24/7/365."

Jake stopped and faced her. "You can hear how ironic you sound saying that after you were shot at with seventeen bullets last night, can't you?"

Alexis's face burned with embarrassment. She'd made a stupid mistake last night and had almost paid for it with Max's life. "I promise not to leave the resort grounds again until the shooter is caught."

Jake took his seat. "I agree the resort is a safe place for you to wait out this threat. I wouldn't want you to bring this danger to Aunt Cat, either."

"I wouldn't want to involve any of you in this." Alexis felt chilled. She pulled her scarlet blazer more tightly around her. "It would destroy me if something happened to you."

"And if anything happened to you, it would destroy *us*." Jake held her eyes, forcing her not to look away. "I understand you prefer to do things on your own. You're stubborn and hardheaded and—"

Ouch. "I prefer independent."

Jake continued as though he hadn't heard her. "—willful. But you've got to let Aunt Cat know what's going on and why. She deserves to know. How would you feel if she were keeping secrets like this from you?"

Alexis's heart stopped at the thought. "I wouldn't be happy about it. But, Jake, how do I tell my mother someone may be trying to kill me? My father died. My sister was killed. How much is too much?"

She dropped her eyes to her desk, but she didn't see the papers on its surface. Instead, she saw her father's and her sister's funerals. She remembered how frightened she'd been that her mother would be the next to leave her. So much fear.

"Your mother's a strong person." Jake's voice was gentle.

"Mom and I have spent so many years—decades—protecting each other. It's a hard habit to break."

"I know, but it's time." Jake shook his head. "Lex, of course Aunt Cat will be worried, but if you don't tell her—if she finds out after the fact or worse from someone else—she'll be worried, angry and hurt. Which would you rather deal with?"

"You're right. I'll call her before lunch." Dread, cold and heavy, was already building in her gut.

"Good." Jake pushed himself to his feet. "In that case, I'll leave so you can make that call."

Alexis stood. "That reminds me, I thought you taught a class on Fridays?"

"It's an afternoon class, which gave me plenty of time to come to your office and chew you out before making the hour drive to the university." Jake stepped aside so Alexis could open the door and lead him from her office.

"Lucky me." Alexis's voice was as dry as the desert dust.

"You're welcome."

Alexis smiled. "I'm grateful. I mean, I don't like having

you call me out, but you're right. Mom and I have to stop keeping secrets under the guise of protecting each other."

Jake wrapped his arm around her shoulders. "You and Aunt Cat have a great relationship."

"I know." She patted Jake's back with her left hand. "So do you and Aunt Suz."

"I can appreciate this won't be an easy conversation to have but I think it will help make your relationship even stronger." Jake dropped his arm.

Alexis snorted. "We'll see about that. I just don't like disappointing her."

Jake stopped and turned to her. "None of this is your fault, Lex. How could you possibly disappoint her?"

Alexis squeezed Jake's right forearm. "You're right. Again. I'll just keep reminding myself I'm not to blame."

"Good. Make that your mantra." Jake started walking again.

As he passed the registration desk, he gave Clarissa a nod and a smile. The young woman blushed and lowered her eyes. Another admirer. Oh, brother. She joined Jake in the L's parking lot. His car was in the space closest to the main building's entrance.

"Drive safely." She gave him a hard hug. "And thank you again for coming to talk with me in person."

"What's family for?" He squeezed her back. "Call me if you need to talk."

"I will." She stepped back and watched Jake get into his car.

He waved before he reversed out of the parking space and drove off.

Alexis straightened her back and squared her shoulders. It was time to rip the bandage off and tell her mother someone wanted her dead.

Chapter Eleven

"How are you feeling?" Max stood on the threshold of Alexis's office late Friday morning. His knuckles still rested against the cool blond wood surface of her door.

Alexis looked up from her laptop. Her welcoming smile made her features glow and filled his body with warmth. It also eased his unrest, most of which had been stirred by the scene he'd witnessed between Alexis and Jake earlier in the parking lot. That had been quite the hug.

"Better." She spun her chair around and gestured for him to take the visitor's seat closest to her. "Please come in. And could you close the door? I don't want anyone to hear us talking about last night."

Her hair was pulled back into her customary bun, revealing her long, elegant neck, as well as her delicate sterling silver earrings and matching necklace. In his mind, he pictured the raven tresses as she'd worn them last night, loose and flowing around her shoulders. Over her ebony shell blouse, her scarlet blazer warmed her golden brown skin.

"Good point." Max shut the door, then settled into the chair.

"How are you?" Alexis asked.

Her office was pleasantly cool. The air smelled faintly of morning coffee, lemon cleaner and wildflowers.

"I feel better as well. Thank you." He rubbed his damp palms on the sides of his pant legs before gripping the chair's arms. "Although I'm sure it'll take a while for us to fully recover from being shot at. We're incredibly lucky."

Max looked into her eyes, searching for… He didn't know what. Some sign of lingering emotions from her meeting with Jake? Longing? Wistfulness? Love? Seeing Alexis in another man's arms had gutted him. Max knew Alexis thought of Jake as a brother. But how did Jake feel about Alexis?

"Yes, we were very fortunate." Alexis picked up a retractable black pen from her desk and rolled it between the palms of both hands. "I didn't thank you properly for once again putting yourself in danger to save my life. Thank you from the bottom of my heart." She smiled. "My mother and Jake thank you, too. Mom wants to send you something more than a card this time."

"Thanks aren't necessary." Max was uncomfortable with the admiration that warmed her hazel eyes to gold. "I did what anyone would have done."

Jake was grateful to him for helping to keep Alexis safe. That meant Alexis had told Jake they'd gone out together. How did the other man feel about that?

Alexis shook her head even as he spoke. "What you did took exceptional courage. Some people would have run—even out of instinct—and left me behind. Instead, you grabbed me and used your body to shield me. If anything had happened to you…" She dropped her eyes as her voice trailed off.

"I'm not a hero, Alexis." Max shifted in his chair. He wanted to put an end to this part of their conversation. "I can't speak to what other people may or may not have done under similar circumstances. All I know is that I wouldn't have been able to live with myself if I hadn't at least tried to help you. That's not the way I was raised."

Admiration softened to humor. "Then maybe my mother should send your parents that fruit basket."

Max widened his eyes, feigning surprise. "Well, if we're talking about fruit baskets, then she should definitely send it to me, especially if it's from the Sedona Family and Community Farmers Market."

Their shared laughter dispelled the rest of Max's unease. He still had lingering doubts about Jake's role in Alexis's life, though. How could he approach his unanswered questions without sounding like a jealous jerk?

Was he being a jealous jerk? The uncertainty was brutal, but this was a new experience for him. He'd always had a hard rule against flirting with women who were already in relationships. If they were happy, he didn't want to sow doubt or undermine their commitment. Although he was still hesitant to be the reason a couple broke up, for Alexis, he'd throw reticence out the window. Max would fight for her love. He wanted to be with her—if that's what she wanted as well. Please let it be what she wanted.

Max sat back in his chair and rested his right ankle on his left knee. "How did your mother take the news about last night's incident?"

"Is *incident* really the right word?" Alexis shivered, putting the pen down. "I'm leaning toward near-death experience. I hated to burden her with it at work, but Jake convinced me I should talk with her before she found out from someone else. And he was right."

"Jake talked you into it? Was that the reason he was here this morning?"

Alexis hesitated, giving him a questioning look. "Did you see him? He didn't mention running into you."

Max fought a losing battle against the heat rising in his cheeks. "I saw the two of you as he was leaving. I didn't want to intrude."

"You wouldn't have been intruding." Alexis waved a dismissive hand. "I'm sure Jake would have liked to have seen you."

Would he, though? "I'm sorry. Perhaps next time. How did Jake find out about the shooting?"

"A friend texted him about it. In his text, he mentioned seeing you there." She gestured toward Max. "Jake put two and two together and was not happy that I hadn't told him about the attack myself."

"I haven't told my family, either." Guilt wrapped around Max like a wet jacket. "I don't know how."

"I understand." Alexis picked up the pen again. "Laura called me last night. I had a feeling she would even though Noah said he'd fill her in on what happened. She wanted to speak with me anyway. She was very upset. I was exhausted after speaking with her, physically and emotionally. Perhaps her reaction is part of the reason I was reluctant to tell my mother."

"Adam called me last night." Max shook his head. "He was angry and shaken. After I calmed him down, I crawled into bed. I didn't want to think or talk about it anymore."

"Exactly." Alexis spread her arms. "It's not that we don't care about our families or that we aren't thinking of them. It's just, how do you tell the people who love you and worry about you all the time that someone's trying to kill you? Fortunately, the media reports didn't include our names. I admit if Jake's friend hadn't seen you, I still wouldn't have told him, my mother or my aunt Suz."

"You've already told your aunt, too?"

"No, but I'm certain my mother has by now. They work

together at the same state agency. They're in different departments, though."

Max rubbed the back of his neck as he imagined filling in his family on the more distressing parts of his working vacation. "My family's in a different time zone. They're probably well into their day. But I doubt the shooting at The Cloisters would have made national news."

"Remember you're a national celebrity." Alexis shrugged. "Is your family on social media?"

"They all are." Max shook his head with a smile. "They compete with each other about followers, likes and reposts."

Alexis chuckled. "But not with you? Why not?"

Embarrassed, Max shrugged. "I'm an introvert in a family of extroverts. Sarah handles all the promotion for me, social media, the website, the fan e-newsletter."

Alexis's eyes dimmed. She dropped them to the pen quickly rotating between her fingers. "We already know one person recognized you at the bar. Suppose others did as well and some of them post about it on social media? Suppose in their posts, they include the fact they saw you at a location where there happened to be a shooting the same night? Your family might see it in their feed. Is that a risk you want to take?"

Max's muscles tensed at the image her words created. "Definitely not."

"Neither would I." Alexis's smile was soft with empathy. "I'll tell you what Jake told me. It's better for you to have that difficult conversation with your family rather than risk their hearing about the shooting from someone else. If that happens, not only will they be frightened for you, but they'll also be hurt and angry with you."

"I don't know how to tell them. Where would I even start?" Max had a fleeting image of his sisters and parents getting on the next flight from New York to Sedona. His family was that overprotective.

"How did you explain the unmarked package that arrived for you?"

Max sighed. He met Alexis's eyes with difficulty. "I didn't."

Alexis's eyes widened. "You didn't tell your family about the creepy box? Do they know about the break-ins?"

Max heard metal tapping nearby and realized he was drumming his fingertips against his chair's arms. He stopped. "They're worried enough about those. I had to talk my sister and her husband out of moving in with me until the thieves are caught."

Alexis's laughter startled him. "I like your family."

"You do? You can have them." Max squashed a smile. "I love them, and I like them, too, even when they're driving me insane. Because of the viral video, I had to tell them about our hiking accident. I didn't want them to stumble across the footage on their socials. As I expected, they freaked out and my busman's holiday almost turned into a family vacation."

Alexis gave him an encouraging smile. "Tell your family everything, Max. The sooner the better. It's not an easy conversation, but you'll feel better afterward."

He pushed himself to his feet, trying to burn the image of her smile on his mind. It would help him get through the upcoming call with his parents.

"GOOD HEAVENS, MAX. Are you all right?" His mother sounded out of breath.

It was late Friday afternoon in New York, which was two hours ahead of Sedona. He'd conference-called his parents after what would have been their lunch breaks. Like

Alexis, he regretted burdening his parents with the news about The Cloisters shooting while they were still at work. But Alexis—and Jake before her, credit where credit was due—was right. He needed to tell his parents rather than risk their hearing about it from someone else.

Max stared at the French doors of his bungalow. Instead of seeing the soaring mountainscape in the distance, he visualized the frowns that were probably deepening the faint lines across his parents' brows. He clenched his right hand at his side, hoping to keep his anxiety from spreading throughout his body.

The conversation had gone pretty much as he'd anticipated. His parents had interrupted with frequent questions. He'd understood their impatience for information. He probably would have done the same thing, but it made his retelling even harder.

"Yes, Mom. I promise I'm fine." Max turned from the breathtaking view to pace the rest of the room.

"I need to sit down." Erika's voice echoed as though she'd put her phone on speaker. Max felt her anxiety through the satellite connection.

"Do the police have any leads?" His father's voice was both angry and impatient. Max imagined MJ was also pacing.

Max rotated his neck, trying to ease his tension. "They have a few theories, but not many solid leads."

"Do you want us with you?" Erika's voice was nearly normal again.

Max smiled. He'd anticipated that reaction as well. "No, thanks, Mom. As I said, the resort grounds are safe."

MJ expelled a breath. Max heard his father's fear and frustration in the sound. "And the Sedona detective—what's his name, Noah?—is keeping the NYPD informed?"

"Yes, Dad." Max stood to pace again. "But the NYPD's investigation has stalled."

"When you get back, you're staying with us until we can move you out of that condo and into somewhere safe." Beneath Erika's voice, Max heard the faint rumble of metal against plastic as though she'd rolled her chair across the plastic runner beneath her desk.

He imagined his tall, slender mother striding the confines of her executive suite, which was in an office building close to their family home in Queens and just a few blocks from his father's company. Max wanted to respond to her comment, but his father spoke first.

"He isn't coming home until this monster is caught." MJ's voice rose and fell in volume. That confirmed Max's suspicion that his father also was pacing while his cell phone was on speaker. A family trait.

Max started to agree with his father.

Erika interrupted. "How do we know this culprit is the same one who's been breaking into his condo?"

Max jumped into the conversation before his window of opportunity closed again. "If I'm the target of the threats here in Sedona, both Noah and the NYPD believe the break-ins are connected. However, there's a chance these threats aren't directed at me. The stalker might have a separate purpose."

Erika sighed again. "Well, whoever they are and whatever they want, let's hope they're caught soon. This has gone on long enough."

MJ grunted. "More than long enough."

Max cleared his throat. "I also wanted you to know my return to New York might be delayed even further."

Erika gasped. "Why? What's wrong now?"

That didn't come out the way he'd intended. Max rushed

to reassure his parents. "Nothing's wrong. Well, nothing else is wrong. But the other producers and I are considering recording the second season of *Cooking for Friends* here."

"Why would you do that?" his father asked.

"Really?" Erika's response carried a wealth of speculation. "Would this change in venue have anything to do with your concierge, Alexis Reed?"

Max shook his head with a smile. "How did you guess, Mom?"

Erika's laughter was delighted and delightful. "It's your texts, silly. 'Alexis and I are going horseback riding. Alexis and I are going hiking.' And on and on. It takes a very special woman to convince my workaholic son to enjoy himself on his working vacation."

MJ chuckled. "Why didn't you tell me about your suspicions?"

"Why couldn't you figure it out?" Erika laughed harder. "Besides, I was waiting for Max to tell us himself. So, Max, tell us about her."

Where should he begin? "Alexis is smart, ambitious, caring. She isn't impressed by my so-called celebrity. In fact, she challenges me. She pushes me."

He loved that and he was starting to believe that wasn't the only thing he loved. His heart beat faster at the thought.

"She sounds remarkable." MJ's tone was warm with approval.

Erika sighed with content. "I'm looking forward to meeting her."

Max's eyebrows rose. "Slow down, Mom. Alexis and I are still getting to know each other. And I want more time with her."

MJ hummed. "And that's why you asked the other producers to consider taping the show there?"

Max wandered his bungalow's great room. "From a business perspective, I think it would be a good touch to locate the show here next season because our focus will be on Southwestern cuisine."

"Ah!" Erika exclaimed. "Because of your cookbook."

"Exactly." Max nodded. "But I won't deny that being with Alexis was the deciding factor."

"Well, between your cookbook's launch and meeting Alexis, I'm looking forward to your show's next season even more now." The smile in Erika's voice eased the weight from Max's shoulders.

"Using the entire season to promote your book is a solid business decision," MJ said. "It would be an even bigger boost to record each episode in front of a live audience."

"We can discuss that later, Dad." Not.

"When will the other producers make their decision?" Erika asked.

"Soon, I hope." Max sighed. "I mean, I know it sounds ridiculous. It feels ridiculous, too, to change my life for a woman I haven't even known for three weeks."

Erika tsked. "Three weeks. Three days. Three hours. Love's on its own schedule. It can take a while or it can be instantaneous, like it was for your father and me."

Max stilled. "It was love at first sight for you and Dad? Why didn't I know this?"

His parents had been happily married for more than thirty-six years. Max and his sisters had assumed his parents had been friends first and love had come later.

"We fell in love right away. When you know, you know." MJ took over the story. "But we waited until our careers were more stable to get married and start a family."

That made sense to Max. His parents were both very career-focused, and had met shortly after graduating from college. In contrast, he and Alexis were already building their careers. But he didn't want to get ahead of himself.

His mother's words claimed his attention again. "Don't worry about the quantity of time you and Alexis spend together. Focus more on the quality of time and on learning the most important things about each other."

Max frowned. "Like what?"

Erika lowered her voice. "What does she think about having children?"

Max closed his eyes and shook his head. "Mom, we're going to have to set some boundaries before you and Alexis meet."

Erika chuckled. "I'm looking forward to it."

That's what Max was afraid of.

"FOR THE SHOOTER to have fired seventeen bullets without any hitting you or Alexis makes me wonder whether the person was trying to kill you or scare you." Adam extended his hand, palm out. "Don't get me wrong. I'm glad neither of you were injured—or worse."

"Thanks for that." Max's voice was dry.

Adam ignored his interruption. "You have to admit it's strange. Either the shooter had never fired a gun before, or they deliberately missed seventeen times."

Max and Adam had finished dinner at Annabeth, the resort's five-star restaurant, Friday evening. The host had led them to Adam's regular table toward the center of the dining area, which had a view of the entire restaurant. They'd both ordered the herb-roasted chicken with asparagus spears, roasted potatoes, white wine and ice water. Max could still smell the cumin, olive oil, oregano and brown sugar.

Noah had been right about Laura demanding a full briefing on the shooting. Afterward, she'd texted the information to Adam and Joshua. Adam had called Max last night to ask three different ways whether Max was all right. He'd then made Max promise neither he nor Alexis would leave the resort grounds again until the stalker was caught and behind bars. Max had noticed there were more security officers patrolling the resort grounds today.

Max drank his ice water. "There's another possibility. The stalker didn't want to be seen. That's why they were in the bushes. They didn't expect Alexis to see their weapon glint under the lamp. Luckily, she did, and we were able to get away."

"That's a good point." Adam sounded pensive, as though he was mulling over Max's theory. "I still can't believe it happened."

"Neither can I." Max set aside his white linen napkin. "But I feel better knowing Noah is on the case. But let's talk about something else, please. Have you identified companies you might be able to go into partnership with?"

Adam sighed, allowing the change of subject. "There are a couple of companies on our list, but we haven't approached any of them yet. I guess a part of us hopes it doesn't come to that."

"I get it." Max inclined his head to indicate their surroundings. "This is your mother's legacy. She left it to you and your siblings. Of course, you wouldn't be in a rush to share it with anyone, much less strangers."

"Exactly. Thank you for understanding." Adam sipped his ice water. "In the meantime, we have another problem."

When it rains, it pours.

"What is it?" Max searched his mind, trying to anticipate what Adam was going to say.

Adam looked around the room. Was he checking on his

customers' satisfaction or making sure no one was listening to their conversation? Or both? Adam lowered his voice. "I think we have a spy at the resort."

If he'd heard that declaration from anyone else, Max would've responded with skepticism. He'd need proof. But he'd known Adam Colton for more than a decade. His friend wasn't given to paranoid delusions. He was the opposite of that.

It angered him that someone Adam trusted would then betray him. "What's happened?"

A cloud swept across Adam's face. "Glenna and Clive have made comments about things they wouldn't have had any reason to be aware of unless someone at the resort had told them. It's suspicious."

Max brought to mind Mariposa employees he'd met during his stay, including Clarissa, Aaron, Roland, Zoe and, of course, Alexis. Could one of them be working against Adam and his siblings? It couldn't be Alexis. Not only was she Laura's friend, in the short time he'd known her, she'd proved her loyalty to the organization.

"But your employees sign nondisclosure agreements."

Adam had explained that, because of the high profile of most of the guests Mariposa attracted, he, Laura and Joshua thought it was important for everyone in the resort's employ to sign a nondisclosure agreement to protect their clients.

"It wouldn't be the first time an employee broke the rules." Adam folded his forearms on the table in front of him. "Alexis just fired someone for noncompliance with our employee rules."

Max clenched his fists as he recalled his encounters with Mark Bower. "And now that employee is suspected of trying to kill her. Could Mark be the spy?"

"I don't think so." The look in Adam's eyes was distant

as though he was accessing a mental list of employees. "Glenna is referencing things that have happened since Mark was dismissed, like Alexis moving into one of the bungalows and Valerie suddenly taking time off. The leak would have to be someone in a position to overhear those conversations. It has to be someone who's here."

"That makes sense." Max continued to process this new, troubling situation. "What do you think Clive and Glenna are up to? Why would they want to have someone spying on the resort?"

Adam sat back against his chair, crossing his arms over his chest. Anger darkened his eyes and tightened his jaw. "They want information they could use against us personally. They also want to damage the resort's reputation."

That was what Max feared as well. "Which would make it harder for you to find a company to go into partnership with."

"Exactly. They're trying to sabotage us, putting us in a position where we'd have to give in to their demands. That's the bottom line."

Max considered his friend's situation in silence. "It's time to fight fire with fire. Since they have a spy, you need one, too."

Chapter Twelve

Max propped his hips against the half patio wall outside his bungalow, waiting for his video call to Sarah to connect early Sunday morning. His eyes took in the mountain ridge in the distance and desert plants around him. It had been a few days since someone had shot at him and Alexis outside The Cloisters. He'd tried to figure out a way to justify meeting Sarah for lunch when someone had made it clear they were determined to hurt him—or worse. Noah had promised to make this threat a priority. In return, Max and Alexis had promised him, Adam and Laura they wouldn't leave the resort again until the stalker was caught.

That meant he had to postpone lunch with Sarah indefinitely.

Sarah finally accepted the connection. Her face was flushed and her red hair tousled, as though she'd rushed to her phone. A cream patio door was framed behind her.

"Max! What a surprise." Sarah combed her fingers through her hair. "Hi. How are you?"

The memory of running from gunfire with Alexis rushed across his mind. Max shook his head to clear his thoughts. "Sarah, I'm afraid I have some bad news. I won't be able to meet you for lunch today."

"What?" Sarah's eyes stretched wide. Her jaw dropped. "Why not?"

"I'm afraid something's come up." He didn't want to discuss the dangers stalking him and Alexis. He'd told his family. He loved them and they had a right to know. Everyone else was on a need-to-know basis and Sarah wasn't on that list.

"*Something's* come up?" Her voice had risen several octaves. Her face was turning pink. "What is this *something*, Max? Does it have anything to do with Alexis Reed?"

Max's muscles stiffened. He didn't like his administrative assistant's tone. His eyes narrowed with a stirring of temper and a breath of outrage. "That's none of your business, Sarah."

"It is if you're breaking our date to spend time with her." Sarah bit the words. Her image shook as though her cell phone was trembling in her grip.

What had gotten into her? Could her family hear her? If so, they must believe, as Steve did, that he and Sarah had more than a professional relationship. For Pete's sake.

"Sarah, this wasn't a date. We don't have that kind of relationship. I was going to have lunch with you because I thought you needed an impartial person to talk with about your divorce. I was trying to be kind." Max heard her sharp intake of breath.

Sarah sniffed. "Well, thanks for that, Max. Thanks a lot. I'm sorry your *kindness* had to be canceled because of *something*."

"This isn't like you, Sarah." Max felt absolved from any feelings of guilt. Relief was the only emotion he had room for now. "I'm going to chalk your behavior up to your pending divorce. Have you heard from Steve? Is there any chance of a reconciliation?"

"For me and Steve?" She wrinkled her nose. "I'm not interested in Steve. Not anymore."

His eyes widened in surprise, then narrowed with confusion. That wasn't the reaction he'd expected from her. If she wasn't upset over her divorce, why did she need someone to talk to?

Max checked the time shown at the top of his cell phone screen. It was almost 9:30 a.m. "I'm sorry to hear you and Steve won't be able to work things out—"

"Are you really?" There was a suggestion in her voice.

"Of course I am." His eyebrows knitted. "I have a great deal of respect for the institution of marriage. My parents have been married for almost forty years. I want a marriage like theirs. I hate to see couples break up."

"That's sweet of you." A faint smile raised the corners of Sarah's thin lips. "But I realized that I'd made a mistake, marrying Steve. I couldn't stay with him anymore. Not when I'm in love with someone else."

He stiffened in surprise and a little disappointment. Perhaps his sisters were right. Perhaps he was a hopeless romantic. He refused to change. "I see. Well, I hope you'll be happy, Sarah. And again, I'm sorry about lunch, but I—"

She interrupted him. "Don't you want to know who I'm in love with?"

Max shook his head. "It's none of my—"

"It's you, Max." Sarah lowered her eyes as though she was suddenly uncertain. Her voice was soft. Her smile was shy. "I'm in love with you. I was going to tell you during our lunch date."

Max froze. He couldn't have heard her correctly. He shook his head in disbelief. "What did you say?"

Her smile grew. "I said I'm in love with you, Max. I've

been in love with you since the first day we met. And I'll love you until the day I die."

Max's head was spinning. Phrases she'd said when she'd told him about her pending divorce came back to him. They were nearly muted beneath the cacophony of screaming voices in his head.

Steve's very jealous of you.

He's convinced we're having an affair.

He really *lost it when you bought me that bracelet.*

Max had one question: Had Steve become jealous of him before or after Sarah told her husband she was in love with Max?

He massaged the back of his neck, trying to ease the pressure building there. Max didn't feel equipped to navigate this emotional minefield. In fairness, he already had a lot on his plate with a stalker doing their very best to kill him and the woman he was falling in love with. He didn't want to hurt Sarah, but he wasn't willing to allow her delusions to continue beyond this phone call.

Max braced himself. He spoke with as much caring as he could muster. "Sarah, I'm sorry, but I don't share your feelings."

"Yes, you do, Max. I know you love me, too."

"No, I don't." Max clenched his left hand, trying to control the impatience that tore through him. "Sarah, I'm your boss. That's all I am. We work together."

"That's not true," she whispered. "You love me, Max. I know you do."

"No, Sarah, I don't."

"Could you…love me…in time?"

"I'm afraid not."

Sarah wiped tears from her eyes with her fingertips. Her nails looked freshly manicured. "We're good together, Max.

I know you know that. Why are you denying it? You're always saying how much you rely on me and how much I help you."

"At work, Sarah." Max heard the bite of impatience in his voice. "We *work* well together. But I don't have those types of feelings for you. We need to keep things strictly professional between us for the good of the show."

"For the good of the show?" Temper hardened her voice. Outrage replaced her tears. "What about *my* well-being, Max?"

He took a mental step back. "I'm sorry if I did something to inadvertently mislead you about my feelings for you. That was never my intention."

Sarah stared at him through the video call screen. Anger built in her eyes. "Are you having a change of heart about me because of her? *Alexis Reed?*"

"Sarah—"

"Whatever you think you have with her now, that won't last." Her voice was almost a sneer. "Your life's in New York—your family, your show, your restaurants, your agent. That woman wouldn't last five minutes in the city."

It was getting harder to care about not hurting Sarah's feelings. "My personal relationships are not your business. If you're incapable of keeping things professional between us, then I'm sorry, Sarah, but I'll have to let you go."

"You're *firing* me?" Sarah's voice leaped up several painful octaves.

"We can't have a professional relationship if we can't keep personal feelings out of the office."

"You're actually firing me." She stared at him in disbelief.

"I regret things are ending this way, but I can't give you what you want."

Her scowl was vicious. "Yes, you can. But for some reason you're enthralled by that concierge. You're wasting your time with her."

Max had had enough. "I'll have my lawyer contact you about your separation agreement. He'll also arrange for you to clean out your office and he'll take your key."

"If that's the way you want it. Fine." She was visibly shaking. Her image on his phone's screen slid from side to side. "There's no reason for me to stay here any longer. I'll return to New York first thing in the morning. Your lawyer can contact me then." Sarah ended the video chat on her final word.

Max closed his eyes and expelled a weighty sigh. That could've gone better although he didn't know how. She'd blindsided him. He stood and walked back into his bungalow. He was confident he'd done the right thing. He and Sarah couldn't have continued to work together if she believed herself to be in love with him. His heart belonged to someone else.

The realization made his legs weak. Max dropped onto the nearest armchair. It was true. Alexis had laid claim to his mind, body and soul from the first time he'd looked into her big, bright eyes. It was irrational. They'd only known each other for three weeks, but he'd fallen completely—hopelessly—in love with her.

Now, what was he going to do about it? His home—his life—was in New York. Hers was here in Sedona almost twenty-four hundred miles away. How was he supposed to make that work?

MAX WAS TEMPTED to ignore the call when his father's number popped up on his cell phone screen late Monday morning. He'd been in such a good mood. He was in the

Annabeth kitchen. The chef had brought back fresh produce from the farmers market. He'd checked and double-checked the recipe he was planning to make for his lunch with Alexis. It was more than her great feedback on his entrées. More than the way she challenged him to get out of his comfort zone. He enjoyed talking with her. He enjoyed being silent with her. He enjoyed *her.* It surprised him how much.

But the call was from his father and MJ wouldn't stop calling. The kitchen staff was preparing for lunch. Shouted commands, clanging pans and chopping knives would make it difficult for Max to hear MJ. Opening the rear exit door, he stepped into April's bright, warm late morning sunshine to take the call.

"Hi, Dad." Max heard soft music in the background on his father's end of the line. MJ had tuned his computer to his favorite jazz website.

"Max!" MJ's booming voice made it seem as though his father was standing beside him. "Have you thought any more about the ideas I gave you for your show? And feel free to take the credit when you present them to your producers."

He smothered a groan. Max had known his father would circle back to his ideas to revamp *Cooking for Friends.* He'd hoped MJ would wait until he'd returned to New York so they could discuss them in person.

"Actually, Dad, I've been focused on the cookbook recipes." He paced the length of the kitchen's exterior wall. It was several yards long, part shade and part sunlight. "I haven't made plans yet for the next season of the show. But I don't think it would be a good idea to make big changes after just one season."

MJ's sigh sounded like disappointment. "Max, you've

got to keep all your projects moving. You can't ignore one in favor of another. I wouldn't have been able to build my production company by focusing on only one movie or TV show at a time."

Max felt nine years old again. "I have a different process. I like to focus on one thing at a time to make sure that thing is done well. Right now, I'm focusing on the cookbook."

And Alexis.

In the almost two weeks—eleven days to be exact—since the shooting at The Cloisters, they'd been spending time together every day. They'd taken the advice of their friends and the police and remained within the security of the resort. Last weekend, they'd gone horseback riding Saturday and hiking again Sunday. His stay was beginning to feel like a real vacation: fun, relaxing and exciting. Thanks to Alexis.

Fortunately, there hadn't been any other attacks or "accidents." Max was glad he and Alexis hadn't had to worry about their well-being. However, the reprieve prompted Alexis to start talking about returning to her condo. His growing feelings for Alexis weren't the reason Max didn't want her to go home. At least, they weren't the only reason. He didn't want Alexis to leave Mariposa because the stalker hadn't been caught yet.

"You sound like your mother." MJ's comment brought Max back to their conversation.

"Mom's a smart woman." Did he sound as defensive as he felt?

"Of course she is." MJ's voice was thick with humor. "She married me, didn't she?"

Max's tension eased. He laughed his appreciation of his father's response. He could imagine MJ behind his heavy oak desk, rocking back on his black faux leather wheeled executive chair and grinning at his own joke.

"Look, Dad, I've got to go. I've got to prepare another entrée. We'll talk about your ideas for the show when I get home, all right?"

MJ sighed. The squeak of his chair carried across the satellite towers. "All right. If you want to put off the show, we can do that."

Max closed his eyes and rubbed the back of his neck. His father had a way of expressing his disappointment without expressing it. "I'm not putting anything off. I'm scheduling myself. I have a lot to do and I'm trying to approach everything in a logical manner."

The silence on the other end of the line felt confused. MJ broke it. "I wasn't criticizing you, son. Your mother's always telling me I should choose my words more carefully."

Good advice. Thanks, Mom.

"I know what I'm doing, Dad."

"I know you do, son. Your mother and I are very proud of you."

Surprise widened Max's eyes and raised his voice a couple of octaves. "You are?"

More confused silence. "Of course I am. Why wouldn't I be? You're intelligent, hardworking, ambitious and the spitting image of me."

Max laughed. "You're proud of me even though I 'could always do better'?"

MJ snorted. "Everyone could always do better. *I* could do better every single day. That doesn't mean we haven't been doing great work."

Max exhaled. "I'm proud of you, too, Dad."

"I know."

Max rolled his eyes although his father couldn't see him.

"Dad, I'm sure Miri and Mel would like to hear you're proud of them, too."

MJ's sigh was long and irritated. "What's wrong with you children? Of course I'm proud of you—all of you. If I weren't, I'd tell you."

Max's heart felt lighter now that his father was expressing his feelings in a way Max could understand. "We get a lot of criticisms from you, Dad. Once in a while, it would be nice to hear the positive reinforcement."

"Point taken. I'll make the effort."

Max grinned. "Thanks. Now I'd better get going. Give Mom my love."

"I will. Keep up the good work, son."

"You, too, Dad." Max disconnected the call.

He let his eyes sweep his surroundings and a smile settled on his lips. His father was proud of him. The day seemed a little brighter, a little more joyful. And the first person he wanted to share that joy with was Alexis.

"As your father said, what's not to be proud of?" Alexis beamed at Max as they sat in her office Monday afternoon. "I'm glad you cleared things up with him."

They'd finished lunch and had packed the dishes on the trolley. Max had made chipotle chicken with citrusy salsa. Alexis had been so enthusiastic about the meal—both the spice level and the side dish—that he'd considered taking a victory lap around her office. Not enough room, though. And she still complained about the presentation: *itty-bitty food on great big plates*. Next time, he'd use smaller dishes.

Max flashed a grin. "Now you're the one being too kind."

Alexis ignored him. "And thanks to you, I'm sure he'll have a similar conversation with your sisters."

"I hope so." Max settled back in his chair, placing his right ankle on his left knee. "It would mean a lot to them."

Alexis's smile faded. Max sensed the shift in her mood, and it worried him. What was on her mind?

She caught and held his eyes. "Noah called me this morning with an update about the case. I told him since I'd see you for lunch, I'd share his news with you."

Max frowned. "Judging by the look on your face, it's not good news."

"No, it's not." She squared her shoulders in her copper cotton long-sleeved blouse. The color made her eyes sparkle. "Noah said he's satisfied he's cleared Mark for the shooting Thursday night. Apparently, Mark has a strong alibi. He was barhopping with a group of friends. Noah checked with all four of them."

Max arched an eyebrow. "Barhopping on a Thursday night?"

Alexis shrugged. "Go figure."

"I sound old." Max sighed. He straightened in his seat and planted both feet on the bamboo flooring. "We can't connect him to the hiking accident, but he's cleared from suspicion for the shooting. So either there are two people out there who want us dead at the same time or someone other than Mark is responsible."

"We're back to square one. I was hoping to go home soon." Alexis crossed her right leg over her left. Tension radiated around her.

Max could feel it across the small conversation table. "I understand this is frustrating. I'm frustrated, too. But I'm glad you have a safe place to stay until the stalker's caught."

"Please don't get me wrong. I'm grateful to be staying at Mariposa." Alexis smoothed her hair, checking the bun at the nape of her neck. "I'm enjoying the bungalow. Who wouldn't like having someone come in and tidy up behind them every day? And you know I love the resort. The views are spectacular. The amenities are wonderful." She spread her arms to encompass their surroundings. "But none of this is home."

"I understand. There's a difference between being on vacation and being displaced because someone's trying to kill you."

"I miss my things. And I really miss my weekly dinners with my mother. Our videoconference dinners aren't the same." Alexis folded her arms beneath her chest. Her body language couldn't be any more closed off.

Max's concern increased. So did his guilt. "I'm sorry. I hate that you're caught up in this."

"Max, we've been through this." Frustration leaked into Alexis's voice. "This is *not* your fault. We don't know which one of us is the target. Maybe *I'm* the one who brought *you* into this. But either way, we're not at fault. The stalker is."

She was right. Max was glad she'd reminded him. "I wish I knew who that was."

"We all wish we knew." Alexis narrowed her eyes as she studied him in silence. "I can't stop thinking there's a connection between these attempts to harm us and whoever broke into your home. Why would they have sent you that package unless they wanted to get your attention?"

"But for what purpose?" Max stood to pace the confines of Alexis's office. "If they wanted to kill me, why didn't they do it in New York? They can't get to me at the resort."

"Maybe they didn't know that."

"I've always thought the thieves were random fans."

"Could random fans get into your secured building?"

"I wouldn't think so." Max spread his hands. "But the police questioned my neighbors and the guards." Alexis's silence seemed to speak volumes. "Just say it. I can tell something's on your mind."

Alexis hesitated. "Has Sarah ever been to your condo?"

Max pushed his hands into the front pockets of his black slacks. "A few times, either to drop something off or pick something up." He couldn't remember the number of times Sarah had come to his building.

"So your security guards are familiar with her." She paused again. "Did you know she's attracted to you?"

Max's muscles stiffened. "Do you think Sarah's the one who broke into my condo and sent the package to me?"

"Yes." She didn't look away.

Max's lips parted in surprise. He stared at Alexis, unable to gather his thoughts. "Sarah's married."

"You told me she's filed for divorce."

"I said I'm in love with you, Max. I've been in love with you since the first day we met. And I'll love you until the day I die."

Max wanted to run from those words. Instead, he paced Alexis's office. "You met Sarah less than three weeks ago. In that time, you recognized something I hadn't picked up on after working with her for more than two years."

"What are you saying?" There was dread in Alexis's words.

Max stood with his back to her. "It never crossed my mind that the obsessive fan who'd broken into my home twice could be Sarah. Nor did I think she could have mailed that box to Mariposa."

Alexis prompted him when he remained silent. "But now you do?"

He drew a sharp breath. The room smelled of cayenne peppers, citrus, tomatoes and wildflowers. "Yesterday, she told me she was in love with me."

"Oh, boy."

"How could she have known I'd be here?" Max turned to Alexis. "I never told her I was coming to Sedona."

"She's your assistant." Alexis's eyes searched his. "Did she have access to your emails or voice mail?"

Max dragged a hand over his hair. "No, I prefer to handle my communication myself. She didn't have any of my passwords. And nothing has ever been taken from my office."

"That's probably because there aren't that many people on your staff. If she took something from work, she'd be one of a handful of people you could accuse. But if something were missing from your home, there would be millions of suspects."

Alexis had a point. Now he felt worse. Max resumed his pacing.

Like her home, Alexis's office was clean and well organized. There were one or two invoices in her inbox. Several letters waited in her outbox, some in internal envelopes and others in Mariposa stationery.

Max's eyes swept her desk and the shelf above her computer, pausing briefly on framed photos he'd admired before. The pictures captured candid images of Alexis's family and friends through the years. She hadn't chosen to be in many of the pictures, which led Max to believe she'd been behind the camera for most of them.

He stopped to study the view from the floor-to-ceiling tinted window to the left of Alexis's desk. The sky was a clear, cerulean blue, dotted with thick white clouds and the peaks of majestic red rock mountains.

"There's no way Sarah could've known about our hike or that we were going to be at The Cloisters Thursday night." Max's thoughts were spinning.

In contrast, Alexis's voice was calm. "And yet somehow she knew we'd been spending time together at the resort."

"She said she'd seen a video of us."

"But there wasn't any such video."

"Why are you so determined to make Sarah a suspect?" He asked the question over his shoulder.

Alexis's sigh was soft and impatient. "It's too much of a coincidence that you're both in Sedona at the same time. Why are you so determined to ignore that?"

"Because I don't want to believe I hired someone who's trying to kill you." Battling frustration, Max scrubbed his palms over his face. "I don't have affairs with married women. Sarah and I have always had a strictly professional relationship. At least, I thought we had. But since we've been here, she's been acting differently toward me. I thought it was the stress of her marriage ending."

"But it wasn't." Alexis made it a statement, not a question. "Did the police question Sarah or anyone on your staff?"

"No, they didn't." That was still a source of frustration. Max understood the theft of an old cell phone and a deodorant stick wasn't a high priority, but someone had invaded his home.

"I think Noah should speak with her."

Max faced Alexis. "Did you tell him your suspicions about her?"

Alexis shook her head. "I wanted to speak with you first."

"Thank you for that." Some of his tension drained. "She may have returned to New York." Max crossed the office to resume his seat at the table. "When I told her I didn't love her, she became very angry. At that point, I realized we couldn't work together any longer. I told her my lawyer would be in touch with a separation agreement for her."

"You fired her?" Alexis's lips parted with surprise.

Agitated, Max spread his arms. "What was I supposed to do? She was bordering on unhinged. I've never seen her like that. She became a completely different person."

"I'm so sorry. Is that the reason you seemed distracted yesterday?"

"It was an uncomfortable situation." Max winced. "Nothing like that had ever happened to me before."

"I'm so sorry." Alexis's eyes were dark with concern. "Why didn't you talk with me about it? Talking often helps people to cope."

"I don't know." Max shrugged restlessly. On second thought, yes, he did. "I was embarrassed. I didn't want to hear you say I handled it badly."

"I understand, but I'm sure you handled it as well as anyone could. It was a difficult situation. I still think Noah should speak with her." Alexis stood, stretching to reach the writing tablet beside her desk phone. It had the Mariposa logo on it. She offered the tablet to Max. "Could you give him Sarah's cell phone number?"

Max took the writing tablet and retrieved his cell from his right front pocket. He wrote Sarah's contact information. "Of course. At least that way, we could put these questions to rest."

He searched for Noah's number in his cell phone. He was sure the detective would clear Sarah's name. Max couldn't believe there was any way he would have hired a killer.

Would he?

Chapter Thirteen

"We can't locate Sarah Harris." Noah looked at the group gathered in the L's small conference room Thursday morning. The detective was wearing a plain gray T-shirt and black straight-legged jeans. "Nor can we find any information that confirms she has relatives in the Sedona area."

Seated beside Max on the right side of the table, Alexis sensed his tension like a wall pushing against her. She wanted to reach out and squeeze his left forearm beneath his pale tan short-sleeved shirt as it lay between them on the rectangular blond wood table. But such a gesture between them wouldn't be appropriate right now.

Noah had asked to meet with Roland, Max, Alexis, Laura, Adam and Joshua to update them on the investigation into the threats against Max and Alexis. It had been three days since Max and Alexis had called Noah to give him Sarah's cell phone number and the highlights—or lowlights—of their last, contentious conversation. Max also had provided nonsensitive information to help the detective find her, including her description, her soon-to-be ex-husband's name and contact numbers, and Sarah's maiden name, Brockman, to help the police department identify her relatives.

"You think she lied about visiting family here?" Alexis

studied Noah seated directly across from her. His tanned features looked strained. His green eyes were hard and focused.

He sighed. "We spoke with Steve Harris Monday. He was positive Sarah didn't have relatives in Sedona."

Max gestured toward Noah seated diagonally across the table. "They've been together since high school. He would know."

Noah continued. "We still spent the past two days calling every Brockman listed in the Sedona area. No one knew a Sarah Harris who grew up in New Jersey and now lives in New York."

Max sat back in his chair, crossing his arms over his chest. "She said she was returning to New York Monday. Maybe she did."

Noah didn't look convinced. "She lied about staying with relatives. I'm not sold on her keeping her word about leaving Sedona. But I'll ask the NYPD to check."

Laura was seated between Adam at the head of the table and Noah on her left. Her violet blouse deepened her blue eyes. "And she hasn't returned any of your calls?"

Noah's expression softened when he met her eyes. "No, she hasn't. We've called early in the morning, late at night and several times throughout the day. We weren't going straight to voice mail, which means she was letting the phone ring. Each time, we left messages. Now her mailbox is full."

Roland was on Alexis's right in his security director's uniform. "She's either ditched her phone or she wants you to think she has. Can you track it?"

Noah gave the security director an appreciative look. "We've requested a warrant for that. Hopefully, the court will approve it."

"We can't forget that Mark Bower's still on the suspect list, too." Max looked from Noah to Alexis. "Sarah didn't have access to the trail, but Mark would have."

"Speaking of tracking cell phones, there's something I've been wondering about." Alexis caught Max's eyes before returning her attention to Noah. "We can't explain how the stalker knew where Max and I would be and when—the hiking trail, The Cloisters."

Max swept his right hand around the table. "The only people we've shared our plans with other than our families have been Adam, Laura and Joshua. Since we'd texted our families, is it possible someone's hacked our phones?"

Noah frowned. He shared a look between Alexis and Max. "I suppose it's possible. Do you both have iPhones?" He waited for their nods of confirmation before leaning into the table. "Find your International Mobile Equipment Identity number under General Settings. Now dial hashtag zero six hashtag into your phone. Does the number that came up match your IMEI?"

"Yes." Alexis nodded. She felt a wave of relief. "Thank you."

"Mine doesn't." Max looked at Noah. "Does that mean someone cloned my phone?"

Noah frowned. "I'm afraid so. Someone's been monitoring every text and call you send and receive."

Seated on Noah's left, Joshua gestured toward Max's phone. "It must have been Sarah. She could've been keeping tabs on you for months. Did you have any idea she'd been spying on you?"

"None." Max looked at Alexis. "I can't wrap my mind around this. How could I have been so blind?"

"You've always been trusting." Adam's voice was low. "But that's not a bad thing."

"It was this time." Max rubbed the back of his neck. "I'm so sorry, Alexis, for putting you in danger."

She couldn't hold back any longer. She leaned forward and squeezed his bicep. "This isn't your fault. You don't have anything to apologize for. This is all Sarah. I'm confident Noah will find her soon and we can start putting this behind us."

His eyes smiled at her before he addressed Noah. "What do we do now?"

Noah nodded toward Max's cell. "First, we break the connection between your phone and whoever's cloned it, presumably Sarah. You'll need to contact the manufacturer's support team."

"I'll do that right away." Max turned off his phone, then slipped it into his front shorts pocket.

A little more of Alexis's tension drained. She glanced around the table at Laura, Adam, Roland, Max and Joshua before meeting Noah's eyes. "Since it sounds like we have a strong suspect for these attacks, could I move back to my home?"

Beside her, Max stiffened. Across the table, Laura frowned. Alexis hoped their reactions wouldn't influence Noah's opinion.

The detective shook his head. "I'm sorry, Alexis. I understand you're getting restless. I would be, too. But it would be best for you to stay at the resort. Neither you nor Max will be safe until we have the stalker in custody." He looked at Joshua to his left, Laura on his right and Adam at the head of the table. "If you don't have any objections."

"None at all." Laura's voice rose above her siblings' responses.

Adam turned to her. "Alexis, Noah's right. Stay here for as long as you need to."

Joshua sat back in his chair. "I agree."

"All right." Alexis struggled to mask her disappointment. At least Laura and Max were happy. "Could I at least resume my Sunday dinners with my mother? Having dinner via videoconference isn't the same."

Noah's eyebrows knitted. "I suppose that would be all right. As long as you don't have the dinners at your home. I doubt the stalker knows where your mother lives."

"I'll call Mom to let her know." Alexis beamed at Max. He didn't seem to share her enthusiasm. Her smile faded.

Noah rose to his feet. "If you don't have any other questions, I'd better get back to work. Thanks for your time."

Roland led the group from the conference room. Laura joined Noah. The Colton brothers followed them.

Max touched Alexis's arm to detain her. "Could we talk in your office?"

"Of course." Alexis noted the somber look in his eyes. This didn't bode well.

MAX FOLLOWED ALEXIS back to her office late Thursday morning. He breathed her scent as he reached forward to open the door for her. With her permission, he closed it again behind them. His eyes swept her slim, toned figure in her black pantsuit as she walked to her chair. She was beautiful, but he couldn't let his attraction to her distract him.

He clenched and unclenched his hands. The conversation they were about to have wouldn't be pleasant. His muscles pushed him to pace her office. But he chose to sit in her visitor's chair instead.

Alexis pulled her executive seat farther under her desk. "What's wrong?"

"I'm concerned about your leaving the resort Sunday evening." Max forced himself to speak calmly even as his pulse galloped with panic at the thought of Alexis being in danger. Again. "We have ideas about who's responsible for the threats, but no one's in custody yet. Suppose the stalker's watching your mother's house?"

"They don't know where she lives." Alexis picked up the pencil on her desk and rolled it between her fingers. "I haven't been to her house since before my accident. The weekend I was injured, my mother and I had dinner at my house."

"I understand you miss your weekly dinners with your mother but the stalker's still running around out there." Max jerked his chin toward the window.

"*Do* you understand?" Alexis's eyes darkened with disappointment. She stared at the pencil as though it could show her the future. "Your stay at the resort was planned. You packed everything you needed for your six-week stay. You know when you're going home, and your family knows when they'll see you again. As much as I love Mariposa, I'm not comfortable living my life day to day. It's been almost three weeks."

Max felt a stab of guilt. He lowered his eyes and stared at the bamboo flooring. "I'm sorry about everything. I'm sorry you're in danger and that your life has been turned upside down." He raised his eyes to hers again. "I know you don't blame me, but I still feel responsible."

"You've really got to get over that." Alexis shook the pen at him. "By assuming responsibility that's not yours, you're absolving the actual guilty party. That's not right."

Max considered her words. "Good point. Thank you."

Alexis searched his features. He didn't know what she was looking for. "I know I pushed you to have Noah add Sarah to the list of people to investigate for these threats. But I hope she's innocent. I don't want her to have lied to you or sabotaged the guardrail or shot at us or cloned your phone. That kind of betrayal would really hurt."

Max was a little overwhelmed hearing the list of grievances he and Alexis had against the stalker. It was long. "I appreciate that but she's already lied to me. I had no idea she had romantic feelings for me."

"You mean a crush on you." Alexis leaned against her chair, still playing with her pencil. "I could tell the first time I met her."

"You could?" Max's eyebrows knitted. "I wish you'd told me."

"I didn't think it was my business." Alexis spread her arms. "But if I had, would you have believed me?"

Max thought about it for a while. "Honestly, no. I don't believe Sarah tampered with the guardrail or shot at us, either. Seriously, we've worked together for more than two years. She's never shown any signs of violence."

Alexis tilted her head. "You don't think she could be the stalker?"

"No, I don't."

"She kept her feelings for you a secret for more than two years." Alexis laid the pencil on her desk. "Don't you think it's possible she kept other things a secret from you, too?"

Max arched an eyebrow. "Like her hobby as a metalsmith or her aspirations to be a sharpshooter?"

"I don't know about the sharpshooter." Alexis's tone was wry. "If that had been her, she fired seventeen bullets without hitting us. Thank God."

He massaged the back of his neck. "I'm sorry. I didn't mean to be short with you."

She gave him a dismissive wave. "I understand. This is a sensitive subject. Someone you know and trust—or trusted—is suspected of trying to kill you."

"And you."

"Do you now think she could be the one who broke into your condo?"

"I don't know. It's possible." Max rubbed his eyes. "I remember her humming songs that were also on my playlist. I thought it was a coincidence." He sprang from his seat, trying to escape his mistakes. He paced Alexis's office. "Adam's right. I'm too trusting. If I'd put all this together before, none of this would have happened."

"Let's not go there." Alexis looked up at him as he paused beside her. "And although I really appreciate your concern, I'm having dinner with my mother—in person—on Sunday."

Gritting his teeth, Max returned to his seat. "Alexis, I—care about you very much. I would never forgive myself if anything happened to you."

Alexis's eyes widened. Was it surprise or pleasure? "I care about you, too, Max. I promise I'll be careful. If you'd like, I'll call you at your bungalow to let you know when I arrive and when I get back." She smiled at him as though she'd offered him the perfect solution.

Not even close. "If you're determined to go off the resort property Sunday, then you leave me no choice."

"What does that mean?" Alexis's tone warned him to proceed with caution.

Max drew a breath. The air was scented with strong coffee and soft wildflowers. "I'm inviting myself to your mother's home for Sunday dinner."

Alexis blinked. "You want to have dinner with Mom and me?"

"That's right. I'd feel better if I were there to watch your back." He hesitated. "If you don't mind."

"Are you kidding?" Alexis clapped her hands together

and laughed. "My mother would love that. She's such a big fan. I can't wait to tell her."

Max smiled, but reluctantly. Alexis's enthusiasm was flattering. And her words were very kind. But they couldn't lose sight of the still-looming threat.

"Slow down, Allyson Felix." Max referenced the track-and-field Olympian. "I'm looking forward to meeting your mother and enjoying her cooking. But we need to be careful. I'll arrange a car service to pick us up from the resort and bring us back after dinner. Sarah—or Mark—may be familiar with your car. In case they're watching the resort, I don't want them to see your car leaving and follow us."

"That's a good idea. Thank you." Alexis reached for the phone on her desk. "I'll call Mom to let her know you're coming."

Max saw the excitement in her eyes. If he'd known how happy his visit would make her, he would have invited himself to their dinner weeks ago.

He stood to leave. "Please let her know I appreciate her hospitality and that I'm looking forward to meeting her."

"Of course." Alexis was waiting for her call to connect.

Max was more agitated as he left Alexis's office than he'd been when he'd arrived. He was going to meet Alexis's mother. Alexis loved her mother. What would he do if her mother didn't like him?

THE ATMOSPHERE IN the conference room Friday morning was electric with curiosity. The table was bathed in the sunlight that slid in through the room's floor-to-ceiling window. Alexis felt as though they were meeting on a stage under a spotlight.

The invitees hadn't been given much information about the purpose of the meeting. The group email had only asked that they join Laura, Adam and Joshua in the conference room at 9:00 a.m. Alexis considered the other Mariposa team members seated around the table. Their positions gave her a hint of the meeting's agenda. She wasn't sure why she'd been asked to attend, but she wanted to help Mariposa in any way she could.

Laura sat at the foot of the table. She wore an A-line soft pink dress and nursed a cup of coffee. Roland was on Laura's left in another crisp security director suit. His right hand was wrapped around a bottle of carbonated soda as though he feared someone would take it from him. Beside Roland, Leticia gave the security director's soda bottle a dubious frown. The personnel director wore a white, red and green floral coatdress. Adam sat at the head of the table in a smoke gray pin-striped suit. Like Laura and Joshua, the eldest Colton sibling had brought a mug of coffee to the meeting. Greg Sumpter, the resort's legal counsel, was on Adam's left. His loud Hawaiian shirt challenged Leticia's attention-grabbing dress. Joshua sat beside Alexis. His tan polo shirt was embroidered with the Mariposa logo.

Adam started the meeting. "We appreciate your dropping everything to join us. This is a very sensitive issue. As such, please do not discuss it with anyone outside of this group or where you could be overheard."

"That sounds serious." Greg was tall and fit with brown hair and green eyes. Alexis couldn't remember ever seeing him in a suit.

"*Very* serious." Joshua glanced at Greg's clothing. "Do you own any quiet shirts?"

The other man crossed his arms over his chest. "Jealous?"

Adam's blue eyes, so like Laura's, moved over them, one

person at a time. "Laura, Josh and I suspect an employee is discussing events that occur at the resort."

Alexis heard the anger and disappointment in his voice.

Leticia straightened on her black-and-sterling-silver chair. Her eyes were wide with shock as they moved from Adam to Joshua and Laura. Her accent exposed her North Carolina roots. "But everyone who works for Mariposa has signed a nondisclosure agreement, including you three."

Greg grunted. "If this is true, it wouldn't be the first time someone violated a nondisclosure agreement. They're legally binding documents but they don't have superpowers."

Roland stroked his goatee. "What kind of 'events'?"

Laura wrapped her palms around her coffee mug as though she was trying to warm herself. "The kind that could damage Mariposa's reputation and make our guests uncomfortable. Details about the investigation into Allyson's murder." She nodded toward Alexis. "The sabotaged guardrail and Max's mysterious box."

Leticia waved her hands. Her long nails were polished red and green. "Okay. But why do you think someone's discussing things that happen *on* the resort with people *outside* of the resort?"

Joshua's tone was dry. "Because Clive and Glenna have made comments and asked things about the resort and those events in particular that tipped us off that they know more than they should."

Adam continued. "But they're coy about where they're getting their information."

Joshua expelled a breath as he leaned against his chair. "We need to get to the bottom of this. We've built this resort on a reputation for security and privacy. This leak is undermining our brand."

Laura looked to Alexis before turning her attention to

the rest of the group. "We've been able to keep these events out of the media so far, but we're running out of time."

Alexis stared into her coffee mug, searching for ideas on how to expose the leaker. She was coming up empty.

Greg's question broke her concentration. "Why don't you plant a false rumor with people who could be the leaker and see which one gets back to Glenna and Clive?"

Alexis looked up from her mug. "I don't know if that would be a good idea." She shared her attention with Laura, Joshua and Adam. "If the media's already giving us extra scrutiny, it wouldn't be a good idea to *add* rumors. We should concentrate on shutting down the leak. Perhaps we find out which employees Clive and Glenna spend the most time with."

"I like that plan." Adam nodded his approval.

"So do I," Joshua agreed.

Laura touched her shoulder. "This is one of the reasons we especially wanted you to join us, Alexis. You have a good rapport with everyone. Could you subtly ask around to see if Glenna or Clive have been spending more time with a particular employee?"

"Of course." She would start with the concierges. For her own peace of mind, she needed to clear her staff as soon as possible.

"Great." Adam shifted his attention to Leticia. "Could you review the personnel files to see if anything jumps out at you?"

Leticia arched a dark eyebrow. "You mean in case some-one would be susceptible to Clive and Glenna bribing them? I'll take a look, but I'm not sure I'll find anything."

Adam's shoulders moved in a restless shrug. "I know it's a long shot, but I appreciate your checking." He moved on to Roland. "We'll keep you apprised of the situation in case we need your help with an internal investigation or if the situation becomes volatile."

Roland inclined his head. "I'd appreciate that."

Adam's eyes dropped to Greg's shirt. His lips twitched as he resisted a smile. "We'll keep you in the loop as well in case we need you to intervene with the media or if we need your legal expertise to remove the employee once they're identified."

"Sounds good." Greg tapped the table.

Adam stood. "That's it, everyone. Again, thank you for your time."

Alexis started to rise. Laura's hand on her shoulder stopped her. "Could you give me a few more minutes, please, Alexis?"

"Sure." She settled back on her chair and watched as Roland, Leticia and Greg filed out of the room.

Adam paused beside her and gave her a warm smile. "Thanks for all you do, Alexis."

Her face heated. "You're very welcome, Adam. If there's anything else you need, please let me know."

"I will." He smiled at Laura before leaving.

Alexis looked up as someone patted her shoulder.

Joshua winked at her. "Great work as usual."

Her face was still warm. "Thank you, Joshua. I appreciate that." After he left, closing the door behind him, she turned to Laura. "What did you want to talk with me about?"

Laura gave her a somber look. "It's official. Cheryl has submitted her paperwork for her retirement."

"That's wonderful. I'm so happy for her." Alexis felt a rush of joy. Cheryl had been with Mariposa almost from its opening day. She was a resort treasure. Then almost immediately, panic set in. She was out of time to prove herself capable and ready to fill the other woman's shoes.

Laura smiled. "So are Adam, Josh and I. Adam's going to send a companywide email Monday, announcing Cheryl's last day, which is April thirtieth. We want to keep the focus on her until then. After she leaves, we're going to announce her replacement."

"You've already made a decision?" Alexis could barely breathe.

"We have." She paused. "Adam, Joshua and I are offering the job to you. We think you would make an excellent event manager. You're thorough, customer-focused and imaginative, and you inspire loyalty in your staff. You'd be perfect for the position."

"What?" Alexis's jaw dropped. Was she floating? "This is wonderful. Laura, thank you so much for this opportunity. I'm thrilled to accept your offer. Thank you."

Laura stood with Alexis and embraced her. "Alexis, I'm so happy for you but I'm even happier for the resort. You're the perfect person to replace Cheryl."

"Thank you so much. This is amazing." Alexis stepped back.

"Remember, please don't tell anyone yet. Cheryl knows we're offering you the position but we're keeping the focus on her for now. We'll announce your promotion May first. Until then, you can tell your mother so you can celebrate." Laura gave her a sly look. "And, if you want, you can celebrate with Max, too."

Alexis smiled. "As it so happens, Max and I are having dinner with my mom Sunday."

Laura gaped at her. "What?" She tugged Alexis back to her seat. "Spill."

Chapter Fourteen

"You didn't have to go to all this trouble for me—the roses, the dinner, the dessert." Alexis sighed as she stood beside Max on his patio late Friday evening. The sound pooled in Max's lower abdomen.

Alexis was wearing her little black dress that skimmed her lithe figure and showed off her shapely calves again. Max had another flashback to her demi-cup black lace bra. He gave himself a mental shake and sharp scolding.

"You keep saying that. It wasn't any trouble. I love to cook. And Annabeth's kitchen had all the ingredients I needed, even for the dessert. And I found itty-bitty plates for the entrée."

Alexis's laughter was soft and low. Max swallowed to ease his dry throat.

The trolley with their meal had been magically cleared away. Only the scents of the garlic and rosemary Cornish game hen, roasted asparagus spears and oyster stuffing remained. He'd made the arrangements for the celebratory meal after Alexis had called to tell him she'd gotten the promotion she'd been working toward. He'd been so happy, he'd been unable to concentrate. All he could think about was doing something to make the day even more special for her.

"Thank you so much for everything." She turned to him. "The meal was delicious. The roses are beautiful, and the company's even better."

The evening's lengthening shadows highlighted her delicate features. Max wanted to caress her cheek, run his fingers through her hair as it flowed in waves to her shoulders. He stuck his hands in the front pockets of his steel gray slacks.

"You're welcome. I know you said we could celebrate your promotion during dinner with your mother on Sunday, but I couldn't wait. I wanted to do something now. And since you're not comfortable dining with me in Annabeth—"

"I've explained employees and guests aren't supposed to fraternize—"

"I know." Max held up his left hand. "The alternative was to have dinner in my bungalow."

"This was so thoughtful of you." Alexis wrapped her arms around herself.

"You're cold. We should go inside." Max placed his hand on the small of her back.

"Not yet." Alexis turned back toward the view. Beyond the red rock mountain ridge, the sun was setting in a wash of indigo, orange and gold. "Let's watch the sunset first."

Max hesitated. He felt her muscles shiver against his palm. "All right." He put his right arm around her shoulders and drew her near to share his body heat.

His temperature rose when she cuddled closer and put her left arm around his waist. Happiness wrapped around him like a soft blanket. He enjoyed the silence as they watched the sun slip behind the mountains.

"What drives you, Alexis?" His voice was low.

She stirred against him. "What do you mean?"

"This promotion was so important to you. You said you don't want to stand still when it comes to your career. You want to keep moving, keep advancing. I admire that about you. I was wondering why. What drives you?"

She was silent for several beats. Was she going to ignore his question?

"An inferiority complex." Her words were so stark and unexpected, Max thought he'd misheard her.

He shook his head in confusion. "Why would you feel inferior to anyone?"

Alexis let her arm drop away from his waist. A cool breeze came between them. "My mother and I didn't have a lot of money. I couldn't afford to go to fancy schools. I went to community college. My wardrobe wasn't full of designer labels. Most of it came from secondhand shops. So I felt I had to prove myself." She shrugged her right shoulder. "I still feel that way. I had to be the valedictorian of my high school class. I had to make the dean's list every semester in college."

"Valedictorian? Dean's list? I feel intimidated." Max was only half joking.

"Oh, please." Alexis gave him the side-eye. "I've read your bio. You've been graduating the top of your class since elementary school."

"Day care, but I don't want to brag."

She laughed as he'd hoped she would. "I've never shared that with anyone before, not even my mother. She's worked so hard and sacrificed so much for me. I didn't want to risk making her feel bad."

"Thank you for sharing your feelings with me. I won't betray your trust." Max's heart was full. He was both proud and humbled by her confidence in him. "May I ask about your father, or is that too personal?"

She arched an eyebrow at him. "You've seen me in my underwear. I think you can ask me about my dad." But she took a deep breath before answering. "He died from cancer when I was seven. My older sister was killed in a hit-and-run by a distracted driver when I was eight."

Max's heart clenched with pain at her loss. "I'm so very sorry, Alexis."

"Thank you." Her voice was husky.

Max felt her struggling with her grief as though she was trying to put it back into a box. He studied her profile, wishing he could say something more meaningful and helpful than "sorry." He reached out to touch her hand. She wrapped her fingers around his and held on.

After another moment of silence, she faced him. "So I told you about my inferiority complex. What's your deep, dark secret?"

Still holding her hand, Max escorted her back into his bungalow. "This is going to sound really stupid." He stepped aside so she could enter first.

She looked at him over her shoulder. "And mine didn't?"

He took a moment to secure the French doors before turning to face her. "I have stage fright."

Alexis stared at him. "You're a celebrity chef. How could you have stage fright?"

He spread his arms. "I told you it was stupid."

"That's not what I meant at all."

Max looked at Alexis, trying to really see her for the first time. The confident woman she projected and the insecurities she tried to hide. "I think, in a way, we're more alike than we may think. You feel like you have to prove yourself. Sometimes I feel like I'm a fraud."

Her eyes stretched wide. "Why would you think that?"

"Sometimes I don't know who I really am." Max moved

his shoulders restlessly. "When people meet me, they see The Celebrity Chef. But I'm just Max. I think that's what's causing my anxiety. Am I giving people what they want? If I am, then am I losing Max?"

Her eyes darkened with pain. For him? "How do you film a weekly TV show with stage fright?"

"It's not easy." His voice was dry. "My mother suggested I pretend I'm in the kitchen of my condo, talking with friends as I get ready for a dinner party. That helps. And the editor does a great job putting the show together in post."

Alexis's smile was tender. "Well, if what we're seeing on TV is you, pretending to be in your kitchen, then what you're giving us is Max, who happens to be a very successful celebrity chef."

Her words made him feel like he could breathe again. "Thank you. I'd never thought of it that way."

"You're amazing. Do you know that? You've managed to create a hit show despite your anxiety."

Max gave her a wry smile. "My father thought the ratings would be even better if I taped the second season in front of a live audience."

Alexis gasped. "Oh, no. He doesn't know about your stage fright?"

Max's smile disappeared. "Absolutely not. I asked my mother never to tell him, either in this life or the next."

Alexis's laughter filled his bungalow and his heart. "I admire you even more now."

He closed the distance between them and took her hand again. "Because I have a successful show?"

She dipped her chin and gave him a chiding look. "Because when you want something, you make it happen even if that means overcoming significant challenges. Not only did you survive but you thrived. You're very impressive."

He stepped even closer, until he felt the warmth of her body, and looked into her eyes. "I feel the same way about you, Alexis Reed. When *you* want something, you make it happen, like your promotions. You've impressed me." His voice was low and deep. He didn't recognize it.

"Is that all I've done?" Her words were barely audible.

"No, it's not." He caressed the side of her face with the backs of his fingers. Her skin was so soft, so smooth, so warm. "You've challenged me. Distracted me. Invaded my thoughts and my dreams." He took the hand he still held and raised it to his shoulder. "And you've made me yearn for you."

Max pressed his mouth to hers. His body tightened at the feel of her soft moist lips against his. He wrapped his arms around her and held her closer. He never wanted to let her go. He wanted to go to sleep with her in his arms and wake up the same way. Max ran his palm down her back and cupped her hips. Alexis moaned deep in her throat. His body burned. She rose up on her toes to fit herself against him. His heart skipped a beat. She opened her mouth to welcome him in. Max swept his tongue past her lips to explore her touch, her taste, her moisture.

Alexis slid her palms up and over his chest to twine around his shoulders. Max shivered under her caress and deepened their kiss. Alexis chased his tongue with her own, taunting and teasing him. She moved against him restlessly. Each wiggle and roll made his pulse pound louder in his head. Alexis raised her left knee along the side of his leg. Max thought his body would spontaneously combust. He cupped the back of her thigh. The feel of her stocking against his palm sketched heated images in his mind. His hand followed the garment under the hem of her dress.

His finger traced its edge between the nylon and her skin. Alexis shivered in his arms like a leaf tossed on a breeze.

She pulled away. "Max." She breathed his name, then stopped.

"Alexis." He forced himself to give her space, but he couldn't let her go. "What is it? You can tell me."

She took another breath and lifted her eyes to his. "You're going back to New York soon. You're going home and my home is here. I'm sorry, but I don't think we should start something we both know can't go anywhere."

He dropped his arms from her waist and took several steps back. His movements were robotic. Max turned to pace away from her. He needed to clear his head.

With his back to her, he nodded. "All right. I respect your feelings." He took a breath, straightened his shoulders and managed to smile. "Let me take you back to your bungalow."

Alexis's smile looked stiffer than his felt. "No, that's all right. It's not far and security is everywhere." She crossed to his side table and collected her purse.

Max followed her. "I'll take you back, Alexis. If I stayed home while you drove a golf cart to your bungalow alone at night, I'd disown myself."

And the cool night air would do him some good.

"RESTAURANTS, COOKING SHOW or cookbook." Catherine sat beside Alexis on her tan sofa late Sunday evening. She leaned forward toward Max seated on the love seat beside her. "Which do you prefer?"

The evening had started on an awkward note. Seated beside Alexis on the back seat of the car service he'd arranged for them, Max had felt Alexis's tension like a third passenger in the sedan. After their heated kiss Friday evening, Max thought they'd needed to spend Saturday apart. Apparently, so had Alexis. Neither had called, texted or tried to see the other.

In other words, Saturday had been horrible. At least from Max's perspective.

Max had missed Alexis more than he could describe. He'd missed hearing her voice, looking into her eyes, seeing her smile, being in her company. Sunday couldn't come fast enough.

But when he saw her again, he'd followed her lead as to how to approach their relationship. Her greeting had been perfunctory. Her smile had been polite but distant. She hadn't touched him. He hadn't touched her either, not even accidentally on purpose. The next move would need to be hers. Or at least that's the mantra he repeated to himself during her mother's fabulous six-course meal.

Catherine had served the sixth course, her homemade pecan pie, with coffee in her spacious living room. She must have worked all weekend, planning and preparing the celebratory dinner for her daughter.

He considered Catherine's question. "The restaurants, show or book? I enjoy them all equally. With the restaurants, I get to cook for people. Through the show, I teach people how to cook for themselves. And I'm having a great time with the cookbook because..." His voice trailed off as his eyes met Alexis's. "Because I enjoy experimenting with new recipes."

Catherine beamed at him. Her smile was as transformative as Alexis's. Max was fascinated, watching mother and daughter next to each other. They looked so much alike: the same lithe, dancer's build, golden brown skin and long-lidded, hazel eyes. They were similarly dressed in dark wide-legged pants and pastel blouses. They even had similar mannerisms. But Catherine's raven hair was a bob that framed her delicate face. Tonight, Alexis wore her hair in loose waves that tumbled to her slender shoulders.

Catherine stood to put her cup and saucer on the blond wood coffee table in front of her. "My friends and I were so excited to learn that your cooking show was extended to a second season. We enjoy trying your recipes during our monthly dinner parties." She returned to the sofa and crossed her left leg over her right. "When are you going to open a restaurant in Sedona?"

"Mom!" Alexis gasped. She sent an apologetic look at Max before addressing her mother. "You just got through the long list of projects Max is juggling. Why are you adding more responsibilities to his list?"

Catherine scowled. "Because it's very expensive to fly to New York every time I want his food."

Max laughed. "Actually, my lawyer and I have been discussing opening a third restaurant. But it's only an idea at this point. I'm using the show and cookbook to help increase demand for the two that I have now. Once the demand has grown, we'll identify a third location."

Catherine raised her hand like a good student asking for the teacher to call on her. "I'm putting in a push for Sedona now."

"I promise to keep it in mind." Max inclined his head. He was at ease in Catherine's company. She was warm and charming. Alexis, on the other hand, was a challenge. In her company, Max was forced to keep his wits about him.

Alexis pinned him with her eyes. "I've read several interviews with you but none of them explain how you got started in your career. They describe how you started your restaurants or your show, but not where you got your love of cooking."

Max cocked his head. "It's interesting that you worded your question that way, my 'love' of cooking. For me, cooking is an expression of love. My family's kitchen was the warmest room in the house. I don't mean the temperature. I mean it's where we spent most of our family time. We started the day together with breakfast. We ended the day together with dinner, and then my parents would go back to work. We celebrated birthdays, holidays, graduations, my parents' anniversary in that kitchen. That's where I found my love of cooking, from my family's kitchen."

"Those sound like wonderful memories." The coolness in Alexis's eyes began to warm. "I agree that cooking is an expression of love."

"Really?" Catherine looked at her daughter as though she didn't know her. "Then why are you always eating burgers and fries?"

Alexis shrugged. "Because I love them."

Catherine put a hand over her face. "I don't know where I went wrong."

Max laughed. "There's nothing wrong with having burgers and fries once in a while. They could be cooked with love, too."

"Ha!" Alexis pumped her fist triumphantly. "And that was from the great Chef Max."

"Fine." Catherine threw up her hands. "I will bow to his greater culinary wisdom. But mark my words. When you love someone, you cook for them. You don't pull up to a fast-food window and place two orders for burgers and fries."

Alexis pulled her attention from Max. Her voice and expression seemed subdued. "I promise, Mom." She stood, gathering the tray that held the remains of their dessert course. "It's getting late. We should be going, but first I'll load the dishwasher."

Max rose, too. "I'll help."

"Oh, no." Catherine and Alexis spoke at once.

Catherine continued. "You're our guest. Please make yourself comfortable. It won't take us long to clean up."

Alexis nodded. "In the meantime, you can request a car service to pick us up. That way, we won't have to wait long for it to arrive."

"A car service?" Catherine waved a dismissive hand at Alexis. "Take my car instead."

Alexis hesitated. Max could sense that she wanted to say yes. "How would you get to work tomorrow?"

"Suz could take me to work in the morning." Catherine spoke over her shoulder as she went to the coat closet near the front door. She pulled her purse down from the top shelf and fished out her car keys. She returned to the living room to give the keys to Alexis. "And she could drive me to the resort to collect my car at the end of the day. It's not a problem. I'd do the same for her."

"If you're sure it's not too much trouble, I'd really appreciate it." Alexis looked at Max. "I'd like to stop by my place to get a couple of things on the way back."

"Of course." Max turned to her mother. "Thank you, Catherine." She'd insisted he call her that. "But you realize now there's nothing to keep me from helping you clean up."

He led the way to her kitchen, trying not to think about what happened the last time he'd stopped by Alexis's condo.

ALEXIS LIVED CLOSE to her mother. Max could probably jog the distance in little more than an hour. It took minutes for Alexis to drive it. Using the electronic device from her purse, she opened her attached garage. She pulled her mother's sedan through, then welcomed Max into her condo.

"Can I get you anything?" Alexis asked over her shoulder.

"No, thank you." Max looked at the soothing tones of her decor. "I don't want to dilute the memory of your mother's six-course meal. Thank you again for letting me invite myself to your Sunday dinner. I had a great time."

"I'm glad." Her face glowed with joy. "I think meeting you was the highlight of my mother's year. Thank you for answering all her questions so graciously."

Let her set the tone.

"I had fun." The room seemed to have gotten warmer. Max put his hands in the front pockets of his dark brown pants. "Your mother asks good questions."

"Yes, she does." Alexis led him into the dining area. "She also has good insights. It must be a maternal superpower."

Max kept his gaze averted from the dining table and the memories it held. He frowned, sensing Alexis's discomfort. "What do you mean?"

She clasped her hands together, then let them drop to her sides. "She said when someone cooks for you that means they love you. My mother and I usually cook our Sunday dinners together. We plan our meals, then we buy our ingredients at the farmers market. We usually go back to her house to cook because she has the bigger kitchen."

"I'm so sorry." Max rubbed his neck, pacing away from her. "This stalking situation has disrupted your life even more than I realized."

"That's not what I'm getting at." Alexis swept her arms before her like a conductor bringing a song to an end. "My mother and I cook for each other every Sunday because we love each other." She took a step toward him. "Friday, you cooked for me."

Max's mind went blank. "Alexis—"

She held up her hand and took another step closer. "We haven't known each other long, less than a month. But I realized yesterday when I had time to think that, even if what we have can't go anywhere, for the rest of my life, I would regret never having been with you."

Max took the final step, removing the distance between them. "So would I." He cupped her cheek with his right hand. "So would I, sweetheart."

He touched his lips to hers. There would be time later to tell Alexis he was falling in love with her. For now, he would show her.

Alexis rose up on her toes and fitted her body to his. She sighed against his lips. Max opened his mouth and let her in. Her exploration was slow and gentle, soft and sweet. Max drew her tighter against him and lost himself in the feel of her. The scent of her.

Her tongue stroked against the roof of his mouth, then withdrew. Needing more, Max followed, sucking it back. Alexis pressed against him, moaning her pleasure. Max captured her tongue again, wanting to hear that sound once more.

Her fingernails pierced his cotton shirt and dug into his shoulders. Max's muscles shivered at the touch. He freed his mouth from hers and buried his face in the thick dark mass of her hair. He breathed deeply, drinking in her scent, soaking up her warmth. He tried to calm his racing pulse. He didn't want to lose control. He wanted this night with her to last.

Alexis's teeth grazed his earlobe. Her voice whispered in his ear. "Take me to bed."

Was he dreaming? Max squeezed his eyes shut as desire tightened his muscles. Those words from her lips were the sweetest sounds he'd ever heard.

"Like music to my ears." He swept Alexis into his arms and carried her through the door he remembered led to her bedroom.

With her hand cupping the back of his neck, she pulled his head down for another mind-blowing kiss. Her taste was intoxicating. It cleared his mind of everything but the two of them. The way they fit together. The way they felt together. The way they tasted together. Nothing had ever been better. Nothing ever would. In her arms, he knew exactly who he was and who he wanted to be: hers.

Max stopped at the foot of her bed and gently released her. Alexis's thigh stroked his hips as her legs lowered to the ground. Max's muscles shook. His blood heated even more.

Breaking their kiss, Alexis leaned back to search his eyes. Her cheeks were flushed like a pink rose. Her eyes shone like stars. Her lips were swollen with passion. "Do you have protection?"

"I do." Thank goodness.

She gave him a smile that made his desire throb. Holding his eyes, Alexis pulled his cream polo shirt from the waistband of his dark brown pants. He felt her palms stroke up and over his torso as she removed it, letting it drop to the floor. Max's stomach muscles trembled. He locked his knees to keep his legs steady.

He removed her mint green blouse. His breath caught when he revealed her demi-cup black lace bra.

Max raised his eyes to hers. "Did you plan this?" His voice was a curious whisper.

She gave him a seductive smile. "It may have been in the back of my mind."

Max swallowed. Hard. He was glad he hadn't known what she was wearing when they'd met at the L. They may never have made it to Sunday dinner. His fingers shook slightly when he reached behind her to unclasp the bra and free her breasts. They were firm, full and round. *Perfection.*

He drew her into his arms, lowering his head for another taste of her lips. The feel of her soft, warm skin rubbing against his bare torso made his body burn and his pulse race. He pressed her closer to him. Alexis raised her arms and wrapped them around his shoulders.

"Alexis." He whispered her name against her lips, still unsure of whether he was in a dream.

ALEXIS DRANK HER name from his tongue. The feel of Max's hardening erection against her stomach made her thighs quiver. She reveled in the feel of his hard, hair-roughened chest pressing against her soft breasts. She felt his nimble fingers at the waistband of her pants, unfastening them and tugging them down. Breaking off their kiss, she quickly helped him. She stripped off her underpants, socks and shoes as well. Then she watched as he removed the rest of his clothing.

His body was art. Alexis's eyes moved over his proud shoulders, sculpted pecs, flat stomach, narrow hips and long, powerful legs.

Dropping to her knees in front of him, Alexis stroked Max's thighs. His muscles were hard and tense beneath her palms. His skin was warm. She reached up and caressed his thickening erection. He was hot, smooth and heavy moving against her palm. Her body moistened. His moan echoed in her ear, emboldening her. Alexis braced both of her hands on Max's thighs, then leaned forward to take him deep into her mouth. The muscles in his legs shook beneath her touch. His harsh breaths urged her on. Alexis drew him in, stroking him with her tongue.

"Stop." Max sounded breathless. Stepping back, he grasped her arms with unsteady hands and helped her to her feet. "You are so beautiful."

Alexis saw her beauty in his eyes.

Max urged her onto the mattress then drew her to the edge of the bed. He knelt in front of her and moved in. Excitement made Alexis's body pulse. She pressed her knees against his sides. Max reached out and cupped his large palms over her sensitive breasts. Her back arched, pressing her against his magical touch. His rough hand smoothed down her torso. Alexis felt her heart beat against it. Her breath came in gasps. Her stomach muscles quivered at his touch. Moisture pooled inside her as desire built.

Max lowered his head to place kisses just beneath her navel. Her legs went lax. His hand cupped the juncture between her thighs. His fingers played tauntingly in her nest of curls. Alexis moved restlessly against the mattress.

"Max. Touch me."

"Where?" His breath blew against her navel.

Alexis whimpered. "There." She lifted her hips, trying to get closer to him. She ground her teeth when he remained out of reach.

"I will, sweetheart."

"Now, Max. I need you now." Her body was moving of its own volition. Her hips pumped. Her back arched. Her body strained.

"Like this?" Max slipped two fingers inside her, stretching her.

Alexis gasped and closed her eyes, pressing her head

back into the mattress. Her muscles clenched around him. Max continued to slide his fingers in and out of her. Her nipples tightened, responding to his rhythmic touches. Her legs parted, urging him to join her.

Max's voice coaxed her. "Look at me, sweetheart."

She opened her eyes and looked at him. The heat in his dark gaze singed her. She'd never felt this rush of heat and need before. The connection was more than physical. It was beyond intense. It was all-consuming.

"Come inside me, Max. I want to feel you in me."

The heat in his eyes blazed brighter. He reached behind him, drawing his wallet from his pants pocket to find his condom. Alexis helped him roll it onto his erection, eager to make this final connection with him. It was the closeness she'd fantasized about. Here, she felt equal. Not less than. Not lacking. Never inferior. In Max's arms, she found a place where she could belong.

He rolled with her onto the bed. Pulling her into his arms, he held her close. Max pressed his lips to hers and entered her with one long, deep thrust.

It was too much.

Alexis's lips parted on a silent gasp. Her body shook and tossed as waves of pleasure rocked her. Max stilled. He tightened his arms around her, caressing her, soothing her until she stopped shaking and could breathe again.

And then he moved once more.

With her. Against her. Deeper and deeper. Max's eyes locked on hers. He slipped his right hand between them and touched her. Alexis moaned as he teased her, stoking the embers that still burned inside. She could feel the moisture flowing from her.

Alexis wrapped her arms and legs around him, holding him even closer. With each of his thrusts, her breasts trembled, rubbing her sensitive nipples against his chest. Alexis arched her back, bringing her breasts closer to Max's lips. He bent his head to suckle first one, then the other. Her nipples pebbled, pleading for more. He kissed them. Alexis twisted and writhed beneath him. Her muscles clenched around his erection, pulling him deeper, holding him tight.

Her pleasure was building to a crescendo. Her hips pumped, greedy for more. Max kissed her again, sliding his tongue into her mouth the way he worked his body into hers. He pressed into her, caressed her. Her muscles tightened and strained, twisting her higher and higher until her restraints broke. His body stiffened. Her muscles tensed. He buried his face in the curve of her neck. She pressed her face against his shoulder and held on tight as they exploded together.

Chapter Fifteen

"There's a video of us at The Cloisters." Alexis handed Max her cell phone Monday morning.

They were standing in the dining area of his bungalow. Alexis was too agitated to sit. She watched him press Play on her cell phone to activate the file. It was a short video. Her body was shaking with outrage. She turned to pace the great room. There was no need for her to watch the clip again. She knew what he would see.

It was a poor-quality video, which was surprising considering even cell phones produced high-quality recordings these days. It started with the interior of The Cloisters. The camera framed a wide shot of the bar. Then it zoomed in on Alexis and Max. Their seats were close. There was an air of intimacy as they talked and laughed together. From the camera angle, it looked as though they were in each other's lap. Several times, the camera closed in on their drinks and the modest neckline of Alexis's dress. The message was a clear condemnation of their behavior and a sly inference on their relationship.

The camera followed them across the bar as they were seated for dinner. The video made an abrupt cut, then ended with Max embracing Alexis in the parking lot. The video title read, "Companionship among the Amenities Offered at Mariposa."

The day had started so well. She and Max had showered together. She'd made him breakfast. Then they'd driven to Mariposa. When they'd arrived at the resort, they'd parted at the parking lot, careful to avoid public displays of affection.

And now this.

Trying to temper her emotions, Alexis drew a deep, steadying breath. Beneath the scent of the fresh-cut flowers in the vases around Max's bungalow, she detected his clean, minty scent. It soothed her, at least for a little while.

Max watched the video in stunned silence. When it ended, anger simmered in his eyes. "This was posted today?" He returned her cell phone.

Alexis pocketed the device. "Yes, I got the alert a few minutes ago."

Max rubbed the back of his neck. He wore a brick red short-sleeved shirt with gray cargo shorts. "How did they know I was a guest at Mariposa?"

Alexis flung her arm in the general direction of the nature trails. "From the hiking accident video. *Celebrity Chef's Heroic Rescue* must have a million views by now." She stopped pacing and covered her face with her left hand. "I can't believe this." She dropped her hand and faced Max. "Did you see anyone at the bar pointing a cell phone at us or any kind of camera at us?"

"No, but that doesn't mean there wasn't one or a dozen nearby." Max continued pacing. "The paparazzi are ubiquitous."

Alexis sighed. "So I've heard. But I can't see them going into the bar to record a video of you, then posting it. The Cloisters is private property. They could be sued."

"You're right." Max paused beside one of the bamboo armchairs, propping his hip against it. "Whoever shot that video wouldn't want to be seen. But why would they wait so long to post it? It's been almost three weeks since we went to The Cloisters."

"Really?" She turned to him in disbelief. "Is that what you got out of this? Why did they wait so long to post such an inflammatory video?"

Max raised his hands in surrender. "Hear me out. If you went to all the trouble to make a secret video designed to show people in a bad light, would you wait three weeks to post it?" He had a point.

"No, I wouldn't."

"Then why would they?" Max gestured toward her front right pocket where she'd stored her cell phone.

"Because the timing is significant." The pieces were coming into place in Alexis's mind. Now if she just knew what the picture was supposed to be. What were they after?

"What's significant about it?" Max straightened from the side of the chair. "Could there be a connection to your promotion?" A flash of worry flew across his dark eyes.

"It could be. But the only person who'd want to hurt me professionally is Mark Bower. At least that I know of."

"And he has an alibi for that Thursday night."

"Besides, the only people who know about my promotion are the Coltons, Cheryl, you, my mother and me. How would the person behind this video have found out?"

The memory of her Friday meeting with the Coltons, Roland, Leticia and Greg wormed its way into her mind. Was it possible that Clive and Glenna's spy was somehow involved in this video post? Was this an attempt by the couple to destroy Mariposa?

Alexis wasn't free to discuss the resort's suspicion that

there was a spy in their midst, not even with Adam's best friend. But if Adam wanted to share the information with Max, then that decision was between the two of them.

Max's voice distracted her from her thoughts. "I don't think there's anything that would connect this timing with my projects."

Alexis nodded distractedly. She took a few more paces around the room, conscious of Max's eyes on her. This wasn't the way she'd planned their "morning after." It had started with plenty of promise for romance. Then it had taken a steep nosedive.

She turned to him and stilled. It would be foolish not to bring up the one person who'd been top of mind in the other threats. "Is there anyway Sarah could be involved?"

He stared at the bamboo flooring as he considered her question. Several seconds, perhaps half a minute, ticked by. "If she was the shooter, I don't think she would've had time to record video from inside the bar, then get in position to try to shoot us."

"I disagree." Alexis shook her head. "She would've had plenty of time while we were eating dinner."

"What about the image of us embracing at the end of the video? How did she get that recording?"

Alexis shrugged. "She could've been hiding somewhere across the street when she took that photo. The police were looking for a shooter, not a celebrity chef fan recording an unauthorized video."

"All good points, but I don't believe Sarah's involved." Max crossed his arms over his chest. "She's returned to New York, remember?"

"Until the NYPD confirms that, I'd rather err on the side of caution." She took a shaky breath. "And if we're right that the motive of their timing was to hurt my promotion, then it looks like they've succeeded."

Max frowned. "What do you mean?"

Alexis let her head drop back as she expelled a frustrated breath. She didn't want to have to deal with this. Not now, not ever.

"I'm going to have to show this video to Laura at least, if not all the Coltons." Alexis strained to keep the panic from her voice. "This video puts Mariposa in a very negative light and it uses me to do that. The inference is that I'm a prostitute. The defamation is intended to hurt me and it's succeeded."

Max joined her, taking both of her hands in his. "I'm so very sorry, sweetheart. When we find the person responsible for this, I promise you, we'll make them pay. I promise."

"How? By suing them and exposing that video to even more people?" Alexis snorted. "Let me sleep on that." She gently drew her hands from Max. "I'd better talk with Laura now. The sooner I get this over with, the better."

"Do you want me to come with you?" His dark eyes searched hers.

Alexis would remember the care and concern in his eyes for the rest of her life. "No, thank you. I'd rather handle this quietly."

He escorted her to the door. "Let me know how it goes and whether you need to talk. Okay?"

"Thanks. I will."

Alexis got back into the golf cart she'd borrowed and returned to the L. She had a pretty good idea of how the fallout from that vile video would affect her professionally. It wasn't going to be good. What she didn't know was how it would affect her and Max personally.

ONCE AGAIN, THE video loaded onto Alexis's cell phone. She sat quietly on one of the burnt-umber guest chairs on the other side of Laura's white modular desk Monday morning. Her friend's office was comfortably cool, but Alexis's palms were sweating. She was so tense, if a breeze blew through the room, she'd shatter into dust. Alexis stared blindly out the window beside Laura's desk, mentally working on a way to explain this media fiasco.

The video started and Laura gasped. "What the—" She cut herself off as the video continued. Had she been reacting to the title screen?

Alexis's stomach muscles were tied in knots. She retreated to her thoughts while she waited for the video to end. It shouldn't be much longer now.

Laura's eyes were wide as she looked from Alexis's phone to Alexis. She'd pressed her hand to her chest over her pale silver blouse. "This is reprehensible."

Her friend's reaction was worse than she'd expected. Alexis wished the floor would open up and consume her. She briefly closed her eyes, swallowing in an effort to ease her suddenly dry throat. "Laura, I'm very sorry. The video's—"

"*You're* sorry?" Laura gasped again. "What do you have to be sorry about?" She returned the phone to Alexis. "You should sue."

The conversation had taken an unexpected turn. Alexis was having trouble keeping up. "You said I should sue?"

"Absolutely." Laura waved a hand toward Alexis's phone. "That's libel. In fact, they've defamed Mariposa, too. I'm going to discuss this with Adam and Josh. I think we should sue."

Alexis held up her hand. "I'm not sure I want to draw additional attention to that video. It's highly insulting."

Laura's voice softened. "I understand, Alexis. But they could be counting on your being too uncomfortable to speak out. You wouldn't be speaking out alone. And they shouldn't be allowed to get away with this."

Alexis's eyes were drawn back to the scene outside the window. The red dirt trails, desert foliage landscaping and the ever-present mountains. "Max thinks I should sue, too."

"He's right." Laura still sounded upset. "I'm going to discuss this with Adam and Josh. Unless they have valid concerns against suing, I'm going to ask Greg to look into this. I won't allow you or Mariposa to be bullied."

Squaring her shoulders, Alexis met Laura's eyes. "I'm sorry my actions have put Mariposa in this position."

Laura frowned and shook her head. "You didn't do anything wrong. I remember the plans we made for you to go to The Cloisters to check out their bartender Kelli Iona. You were doing me a favor and I'm grateful to you. That ridiculous video is deliberately and maliciously misrepresenting the purpose for your visit."

Alexis felt weak with relief. "Thank you for understanding and believing in me."

"Do you think I don't know you?" Laura giggled. "You don't have anything to worry about."

Or at least, there wasn't anything *more* for her to worry about. "I appreciate that."

Laura sobered. "Do you have any idea who could be behind the video post?"

Alexis crossed her right leg over her left and leaned forward. "I met with Max right before I came here. We discussed Mark Bower and Sarah Harris. It could also be Clive and Glenna. Max thinks it could be the paparazzi."

"You don't sound like you agree with that last one."

Laura stretched forward and pulled a pencil from her holder. She wrote down their brief list of names.

Alexis spread her hands. "I think it's a long shot."

Laura nodded. "But this is a good start. I'll share these names with Noah. He'll probably want to speak with both of you."

"I'm happy to speak with Noah, if he thinks it will help." Alexis shrugged. "But I don't know what else we could add. I feel helpless. Someone's trying to harm me, but I don't know who or why. You'd think if someone hated you enough to want to harm you, you'd have some idea of who that person was."

"This situation is very scary. We have to do everything we can to keep you and Max safe."

"Thank you." Alexis exhaled a frustrated sigh. "I want this to be over so we can go back to normal."

Laura leaned into her desk, folding her arms on its surface. "We all do. We're worried about you and Max."

"That makes me feel worse, knowing I'm the cause of other people's anxiety. Getting the promotion was a bright spot in all of this. I would've been devastated if I'd lost that opportunity, especially over that defamatory video."

Laura looked shocked. "Even if your visit to The Cloisters wasn't work-related, I'm not going to hold you accountable for what you do in your private life—unless it's illegal. And falling in love isn't illegal."

Alexis gaped. "Well, I don't know if you could say—"

"Don't try to deny it." Laura held out a hand, stopping her. "I've seen the way the two of you are together and the looks between you. I'm very happy for you."

Alexis sighed, dropping her eyes to the bamboo flooring. "I don't know if there's anything to be happy about. He's going back to New York in two weeks."

"Alexis, you're the most determined person I've ever met. We've had clients who've asked for the impossible and you've never blinked. You find a way to make it happen. I know you." Laura pointed at her. "If you want something, you'll make it happen. If you want this relationship to work, you'll make it work."

Her friend made it sound so easy. Alexis wanted to believe it could be—but suppose it wasn't. "A relationship involves two people. Suppose *I* want it to work, but it's not as important to him."

"Then that would make him a fool."

Alexis gave the other woman a chiding look. "Laura—"

Laura sat straighter on her chair. "I'm serious, Alexis. You're intelligent, kind, hardworking, ambitious and loyal."

"You make me sound like a Saint Bernard."

Laura ignored her. "If he doesn't see that in you and do everything he can to build a life with you, then he's a fool who doesn't deserve you."

Alexis smiled as she stood to leave. "I appreciate the pep talk."

Hopefully, she won't need it again in two weeks.

"SOMEONE TOOK VIDEO of you and Alexis at The Cloisters, then posted it online?" Adam stood still beside Max. His eyes were wide with disbelief and outrage. "That's a massive invasion of privacy. You should sue."

"That's what I think, but Alexis is embarrassed by the video." Max started walking again. Adam kept pace with him.

They were strolling the resort grounds Monday morning. Mariposa was picturesque. A mixture of delicate vistas and bold terrain. This morning, a subtle, warm breeze pushed webs of cirrus clouds across the bright blue sky.

Max thought being outdoors would help clear his mind. It might also help Adam. Since he arrived at the resort, Max had sensed something had been weighing on his friend's mind beyond the threats from his father. Adam had dodged every attempt he'd made to get him to open up, though.

"I'll talk with Laura and Josh about it." Adam sounded annoyed and determined. "Unless they have a substantial objection, I'll speak with Greg about filing a suit. You think Mark or Sarah might be involved?"

"It also might have been a member of the paparazzi." Activity near the outdoor pool drew Max's attention. Private cabanas and deck chairs surrounded the large outdoor pool. A stunning view of the surrounding rock formations stood in the background.

"It could also be an attempt by Clive and Glenna to undermine Mariposa's reputation." Adam's statement drew Max's attention back to their conversation. "Have you given this information to Noah?"

Max was irritated that he hadn't thought of that himself. "No, I've been so concerned about Alexis's reaction to that video. I didn't think about updating Noah. I'll do that as soon as I get back to my bungalow."

Adam glanced at him. "Do you want me on the call with you? You seem a little distracted."

Max rubbed the back of his neck. The restless feeling was building again. "I'm supposed to leave in two weeks. Suppose the case isn't solved by then? I can't stay here indefinitely, but I can't leave while Alexis is still in danger."

"You're my best friend, Max." Adam stopped again, turning to face him. "Your safety is very important to me. Stay here as long as you need to."

"I appreciate that, Adam." Max started moving again. He

couldn't control the frustration in his tone. "But the sooner this case is solved, the sooner everyone will be safe."

"By 'everyone' you mean Alexis."

"If Sarah's the stalker as we suspect, then Alexis is in danger because of me." The thought filled him with anger and shame.

"You're wrong." Adam's voice was firm. "If Sarah's behind these attacks, then Alexis is in danger because of *Sarah*."

"I'm not completely blameless. If I hadn't been so blind, I'd have realized Sarah had issues." Max surveyed the pathways, buildings and bungalows in the immediate area.

Was it his imagination or were there more security guards on the grounds lately? Was it all because of the threats or was something more going on?

Adam's assessment of their surroundings seemed more critical than admiring. Was he checking to see whether repairs or improvements were needed? Max thought everything looked perfect.

Adam addressed Max. "I hope the case is solved before you leave. I hope it's solved today. But what then? Will you and Alexis keep seeing each other?"

Max blew a breath. "I want that very much, but my life is in New York, and she seems rooted in Sedona."

Adam chuckled. "You wouldn't be the only couple in history who'd need to manage a long-distance relationship. It's not ideal, but other people have made it work. If she's important to you, you can make it work, too."

"Distance isn't the only problem." Max glanced toward the hiking trails far in the background. Even though he and Alexis had gone hiking after the accident, he didn't think he could look at a trail without remembering her fall. "I'm growing the restaurants, starting a second season of the show and I have my first-ever publishing contract. I don't know if this is the best time for me to start a relationship, especially a long-distance one on different time zones."

He and Adam walked together in silence for several strides, each caught up in their own thoughts. Usually, physical activity helped him think. It put things in perspective and made him feel better. That wasn't happening today. He still felt overwhelmed, agitated and lost.

Adam finally broke the companionable silence. "Max, I'm going to give you some advice—don't make the same mistake I did."

"Which one are you talking about?"

Adam gave him a sour look before facing forward again. "I've seen you and Alexis together. There's a strong connection between the two of you. Laura and I were right. You make a great couple."

Max stopped in his tracks. "You set us up?"

"Of course we did." Adam waved his hand. "Keep up. We all think Alexis is a wonderful person. If you agree, you need to find a way to make a relationship with her work. There's more to life than your career. Success doesn't mean anything if you don't have someone you love—and who loves you back—to share it with."

"You're thinking about Paige, aren't you?"

Adam sighed. "I have a lot of regrets in my life. I think not pursuing a relationship with her is the biggest one."

Max silently agreed with his friend. "What happened between you?"

Adam's shrug was more of a restless movement than a gesture of confusion. "I thought my family needed me and I didn't want to hold Paige back. You and Alexis are in a different place in your lives and careers than Paige and I were. Still, don't make the same mistake I made. Don't turn your back on happiness."

Max knew that was the most he'd get out of his friend on the topic of Paige Barnes, at least for today.

But his friend was right. Alexis was special. She was worth whatever effort was necessary to make a relationship with her work. She was the kind of woman he'd change his life for.

He needed to tell her that.

Chapter Sixteen

Why was her condo's management office calling her at work in the middle of the morning?

Alexis accepted the call on her work cell phone late Monday morning. "This is Alexis Reed. How can I help you?"

"Ms. Reed, this is Orlie. I'm new with the Red Dust Realty Property Management Group Office. I'm afraid I have some bad news for you, ma'am. Your condo was broken into this morning."

"Oh, no." It doesn't rain, but it pours. Alexis stood, preparing to leave her office. "How much damage did they do?" She tapped some keys to lock her computer.

"I'm afraid quite a bit, ma'am." Orlie's tone was full of regret. "The police are here with me in the management office. I know we're interrupting you at work right now, ma'am, and I apologize for—"

"No, I appreciate your call, Orlie." Alexis grabbed her bag from her top desk drawer.

Was it possible the break-in had something to do with the stalker? Alexis didn't believe in coincidences.

"It's no problem, ma'am. But do you think you might be able to get away for a short bit? The police would like to get a report from you about what the thieves might have taken."

"I'm on my way, Orlie. I should be there in about twenty minutes."

Orlie breathed a sigh of relief. "Oh, that's wonderful, ma'am. I appreciate your time."

"And I appreciate your assistance. Thank you, Orlie. I'll see you soon."

Alexis hurried out of her office. She sent a text to Laura as she strode down the hall. Her boss needed to know she was leaving the office to deal with a home emergency. Under the circumstances, Alexis was sure Laura would understand.

She paused briefly to leave a message with one of the clerks on duty at the registration desk. "Hey, Clarissa. My condo manager just called. Someone broke into my unit."

Clarissa's naturally sunny disposition clouded over at the news. "Gosh, I'm sorry, Alexis."

"Thank you. I sent Laura a text about it and I'm on my way to check it out."

"Okay. Be careful." Clarissa waved. "Drive safely."

Aware that Sarah, Mark or some yet-unknown stalker suspect could be watching the resort, Alexis drove her mother's car. She should be back in plenty of time to return the vehicle to Catherine. All the way to her condo, Alexis chided herself for the break-in. Although she didn't know what more she could've done. She'd put a hold on her mail, left the exterior lights on, left a couple of interior lights on and asked her mother to drive by at least once a day.

She wished she'd called Max before she'd left, but she'd been in a hurry to deal with her condo situation. She'd call him after she spoke with Orlie and the police.

Alexis arrived at her condo in less than the twenty minutes she'd promised Orlie. She slowed as she approached the driveway to her garage. That was strange. When she'd asked how much damage had been done, Orlie had replied, "Quite a bit." Leaning forward in the driver's seat, Alexis scrutinized her condo. It didn't look damaged at all. The garage door and all the windows were intact. Her front door…was it ajar?

What was that about? Were the police holding a sale with the remainder of her belongings?

Alexis parked her mother's compact sedan in her driveway instead of opening the garage. She was anxious to lock her condo. She jogged up the four steps to the front door. It was open perhaps three inches. Alexis cautiously pushed it open all the way. She waited to see whether an intruder would welcome her into her own home. Nothing.

She stepped over the threshold. Still nothing. No police officer. No property manager. Alexis started to feel uneasy. She wasn't convinced her muscles would listen to her if she urged them to move one more time. But they did.

Another, longer step placed her in the entryway. The door slammed behind her. Alexis jumped a foot off the floor and spun toward the sound. Sarah Harris stood in front of the now-closed door. The tall, full-figured woman wore black biking shorts that ended at her knees and a midriff-baring blue cap-sleeved cropped shirt. In her right hand, she held what appeared to be the largest knife from Alexis's butcher's block. Her pale round face was a mask of jealousy and anger.

Alexis's shaking started slowly but was building. She exhorted herself to remain calm and confident. "Good morning, Sarah. So you do know where I live. I'd wondered."

Without a word or a sound, Sarah charged at Alexis,

knife raised. Shock gripped her. She quickly shrugged it off. Fight or flight? She'd choose fight every time. She had no doubt if she tried to run from Sarah, the other woman would stab her in the back. That's not the way she imagined herself dying.

Alexis grabbed Sarah's knife arm with both of her hands. "Drop the knife, Sarah! What good is killing me going to do?"

No response. Instead, Sarah grunted, growled and panted like a person possessed.

Alexis had never been so afraid in her life. Not even when she'd fallen off the side of the cliff or when she was being shot at. Was that because in both cases, she hadn't been alone? Max had been with her.

Alexis battled fear and Sarah. The other woman was as strong as she looked. Maybe stronger. Alexis could barely move her. She gripped the other woman's arm as hard as she could with both of her hands. Sarah would not let go. She squeezed and squeezed and squeezed. She tried to hurt Sarah to force her to drop the knife. It wasn't working.

"You pretended to be Orlie to lure me here?" Between terror and exertion, she barely had breath to speak.

Sarah replied with more grunts, growls and pants. She brought her other arm into the struggle. She seemed to want to drive the knife into Alexis's chest. Alexis saw the bloodthirst in Sarah's eyes. They were wide and filled with hate. The pupils were dilated. Alexis was losing ground. The knife was coming closer and closer to her skin. In desperation, she kicked out. Sarah lost her balance, knocking over a chair. Falling to the floor, she finally released the knife.

Alexis kicked it away. She dropped to the floor, straddling Sarah's hips and pinning her arms down. "What is wrong with you? What do you want?"

"To kill you." Sarah spoke in a growl.

Alexis had deduced that much. "Why?"

"You stole my man and my job. I. Am. Going. To. Kill. You."

Sarah surged up, dislodging Alexis. Alexis's flailing arms knocked over another chair. Was Sarah's delusion giving her strength? Sarah reached for the knife. Knowing if Sarah reclaimed the weapon, she was going to die, Alexis struggled to drag the taller, stronger woman back. She grabbed Sarah's arm and caught her bracelet. The jewelry broke in her hand.

Sarah's scream of rage came from deep inside her. The sound was like that of a mortally wounded wild beast. Alexis's blood ran cold. Sarah pushed her backward. She saw the other woman's fist coming toward her. She tried to block it, but Sarah was too fast. Alexis's head snapped back. Everything went dark.

Chapter Seventeen

Max knocked briefly on Laura's office door. "Good morning, Laura. I'm sorry to interrupt you, but have you seen Alexis? She isn't in her office or her bungalow."

Laura's concerned expression made Max worry more. "She sent me a text. Someone broke into her condo. She's meeting with the police at the condo manager's office."

A break-in. Guilt weighed even more heavily on him. He crossed the threshold into Laura's office. "How long ago did she send the text?"

Laura checked her cell phone. "About thirty minutes ago. She should've reached her condo by now. I can text her for an update."

"No, that's okay." He stepped back, preparing to leave. *A break-in? When a stalker was after her?* "I'll call her. I had my service provider help me reset my cell phone."

Laura gave him a knowing smile. "Would you rather go to her?"

"Yes, I would." Max shrugged. He was restless. Something didn't feel right. He felt an urgent need to see Alexis. Now. "Between that video and this break-in, she's had a tough morning. I'd like to be with her. Unfortunately, that's not possible because I don't have a car."

"That's sweet." Laura's smile widened. "And I would

love it if my friend had someone with her to help her deal with the fallout from this break-in. Why don't you borrow a Mariposa jeep? It's a twenty-minute drive. I'll call the grounds service and ask them to lend you one."

Max's body eased with relief. "Thanks, Laura. I appreciate that."

He drove his golf cart to the grounds department. The young woman who set him up with one of their jeeps looked like a college student. Max was fairly certain he could find Alexis's condo, but he didn't have time to waste. He used an app on his phone to direct him.

He arrived in a little more than twenty minutes. What he found made his blood run cold. No one was around; not the police, condo management or Alexis. Her garage and front doors were wide open. There wasn't a car in the driveway, garage or parked on the street.

What was going on? Where was Alexis's car?

Max jogged up the front steps. He raised his hand to knock on the door—and froze. Several chairs had fallen over. Or had they been thrown over?

"Alexis?" He entered the condo, careful not to touch anything. "Alexis?"

Panic was trying to grab him. He beat it back. Max searched her bedroom, the bathrooms, the dining area and the kitchen. Nothing. He checked the area near the fallen chairs. On the floor, half-hidden by one of the chairs, was one of the bracelets he'd given to the women on his show's production crew.

Sarah.

It was getting harder to stave off the panic.

Max used one of Alexis's paper towels to handle the broken bracelet, then went in search of the condo office.

It was dark, dusty, stifling and stank of cigars. He tapped the service bell twice for assistance.

An older woman walked up to the scarred and dusty desk. Her nametag read Orlie. "I heard you the first time. Whaddya need?"

He took a breath and forced himself to speak patiently. "One of your tenants said you'd contacted her at work earlier this morning to report she'd had a break-in."

Orlie was shaking her head before Max had finished speaking. "Not me."

Ice collected in his veins. "Are you sure? The tenant is Alexis Reed."

Orlie frowned at him. "Well, I don't know who'd have told you all that bunk, but *I'm* telling you, we haven't had any break-ins since I've worked here. Someone's got their wires crossed. Anythin' else?"

Max's heart was pounding. Thoughts were screaming across his mind. "No, nothing else. Thank you."

He pushed his way out of the management office and got Laura on the phone.

"Hi, how is she?"

Max's voice was grim. "She's missing."

"What?"

"The condo manager said she never called Alexis. There haven't been any break-ins at the condos."

Laura gasped. "Do you think the stalker has her?"

Max thought of the broken bracelet in his shorts pocket. "I know she does. I need to find her."

"Wait." Laura's voice was breathless. "We gave each other permission to use the locator app to find our phones."

"Thank goodness." Max climbed back into the jeep.

"Come on. Come on." Laura spoke under her breath.

"Got it! I'll text her coordinates to you and Noah. Max, please find her."

"I will." His words were an oath and a prayer.

Chapter Eighteen

"Sarah! What are you doing?" Max raced through the trees into the clearing.

The scene unfolding in front of his eyes had been pulled from his worst nightmare. Alexis knelt at the end of a cliff. Max knew a rock-filled river lay at its base. She'd been gagged. Duct tape bound her arms behind her back. Sarah stood over her. She held a gun against the back of Alexis's head.

Max had never known he could be terrified and enraged at the same time. He drew a deep breath to settle his nerves. The solid scents of desert foliage and red dirt steadied him. What was he supposed to do? Culinary school didn't offer classes on de-escalating hostage situations. Frantic, he searched his mind for a plan. Two things were helping him keep it together. The first was his love for Alexis. He needed this woman in his life. The second was the knowledge that Noah was on his way. If he could keep Sarah talking until the cavalry arrived, Alexis would get out of this alive

"Sarah!" He called to her again as he ran toward her and Alexis. "What are you doing?"

"Max?" Sarah jerked Alexis to her feet. "Why are you here, Max?"

Alexis struggled to get her feet under her. Max gritted his teeth at Sara's continued mistreatment of her. Her gold pantsuit was torn and covered in dust as though she'd fallen several times during the hike to this area. Her arms and cheeks were scratched. One of her shoes was missing.

"You know why I'm here." Max walked closer. Only thirty yards separated them now. But it was still too far. He had to get a better look at Alexis. Was that a bruise on her jaw?

Sarah's smile was bitter. "Oh, I get it. You're here for *me*. Right? Because you care so much about *me*. Because *I'm* the one you really love. And I was wrong to think you were in love with Alexis." Her words taunted him. "Were you going to use that script, Max?"

"No, Sarah." Max clenched his fists at his sides. "I'm here for Alexis. Let her go!"

"No!" Sarah growled the word in a voice Max didn't recognize. "Why should I let her go? Why do you care about *her* and not *me*?"

"For one thing, she wouldn't try to kill the woman I love." Max paced forward. In his peripheral vision, he saw Alexis look at him as though surprised, but he couldn't think about that now.

Sarah held the gun in the air and pulled the trigger. "Don't come any closer or the next one won't be a warning shot."

Max's temper spiked in equal measure to his fear. "What do you want, Sarah? Why are you doing this?"

I can't keep her talking for much longer. Where is Noah?

"Why am *I* doing this?" Sarah screeched. "This isn't *my* fault. This is *your* fault. I did everything for you! Everything! I kept your schedule. I brought your supplies. I made your appointments. You said I was indispensable."

Max frowned. "That was your job, Sarah. You got paid to do those things."

She ignored him. "I even ended my marriage for you. And for what? So you could spend time with some cheap woman you got from that resort?" Sarah waved the gun toward Alexis.

Max's heart nearly stopped. His eyes flew to Alexis. She was glaring at Sarah. She must have realized as Max had that Sarah was indeed the person behind the defamatory video.

They could deal with that later. For now, Max needed to know that she was all right. "Put the gun down, Sarah. *Now.* And let Alexis go." He was so angry. And so afraid. He wasn't doing this right.

Dear God, please don't let me get Alexis killed.

"I will not." Her voice was thick with hatred. "You betrayed me."

"If you think I betrayed you, then deal with me and let Alexis go. Take me!" Max saw Alexis's eyes widen. He heard her voice in his head, *Are you crazy?*

"Maybe I should kill both of you." Sarah's smile was mean.

Max was winging this. "That would be in keeping with your deceit."

"What?" Sarah lowered the gun. "How have I deceived you?"

Max walked forward. "You claim to love me, but you don't. You love The Celebrity Chef. You love the fame and fortune. The perks that come with the persona. But you don't know anything about Max."

"That's not true." She waved the gun at him. "I've read every interview about you. I know everything there is to know about you." Sarah pointed the gun at the sky and fired another bullet. "Stop! Moving!"

Max stopped. "You know everything about me? Then tell me, why did I become a chef?"

Sarah frowned. "You already know why you became a chef."

Max spread his arms. "I want to hear it from you." *Please, God, let this work.*

Sarah looked at Alexis, then back to Max. "You became a chef because you wanted to open a restaurant."

"That's not true." Max shook his head. "So you see? You don't love me. You only think you do. Let Alexis go."

"I do love you!" Sarah screamed. "Why won't you believe me?"

"Police! Freeze!" Noah's voice carried from the tree line behind Max. It was loud and firm.

Max heard the detective's footsteps as he ran forward to join him. Relief lifted the weight from Max's back. He started to turn toward Noah, but Sarah's scream distracted him.

"Why won't you believe me?" She pointed her gun at him.

Before Max or Noah could react, Alexis launched herself at Sarah, knocking her to the ground as the gun went off.

The sound of that discharge would feature in Max's night terrors for years.

"Alexis!" Max charged toward her. Her body was so still as she lay on top of Sarah.

Max dropped to his knees beside her as Noah reached Sarah. The detective pulled Sarah out from under Alexis and took her into custody.

"Alexis. Sweetheart, are you all right?" Max searched

her for injuries. He found scratches and bruises, but no bullet wounds. Thank God.

Alexis was trying to talk through the duct tape Sarah had used to gag her.

"Sweetheart, this is going to hurt." Max took a corner of the tape with his still-shaking fingers and pulled as fast as he could.

"Ow." Alexis gasped. Her hands flew to her face to rub her cheeks. She scowled at Max. "I said, please take me home."

Noah returned, hunkering down beside them. He held up a retracting knife. "What say we cut you loose first."

Max turned to him. "Thank you, Noah. For everything."

Noah smiled at him as he cut Alexis free. "I think Alexis is the one you should thank. She saved your life." He straightened and disappeared.

Max helped Alexis to stand. "Alexis." He had no other words.

She cupped the side of his face. "You came for me. Thank you."

Wrapping his arms around her, he lifted her to his lips and kissed her until their fears drained away.

Chapter Nineteen

"When I heard your voice shouting at Sarah, I wanted to cry with relief." Alexis shivered at the memory. Max tightened his arms around her. "But at the same time, I wanted to scream at you to run away. I didn't want you putting yourself in danger. Again."

"There was no way I was leaving without you." Max could no longer even imagine a life without her. They sat wrapped in each other's arms on Alexis's love seat Monday evening.

He gently took Alexis's small, pointed chin, turning her face into the light so he could better see the bruise on her jawline.

"Sarah was freakishly strong." Alexis sounded tired. "And she'd become unhinged. I wonder what led to that."

"I don't know if we'll ever learn the answer." Max felt a wave of sadness. Had she always been troubled? If so, why hadn't he noticed it during the two years they'd worked together.

Alexis's condo was eerily quiet in the aftermath of the parade of family and friends who'd come to check on her once they'd heard about her kidnapping. The well-wishers included her mother and her aunt Suz, Jake, Laura, Adam, Joshua, Roland, Clarissa and a number of other Mariposa colleagues. Some had brought flowers, cards or candies. A couple of people had shown up with burgers and fries.

Max put his arms around Alexis again, careful not to hurt her. Her body was soft and warm against his, reassuring him she was real, and she was here. "I've never been so afraid in my life as I was when I saw Sarah holding that gun on you and realized she planned to throw you over the cliff."

Alexis shivered again in his embrace. "And I've never been so afraid as I was when I heard you offer to take my place." She tilted her head up to hold his eyes. "Please don't ever do that again."

"Hopefully, I'll never have another opportunity." Max kissed the top of her head. He kept touching and kissing her. Was he comforting her or himself?

"I'd hoped once the case was solved, everything would return to normal." Alexis drew a shaky breath. "But I have a feeling I won't feel normal for a while."

"Neither will I. But we'll get through this together." Max caught his breath at the hope in Alexis's eyes.

She raised her arm and stroked a finger down the right side of his mouth. "I hope it won't be too long before I see that dimple again." Her words made him smile. "Ah. There it is."

He kissed her forehead. "Your wish is my command."

Silence lingered over them for moments. It felt comfortable to lean on each other as they sank into their own thoughts.

Alexis sighed. "Max?"

"Hmm?"

"When Sarah asked why you loved me and not her, you said because I wouldn't try to kill the woman you love."

Max's muscles tensed in preparation for her obvious

question. He prompted her when she remained silent. "That's right."

Alexis cleared her throat. "Did you say that because you were trying to save my life, or did you say that because you're in love with me?"

Max shifted to face her. His arms were cold without her in them, so he took her hands. "Alexis Reed, I fell in love with you the first moment I met you. Like a fool, I didn't want it to be true. I should have been smart enough to realize it without your being in a life-or-death situation." He paused to help Alexis wipe the tears from her cheeks. Were those tears of joy or regret? He grasped his courage in both hands and continued. "You once said the two of us want different things. I don't think that's true. I think we want the same thing—to be together. And we're the kind of people when we want something, we make it happen. Alexis, I've never wanted anything more than to have you in my life."

Alexis gave a watery laugh. "I confess, I don't think I fell in love with you in the *first* moment we met, but I fell pretty quickly."

Max kissed the back of her right hand. "I know how much you love Sedona."

"And I know your family, home and work are all in New York." She sounded disappointed.

Max smiled. "My family could come to visit. In fact, my mother's excited to spend time at Mariposa. And although my work is primarily in New York, that doesn't mean it can't be moved, at least temporarily."

Alexis gave him a curious smile. "What are you saying?"

"The producers have agreed to film the second season of *Cooking for Friends* here in Sedona."

Alexis's eyes widened. "They did?"

Max nodded. "I floated the idea to them a couple of

days after the shooting, when I realized I'd fallen in love with you."

Alexis gasped with pleasure. She launched herself into his arms and covered his face with kisses in between exclamations of joy. "This is so wonderful. My mother will be thrilled. I can't believe you'd do something like this. Did you do this just for me?"

Max smiled into her eyes. "I did this for us." He grew serious. "You're my heart. You're my world. You're the one I want standing beside me in good times and in bad. I would change my life to be with you, Alexis."

Alexis wiped the tears from her eyes. "Maxwell Powell III." She paused when he chuckled. "You're everything to me. And I would willingly change my life to be with you, including eating itty-bitty food on great big plates."

"Now, that's love." Max pressed his lips to hers and tasted their forever.

* * * * *